I'LL FIND YOU

Vaguely, Callie realized something had been bumping against the boat. She started to turn back, fired by the certainty that Teresa was taking Tucker away, when the woman in the boat next to her let out a scream that sounded like a siren. A chill ran up Callie's back. She shot a glance at the woman and saw her stumble back from the edge of the boat, her hands clasped to her chest while the man tried to steady her. Her gaze was fixated on the water.

A body floated into the light. Not a swimmer. Someone wrapped in a black dress and sweater. As Callie watched, the face turned slowly upward, mouth open, dark reddish-blond tresses sliding across the slackened flesh of a familiar face. . . .

Books by Nancy Bush

CANDY APPLE RED

ELECTRIC BLUE

ULTRAVIOLET

WICKED GAME

WICKED LIES

SOMETHING WICKED

UNSEEN

BLIND SPOT

HUSH

NOWHERE TO RUN

NOWHERE TO HIDE

NOWHERE SAFE

SINISTER

I'LL FIND YOU

Published by Kensington Publishing Corporation

I'll Find You

NANCY BUSH

ZEBRA BOOKS
KENSINGTON PUBLISHING CORP.
http://www.kensingtonbooks.com

ZEBRA BOOKS are published by

Kensington Publishing Corp.
119 West 40th Street
New York, NY 10018

All Kensington titles, imprints and distributed lines are available at special quantity discounts for bulk purchases for sales
promotion, premiums, fund-raising, educational or institu-
tional use.

Special book excerpts or customized printings can also
be created to fit specific needs. For details, write or phone
the office of the Kensington Special Sales Manager.
Attn.: Special Sales Department. Kensington Publishing
Corp., 119 West 40th Street, New York, NY 10018. Phone:
1-800-221-2647.

Zebra and the Z logo Reg. U.S. Pat. & TM Off.

First Printing: July 2014
ISBN-13: 978-1-4201-3462-9
ISBN-10: 1-4201-3462-0

First Electronic Edition: July 2014
eISBN-13: 978-1-4201-3463-6
eISBN-10: 1-4201-3463-9

10 9 8 7 6 5 4 3 2 1

Printed in the United States of America

Prologue

Dark. Hot. Driving faster than she should but she had to keep up with their car. She'd made an unforgivable mistake—a calculated risk, really; several of them, if the truth were known—and it had come back to bite her in the ass. But she'd been new to the game then. Hadn't known what she wanted, other than him. Couldn't be blamed for that. *Couldn't* . . .

A chill stole into her heart as she pressed her toe to the accelerator. Her hands were slick on the wheel. Carefully she wiped them, one at a time, on her jeans. Had to concentrate. Had to get this right. Already it was a problem that there were two heads in the car in front of her, not one, but too damn bad.

Her mind wavered. Cast back to that night when she'd become his again. The feel of the chain he'd draped around her neck, the weight of the ankh cross. The pressure of the links as he twisted it until her skin pinched and her breath lay trapped in her throat.

"Who am I?" he whispered.

"The Messiah."

"Who are you?"

"Your handmaiden. I love you. I've always loved you."

"Liar."

"I just lost my way for a while, but I'm back."

"Will you obey me?"

"I'll do anything you ask." *Almost anything.*

"You've left things very messy."

"I know. I'll clean up everything." *Almost everything.*

He relaxed the chain ever so slowly, then drew back and touched the cross around his own neck. This, too, was part of the ever-changing rituals he expected them to all participate in. The gold ankh shimmered dully in the light and she stared at it hard, promising herself that she would do everything he wanted of her. *Almost everything.*

Now the black Mercedes ahead of her had reached Mulholland Drive. She knew where they were heading. She knew where the turn would be, where the road pushed out around the cliff, where the rail was no barrier at all. Dead Man's Curve. Maybe not called that, exactly, but close enough.

Her vehicle was a ten-year-old Ford Explorer. Brownish. Stolen. He'd given it to her for this express purpose. All she had to do was follow through.

But it wasn't supposed to be *two heads.* Worry gnawed at her brain. Someone who wasn't supposed to be targeted would die tonight because of her. She'd killed before and had even enjoyed it a little—maybe more than a little if the asshole truly deserved it—but she had never murdered an innocent. But then who was to say the other person was innocent?

Her mouth was Sahara dry. Her heart beat hard and slow, thumping in her ears with the precision of a metronome. Deafening her. She felt like she was floating.

They were traveling fast. Too fast. If she wasn't careful she could lose control of her own vehicle. It was almost as if the people ahead of her knew the danger creeping up on them. Did they? *Could they?*

She focused on the driver, knew that he liked speed and risk, loved to push himself. She could see the second head—the woman's—turn as she flashed at him in anger. She clearly didn't feel the same way, but her quarry's response was to accelerate even more.

A grim smile touched her lips. Carefully, she pressed her toe down farther and the SUV jumped forward. Did he know they were being followed? She doubted it. He was a narcissistic fool, believed himself infallible. She'd known that from the first time she met him in the dim light of the bar, the way his gaze had caressed her. She'd known just how to play him.

But now she had to time this right. Had to move up closer. They were almost there. The curve was coming up.

She glanced around anxiously. If a car approached in the opposite lane at the point of impact she would be lost. Likely to go over the edge herself. Her SUV gained on the Mercedes as she pushed it to reckless speed. The woman passenger looked back in fear as she bore down on them, her face white, her mouth opening in a scream.

And then her Explorer was on them. Deliberately she clipped the rear of their car, aiming for the back end of the driver's side.

Bam! The Mercedes whipped around as if spun by a hand on a roulette wheel, then slewed sideways. The man overcorrected and the car swung back, shimmying as it hit the rail. It went airborne so fast that even she gasped in surprise. She felt a moment's jubilation until she saw the third head lift from the backseat. A small head.

What? What!

The boy was in the car? *NO! NO!*

Oh, God. Oh, God. NO! He wasn't supposed to be with them!

It felt like the Mercedes hung in the air forever. She was screaming herself as it smashed into the ground with a sickening crunch. Her own vehicle was shuddering and rotating. She wrestled the SUV around, the world spinning. She barely managed to stop its dizzying turn and straighten it out. Keep it, too, from sailing over the edge as it charged forward. Distantly, she felt her arms aching from the effort. But the *boy. The boy* . . .

Her Explorer flew around the next corner, hung on to the road. No traffic. A miracle. She stood on the brakes, shuddering violently to a stop. Pulled off at the first place she could, a small strip of dirt on the side of the road.

No . . . no . . .

She had to go back. *Had to.* It was dangerous. Foolhardly. Suicidal. Undoubtedly someone—there were houses there, nestled into the cliffside far below—had seen the vehicle launch over the edge, heard it as it smashed downward. But the *boy.*

She ran back to the site of the crash. An eerie calmness held. There was no evidence of the accident from up here apart from the missing chunk of rail that looked like it could have given way weeks, months, years earlier.

Heart in her throat, she scrambled over the edge and down the cliff. It wasn't easy. It wasn't safe. Her hands were ripped and bloodied by the bushes and limbs as her sneakers slid in the dried, loose dirt. She approached the car cautiously. The Mercedes lay on its side, wheels spinning, headlights aimed at a distant land far below and the snake of glittering headlights in the valley. The vehicle had been caught by a stump and scraggly line of twisted trees. All that had saved it from tumbling down the cliff. Lucky, she thought with a swept-in breath. Maybe still alive.

She saw the boy first. Lying still. Quiet. His booster seat flung to one side. Her heart sank at his body, limp and motionless. Tears filled her eyes as she ran to him. She searched for a pulse and found none. A cry wrenched from her soul. It wasn't supposed to happen this way! Glancing up, she focused on the car. The woman was tangled up, flopped like a marionette, slung up inside the passenger seat belt, which had restrained her, the airbag crushed up against her.

And the man. The reason she'd been sent on this quest. To right the wrong she'd done to Andre . . . The Messiah, she reminded herself, though she had trouble remembering the name he liked to be called in front of the other handmaidens, was resentful of it.

Her quarry was on the ground a few feet from the boy, lying on his back. His eyes were open, reflecting a strip of moonlight. He focused on her and her blood ran cold. *Alive.*

They looked at each other and he lifted up a hand, as if he planned to reach for her. "Martinique," he said.

Her heart thudded hard in her chest. She remembered clinking her mai tai to his, the sight of the roll of bills he pulled from his pocket, the feel of him inside her while he moaned and thrashed above her and she thought of all the beautiful things she'd dreamed that his money could buy her.

With a last inhaled breath and then a slow expelling of air, he died.

She looked away from him and back to the boy.

I did this. I did this. . . .

No, he *did this,* she told herself. *Andre. The Messiah,* she thought with hot fury. It was his fault.

And he'll do it to your boy, too, she thought.

Her son.

One of the very messy things she'd left behind.

Headlights flashed up above on the road. Quickly, she pocketed his cell phone, which had incongruously landed above his head, then she carefully picked her way farther down the hillside and along the side of the cliff. Little by little, she inched down the steep incline to one of the backyards of several houses far below Mulholland, one that was completely dark. Briefly she thought about possible fingerprints on the steering wheel. She should have worn gloves. She hadn't really believed she would go through with it.

Too late now.

By the time she'd worked her way onto the lower road she could hear the police sirens. It took her another two hours, mostly ducking out of sight, before she came to a place she could hail a taxi far from the crash site. Then was driven to a bus stop a few miles from the house she shared with Andre and the fucking handmaidens. She walked those last miles, but it wouldn't hurt for the cabbie to think she was waiting for a bus.

She entered with her key through the front door, dusty, scratched and soul-sick, and immediately realized they were all in the ceremony room. That meant they'd be wearing their white robes. She had truly loved Andre once. Back when they were a reckless team of two, making their way from chump to chump. But things had changed. Andre had changed, become The Messiah.

She wanted to spit and had to contain her emotions. Still, the rituals of being a handmaiden made her grind her teeth and furthered her resolve to run away with her boy.

Could she do it? Could she make the break? Was it the right time?

Naomi, the biggest and baddest of the handmaidens, her dusty blond hair in cornrows, her 'tude that of a street kid though Teresa had heard she'd come straight from the middle class, caught sight of her before she could sneak to her room. Naomi pointed at her even while the others were chanting and undoubtedly holding hands in a semicircle, making sure everyone knew she'd returned. Sometimes Andre would select one of them for a sex act while he was under the spell of his own beliefs, laying the joyous one down on the mats, letting them all watch. Her lip curled at the thought but she nodded to Naomi and hurried to strip naked and then slip the white robe over her head. By the time she was at the ceremony room and had taken her designated spot to Naomi's right, her facial expressions were under control, though she could feel an uncontrollable quiver in her thighs and running down her legs. Fear. If she left and he came to find her . . . what would he do to her? What would he do to her boy?

"You," Andre said in a worshipful tone, curling a finger at her to come join him. He had that dazed, rapturous look on his face that caused the other handmaidens to begin chanting louder.

I can't, she thought. Then, a sterner voice within her own self said, *You will.*

Andre gathered up the hem of her robe and pulled the garment over her head, then stripped off his own. He lay her down on the mat and covered her body with his own, and as the handmaidens' voices reached a crescendo and Andre roughly slid inside her, she closed her eyes and reminded herself that she had loved him once . . . that this was just another test she must endure to keep up the charade . . . that all she had to do was play along and ignore the rapturous madness in his eyes . . . that nothing was as important as saving her son.

PART I

Chapter One

Callie Cantrell slid open the door to her balcony and immediately felt the sweltering humidity of Martinique. She'd grown accustomed to it these past months, though when she'd first arrived on the Caribbean island she'd been limp, exhausted, and certain she would never become acclimated.

Or maybe that was just because she was mentally and physically spent. Numb. Lost. She'd lived in Los Angeles for most of her adult life and normally would have been able to handle the change in temperature, but ever since Sean's death nothing was normal.

One year ago. A little over, now.

Leaning her forearms on the wrought-iron railing, she purposely pushed those dark and anxious thoughts aside, like she'd done nearly every moment since she'd decided she wanted to try to get better, to try to live again. Dwelling on his death was dangerous to her. She hadn't needed a therapist to tell her that, but she'd needed one to bring her back from the edge, to help her begin the journey into the next phase of her life, to convince her she still had a life.

It had taken a month in a hospital and then continual sessions with Dr. Rasmussen to get her to start eating again, get her out of the house she'd shared with her husband and son, get her to accept that this was her new reality. She hadn't truly been suicidal, though they'd thought she was. She'd simply been too destroyed to function in any positive capacity. Depression. Survivor's guilt. Abject misery. Yep, she had them all. When she'd finally gotten up the gumption to take charge of her life, she'd told the Cantrell family lawyer that she was going to the island of Martinique for an indefinite stay. He'd objected. It was too soon. She was too fragile. What would he tell Derek and Diane, Jonathan's grasping brother and sister? When was she coming back?

Now she gazed over the rooftops of the apartments and tenements on the hill below her, looking beyond the tell-tale signs of humanity toward the crystalline waters of Fort-de-France Bay. She should really appreciate its beauty more than she did, although she did recognize that the slow pace, French language, and sense of being in a different world were helping her slowly come back.

"Callie! Callie!"

Looking below, down the crooked cobblestone alley that led to the road, she saw a little boy, no more than five years old, racing around the corner waving his dust-grimed arm frantically.

Callie grinned and waved back. Tucker, the only other resident of the area she knew who spoke her language, was heading in her direction full tilt. "What are you doing up so early?" Callie called, leaning over the rail.

"I come to see you." He flashed her a huge smile and scampered up the cracked concrete steps to the apartment house's front door.

Callie walked back inside and wondered, not for the first time, how Tucker could have so much freedom. It was barely six A.M., for Pete's sake, and the child ran loose among Martinique's narrow streets and alleys until way after dark. Callie rarely saw Tucker with an adult, and she'd only met his mother once. Aimee Thomas had regarded Callie with suspicion and had ordered in French—Martinique's native tongue—for Tucker to leave the room. She then explained in broken English to Callie that she was Tucker's mother and that she had tried very hard to keep him in line but it was difficult. She didn't mention Tucker's father, and Callie couldn't tell if there even was one.

Callie had privately felt Aimee was just making excuses for being so lax, but since she hadn't wanted to alienate herself from her she kept her opinions to herself. Tucker was too important to Callie for her to object too strongly. In fact, Callie realized, Tucker was the reason she was still here, almost a month after her initial date of departure. Was he a replacement for the son she'd lost? Almost assuredly, but in that she didn't give a damn. If she wanted to lavish all her love and attention on the boy, what the hell was wrong with that? And Tucker's innocence and unbridled enthusiasm were a tonic she eagerly drank. She was slowly, ever so slowly, getting better.

Tucker impatiently rattled her apartment door and Callie hollered, "Hold on. I'm coming."

"Hurry! I brung you something."

"That's 'brought,' Tucker, and no, I will not accept any more gifts. You've got to take this one back," Callie said sternly, glancing toward her bedroom and the bracelet on her dresser as she made her way to the front door.

She slipped the chain off the lock and opened the door. Tucker, like the bundle of pure energy he was, hurled himself inside and held out his hand triumphantly. "See?" he demanded.

Cupped between his palms was a tiny, bluish-tinted starfish.

"Ahhh . . ." Callie put the starfish in her own palm, examining it critically as she looped an arm around Tucker's thin shoulders. "You've been beachcombing."

"Yesterday. And I goes today, too."

"You're going today?"

Tucker bobbed his dark head. His eyes were a fine, clear blue and they stood out dramatically against his dark hair and skin. Callie had grown used to the way he mangled his verbs; in fact, it was amazing he spoke English as well as he did, considering his mother was so poor at it. Or at least that's what she wanted Callie to believe.

"I go to the pier and waits around." Tucker glanced over his shoulder as if he expected someone to materialize in the open doorway. He moved still closer to Callie. "I have to go first with *Maman*, though."

Tucker's dislike of doing anything with his mother was another piece of a growing puzzle. *It's none of your affair,* she reminded herself, but she hugged Tucker extra hard. "Well, I have to go out this morning too," she said, straightening. "I'm going grocery shopping and I promise to bring you back something from the bakery."

"Chocolate?"

"You bet."

"You bet," he repeated, grinning.

She laughed, surprising herself. When was the last time she'd done that?

"Take me with you," he said suddenly, begging her with those beautiful eyes.

Callie had to fight herself from buckling under. "You are a heartbreaker," she scolded him lightly. "But your mom's waiting for you and I've got a million and one things to do that you'd think would be no fun. Now," she added briskly, before he could put forth another protest and weaken her resolve, "let's talk about that other gift you gave me. The one I have to give back." She strode into her bedroom and picked up the unusual silver bracelet with its rings of purple stones— *They couldn't be amethysts, could they?*—that Tucker had bestowed upon her. Callie had been bowled over by the gift and done her best to refuse it. From all accounts Tucker lived in near squalor, and when he'd unceremoniously dropped the bracelet in her lap one afternoon, Callie had done a classic double take. She was certainly no expert, but . . . even if it was a fake, it was an expensive one. It must belong to his mother. She'd tried to refuse but Tucker had been adamant, his eyes filling with unshed tears at her insistence that she couldn't accept it. Sick at heart that she'd hurt his feelings, Callie had said she would keep the bracelet for a few days. Those few days had passed and now she was anxious to give it back.

She stretched out her arm to him, the bracelet hanging from her fingers. "It's beautiful and I love it, but it's too expensive of a gift." She wondered again how he'd ever come to possess it, then decided she was probably better off not knowing.

"You don't wear it," he said, hurt.

"I can't. It's too precious. I think you should . . . give it back to your mother."

"It mine!" he said swiftly, almost angrily. "You wear it."

Callie stared at him in consternation. Something wasn't quite right, but she couldn't figure out what it was.

"I'll wear it today," Callie said, as a means to pacify him, "but only if you promise to take it back later. Deal?" She passed the bracelet to her left hand and stuck out her right.

Normally Tucker jumped at her Americanisms, soaking them up and adding them to his vocabulary. But now Tucker just stood in injured silence, his gaze on the floor. Callie squatted down to his level and lifted his chin. "If I could, I would wear your gift every day. Believe me. But sometimes adults can't accept certain gifts. It just wouldn't be right. What would your mother think if she knew you gave me this bracelet?"

"It mine," Tucker insisted again, but doubt had crept into his tone.

"If I put it on now, promise me you'll let me give it back later." She waggled the fingers of her right hand and he reluctantly reached out and shook it.

"Deal," he mumbled.

"Good. Then I'll put it on right now." Callie ran the bracelet up her left arm and gave Tucker a quick kiss on the top of his head. "Now scoot home before we get in hot water with Aimee."

She put her palms on his shoulders and turned him in the direction of the door, but he twisted his neck around. "Hot water?" he asked.

"Just another expression. It means 'big trouble'—the kind that neither of us wants."

"Hot water," he repeated, turning fully around again to face her, his expression lightening.

"You just love those idioms," she said, laughter in her voice. "I think—" she began, when he suddenly threw his arms around her waist and pressed his face into her stomach, his thin body tense with emotion. They stood in silence for a moment and Callie felt her heart beat painfully in her chest. She had to leave very soon, she realized, or it would be impossible to. It nearly was already. She thought of Sean and for a terrible moment couldn't picture his face. All she could see was Tucker and it stopped the breath in her throat.

Tucker ended the embrace a moment later. He was quick to display affection but also quick to sense when he needed to pull back. With a wave and slight smile he headed out the door, the clattering of his footsteps down the wooden stairs sounding more like an army than just one small boy.

"Let me walk you home!" she called after him.

But it was already too late to catch up with him. Curbing her natural instinct to mother him, Callie pulled herself together and let him go. This was his accepted way of life. He would be on his own again—alone—soon enough anyway. It was crazy, but it was out of her hands.

She inhaled deeply, then let out a slow breath. Tucker belonged to Aimee and not to her. He was an endearing boy, but she was nothing other than a friend to him. This was a transitory relationship, one that had certainly done its magic in bringing her back to the land of the living, but she couldn't build on it.

Though Callie understood perfectly why she found Tucker so attractive, she was less sure of why he had been drawn to her. She was just another tourist in a city overflowing with them, and though she had purposely moved from her hotel, stretching her meager French vocabulary to rent this apartment on the hill above Fort-de-France, that was the only remarkable aspect about her.

Grabbing up the plastic beach bag she used as a carryall, she stepped onto the third-floor landing, locked the door, then headed down the stairs and out to the narrow, cobblestone street lined with tall, whitewashed buildings that meandered down the hill.

She planned to go to the open market and buy some produce, maybe a bouquet of flowers. Ever since the accident, she'd felt like she was in a colorless world and subconsciously the part of herself that had been buried so long but was determined to survive gravitated to bright hues.

As she walked along she felt a shiver shimmy down her spine, as if someone were spying on her. Immediately she looked behind herself but the street was empty.

Something's wrong, she told herself, then just as deliberately shoved the thought aside, one she kept having no matter what she seemed to do. Of course something was wrong. Her whole world had been upended and torn apart. That was it. That was all. That was enough.

Yet . . .

From the moment she'd first woken up in the hospital, bleary and confused, she'd felt there was something she was missing. Something she'd forgotten or had almost known, and she kept experiencing a kind of déjà vu in odd moments. When she was reading the overhead menu at a coffee shop. When she was pulling money from her wallet. Each time she fought the emotional wrench of saying good-bye to Tucker and then turning her thoughts to her own life.

She had no memory of the accident itself, a common occurrence she'd been told, but she could remember the sense of anxiety and uneasiness that had plagued her for weeks prior to the accident. Was it because Jonathan had turned so mean-spirited and reckless? Was it her fear that he was keeping something from her? Or was it because of this *something* she'd known and then forgotten, something that felt like it was teasing just outside her consciousness? A sense that if she fell into a half dream it might well to the surface and she might be able to reach out and grab it?

Now, as she reached the open market, she shook her head, like she had so many times before. The harder she tried to nab it, the farther it seemed to recede from her grasp.

Someday, she told herself, fighting back the building frustration, but her mind wouldn't quit traveling down that twisted path. She'd been told their car plunged off a cliff as they were driving on Mulholland. No one knew quite how it had happened but Callie, even though she couldn't fully remember, simply blamed Jonathan for driving too fast. He was always driving too fast. And yes, she'd heard that there was another car abandoned at the scene. A stolen car with a broken headlight and smashed right, front fender. The theory was the two cars had been racing. She'd adamantly refused to believe Jonathan would have raced someone with both Sean and her in the car, but then, how much had she really known about the man she'd married?

She'd also been told she was lucky to be alive. Maybe . . . but she'd wished, more than once, that she had died with Sean. Those months afterward, the excruciating minutes that ticked by so slowly while she recovered from broken ribs and lacerations along her right arm and torso, had been long and hard. And then the month in the mental ward . . .

Jonathan's sister and brother, Diane and Derek Cantrell, had taken care of the funeral arrangements. Callie, who barely knew them, vaguely registered their hostility, thinking they blamed her for their brother's death. Later, she'd come to realize that they blamed her for inheriting the Cantrell family fortune. Later still, she discovered that fortune was about a tenth what it had once been, that Jonathan had practically run the company into the ground. She'd been thinking of taking a trip to Martinique, to the island where she and Jonathan honeymooned and Sean was conceived, a vague plan that had roots in the fact that she wanted to just run away. With Diane and Derek's increasingly hostile attitude after they examined Jonathan's financial records and realized the money just wasn't there, Callie had taken off. She had kept her own checking account and she used funds she'd saved on her own.

She told William Lister, a man she'd felt she could trust even though he was the Cantrell family attorney, that she was leaving on a trip. She didn't tell him where. He advised her against it; there were a dozen legal matters to attend to, to which Callie told him that Diane and Derek could have everything, save what she had in her own account. She didn't care. She just needed to leave.

Derek caught up with her before she took off and tried to wheedle out of her where she was going. He intimated that she was stealing their inheritance, which pissed her off no end. She didn't give a damn about the money, or him, or anyone. She'd lost the only person who was important to her. Derek also implied that Jonathan had bought her jewels and designer clothes and other lavish gifts. That's where he felt the money had gone, and he wanted those gifts returned.

To that Callie said, "Bite me." She didn't have the money or the mythical gifts. She took off for Martinique and left her cell phone behind so they couldn't reach her. She was sick of the lot of them. In the end she'd called Lister a time or two, mostly to let him know she was still alive and okay and to keep him from sending the hounds after her.

Callie sensed there was a lot she didn't know about her husband, but she wasn't even certain she wanted to know what it was. Maybe that was why her mind shied away from whatever it was she couldn't grasp. Whatever the case, she'd spent the last month finishing the recovery that had started within the walls of Del Amo Hospital. She wasn't her old self; that person had died an unlamented death somewhere along the way. She was someone new, someone stronger. Someone who planned to make much better choices from here on out.

He watched the young woman with the red-tinged, blond hair weave through the open market and held his breath, a surge of hot fury licking through his veins. He'd been accused of being cold and heartless by women before, maybe he had been with them, but right now he was churning with rage, his insides hot lava.

His eyes followed her as she picked up several mangos and a papaya and then moved on to examine an array of tropical flowers. He saw her fingers reach out and gently touch a blood red anthurium and fought back the urge to grab her hard and shake her until something fell loose.

Not yet, he told himself. *Not here.*

He traced her movements as she made her purchases, then slipped in behind her as she walked away, her carryall laden with fresh fruit and vegetables, the nodding heads of birds of paradise and tiger lilies almost like a beckoning hand. He followed carefully behind her and realized she was heading toward the bay.

* * *

The early-morning stillness of Fort-de-France Bay seeped seductively into Callie's consciousness. Her senses were lulled, attuned only to the heat, the silence, and most of all the view, as she stood on the pier and watched the ferryboat load visitors for the thirty-minute voyage from Fort-de-France to Pointe du Bout, the tourist resort on the other side of the bay.

Her carryall was loaded with groceries, and she had only one stop left to make: the bakery. But she couldn't find the energy to move. Stretching her bare arms skyward, she felt the sun soak deep into her skin. Smiling, she squinted against the blinding dazzle of light on the water.

An inflatable boat at the end of another pier was being stowed with provisions, and Callie watched the two men doing the loading without really seeing them. Her thoughts were far away. That same elusive memory was teasing at the back of her mind. She ignored it, unwilling to frustrate herself with being incapable of grasping it, and kept her gaze on the small rubber launch as it roared to life and pulled away from the shore. Her line of sight took in a trim white and royal-blue sailboat anchored in the bay. Small waves from the wake of other boats slapped against the sailboat's gleaming hull, and a man on deck moved to the rope ladder near the stern, leaning down to help load provisions from the approaching inflatable raft.

Callie's scalp prickled and she looked around. A man and woman were walking along the dock, arm in arm, and a female jogger with a long-limbed reddish dog trotting beside her swept off to her right. A deeply tanned man about a quarter-mile down the shore held a pair of binoculars to his eyes, the binoculars trained on that same sailboat. She glanced back to the sailboat herself and didn't see the same binoculars sweep the shore, pass by her once, then casually pass by her again.

Callie closed her eyes and inhaled the heady, salt-laden air. Hearing the launch rev to life once more, she slowly lifted her lids and watched the rubber craft motor back to the pier, a frothy wake fanning out behind it. To her surprise one of the men looked up, saw her, and began to wave frantically.

She glanced around. She was the only person in sight. Did she know this man? She didn't think so. He had a grizzled beard and bulky build, and even from a distance she could see how dirty his clothes were. Then he put his hands to his lips and threw her an expansive kiss, arms spread wide, his mouth split by a wide grin.

She smiled back. Of course the man was a stranger. A Frenchman. She'd just been the recipient of his romantic enthusiasm.

She lifted her hand and waved a bit self-consciously. Tucker's bracelet caught the sunlight and threw bright, lavender pinpoints of light in an arc around her. The man in the launch waved again and then the small boat reached the pier and the two men began hauling on more provisions.

Callie looked at her watch. It was time to get moving if she planned to do anything more than hang around the piers. Turning away from the bay, she walked back toward the center of the city.

Feeling something on the back of her neck, she glanced behind herself, her heart suddenly galloping. But it was the same scene. Nothing had changed except the jogger and dog had disappeared around the curve of the pier. The man who'd been watching the sailboat was tucking his binoculars into their case and turning the other way.

Fort-de-France was a thriving metropolis, its streets so narrow that cars parked on the sidewalks, forcing the pedestrians to spill into the street. It was early enough, as Callie headed north, that she wasn't battling a crowd of people and cars. Her progress was rapid and she arrived at the tiny bakery within minutes.

"Bonjour," she said to the woman behind the counter.

"Bonjour." The woman smiled distractedly and waited for Callie to make a selection.

There were pastries of every kind. Flaky Napoleons layered with custard, cone-shaped scones filled with coconut crème, pineapple tarts, croissants, crusty loaves of bread. Callie's French couldn't stand the test of such exotic names and she pointed to several crème-filled items, unable to resist buying several.

"Thank you. *Merci."* Callie picked up the bag and settled it into the trusty plastic carryall. Since she had no car she walked everywhere, and after she had found herself an apartment a mile from the city center she learned to limit her purchases to what she could comfortably carry.

The sun was already hot as she headed up the hill toward her apartment. Shifting the bag from one hand to the other, she trekked along until the sidewalks of Fort-de-France gave way to the steep, narrow roadway that led back to the less congested street fronting her apartment. Traffic was thick, and she turned at the first street that could take her away from the main thoroughfare.

A trickle of sweat ran down her spine as she hiked upward. Looking back down the hill, she saw the ferry, shrunk by distance, returning across the bay from Pointe du Bout. Even from this distance she could discern many of the major hotels and tourist resorts that ringed this side of the bay, their white sand beaches sloping into the sea. When Callie and Jonathan had come to Martinique on their honeymoon, they'd stayed at one of those hotels. This time she'd steered clear of them. She asked herself for about the millionth time why she'd chosen Martinique when it held such a dubious memory for her, but she had no answer to that. It was a pretty place. More tropical than Los Angeles. She hadn't traveled a lot, apart from moving from a suburb of Chicago to the West Coast after a man she'd thought she wanted to marry. It was Bryan's dream to work as an actor and Callie's dream to be with Bryan. Neither had worked out.

Tired, she paused for breath, setting down her bag and wiping perspiration from her forehead. It was damn hot. The kind of thick, tropical heat heavy with humidity that stole your breath and weighted down your limbs. Resolutely straightening her shoulders, Callie trudged on again. As the noise of Fort-de-France receded behind her, she almost felt alone on the planet. The only other person in view was a man walking some distance behind her. He looked familiar and her heart jolted before she realized he was only the man who'd been watching the sailboat, his small binoculars tucked into his belt. He was staring into the screen of his cell phone, his forward motion kind of haphazard as his attention was on his phone.

Texting, she assumed, thinking of the disposable phone she'd purchased, then shoved in a drawer. She'd made a few calls since she'd been here, couldn't act completely like she was a missing person. The few times her phone had rung she'd known it was William Lister or a wrong number. She didn't answer either way. She didn't have anything to say to Lister. She would deal with him and the rest of Jonathan's family when she was darn good and ready. She'd given them everything they wanted, and if they would just leave her alone, she would be back soon enough anyway.

And you'll leave Tucker.

She couldn't think about that now. Couldn't. Think. About it.

Cutting across a weed-choked lawn, she took a shortcut the rest of the way. The sun was shining brightly as she turned a corner, walked along a cracked, narrow sidewalk, then ducked into the alley between her apartment building and the one next door.

* * *

Where the hell is she going?

He kept a careful distance behind, his gaze not on the smartphone in his hand but on her tan legs and the swaying hem of her gauzy white sundress. He'd been looking for her for over a week, trolling a particular Internet café, making discreet inquiries, getting nowhere. Then she'd turned up at the market and walked down to the pier, big as you please. Soaking in the sights like every other tourist, her crown of hair shining beneath the blazing sun.

He wanted to kill her with his bare hands.

"Don't do anything rash," Victoria had warned him in her tight-lipped way. "If you have to bargain with her, okay. But don't antagonize her any further."

Like he needed to be told what to do. He'd done plenty of surveillance. Had enough years with the LAPD to be considered an old hand.

Still, Victoria was right in one respect: he wanted to shake the woman until she fell into pieces. He wanted to shatter her self-indulgent world and leave her in the rubble. There would be no bargaining as far as he was concerned. Victoria knew that, but she always tried to make everything sound so civilized. But the only way to deal with *her* was by bringing things down to a level she could understand.

Bargaining was for beggars. Now was the time for action.

The bitch was in his sights.

Callie stopped again, halfway through the alley, arms aching. She set down her carryall and swept a hand through her hair, making a face at its long, untamed style. When she got back to LA she was going to cut it short. A new life and a new look. Maybe she'd get her master's and apply for a real teaching job.

Hoisting her bag once more, Callie continued on the sun-cracked dirt path between the buildings. She met no one and the silence was unbroken as she walked on. The sun reflected off the white walls and prickled her scalp. The air felt like a hot blanket. She blew on straggles of hair that fell into her eyes and thought about the pitcher of iced lemonade that awaited her in her tiny refrigerator.

A pebble lodged itself in her sandal and she stopped, lifting her foot and wiggling her toes. Lemonade and croissants at the little table on her balcony, she told herself. Maybe she would even splurge and try one of the gooey pastries she'd gotten for Tucker. Maybe he would even come back and share with—

"So, Martinique, huh?" a cold, male voice asked. "Must be a reason."

Callie nearly jumped from her skin. He'd made no sound and she'd thought she was alone. Before she could respond a hand grabbed her upper arm and twisted her around until her back was pressed against the west building's hot wall.

"Wh-what?" Callie stared at him and the air rushed from her lungs. Deeply tanned. Hard jaw, mouth, and eyes. The man with the binoculars. "Let go of me!"

"Where's the boy?" he gritted out.

"The boy?" she repeated blankly.

"Stephen Tucker Laughlin. Your son, Teresa. Where is he?"

Chapter Two

Your son.

The words stopped her cold. Stephen Tucker . . . ? Tucker? He meant *Tucker?* Her head swam. Tucker wasn't her son. Her son was gone.

He shook her hard. "You're not going to faint," he warned.

No, she wasn't going to faint. But was that the truth? She felt like she could faint.

Teresa. He'd called her Teresa?

"Where is he?" he demanded again.

Her heart raced with fear. Her mind was dull and sluggish. With a feeling of unreality Callie stared at the man. There was a grimness of purpose around his mouth that chilled her blood. She tried to capture her scattered wits. "Who are you?" she managed to get out.

"Make a guess."

"What? I can't . . . I don't think—"

"Take a good, hard look."

Callie could do little else. His face, tanned to the color of teak, was within inches of hers. His eyes were bluer than her own, with thick, dark lashes and tiny white lines edging from the corners where the sun never reached.

Dark hair framed a lean, savage face; she was certain his
nose had been broken more than once. His mouth was
wide and sensual and she thought a bit cruel; his jaw, firm
and jutting, sported a dark growth of beard. He looked
handsome, dangerous, and determined.

And he scared the living shit out of her. "What—do you
want?"

"Show me the boy."

Did he mean Tucker? He must. His hand still held her left
wrist. The grip was tight and hurting, and only the solid wall
behind her back kept her on her feet. "I don't know you."

"Not yet."

She didn't like the implied threat in his tone. "I don't
know who you think I am, but you're mistaken."

His fingers flexed and tightened on her wrist. "People tell
me I look like Stephen. Personally, I've never thought there
was much resemblance. What do you think?" He leaned in so
close that she could see the individual hairs of the stubble on
his chin.

"Stephen . . . ?" His grip tightened but she was at a loss.
"I don't know any Stephen. You—you have to let me go."

"I have to?" he challenged.

"When you realize the mistake you've made, you'll . . ."
Be sorry. That sounded so overly dramatic she couldn't make
herself say it. "Just let me go."

She realized belatedly that her free hand was still gripped
around her carryall, as if her very life depended on it.
Slowly she dropped it to the ground. If he was looking for
Tucker, she wasn't going to give him away. "I don't know any
boy." She glanced down at the carryall, anything to keep
from looking at him directly. "I have some cash with me—
not much—maybe enough . . ."

"Goddammit, Teresa." He gave her another shake. "Do I
have to drag it out of you?"

"My name's Callie. You've got me mixed up with someone else."

He swore tightly, beneath his breath, then grabbed her right wrist, too, pinning her flat against the wall. Both of her wrists were down by her waist but now he twisted up her left arm, pulling it forward until the bracelet Tucker had given her was at eye level between them.

"What about this?" he asked, meaning the bracelet.

Callie stared into his eyes with growing panic. All she could think about was Tucker and the bracelet. It was valuable. It must be! How had he gotten it? And how did this man know about it?

She suddenly didn't care what he wanted. She didn't care who he was. But if he tried to steal Tucker's bracelet from her he'd be in for the fight of his life. She'd rather die than let him take it from her.

"Let go of me," she said tautly, jerking at her left arm. But his grip was too strong, his fingers too tight around her wrist. She glared at him, matching his savagery with her own growing anger.

"Looks like I struck a nerve," he said with a smugness that infuriated Callie. "We both know where you got the bracelet."

"Yeah?"

He nodded.

"Well, if you know how I got it, you're a mind reader."

"Stephen gave it to you."

"No." But uncertainty flickered through her. Stephen *Tucker* Laughlin. That's who he'd said he was looking for.

"Or you stole it from him," he added easily. "Victoria probably gave you too much of a pass on that one."

Is Tucker this Stephen Tucker Laughlin he's looking for?

"Who *are* you?" she asked.

"The black sheep of the family. If you try hard enough, I'm sure you'll figure it out."

He clearly thought she was someone else, and she already understood she wouldn't be able to convince him of that fact. And he also wasn't going to listen to her, no matter what she said. It was insane and she felt panic rise inside her.

She hauled back and kicked him as hard as she could, connecting with his shin. He cursed viciously but didn't release her. Callie tried to kick another time but suddenly she was slammed hard against the wall again. The air shot from her lungs and she inhaled like she was starved for air. His full weight was pressed against her.

"I'm not Teresa," Callie gasped. "In my wallet . . . my identification . . . you'll see."

"Shut up," he growled furiously. "I *know* you. So help me, before this is over you're going to know me, too."

"It's a mistake . . . it's a mistake."

She could hear the hard pounding of his heart as if it were in her own ears. Her own pulse beat in rapid tandem. She hadn't been this close to a man since Jonathan. Hadn't wanted to be. The bizarre events that had led to this encounter only added to the intensity.

A scream rose in her throat, but as if he sensed it his grip changed and one hand pushed down on her collarbone, the fingers lightly creeping toward her throat.

"Don't," he said softly.

"You're scaring me." Tears built behind her eyes.

"That's the idea," he muttered grimly.

A sound caught their attention. At the north end of the alleyway, two young men were just entering.

Thank God. Callie could have wept with joy. Salvation was at hand.

But then she met the eyes of her captor and they read each other's mind at the same moment, Callie gauging just when to cry for help, her attacker wondering how to silence her.

She opened her mouth, but her cry was extinguished as his mouth suddenly descended on hers, grinding down on her, cutting off her breath. As a kiss it left a lot to be desired, but as a means of keeping her quiet it was quite effective. She made choking sounds that could have meant anything, and though she tried to push him away she was helpless against his weight and the surprise of his unexpected maneuver.

She pounded on his back but he was impervious to the action. The fingers of his right hand held her face a prisoner.

There was no passion in the kiss, just a steely determination that Callie found more frightening than anything he'd done so far. He loathed what he was doing; she could feel it in the tight, unyielding contours of his lips, the tense hostility that radiated from every pore. If this was the way he felt about the mysterious Teresa, Callie found herself glad she wasn't in the other woman's shoes.

Except she was—sort of. At least *he* thought she was.

Teresa . . . Jonathan had called her Teresa the first time they met . . . that was the name, wasn't it? Or had it been Marissa . . . ?

The missing piece dancing outside her memory floated within reach. *Something about Teresa?* Immediately it slid out of reach again.

One of his hands was wound in her hair and her head was trapped. The two teenagers whistled as they walked by. Callie wondered if she twisted, flailed, and sought escape, they would even consider she was a woman in trouble. She was aware of how much this kiss might look like an act of passion.

As soon as the young men were out of earshot, Callie's captor released her lips as if she burned his touch.

"Don't," he warned.

"I wasn't going to do anything." Actually, she'd been thinking about slapping him and letting loose a bloodcurdling scream at the same time. Instinct warned her against antagonizing him further, however. This man was no ordinary hoodlum. And by his accent he was obviously American, like herself. He truly believed he'd found Teresa. If he would just give her a chance to explain, maybe he would leave her alone. He wasn't a threat to Callie Cantrell, so it was better . . . smarter . . . to play along.

"Where's the boy?" he asked again. "Tell me."

She knew with bone-deep certainty now that he meant Tucker. Had to be. There were only so many coincidences she could believe in. Had Tucker, or this Teresa person, stolen the bracelet from him? Was that it? Not that she gave a damn, but she wasn't going to reveal anything to him that might put Tucker in danger.

"Listen to me. Just listen," she added tautly when she saw more impatience cross his face. "I'm not Teresa, whoever she is. I'm Callie, Callie Cant—" She cut herself off at the last minute, realizing it wasn't beyond probability that he knew exactly who she was and that this whole scenario was an act. She was, after all, Jonathan Cantrell's widow, and though Jonathan had run through a substantial portion of the Cantrell fortune, this man might not know that. In essence, she was the heir of what remained and maybe he knew that, too.

Is this what you can't remember? she asked herself. *Is this what Jonathan was hiding?* "I'm not Teresa," she said again, firmly. "I don't know you, and I really resent the way you've accosted me. I'm a tourist. On vacation. That's all. Now, get the hell away from me."

"You're not Teresa."

She shook her head.

"You just happen to be wearing a Laughlin family heirloom."

The bracelet burned on her arm. "I don't know about that."

"You don't?"

"No," she said firmly.

"If I didn't have the evidence that said otherwise, I might even believe you."

"You're lying. You won't believe me no matter what I say."

He looked faintly surprised by her challenge. "You got me there."

"Look at my identification, for God's sake!" she demanded, throwing caution to the wind. If he was really after Cantrell money, no amount of lying about who she was could save her now. "My wallet's in my bag."

"Fake identification's not beyond your capabilities."

"Oh, please."

"I'll look at it when we get to your place."

"My place?"

He'd been looking in the direction the teenagers had taken, as if considering where to go from here. Now his dark head turned back to her. "Your place."

"We're not going to my place," she stated firmly. "I'm not who you think I am."

"I know who you are," he ground back at her again.

Callie realized there was nothing she could say. This stranger was convinced she was someone else. He truly believed she was this Teresa person and he wasn't going to listen to reason. What the hell was she supposed to do?

What if Tucker is waiting for you?

"You're crazy," she whispered.

"Take me to the boy and I'll go away."

His grip had weakened slightly after the kiss. Callie pretended to consider his demand, inwardly counting her own heartbeats. She twisted from his grasp and jumped away in one swift movement, racing for the end of the alley with all her might.

One thought in her mind: *Run!*

She could feel him gaining on her as the wind streaked past her ears. She felt fingertips brush her back and she leapt forward, crashing down on one unsteady ankle. Her sandal caught a cobblestone and she flew forward.

Her face hit the ground and her chin jarred with the

impact. She saw stars and for one, wild moment prayed she could be hurt, at least rendered unconscious.

Except he would probably just pick her up and kidnap her.

He was beside her in a moment, turning her over gently. She groaned and closed her own eyes against the concerned blue eyes that seemed to peer into her soul.

"Damn it, Teresa. Goddammit." He expelled his breath and she felt it on her throat. "For chrissakes, just stop. You can't just run away with Tucker."

"You're going to be so sorry." She didn't open her eyes, but there was steel in her unsteady voice.

"I'm going to stick to you like glue until you give him up. Where is he? Tell me, and I'll let you go."

Callie was unable to answer him. She realized she was losing her fear of him. He wanted Tucker. Keeping her eyes squeezed shut, she thought of a dozen responses that continually boiled down to the one that finally passed her lips, "Screw you."

He hauled her back up as if she were weightless. Then he half-carried her toward the end of the alley. She toyed with the idea of making another break for it, but she was seized by a wave of dizziness.

"You okay?" he asked tautly, the words dragged out of him as he set her on her feet.

"No." She was hanging on to him as if her life depended on it, her fingers clenched into the fabric of his shirt.

"It's reaction," he said when she couldn't continue.

Bastard.

They stood there a moment. Callie could hear her stuttered breathing and feel his anger and indecision.

"Just stand here a minute and don't talk," he said. "You'll be all right."

She snorted in disbelief. Who was he kidding? She didn't think she'd ever be all right again.

Her head slowly cleared and she abruptly let go of his

support. When she did, his arms dropped away from her with undisguised relief, though he kept a hard eye on her. Callie felt a prickle of annoyance. She hadn't asked for this; he'd forced it on her. And if he found touching her so offensive he shouldn't have accosted her in the first place.

He was warily watching her, probably wondering if she would run, fall, attack him, or God knew what.

Reaction was indeed setting in—only it wasn't reaction from the fall, it was reaction to the whole situation—to him, to everything. Callie leaned a trembling palm against the wall of her apartment building. "Leave me alone," she rasped out. "I don't know what you're talking about . . . and you hurt me."

For the first time she witnessed some uncertainty in his expression. "You kicked me and—"

"You *hurt* me," she repeated on a hiccup. For good measure she leaned her cheek against the hot wall and closed her eyes. She could feel her body tremble and she added a little stuttering intake of breath, hoping he felt terrible.

"Aww hell," he muttered. Then, "Don't try to run away again."

"I'll be lucky to walk with the aid of a cane," she said, working up to tears. If she could just squeeze out a few maybe he'd realize what he'd done to her, how much he'd scared her.

There was definitely a hesitation. Good. She wanted him to think she was worse than she was. And he *had* scared her. And her jaw and head hurt and her knee was scraped, and that was his fault too. Her eyes burned and tears reached her lashes.

"I know your games," he said. "Stephen told me. Victoria said something too."

"I thought you were looking for Stephen."

"Not the boy." He sounded like he was holding on to his patience with an effort. "Stephen. Your husband."

She cracked open an eye and saw that he was watching a tear slide down her cheek. "My husband?"

He met her gaze. "Man, your act is getting old."

"Just leave me alone."

"Show me Tucker and I'll be glad to."

"I don't know what you're talking about. I don't know you."

"Fine. I'll play. I'm West." When she continued to regard him blankly, he shook his head and said, "You're a lot better than I expected."

"I'm not this Teresa, and I've never heard of you in my life, Mr. West."

"Laughlin," he corrected. "First name's West."

"Whatever."

She gazed down the alley and saw her carryall where she'd dropped it before she ran. It had gotten knocked over in their skirmish and birds of paradise lay with bent stems, making it seem like their necks were broken. The lilies hadn't fared much better. They were scattered haphazardly. Tucker's chocolate pastry lay smashed and dusty to one side. Callie tried to marshal her strength for another attempt at escape but, though she managed to push herself away from the wall, she was too limp-muscled to run. What was the point anyway? He would catch her even if she was at her best form, he'd already proven that.

She thought briefly about screaming *"Police!"* and wondered if that would do any good. Would anyone even hear her? And did she want to get further embroiled in this? Bring in the authorities and have this bastard arrested for accosting her? He would tell his story and likely find Tucker anyway. A better way of dealing with him might be to try talking to him reasonably. He hadn't listened to her so far, but she sensed he wasn't as threatening as he'd been initially. She'd thrown him off balance and even the most stubborn person would lose conviction if faced with overwhelming evidence. He couldn't believe she was Teresa forever.

Callie hadn't noticed her own condition until that moment. Her white dress was filthy, her arms and legs streaked with dust and sweat. She could just imagine what kind of state her hair was in. Only the bracelet on her arm appeared as clean and beautiful as it had been when she'd put it on this morning. She wished she'd left it at the apartment. Good God, was it really valuable?

Gingerly she took a step, realized she wasn't going to fall apart, then took another, straightening her shoulders. West eyed her carefully.

"I'm going to get my bag," she said.

"You need some help?"

She threw him a dark look, then hobbled over to the bag. He followed closely, as if afraid she would make another break for it. Like she had the strength.

She picked up the lilies and stuffed them back in the bag. "I'm not interested in talking to you, Mr. Laughlin. I'm not Teresa. I don't know how many times I can say it."

"Just take me to the boy and we'll figure this out. You're his mother. You hold all the cards. I just want to see him."

"Bullshit. You clearly want something more." She slid the carryall up her arm, aware of how heavy it felt. Reaction, indeed. "I'm not anyone's mother," she added. *Not anymore.*

"You live in one of these buildings?"

"You think I'd take you to my place after you attacked me?" she demanded.

"I didn't attack you. You ran away. I was—"

"You chased me down and threw me on the ground."

"You tripped!"

"That's not how I remember it."

"Wow."

"You want to talk? You want to learn who I really am?

Fine. Let's go somewhere else, but I'm not taking you to my place."

"I'm not going to hurt you," he said.

"Oh, yeah, I believe that."

He swore softly under his breath, but asked, "Where do you want to go, then?"

"Somewhere public." She carefully touched her chin. "I'm not feeling the best and I'd like something cool to drink."

His gaze slid over her tangled hair and dirt-smudged dress. He clearly wanted to argue but he only said, "We'll go to my hotel."

"Oh, sure." Callie almost laughed. Still, it was imperative that she get him as far away from Tucker as possible. As she tried to figure out what to do, the ferry horn blasted twice.

Pointe du Bout. Across the bay.

"We can go to Bakoua Beach, in Pointe du Bout," Callie said, seeing West's head swivel sharply to stare at her. "I've stayed there," she explained a trifle defensively. "There's an outdoor restaurant where we can talk privately. I realize it's on the other side of the bay but I would feel comfortable there."

And it's miles away from Tucker.

West considered a moment. She thought he was going to refuse her, but then he shrugged and said, "Bakoua it is."

Chapter Three

Sometimes you have to make things happen. If you don't press, if you don't push, then you're going to be waiting a lifetime for the good things. The things you deserve. The things you need. I can't tell you how much time has gone by while others around me keep getting richer, in every way. I've got the momentum now, though. I'm aimed, cocked, and ready to fire.

And if some of you fall beneath the spray of my ammo, too fucking bad.

It's my time to hunt.

Teresa tiptoed inside the house, closing the front door behind herself, cringing as it softly clicked into place, the faint noise sounding like a pistol shot to her own ears. It was early, not the crack of dawn but definitely on the early side for Andre and the handmaidens. She'd stayed out all night on purpose. The walls of the place were closing in on her and at night, sometimes, she bit down hard on the top blanket to keep from screaming, clenching the fabric between her teeth for hours until her jaw weakened and exhaustion overtook her.

It was harder and harder to remember how much she'd loved him. How much he'd meant to her in the beginning. How there was no Teresa without him. She was a vessel that only he could fill. She was empty when she was away from him.

At first she'd thought she was stealing him away from other women, keeping him for herself. She'd wanted him so much. She was happy and triumphant. There was no one on the planet as lucky and loved as she was. Even when he'd been circling the first handmaiden, she hadn't really been worried. Men were cheaters by nature, but she was confident that he would always come back to her. That this obsession with someone new would only be temporary.

She'd gone to Stephen at his behest, and she'd played the part so well that sometimes she'd even felt like she loved Stephen too. She had, as it turned out, but she hadn't realized that until much later . . . until it was too late. By then Stephen was gone and it was her fault as much as anyone's. If she could turn the clock back, she would. She wished her younger self hadn't believed in Andre so desperately. It would sure as hell have saved her a lot of grief now.

"Sneaking in?"

She froze at his voice, her hand flying to her chest. There were shadows in the house. All the shades were still down and only faint morning light reached around them.

He materialized from one of the open doorways that stretched down the hall, moving like a cat. She caught the glint of the ankh against his bare chest. She held her breath for a moment, then said, "I was . . . doing my job."

"What about the wife?"

Teresa was "dating" an older married man whose wife held the purse strings. Andre wanted her to take him for all he was worth. In fact, he was downright vicious about it and Teresa knew why. But though the mark was more than willing to rob his wife blind for Teresa, it was difficult for him to slide money out of her control.

And always, always, the wife expected him home in her bed. There was no spending the night between him and his lover, much to his chagrin and Teresa's relief. Though she couldn't tell Andre, she was no longer even trying to keep the con going.

"I was at the Santa Monica pier . . ."

"All night? You were supposed to be in my bed."

"I thought . . ."

"What?"

"I thought you'd chosen Daniella. Last night."

"Who were you really with?" His tone was light but she knew better than to trust it.

"I wouldn't be with anyone but you." This was the truth, at least. She would only be with someone if he ordered it—so far, anyway—though she was planning a new and different future for the next part of her life. She just couldn't let him know. The consequences would be dire. And he was so good at always discerning the truth that she was certain he would know she wasn't lying. *Please, God, let him hear the truth. Don't let this be the time he doesn't believe me.* "I was at the pier, and then I was driving around."

"Something bothering you?"

"No . . ."

"That child?"

Her gaze flew to his face. He knew how she felt about the Cantrell boy? It had been so long since she'd had an actual conversation with Andre that she didn't trust this was real.

"It won't be long now," he whispered, running his hands down her arms.

Andre always promised that this life with the other handmaidens was temporary, that there was some ultimate goal that only he and she would share. But she sensed he told the rest of them the same thing.

"Ever since the accident, I've lost heart," she admitted carefully.

"You know it had to be done. You know why."

She nodded. Jonathan Cantrell had become a problem for Andre.

"You'll enjoy it again."

Teresa felt a quiver go down her legs. The worst of it was that he might be right. The high that came from fooling men, using them, bringing about their downfall . . . even the regret she felt over the Cantrell boy and other deaths she'd caused might not be enough to stop her. She had to stop herself or it wouldn't happen.

To do that, she had to get away from Andre's encouragement.

"You've lost your cross," he said.

Her hand flew to her throat. No, she hadn't lost it. She'd squirreled it away in a safe place. She nodded, afraid to speak because she was the only handmaiden to whom he'd given an ankh. It was an honor and a privilege . . . except she didn't believe in any of it anymore. She didn't believe in Andre.

His hand clasped hers, hard, and he led her away to his bedroom. The thought of having sex with him made her feet slow, and for once Teresa wished one of the handmaidens was waiting in the room as well, but it was not to be. She and Andre were alone.

As he stripped off her clothes and slipped the chain over her head, she thought of the money and passport she had hidden away. She had to leave soon or forever be in this limbo, away from her son, away from any chance at a normal life.

In her mind's eye she was inside a silver bird, flying far, far away.

The Bakoua Beach Hotel was renowned, a bit exclusive, and the perfect place to dissuade West from making any more threatening moves. She could even check in for the night if she had to, Callie reasoned. Whatever it took to keep West from Tucker.

She tried to dust herself off as they walked back toward the main road.

"You want to change?" West suggested, but Callie shook her head.

"All I want to do is sit. If you could get a taxi . . . ?"

He probably thought it was odd that she wasn't concerned with vanity. Maybe he would believe she was just too undone and passive to care. Whatever the case, he didn't argue. Instead, he suggested that Callie sit on the curb as he signaled for a cab. Eventually, one of the drivers spied them and motioned that he would pick them up after he dropped off his passengers.

A few minutes later the taxi pulled up beside them. West tucked a hand under Callie's upper arm and helped her to her feet. As soon as she was upright she pulled her arm from his grasp, catching sight of the driver's faint smile. Probably thought it was a lovers' quarrel. She couldn't wait to hear West's apology when he found out she really was Callie Cantrell.

"Bakoua Beach, *s'il vous plaît*," Callie said before West could give any other instructions. She didn't trust him, though she sensed he wasn't really interested in harming her. Or was that being too trusting?

He climbed in the backseat beside her, and, as the taxi pulled away, Callie let her muscles go limp and leaned her head back against the cushion. The drive was a little more than thirty minutes. She kept her eyes closed throughout the trip, only opening them once to catch a glimpse of the blue-green water of Fort-de-France Bay and the Caribbean Sea beyond between the stretches of hills, palms, and buildings.

When she'd left her cell phone and life behind in Los Angeles, she'd never thought she would need it to prove who she was. She considered pulling her wallet out and showing it to West but decided it would be better to wait until they could speak privately. Besides, she owed him nothing and the more miles they put between Tucker and him the better. If he wanted to keep thinking she was Teresa, have at it. She didn't need to be helpful.

And besides, she was really growing curious about West Laughlin and his search for his brother's son. If he was looking for Tucker, *her* Tucker, then she sure as hell wanted to know what this was all about. He wasn't the only one who sought answers.

The taxi pulled into the sweeping drive in front of the Bakoua Beach. West paid the fare, then guided Callie inside, his hand at her elbow. This time she didn't pull away as they walked through the open-air lobby, past the woman at the reception desk, around the circular, outdoor bar and to the steps that led to the beach.

The hotel was built into a hillside, the main reception area a level above the pool, the pool above the cabanas, the cabanas and restaurant above the beach. West took Callie to the restaurant, but the amount of stairs she had to climb down took their toll, and by the time he pulled back her chair her knees were trembling.

"Thé glacé," he said to the waitress as he sat down across from Callie. He raised two fingers. *"Deux."*

Iced tea. Callie wondered just how good his command of the French language was. Maybe better than her own?

"You look like you're going to faint," West said, his gaze moving over her pale face.

"I never faint."

"You're bleeding."

She followed his gaze and realized a thin line of blood had run down her right leg. "My knee," she said, pulling up her skirt to above the injury. The skin was scraped and there was a small, deeper cut in her flesh.

He was silent for long moments.

"What?" she asked.

He didn't answer but she could tell he was disturbed that she was hurt. Well, good. He should be. Taking her own fate into her hands Callie dug through her carryall and pulled out her wallet, unclasped it, and shoved her California driver's license in front of his face.

The iced tea came as he was looking at her picture. "Take it," she told him, slapping the wallet in his hands. "Rob me blind."

Callie reached for her glass and sat back. She glanced over at him, focusing at the dark, silky hair at his crown as he continued to gaze down at her picture. When she felt as if an eternity had come and gone and still he didn't speak, she lost patience and demanded, "Well?"

His brows were knit in concentration, and a trickle of sweat ran down the curve of his jaw.

"See my name and picture?" she demanded.

He lifted his eyes and glanced at the bracelet. Then he looked at her identification again.

Callie realized, in a distant part of her mind, that this was the longest she'd gone without thinking about Sean since his death. She stuffed that thought aside to dissect it later and said, "If my license is good enough for the state of California, it ought to be good enough for you."

He didn't answer.

Callie fought back another smart comment, deciding if this was a silent battle of wills, she could play. He ignored her credit cards and the crinkled edges of the euros shoved into her wallet. His expression gave no clue to his thoughts.

At long last he said, "You applied for this driver's license less than a year ago."

"It's a renewal." At his renewed silence she couldn't help herself from adding, "It is. I've lived in California since I was twenty. Before I was Callie Cantrell I was Callie Shipley."

"You're married?"

"I'm a widow."

He scowled and instantly his behavior changed. "I know," he said darkly. "I know what you did."

Callie narrowed her gaze at him. "You know I'm not this Teresa you're looking for."

"Then you're her twin."

"Fine," she snapped.

He made a sharp movement with his arm, closed her wallet, and dropped it back into her carryall. "I could almost believe you if I didn't know better," he said. "That lost and miserable act is hard to resist."

"I think you're the kind of person who can't admit they're wrong."

He inclined his head. "Probably. But you have the bracelet."

"I'm not Teresa."

"Where's your son?" he demanded.

Her gut twisted. Carefully, lest emotion got the better of her, she said, "The only son I ever had is dead."

His head jerked up and he gave her a sharp look. "Dead?"

"Don't worry. He's not the boy you're looking for." Her voice was brittle. "He was *my* son. He has nothing to do with you and this Teresa person. He only mattered to me." She swallowed hard, sensing she could break down if she wasn't careful.

He was watching her with a mixture of fascination and horror, as if he couldn't turn away.

"I don't know you," she insisted. "I don't know the boy you're looking for."

"Why did you come here with me, then?"

"Did I have a choice?" She was outraged. "What are you talking about?"

"You haven't tried to call the police. You didn't want me to go to your place, and you took me all the way to this particular hotel."

"Don't put this on me," Callie said, slightly alarmed.

"You've got some agenda going. If you're not Teresa, you're involved at some level, so start telling the truth."

"I *am* telling you the truth! I'm Callie Cantrell."

"Okay."

Callie stopped short. "Okay?"

"If you're Callie Cantrell, tell me about her. Convince me you're not the woman who married my brother and had a child with him. You're not the woman who took off after Stephen's death, with the bracelet, maybe to avoid questions about his death."

"What?"

"You're not Teresa DuPres Laughlin, even though you look just like her."

Callie suddenly understood West Laughlin's smoldering anger. Shaken, she said, "I'm not her. I was married to Jonathan Cantrell. We had a son. Sean. Jonathan and Sean both died in a car accident on Mulholland almost exactly a year ago. I have a series of scars down my right side from the same accident that killed them. I've been told I was lucky I survived, but I don't feel lucky. I feel miserable. And lost.

And sometimes—most times—I wish I'd died with them."
They stared at each other. She could tell her words got to
him and added, "I'm sorry about your brother, but I don't
know Teresa."

"I just want to find Stephen's son. I want to make sure
he's safe."

"I don't believe you."

"What?" He was taken aback.

"I think you're the one with the agenda."

He put his face within inches of hers. "I cared about my
brother, and I care about his son."

His voice had lowered to a whisper, but that took nothing
away from its intensity. On the contrary, every syllable
seemed to hammer into her brain. Callie held his gaze with
an effort. The pain in her jaw from the fall had created an
overall headache and she wasn't sure how much more of this
she could take.

"What's the matter?" he asked suddenly.

"Nothing."

"Don't give me that. You look terrible."

Was that a news bulletin? Of course she looked terrible.
He'd frightened her—*terrorized* her—chased after her and
scared her. How could she look any other way?

"Your jaw?" he asked, frowning.

"Yes, my jaw. My whole head hurts. Everything hurts."
When West made an impatient gesture, she embellished,
"It's killing me," then lifted a hand to cup her chin, wincing
a little.

"It's your own fault," he said tersely.

"It's *your* fault. You tackled me and I went facedown."

"You ran away. I never meant to hurt you."

"As I recall it, you said you wanted to kill me."

"Maybe you should lie down," he said, ignoring her jibe.

"Maybe I should go home?"

He smiled faintly, then sobered as he witnessed her flash of spirit give way to what he thought was pain. He looked down at the table and she sensed he was indecisive about what to do with her. She had a mental image of what he was seeing and understood his doubts. She probably looked like death itself.

"If you're not Teresa, you look enough like her to be her double. And the bracelet . . ." he said, trailing off as the waitress approached their table.

Callie asked for more tea and West ordered the continental breakfast tray for two.

As the waitress left, Callie realized how hungry she was. She'd missed breakfast and now it was lunchtime.

"If Stephen didn't give you the bracelet, where did you get it?" West asked.

Tricky territory. "It was—a gift from a friend."

"What friend?"

"Just someone I know."

"Who?"

"Her name is Aimee," she said, telling a half-truth. As soon as she'd said it she wished she'd come up with something else.

"Aimee," he said doubtfully after a long moment.

"That's right."

He shook his head. "There was an accident on Mulholland last year."

"Yes . . ."

"It just so happens I'm from Los Angeles too."

"Really." She found that faintly disturbing.

"You just decided to vacation on Martinique?"

"I came here on my honeymoon. With Jonathan," she reiterated.

"When was that?"

"Five . . . no, almost six years ago."

A tray of croissants, jellies, butter, and fresh pineapple rings arrived at that moment. Two more tall glasses of iced tea were put down in front of them and Callie felt her sinking spirits revive at the sight of food.

West didn't touch the tray. He was distant and remote, staring moodily across the water toward Fort-de-France. "You never met Stephen Laughlin?"

"No. I don't know Stephen—your brother, you said?— and I don't know you." Callie plucked up a croissant and began to butter it.

"Half brother," West said.

"Still don't know him."

"There aren't two women who look like you with that bracelet on this island."

"Probably not. But I'm not Teresa. If you don't believe my identification, then, I don't know. . . ." She broke off.

West leaned forward. "What?" he asked softly.

"You can call William Lister, the Cantrell family attorney. He'll tell you who I am. He knows I'm here. I'll give you the number."

"Family attorney, huh?"

"That's right. He'll tell you everything about me you need to know. Are you ready to write this down, or put it on your phone?"

West pulled out his cell phone. "You know your attorney's number by heart?"

"Well, yes," she said.

"You must have a close relationship," he said dryly. "I expected you to pull out your cell phone."

"I don't have a cell phone."

"Really?"

"Not everyone does," she pointed out.

"Yeah, but you look like the kind of woman who would."

"You make a lot of assumptions. What kind of job do you have?" she asked.

"I'm currently unemployed."

"Really."

He nodded, apparently unwilling to give her any further information. Callie told him the digits, making certain he repeated them back to her. "It's William's office number so his receptionist will probably answer."

"Who gave you the bracelet?" he asked again as he plugged the number into his call list.

"You think I'll have a different answer if you just keep asking?"

He lifted his head and half-smiled. But then he said, "That bracelet's a family heirloom. My grandmother's. And it's been missing since Teresa took off."

Callie didn't know how to respond. No wonder he thought she was Teresa.

Teresa . . .

Was there any chance *Teresa* was the name Jonathan had called her when they'd first met? Was that just coincidental, something she was trying to make up inside her mind? A connection that wasn't there?

She recalled it feeling strange, at the time, all the attention the wealthy and charming Jonathan Cantrell had suddenly showered on her. She'd been walking out of a coffee shop when he practically ran into her. Steadying her by her arms as she juggled her paper coffee cup, he'd said a name, then had caught himself up as if he'd just snapped out of a dream. He apologized for almost knocking her down and insisted on helping her to her seat. He'd been charming and good-looking, and wore designer label chinos, shirts, and deck shoes with ease. He'd sat down with her at the metal table for two and coaxed her cell number from her with very little effort, and then had pursued her as if she were the jewel in the crown. In a matter of months he'd gotten down on one knee and proposed and Callie, a teaching assistant at a nearby school who'd been thinking about going for her master's to become a full-fledged teacher, had accepted with tears in her eyes. The only relationship she'd really had was with Bryan. Bryan had followed his dream while Callie tutored, waited tables, and generally put her life on hold for him. It was years before she could make a final break, and only then when she learned he'd been seeing another wannabe actress who just happened to be pregnant with Bryan's child.

She was about a year out of that relationship when she met Jonathan. It was a fairy tale from the beginning. The handsome prince saving the drifting, slightly lost midtwenties gal with the red-gold hair. Except nothing about their marriage was magical except Sean.

Teresa . . . or Marissa . . . ?

She remembered Jonathan calling out to her and literally running into her, almost as if he'd done it on purpose. She recalled wondering if it was some ploy on his part. A way to meet women by practically knocking them off their feet. Hey, it was Los Angeles and she'd seen a lot of crazy things.

Her mind reached for that missing piece again. She failed, as ever, to grasp it, but a deep recognition filled her. There *was* a connection. Something . . . something . . . and thinking of Jonathan, and the name Teresa, brought it closer. Had Jonathan seen something of this Teresa in her? Was that why he'd been so eager to make her acquaintance in the first place? God, she wished she could remember fully, but there were big blanks in her memory since the accident. She'd tried to believe they were the result of her injuries, and maybe they were, but she'd needed time at Del Amo to put herself right mentally and emotionally.

Or maybe she was just trying to force a connection as

much as West Laughlin was, in order to make sense of everything.

West's jaw was slid to one side, as if he were fighting back something he wanted to say.

"Tell me about West Laughlin," she said.

"You really don't know who I am?"

"I thought we'd established that I'm not Teresa."

"Like I told you, I'm the black sheep of the family."

"That's all I get? How come you're unemployed, Mr. Laughlin?"

"Mr. Laughlin," he repeated ironically. "Okay . . . Ms. Cantrell . . . I got myself fired from the LAPD. They call it furloughed, but I pissed off my captain and he's trying really hard to keep me from getting rehired."

"What did you do?"

"Broke off a relationship with his daughter."

"Oh, really. That doesn't sound like something that would hold up."

West grinned for the first time, and Callie looked away, concentrating hard on the horizon instead of that devastating smile. She didn't like this man, she reminded herself. All she wanted was information from him that might explain something about Tucker.

"It wouldn't," he admitted. "But I didn't really give a damn at the time. My grandmother, Victoria, has believed for years that Teresa had something to do with Stephen's death. I always thought it was just that she wanted her grandson back. Tucker. Kinda had my own issues and ignored her, which is how she'd treated me most of my life. But then, some things happened and I wanted to make sure Tucker was okay too."

"Why are you looking for Teresa in Martinique?"

"The e-mail trail on Victoria's computer. Teresa tried to

wipe it off, but it was still there. I got the right people to find a way in and see what was written. There wasn't much."

"You know the right people."

"I know tech people," he said. "The e-mail went to an Internet café in Fort-de-France. I've already been there but no one remembers anything and it was a while ago."

He was watching her closely as he gave her this information, as if expecting her to jump up and scream, "You got me!" She shook her head and said, "Still not me."

"You were on the pier this morning, wearing the bracelet." His gaze drifted upward. "You didn't even change the color of your hair."

"You've never actually met this Teresa," she said.

"No, but I've got a picture."

"You do?" she asked in a tone that suggested he'd been holding out on her.

He pulled out his cell phone, touched the screen for the photo app, and scrolled until he came to a picture. He then held the phone up so she could see. Callie shaded her eyes from the bright sun and examined the image on the screen. It was a picture of a man and a woman standing beside each other in front of a rambling, two-story house with a wide, covered porch that looked straight out of the Old West.

"Victoria said that it was taken shortly after the wedding," he explained. "I scanned it and put it on my phone after she asked me to find you and the boy." At her studied silence, he added, "It's the best I could do."

Callie was only half-listening. The young woman in the picture was definitely not her, though she did bear a striking resemblance. It was the hair that was the same, distinctive, and their body type. Facially, it was difficult to tell as the woman was looking into the sun, squinting against the glare. Callie estimated her age in the midtwenties and as

Callie herself was over thirty, she asked, "How old is this photograph?"

"It was taken about five years ago."

"Well, it's not me. I see the resemblance, but it's not me." It didn't look anything like Aimee, either. "Who's the guy? Your brother?" She turned her attention to the man in the picture standing next to Teresa, his arm wrapped protectively around her waist. He was dark, like West, with a serious face, but otherwise there was little resemblance.

"Half brother," he said again.

"And Victoria's your grandmother?" Callie asked.

"The Laughlin matriarch," he agreed.

"And she put you on this quest?"

West held out his hand for the phone. "That's right."

"Maybe you should call her and let me talk to her," Callie suggested. "She knew Teresa. She should know I'm not her, right?"

"Maybe if she met you in the flesh. She's in her eighties, and my phone's not working internationally," he said. "Tried to set it up before I left, but apparently there's some hiccup."

"So, where are these tech people when you need them," she murmured dryly as she handed his phone back to him.

"Yeah, well . . ." He gazed around the restaurant as if seeing it for the first time. "I'm halfway convinced you're not Teresa."

"Only halfway? Really?"

"Tell me who really gave you the bracelet. Lead me down that path the right way. Convince me I'm wrong, and I'll apologize and go away."

Far across the bay a flock of gulls swooped down, crying plaintively. Callie watched a ferry chug toward the Pointe du Bout terminal and silently wondered what she could say that would still keep Tucker safe. A part of her believed him halfway as well.

She reached for her iced tea, thinking hard. She recalled the first few times she'd met Tucker. The way he'd meditatively rubbed Callie's red-gold hair between his fingers and wrapped his arms around her like he never wanted to let go, a behavior she'd unabashedly encouraged. If she accepted what he was saying, then it seemed probably that Aimee was not Tucker's mother, that this mysterious Teresa was, and that Callie wasn't the only one using someone as an emotional surrogate. Tucker was using her for the same purpose.

the many terrible things she'd done since to keep him safe and off Andre's radar.

If Andre knew about him, he would kill Tucker.

Her heart started pounding from the direction of her thoughts, and she studiously and firmly shut her mind down. She'd learned to compartmentalize with greater and greater efficiency over the years and could almost make herself believe she lived a different life. If called upon, she could give one helluva performance, Oscar-winning, really, because it was less about acting and more about believing.

But how had she so foolishly believed in Andre? At one time he'd filled her thoughts, her heart, all her needs. If he'd been lost to her then, she might have killed herself like some tragic Juliet. She knew this to be true. She just couldn't believe it any longer. *Couldn't* feel it.

Tucker had done that to her. Her love for him was bigger than anything else. Had changed her. And it was such a fluke, the pregnancy. Not part of the plan, not part of her aim, her job. As soon as he was born there was a shift inside her. Afterward, even though she'd kept doing Andre's bidding, playing her part, she'd kept the fact that she'd borne a child a secret from him. Even after Stephen's death—especially after Stephen's death—she'd had to come up with a plan for the future, one that didn't include Andre. She'd done the only thing she could think of: she'd entrusted her son to the care of someone she believed in.

But she was going back for him soon. Tonight, maybe.

Cracking open an eye, she slid a look toward Andre. Her heart clutched and she gave a little gasp to see he was wide awake as well and staring at her speculatively. Lifting the arm he'd held possessively around her, he ran his index finger down her arm, sending an arctic chill through her that it took her considerable skill as a con artist to hide.

"You're going to have to start being more honest with me,

Teresa," he said with that faint smile that spelled trouble for her in the future.

"About what?" *When in doubt, pretend ignorance.*

"About last night, for starters."

"I went to the Boathouse to meet him and he came in, but he brought his wife with him."

"And then what?" he asked silkily.

"I followed them back to their Laguna house." She mentally crossed her fingers against the lie. The Laguna Beach house was several hours' south and she hadn't been anywhere near it, but she was counting on its distance to keep one of Andre's spies—Naomi, probably, or maybe that psychotic bitch, Jerrilyn—from tracking her. "I might . . . be able to break in sometime . . . ?" she suggested.

"Do you want to?" he asked, climbing atop her.

An automatic protest fought its way up her throat. There was a time when she'd panted for his lovemaking. Back in the day when they were a team. Andre was a good lover when he wanted to be, and in the beginning he'd been just about perfect. But everything had changed since then. His style had definitely altered and now there was more impatience and dominance than any desire to please her. Maybe, with the other handmaidens so available, he just didn't try as hard. Or maybe the frustration that had always fed him was growing too huge and he couldn't be bothered with anything but his own, immediate pleasure.

He reached up and pulled the chain that held his ankh from around his neck, then slid the cross along her cheek and to her mouth. Then he pressed down harder until the ankh's metal sides dug painfully into her bottom lip. Hard. A rise of panic made her insides quiver. She breathed in air through her nose and met his gaze deliberately. She had to act like her old self or he would know how much she'd changed.

"You have to stop lying," he said.

Carefully, slowly, he pulled the ankh away and replaced it on the nightstand. She automatically sucked her bottom lip into her mouth. She could feel fury licking its way inside her; a hot wind that could consume her if she let it.

"Where were you?"

"I told you."

He shook his head slowly. He'd taken his hair out of its band and it hung around his face. "You shouldn't make me discipline you," he said, sounding like a weary parent.

"I'm sorry," she said. Her plan to leave became more cemented.

His hands slid down her body and he fit himself in the cradle of her thighs. They looked at each other and Teresa kept her face carefully expressionless.

Tonight, she thought. *I'm leaving tonight.*

Time was passing and Callie had managed to avoid his question about the bracelet, sticking with her story that a friend had given it to her. But he was right in that being the sticking point. If it was indeed the Laughlin heirloom, then it must have come through Teresa and logically that made her Tucker's mother.

But where was she? And who was Aimee?

She knew West was biding his time, waiting for her to cough up the truth. Did she want to? Not yet . . . not until she knew what it would mean for her to give up Tucker.

"Well, I think it has to all be a strange coincidence," Callie said. "If there's a connection, I don't know what it is."

"You came here on your honeymoon."

"Well . . . yes."

"That's why you chose Martinique now. Why you came back here."

"That's right." She didn't like the careful way he was

approaching some train of thought that was clearly behind his questions.

"The accident, where your husband and son were killed . . ."

Callie took a careful breath. "You want to know about it?"

"I just want to know how you ended up here with the Laughlin bracelet."

"I only have your word it's a family heirloom," she pointed out.

"True enough."

Callie shook her head. She needed to end this conversation and get back to her apartment, find Tucker, and most of all, keep him safe. She said with as little emotion as she could, "They said another car struck us and sent our car over the cliff. Sean and Jonathan died at the scene. I was taken to a hospital."

"They said?"

"The police. Whoever investigated the crash."

"Do you know who that is?"

"You mean the policeman? No. I was in a hospital, and then I was . . ." *Grief-stricken . . . sick with guilt and failure and pure misery.* She had to bite down hard on her lip to keep from going into that abyss again, the one that was always waiting for her. She waited till the tide receded a bit, then managed to say in a nearly normal voice, "Nothing was the same. They were gone and I didn't care how it happened. All that mattered was they were no longer with me."

Callie squeezed her hands tightly together, damn near cutting off the blood flow. It was an effort to get herself to loosen her grip.

"I'm sorry," he said, sounding like he meant it.

No, she thought. *Don't be nice to me. Don't act like you care.* She could manage if people weren't nice to her, but if they were she lost all of her defenses. And she couldn't afford to break down completely like she had when the realization had crashed down on her. She'd been a blithering idiot. Completely undone. And she'd ended up hiding from reality for a while.

"I was just wondering who checked out the crash."

"I don't know. LAPD . . . you probably have a better idea than I do."

"Your husband chose Martinique for your honeymoon?" he asked.

"We chose it together."

But had they? Callie remembered the brochures Jonathan had brought from the travel agency, and the way they'd bent their heads over the Internet together, planning for their future. Callie had been too happy to pay much attention to honeymoon plans. There was a wedding to plan, and even though they'd kept it small—both of them had definitely wanted that—it had required the requisite organization, list making, phone calling and e-mailing. She hadn't questioned Jonathan's choice of Martinique, but now she wondered.

The reason she'd come back here was more because Sean had been conceived on their honeymoon, not because the trip itself had been such a fabulous time. She recalled distinctly how Jonathan would wander away from her and she would find him in the hotel bar, passing the time with the bartender and waitstaff. Yes, he made love to her and they had dinners together, but she'd sun-bathed alone a lot of the time, and she'd felt the first twinges of worry that she didn't know her new husband at all.

Jonathan Cantrell had swept her off her feet, and she'd been flattered and overwhelmed by his good looks and wealth. She'd wanted so much to believe that he truly wanted her that she'd shut down her radar and fallen in love with him hard and fast. Or at least that's what she'd told herself after Bryan left her.

Looking for love in all the wrong places.

Sean was the only reason she hadn't left Jonathan in the years after the marriage. Jonathan didn't love her, maybe hadn't ever, and she kinda thought she'd made herself believe she was in love with him. In truth, neither of them had known each other very well.

"Jonathan and I honeymooned here." She swept an arm to encompass the grounds.

"At the Bakoua Beach?"

"Yep."

She wondered what time it was. Early afternoon, maybe two? It was time she got away from him. "Your turn," she said. "You were let go for breaking up with your captain's daughter."

"Not the official reason," he reminded.

"What was the official reason?"

"Captain Paulsen said I was too aggressive during an investigation."

Her eyes moved to the small smear of dried blood on her leg. "Imagine that."

"It wouldn't have mattered what it was, it was just to punish me. But then Victoria laid down a convincing case and I didn't give a damn about anything but finding Teresa and Tucker."

"You said something new came to light."

"Yeah, well . . ." He clearly didn't want to talk about it. Instead, he said, "Teresa barely stuck around long enough to make Stephen's funeral before she took Tucker away. Victoria always blamed her, but it was all conjecture. Everyone thought my grandmother was old and just making it all up, though she's always been sharp as a tack. It took a lot for her to finally ask me to help her, since we've never been on close terms. That's how much she wants Tucker."

"She thinks Teresa's to blame?"

"She thinks Teresa had a hand in the accident that killed Stephen."

"And you do too?" No wonder he'd been so harsh in the beginning.

"She's got some things to answer for. She didn't waste a lot of tears over Stephen, and she took off with his son almost from the moment he was gone. She's been missing ever since, probably by design."

"You must have something more . . . ?"

"Suspicions. I just want to find her. Even if she's not to blame, she's completely self-serving, and I want to make sure Stephen's son is okay. That's what Victoria says she wants too, though I think she'd like Teresa to be declared an unfit mother."

"What happened to Stephen?"

"A hunting accident. He was out with a friend. Something happened and Stephen got in the way when the friend's rifle discharged. Shot him in the chest. Devastated the friend."

"But . . ."

"I know. How is Teresa responsible. Victoria says she was having an affair with the friend. His name's Edmund Mikkels."

"And she got him to *kill* your brother?"

"Half brother. Not necessarily, but I believe she had an affair with Edmund. That's just how she operates."

"No wonder you wanted to kill me," Callie murmured. "Well, I'm not her. I don't have anything to do with any of this."

His gaze, which had been centered on her face, slowly moved to the bracelet at her wrist. "Where can I find this Aimee?" he asked.

Callie struggled with herself. She wanted to tell him. She wanted to trust in him implicitly, but she wasn't exactly batting a thousand when it came to her judgment of men. "All right, I lied. I picked the bracelet up at a pawnshop."

The words were out before she even thought them through. *Careful,* she warned herself, wishing she could take them back.

"What pawnshop?"

"I—hmmm. It was in Barbados. I flew there first, for a couple of days, and the bracelet was on display in the window."

"Barbados?"

"Yes."

Lies, lies, and more lies. After giving him a straightforward and credible story about her past now she was lying. And she was such a terrible liar! But she wasn't about to bring up Tucker yet. She believed him, to a point. Believed that, like herself, he'd doled her partial truths, and until she knew the whole story, she wasn't going to say anything that she didn't need to.

"Stephen gave Teresa that bracelet or she took it," he insisted in a low voice.

"Maybe she pawned it," Callie said.

"I don't think so."

Callie felt as if a cold hand had traced a line down her back. She'd made a whopping mistake. He knew she was lying.

"Who's the friend who gave it to you?" he asked.

"I just said—"

"I'll believe the first story."

"Well, I can't help that."

They were at an impasse. "All right. I'll take you back and we can figure the rest out."

"What do you mean?"

He made an impatient sound. "What do you think I mean? I mean, you're my connection to Tucker and Teresa. You need to get back and take care of yourself, and I need to repay you for all the trouble I've caused."

"I'm fine. Truly."

"You took a hit and you're scraped up—"

"A misunderstanding."

"You said I attacked you," he reminded her.

"Well, I didn't mean that, I was just trying to . . . goad you. But you're absolutely right. I did this to myself."

"What the hell's going on?" he asked. "You're being awfully agreeable." He was looking at her with the same narrow-eyed suspicion he had earlier.

And suddenly she was done. Reaction, or the realization that anything she said to this man was dangerous until she had more information—both, probably—caused her to just shut down. Whatever interest she'd had in talking to him, and there had been some, she could admit that, she now felt none. She needed to leave. Get away from him. Pull herself together and keep Tucker safe.

"I'll just use the bathroom to clean up." She got to her feet and dusted herself off.

He rose to his feet to help her up the stairs but she waved him away as she picked up her carryall. In truth, her head had been filled with a dull ache for a while now.

"I'll be a while," she said.

"All right. I'll wait at the bar."

"No, I'll come back." She moved lithely away from him, pretending she wasn't starting to feel the mass of bruises that were settling in from her earlier fall.

She wished she had a way to call Tucker on the phone, or at least Aimee, but she didn't know their number, whether they had a phone, or a cell, or anything. She knew next to nothing about them other than Tucker was a sweet little boy she would lay down her life to protect, if necessary.

West stared after the woman who looked so much like Teresa. She'd lied to him, was still lying to him. The needle on his bullshit meter was flickering in the red, and he trusted his instincts completely. He'd been a cop for too many years to be bamboozled by an amateurish liar.

And Callie Cantrell, if that was truly who she was, was most definitely lying. About the bracelet for certain. There was no goddamned pawnshop in Barbados or anywhere else that had this piece, unless Teresa had pawned it herself, and that chance was slim to none. The bracelet was part of the Laughlin family collection that was catalogued, insured, and kept in a safe-deposit box. He might not be a true member of the family, at least in his grandmother's eyes, but he sure as hell had been tutored in what they possessed, by his mother, his father, and Victoria, too.

It was probably closer to the truth that she'd gotten the bracelet from her friend, Aimee, if she was truly Callie Cantrell.

Well, fine. He'd figure it out one way or another. And he'd lied to her, as well. His cell phone worked internationally. He wouldn't have come all this way without making certain he could communicate at will. He just hadn't wanted to stop and call anyone on her behalf until he was completely certain she wasn't Teresa.

And she wasn't Teresa. That didn't track. But how could this doppelgänger with the Laughlin bracelet not be involved? That really didn't track. So, how did she fit into this puzzle? His gut told him she was involved in Stephen Tucker's abduction somehow.

Reaching into his pocket, he fingered his phone. He could call the number of the attorney she'd given him. Or he could call Dorcas at the department and get the details about the fatal accident on Mulholland that had killed a father and son. See if their name was Cantrell. See if a woman named Callie Cantrell had survived.

Pulling out his phone, he glanced at the time. Two thirty, and the day felt like it was getting hotter. Thank God for the breeze off the bay.

* * *

How much time did she have? Ten minutes? Five? Callie
sluiced water on her face, thought about cleaning herself
up more, then glanced at her image in the mirror. Lines of
strain had formed around her mouth. Her eyes were wide
and slightly anxious. Well, no shit. She'd done okay with
him, but now that she was free she wanted to run screaming
out of here.

Quickly, she tucked the carryall over her shoulder and left
the ladies' room, turning toward the front of the hotel and the
outdoor portico where taxis and rental vehicles vied to drop
off or pick up hotel patrons. The doorman saw her and inter-
preted that she wanted a taxi without her even saying so, opening the door of one that had just pulled in with a flourish.

"Fort-de-France," she told the driver, searching in her
purse for a tip. She thanked the doorman, shoving several
bills into his hand before sliding into the backseat. "Please,
hurry. *S'il vous plaît.*"

The cabbie nodded and they were on their way. As they
sped off, her eye fell to Fort-de-France Bay and the ferry
churning its way toward Pointe du Bout.

"Wait . . ." she said.

Chapter Five

Just after noon in Los Angeles the clouds opened up and poured rain down in torrents. It never rained in LA except when it did and then it blasted down in sheets. Andre walked out into the October downpour utterly naked and turned his face to the heavens. It was cold, hard, and nothing like Papeete weather, or anywhere else on Tahiti, but it was sharper and more cleansing.

He was, after all, The Messiah. Meant for greatness, and if those conniving bitches, the handmaidens, could ever put together an original thought among them they would see him for what he was. Oh, he sensed their playacting. They thought themselves so cagey and clever, but they were empty-headed vessels just made for filling up, then winding up, then setting on their way to do his bidding.

Rain ran over his upturned face and down his chest and the dark, thick strands of his shoulder-length hair. He could smell the sea from where he stood, a briny, frigid scent unlike the musty, luscious heat that came off the South Pacific. He'd been in the States for almost ten years and he was closer to fulfilling his mission than he'd ever been, but there were still hurdles to be leaped, misfortunes to be avenged, people to kill.

There was also a long list of those who'd dismissed him, and he would not be dismissed. They didn't know him as The Messiah, but they would soon. And then he could dispense with the handmaidens. Clarice, that mealy-mouthed piece of meat, had once had the nerve to question his title.

"There's only one true messiah," she'd said, her expression troubled, her body tight with fear and rebellion. "And that's God."

He'd punished her for that. It had to be done. And though she'd cried and curled up in a ball from the rough sex and solitary confinement, she'd never questioned him again. Neither had any of the others, who'd kept their eyes downcast and swore how much they loved him. *Lies!* But he'd pretended to believe them all. When he'd released Clarice from her confinement and then used some of the money to shower her with clothes, jewelry, and gifts, she'd glowed under all the deliberate one-on-one he'd shown her. The other handmaidens had been bright green with jealousy. And everything had gone back to the way it should be.

At least that's what they would have him believe, though he sensed, very clearly, that there was a change afoot. Clarice had openly defied him, although Teresa had been pulling back for a long time.

He shook his head, water spraying in all directions. There were houses on all sides of their rental, but they were bungalows whose windows could not see over the tall fence. No one could see him standing naked in the rain. It was too bad they needed privacy because the thought of prying eyes brought his penis erect. He smiled as he thought of how much he would like to have them watch.

But he couldn't bring attention to their way of life. He needed obscurity as he moved forward in his plan. The handmaidens didn't know it, but the endgame was nigh. The pyramid was being dismantled; the lower levels had been taken out first, peripheral players who'd nevertheless been in his way as he ascended to the top level.

And once he was there—once he was standing on the pinnacle—then he truly would be The Messiah and he would have no more need for the handmaidens. He would also be wealthy, respected, and in his rightful place. They thought they could take it from him, but they were wrong.

"Andre?"

Daniella's voice scraped along his nerves. He fought back a surge of anger as the sliding door slid open and she stepped cautiously outside, hovering under the eave to keep from being drenched by rain. She was the smallest and plainest of the handmaidens. He would never have accepted her if he hadn't needed someone with her attributes. Someone nonthreatening, non-memorable, almost nonexistent. Someone incredibly malleable who would scarcely cause a ripple of interest once she was gone for good.

"Irene called about the rent," she said, clicking her teeth in that annoying way she had when she was nervous. "I think maybe Robert put her up to it."

"You think?" he questioned.

Flustered, she said, "No . . . I mean . . . you said her son was a growing problem."

"I did say that," he agreed, and she bobbed her head eagerly, afraid. His good mood vanished as he considered the addled old woman who was their landlord and whose son was trying to take over her finances. He wished Irene Lumpkin would just die and be done with it . . . except that he liked the house, and if she died, Robert would take over and sell the place as fast as he could. And they didn't have enough money to buy it . . . not yet, anyway . . . though soon . . . soon . . . damn southern California real estate prices. It was robbery, plain and simple.

"She said she wanted the rent by four o'clock today," Daniella added diffidently. "Can . . . can I get it to her?"

Daniella was the face of their home. Irene thought she lived in the house with her sisters. No one knew about Andre. Daniella kept the fact that a man lived in the house secret, which was one of the reasons Robert Lumpkin felt he could maneuver things his way.

Andre hadn't planned another killing for the immediate future. He didn't want anything to disrupt the momentum of his plan. But then again, he couldn't have a piece of excrement like Robert Lumpkin mucking things up.

There was cash in the safe. More than enough for the rent, but the supply was dwindling. Shooing Daniella back inside, Andre then stalked to his bedroom where Teresa was still lying in his bed. What was wrong with that woman? One moment she was sneaking in and doing his bidding with energy to burn, the next she was a lump of meat.

"Get up," he snarled. She roused herself with an effort and staggered out of the room.

He then went to the safe and twirled the combination after a quick look over his shoulder to see if any of the handmaidens were there. He loved them dearly, in his way, but they couldn't know how to get to the money. He couldn't trust them. They were children, really.

Pulling out one of the stacks of cash, he gloomily considered the safe-deposit box at the bank where most of the rest of the cash was hidden. He had a bank account under his real name; one of the only good things his father had done was get him a Social Security Number. He'd opened the account years earlier on one of the few trips he'd taken to the States about ten years before his final return.

Selecting several thick rolls, he tucked most of the money in the zippered pockets of one of his jackets, then

gave Daniella enough for the rent and told her to drop it at the
Lumpkin house. "Take the Chevy," he said, the least auspi-
cious of the three cars they were currently using. Its plates
were good for another three months. "Don't give the money
to Robert. Only Irene."

"But Robert always answers the door," she whined.

Andre ground his teeth together and nodded once, allowing her to give the cash to Irene's son, and Daniella scooted
for the door.

He watched her leave and his thoughts turned to the rest
of the handmaidens, wondering which one would be best to
strike up an acquaintance with the fat and greedy Robert
Lumpkin. He'd only seen Daniella up close and personal, so
it could be any one of them: Clarice, Teresa, Jerrilyn, or
Naomi. Tall, statuesque, and stern Naomi might be too
much for him, and Teresa was off her game. Clarice, maybe,
although she had that streak of religion that made him want
to strangle her. Jerrilyn. She was on another job, but she
could probably fit Robert Lumpkin in too. But she wasn't
perfect either. Too unpredictable and self-indulgent. Still,
she'd been the one with the best results, if you discounted
Teresa.

Fleetingly he thought of women he'd had before Teresa.
To a one they'd been possessive, would never have understood about the handmaidens. They thought it was cheating,
when he was with another woman, and he'd parted with each
of them quickly. Like so many things, they were from another time, another place, another life. Before Teresa and
Martinique, before California, before his plan had crystallized. The dark days before he'd truly understood his calling.

Andre's thoughts touched briefly on his father and he
scowled, feeling a renewed spurt of fury lick through him.
The man had dragged his wife and young son all over the
South Pacific, beating both of them when he was drunk and
stupid, which was more times than he was sober. Andre had

been forced to kill him to save his mother and himself. By then they'd been in Tahiti, and though there had been an investigation into the drowning victim's death, no one suspected the nine-year-old boy who'd lured his drunken father to the sea, smacked him with a rock, and held his unconscious body underwater.

It had been necessary, and though Andre's mother suspected, she never said anything. After her death, which he'd never quite understood—she'd just given up the will to live—he'd found the documents that explained who he was and he'd realized that he was meant for greatness. It was his heritage, his destiny. He stayed with a series of foster families until he was sixteen, then started grifting.

He ran through a slew of women until he found Teresa. He remembered being bowled over the first time he'd seen her, even though she tried to pull a con on him. But he was ahead of her at that game, and as soon as she realized that fact, they became compatriots and lovers. Both hungry for money and each other. Perfect partners. Together they worked wealthy patrons at a number of the finer hotels and then, when they'd picked the area clean, so to speak, they moved on to California. Teresa didn't know his ultimate plans, but she'd left Martinique before she was caught or snitched on by people who swore to be their friends, but who would sell you out in a heartbeat.

No one could be trusted. Not even Teresa any longer . . . especially not Teresa.

Now, seating himself cross-legged on his bedroom floor, he closed his eyes and pressed his palms together, imagining the doughy, mean-spirited face of Robert Lumpkin. For long moments he drove killing thoughts into the man's dark heart.

You are targeted for death, Robert Lumpkin.

He stayed in the same position until he felt the beginnings of a blinding headache. They were happening more frequently and though he'd shoved off Clarice's concern—she'd caught him damn near unconscious one day—he knew he had to get to his endgame soon. He needed a medical doctor but didn't trust anyone, didn't want to give away where he lived.

A long time later he got to his feet and headed for a shower, his headache breaking up.

He would call Jerrilyn.

West kicked himself all the way back to Fort-de-France. He'd waited far too long for Callie to reappear, trusting that she was who she'd said she was, never dreaming she would slip out the front of the hotel and disappear. God. If he'd thought about throttling her before, now he really wanted to. Except it was his fault.

Realizing she wasn't coming back, he'd tried to talk to the doorman who'd clammed up quick when he'd witnessed West's temper. But she had to have taken a cab, and so he was doing the same, hoping he was close enough behind to catch up to her before she disappeared into one of the many apartment buildings around the alley where he'd first accosted her. Yeah, he felt a little bad about the way he'd treated her, purposely trying to scare her, but so what. Now she was in the wind. And he'd let her go. It was his fault, no one else's. If she decided to hole up inside her apartment, it could be a while before he found her again, but he would find her. Damn. He shouldn't have trusted her an inch. What the hell was wrong with him?

You liked her.

He swore under his breath. Yeah, he'd liked her. Just like his brother had.

She's not Teresa. But she's . . . someone who could be equally as deceptive.

His ego had taken a direct hit. After Roxanne and their

messy on-again, off-again relationship, he'd believed himself wise to the lures of the female sex, but hell . . . he was just as stupid and clueless as he'd been before. Grabbing up his cell phone, he put a call in to Pete Dorcas's mobile. When he got his old partner's voice mail, he debated on even leaving a message, then said tersely, "Hey, I need your help. You remember that crash off Mulholland last year, the father and son were killed, mother survived. Get me as much information on that as you can. Thanks. I owe you."

He gazed out the window at the passing landscape. "God. Damn," he said through gritted teeth.

Callie's heart was beating unevenly as she walked along the dock, and she had to repress the urge to look over her shoulder. She was not a superstitious person but she couldn't control the feeling of urgency that assailed her. She had to get back to Tucker. Immediately. Without West Laughlin.

Aimee Thomas wasn't Tucker's mother. Teresa was. Had to be. And it explained why Tucker spoke such excellent English while Aimee spoke only a few words, or at least that was what she would have Callie believe. Though Callie had only met her once, Aimee had seemed overly wary of her. Callie had found that odd since Aimee let Tucker wander the streets with his friends as if he were years older, a freedom that drove Callie half crazy.

Had Teresa stowed Tucker with Aimee? Were they friends? Had they known each other for years? West said there were e-mails from Teresa to someone who had picked them up at an Internet café several years earlier. Was it Aimee? Who maybe now possessed a smartphone and picked up her e-mail that way . . . or who texted?

Why had Teresa left Tucker with Aimee? Was she maybe on the run? Because she had something to do with her husband's death? Was West's grandmother right, or was she elderly and paranoid?

Or maybe Teresa just stashed Tucker with Aimee because he was an encumbrance? *Where was she?*

Now she did glance over her shoulder. The taxi driver had left her at the hub of the tourist shops scattered along the periphery of the Pointe du Bout marina's docks. There were people behind her but none that she recognized. She glanced both left and right but saw no sight of an angry West Laughlin chasing her. In front of her were the narrow white spires and rigging of the sailboats that created a mesh against the cloudless blue sky.

Stephen Tucker Laughlin. West Laughlin's nephew. Was he really *her* Tucker?

He gave you the bracelet, she reminded herself.

The ferry horn blasted twice and Callie hurried down the pier. Once more she glanced nervously behind herself, but she was still alone. The sun hit the amethyst gems and made them sparkle. She slipped off the bracelet and put it deep inside her carryall. If it was an heirloom, she sure as hell didn't want it to be seen any longer. She didn't even want it in her possession, but what should she do? Give it to West? Or give it back to Aimee, since Tucker wouldn't take it?

She ground her teeth together. She didn't want to give it to Aimee, after what West had said.

It seemed to take forever for the people to empty the ferry. Callie stood in the crush of tourists eager to visit Fort-de-France. Stepping onto the boat, she hazarded one more glance at the pier. Nothing. The ghosts were all in her own mind.

When the engines changed and the ferry began to pull back into the bay, Callie was on the aft deck, one hand gripped tightly around the wide white railing. She held her breath until they were underway. She wouldn't fool him for long. She knew that without being told.

She just needed a little time to get back to Fort-de-France and find Tucker before West Laughlin did.

Teresa could hear Andre talking on his cell to Jerrilyn about Robert Lumpkin and thanked her lucky stars that he hadn't put her on that job. It was a bit of a worry, actually, that he'd chosen Jerrilyn over her in that she was the natural choice. Was he onto her? Aware that she had other plans? Did he have some other job for her?

She was lying on the couch, pretending to be asleep, when she heard him walk over toward her.

"You gonna sleep all day?" he demanded, irked.

Carefully, Teresa opened her eyes and drew herself into a sitting position. Andre was dressed in light pants and a white shirt. His hair was pulled back in a low ponytail, held by a thong of leather. He looked handsome and serious, and briefly she remembered why she'd been so enamored of him, why she'd done all the things she'd done on his behalf.

"I need you to take care of a problem for me."

"I thought I heard you talking to Jerrilyn."

"She's busy," he clipped out.

"What is it?" she asked carefully. She wanted to leave tonight. She was pretending to be napping while her brain was churning, her stomach clenched with anxiety.

"I need you to neutralize Robert Lumpkin."

Her heart sank. Ever since she'd caused the death of Jonathan's son, she'd been unable to follow through with all of Andre's orders. She'd explained why and he'd pretended to understand, had given her jobs that didn't require her to kill anyone else, but now she knew that time of reprieve was over.

His face flashed with annoyance. "Daniella took the rent to him and is watching Irene's house. When Lumpkin leaves, she'll let me know where he's gone and I want you on him. Do you understand?"

She nodded.

"Say it."

"Yes, I understand."

"*Say it!*"

"Yes, Messiah. I understand," Teresa said woodenly, the words ashes in her mouth.

He eyed her with suspicion but Teresa pretended not to notice.

"Make it happen tonight."

On leaden feet, Teresa went to the closet she shared with Jerrilyn, passing by Naomi, who gave her a sympathetic look that Teresa knew to be a fake. None of them cared a whit about any of the others.

She took a shower, dried her hair, and applied a thick coating of foundation, then overplayed her eyeliner, lashes, and lipstick. She added a liberal coating of blush as well. She knew enough about Robert Lumpkin from what Daniella had described over the last several years to suspect he wanted pizzazz over elegance. "His eyes are all over my tits every time I hand him the rent," she'd said, "and he always waits to close the door when I'm leaving. I looked back once. His eyes were glued to my ass. He's round and losing his hair, which he's got in a comb-over. He's pathetic and he knows it."

Subtlety would not be the way to go to catch his attention.

When Teresa was ready, she sat down at the table where they took all their meals. It could be a long wait, depending on when Lumpkin decided to leave his mother's house. Maybe it wouldn't even happen today, but in any case she had to be ready at a moment's notice.

As she sat there, she felt a slow, heavy beat begin inside her chest. It was a familiar friend. Oh, she could posture all she wanted, she could feel the throb of anticipation. Adrenaline junkie. That's what she was, and though she never, ever wanted to hurt an innocent, the thought of taking care of an asshole like Robert Lumpkin got her juices flowing.

Raising her eyes, she saw that Andre was watching her across the table, his arms crossed over his chest. As if he knew what she was feeling, he smiled with approval.

I'm leaving you, she thought. *For good this time. It's not the same anymore.*

You're not the same.

But she smiled back in understanding, letting him believe she was back in the fold. And just because she resented having to do his bidding one last time didn't mean she couldn't enjoy it. She would just do it her way.

Callie stepped off the ferry into long afternoon shadows. Her apartment wasn't near the pier so she gazed around for a taxi, lifting her arm and shading her eyes against the sun. West Laughlin was going to have a cow when he realized she was gone.

"He's going to think you're Teresa again," she said aloud, dropping her arm.

Though she was desperate to find Tucker, she had to hold herself back, think it through. It was best if she stayed away from him with West Laughlin circling around, unless she got there right now, before West had time to get back to Fort-de-France.

But maybe he already has.

She hesitated in indecision. A cab ride would be quicker than the ferry, which trundled along on its own schedule. It would be better if she didn't go anywhere near her apartment. The chance of running into West or Tucker was too great. Maybe she could walk around for a while, go to a different hotel somewhere nearby.

She thought longingly of her cell phone, tossed into the back of one of her drawers. But who would she call anyway? William? He wouldn't be interested in anything but getting her back to LA to deal with the ever-clamoring Cantrells. Jonathan had made out a will and left everything to Sean, but it had bounced back to Callie when Sean had died at the same time. There hadn't been any peace from Derek or Diane ever since, but too damn bad. She hadn't much cared at the time; she didn't care much now.

She realized how much she'd been cut off from people she knew. Friends whom she'd let drift away when she'd followed blindly after Bryan to Los Angeles. People she'd met from work whom she'd lost contact with after she married Jonathan. She was alone to fight her own battles . . . and possibly Tucker's.

Should she go to his house? She wanted to confront Aimee, but she could unknowingly lead West Laughlin right to Tucker.

She was walking through the crowded pier, getting jostled by elbows. She felt a particularly hard shove and suddenly her bag wasn't on her arm. She grabbed at it instinctively, catching a handle, and realized a young man was holding onto the other side and trying to yank it from her grasp. "Hey!" she yelled, shocked, jerking back with all her might. "Stop! *Thief!*"

The boy let go and ran as people turned and stared. Shaken, Callie clutched the bag close to her chest. She'd always known to be careful in the crowds. She'd heard tales of wharf rats stealing purses, cell phones, and passports. It was a hazard in most crowded tourist areas.

She was lucky she still had her carryall, ID, credit cards, and the *bracelet*. Quickly, frantically, she searched through the carryall, her hands clasping over the hard-edged gems. Thank you, God. Her pounding heart threatened to overtake her. Feeling weak, she walked to a bench on the edge of the pier. Maybe the bracelet was safer on her arm. It had a hidden clasp that had to be undone to release it. It seemed counterintuitive, but her carryall was like a beacon to would-be thieves. Carefully, watching the people strolling by, she slipped the bracelet back on her arm, clasped it, and then kept touching it to make sure it was there, clutching the carryall to her chest. She needed to go home. Needed to pull herself together. No more walking aimlessly around.

She needed a ride home and for that she had to get to the main street and access to a taxi. At this time of day, rush hour, it was difficult to walk to her apartment. Weaving her way through the sauntering crowd, she held tight to her carryall, her arm imprisoning it close to her body. There was no reason to feel so paranoid about Tucker, she reminded herself. He was safe, well, and very possibly loitering impatiently around her apartment. She'd promised him a treat from the bakery and he was unlikely to forget even though the pastry was crushed and left on the pavement.

It took a while to work her way from the pier and pedestrians, reach the street, and lift an arm for a taxi. It was a hopeless gesture. The traffic whizzing down the four-lane street wouldn't slow down for anything short of a ten-car pile-up. Callie gritted her teeth and waited for the traffic light to change. She wasn't near a crosswalk, but if she could make her way to the median in the center, then hurry across the other lanes, she could get to the taxi stand.

The light changed from green to yellow, then to red. She gripped her carryall tighter, waiting for the traffic to slow. It seemed to take an eternity. Finally she dared to step off the curb, only to be blasted by a dozen horns, the driver nearest shaking his fist outside the window and yelling at her in rapid-fire French.

Ignoring him, Callie darted between the cars, reached the median, glanced toward the traffic light, and saw it change to green again.

"Hey! You!"

The hairs on the back of her neck rose. She whipped around, certain it was West.

But no, another driver was jabbing his finger in the direction of the light, his face a dark scowl. Not heeding his warning, she quickly zigzagged her way through the other cars before they got into gear.

She cut across the park on the edge of the outdoor tourist market to the small, in-cut road used as a taxi station. The station was empty.

Forced to wait or walk up the hill alone, Callie wrapped her arms around herself and tried not to pace. A chill had settled between her shoulder blades though the temperature was still warm. She shot a glance back toward the ferry dock and got a jolt when she saw a man looking up at her through binoculars.

West. No. Just a tourist.

"*Bonsoir*, Madame."

She nearly jumped from her skin at the friendly greeting. A tall, silver-haired gentleman in a suit stood beside her, and she smiled faintly as she realized he, too, was waiting for a taxi.

"*Bonsoir,*" she answered.

"You're American," he said in a French accent, and Callie only nodded. The last thing she wanted was to get embroiled in a conversation with a stranger.

All she could think about was Tucker.

"You are alone," he said with obvious concern, and for once Callie grew impatient with the gallantry of the French.

"Not really alone. Just on my way home. I've been . . . shopping."

He glanced at her plastic bag, and Callie remembered what she looked like: torn, dirty, and scraped. Though she'd brushed the dust off her arms and legs, the grime on her white dress was distinguishable even beneath the shadows of the tall buildings.

And her hair. It would be a miracle if she ever got the tangles out. With sinking realization she wondered if he could see the bruise developing on her jaw.

She opened her mouth to come up with some explanation just as a taxi slipped into the narrow roadway.

"Please." The gentleman gestured her forward, opening the taxi door for her.

Callie gave him a slight nod and slid into the seat of the taxi. "I live up the hill," she said to the driver, bending forward so he could hear her over the noise. She pointed in the direction she meant.

The driver nodded his understanding. The silver-haired gentleman lifted a hand and said, *"Au revoir, jolie femme."*

Callie smiled. *"Merci, au revoir,"* she said out the window, then the taxi was speeding away from the curb and the city of Fort-de-France.

Good-bye, pretty woman. She doubted she looked all that pretty right now.

Safe inside the vehicle, she felt close to exhaustion. Away from West Laughlin's powerful influence she realized what a bully he'd been, forcing himself on her like that. She was glad to be away from him. Hoped to hell he couldn't find her again.

"Go back to LA," Callie muttered aloud.

"Eh?" The taxi driver cocked his head.

"Nothing. Turn right . . . there."

The taxi swung into the narrow cobblestone street that fronted her building. Callie paid the fare with a surreptitious glance in both directions. No one there, thank God.

Quickly, she crossed the street and let herself inside. No small boy greeted her as she mounted the stairs, and though she knew she should be relieved that Tucker wasn't waiting outside her apartment, her heart was curiously heavy as she unlocked her apartment door and closed it gently behind her.

The silence of the pastel-green rooms enveloped her. A silence she'd grown familiar with. She headed straight for the shower, stripping off her clothes and turning on the spray as hot as she could get it, which wasn't saying a lot. She stood under the showering water until it was too cold to stand any longer.

Drying off, she wrapped her hair in the towel, then walked to the mirror above the chipped, white bureau. Naked, she could see every bruise and cut. Had that just happened this morning? It already felt like a lifetime ago.

Opening the bureau drawer she dug through her shorts and tops to find the cell phone and checked to see if it was charged. Barely, but enough for what she needed. She placed a call and when it was picked up, said, "Hello, Angie. It's Callie Cantrell. Is William in?"

Chapter Six

West waited in the shadows of Callie's street. He'd seen the taxi turn the corner and drop her off but he'd stayed hidden in the alcove of the front door of one of the buildings. He couldn't see which exact building she'd entered, but he knew it was one of three. As the cab left he moved from his hiding spot, his shoes scuffing on the uneven cobblestones. It was dark and quiet along the street, the sultry evening air heavy with the smell of frying fish and the omnipresent tang of brine lifting off the bay.

He barely noticed. He was in a sullen rage that was almost entirely self-directed. *Almost* because a portion of his anger was meant for Callie Cantrell. A muscle jerked beside his jaw. Whoever the hell she was, she had something to hide, and she'd played him but good. It wasn't often he found himself in this position. He was a pretty damn effective investigator and the fact he'd begun to believe her, against all signs to the contrary, stung mightily.

But hell . . . he had to let that go.

A light from a third-floor window switched on, spilling a trail of illumination over a wrought-iron balcony and into the street. West's eyes were irresistibly drawn. He inhaled a sharp breath when he saw a female silhouette inside before the tiny gap in the curtains was twitched shut.

Callie . . .

He pressed himself back into the alcove. She hadn't seen him and he wasn't about to give himself away now, not yet. Not until he'd had some time to think.

He was aware that at that moment his interest in her was dangerous. Somehow she'd gotten under his skin in a way he would not have believed possible. A hot awareness licked through him that he recognized as the early stages of desire and he wondered about his own sanity. He had a new understanding as to why his brother had been so enamored of Teresa. Callie might not be Teresa, but she looked just like her. And maybe she knew Teresa, maybe had even posed as her once or twice? There was some reason they were practically twins and both connected to Martinique.

Whatever the case, the woman on the third floor was involved up to her eyebrows, at least at some level; he could feel it.

Callie ran the brush through her wet hair, shooting a glance at the cell phone she'd carelessly tossed on the bed. William had been on another line, and though Angie had assured her he was very eager to talk to her and would she please, please, please stay on the line, Callie told her to have him call her back. She'd put on another sundress, this one a pale pink that didn't clash with her hair.

Setting down the brush, she walked into the living room, lost in thought. Her eye fell on the tiny gap in the balcony curtains and she stepped forward and switched them closed at the same moment her cell phone started ringing. She hurried back and picked it up on the fourth ring.

"William," she greeted him, but that's all she got out before he ran her over.

"You said you wanted the estate all wrapped up, but there are papers you need to sign to finalize the transfer to Diane and Derek."

"I thought I signed everything."

"We need to straighten this out," he said, sounding on his own path. "Your belongings are still in the house."

"I know." She could imagine Diane and Derek having conniption fits about not being able to take possession of the house. "I've just got a few things to wrap up, and I'll be back."

"Have you spoken to Dr. Rasmussen?"

Callie tried to hide her impatience. Bringing up her psychiatrist was a calculated move on his part. "I am better, William."

"Good. That's good."

"I'll see her when I get back, but being here's been the best thing for me. William, listen," she said before he could hit her with anything else. "Can you find out some information for me about a family named Laughlin who live somewhere around the LA area, I think? Victoria Laughlin is the matriarch. She had a grandson named Stephen who's deceased, and another named West who was with the LAPD up until recently."

"Why do you want to know?"

"I just do. I promise I'll be back soon, but if you could find out anything. Google the names, maybe. I don't have Internet service."

There was a hesitation and she could picture him smoothing the sides of his silver hair. "Sure, I can do that. Is there something I can tell Derek and Diane?"

"Tell them I'll be there soon," she stated flatly.

"Did you know Jonathan took out a mortgage on the house?" he suddenly put in.

"Yes. He took care of all the finances, but yes. He told me about the mortgage."

"You know he wasn't really in a position to mortgage the house," William said. "Legally, the house was in his name, but it should have been in the family trust."

"There's nothing I can do about that."

"Find the paperwork, when you get back. That's what you can do. There was a . . . well, I don't want to call it a mistake, because we really don't know what Conrad had in mind, but Jonathan shouldn't have been able to take out that mortgage."

"All right, I will." She just wanted to get off the phone now.

"I wasn't the attorney when Jonathan's father was alive, but Derek and Diane always had the understanding that the family home was theirs along with Jonathan, and if any of them were deceased, it would not go to their spouses or heirs."

"I know." Callie resisted the temptation to snap back at him. "I'll take care of it all."

"So, you aren't aware of what Jonathan did with the money he borrowed?"

"You would know better than I." William's firm, along with the Cantrells' CPA, had filed their tax return and all the requisite forms.

"Maybe he made an investment of some kind?"

"If he did I don't know anything about it."

"Possibly there's a separate bank account?"

"If I knew anything, I'd tell you. Jonathan didn't share. You know that."

"I do. But I'd like to avert a lawsuit between Derek and Diane and you."

"They're threatening to sue?" She was taken aback. She'd done everything they'd asked of her and more, and she hadn't left until the last *t* was crossed, the last *i* dotted, or so she'd thought. *They think I took the money*, she realized and felt her cheeks warm with anger.

"We're just looking for the paper trail."

"Maybe he spent the money," she tossed out. "He liked nice things."

"When you get back, maybe you could check his papers again."

"Sure." As if she hadn't checked and checked and checked. But this conversation would keep going in circles if she let it, and she wasn't interested in continuing. "See what you can find on the Laughlins. Thanks. Bye."

She clicked off, irked, then made herself think about leaving Martinique and going back to LA. Her chest tightened. She couldn't bear the thought of leaving Tucker, and how could she go now anyway, when West Laughlin constituted a threat to him?

She paced to the balcony, then back across the room. Was West out there somewhere, even now, waiting for her to show him the way to Tucker's?

Maybe. Probably. If not yet, then he would be soon. He knew approximately where she lived.

Sitting down on the edge of a chair, she twisted the bracelet around her arm. Tucker had given it to her and wouldn't take it back. Had he stolen it from Aimee or his mother? She needed to give it back. Pretty as it was, it was beginning to feel like a curse. She wanted to rid herself of it once and for all.

West waited, wondering if he should confront Callie. It was after six o'clock and he was hungry, tired, and frustrated.

The tea and croissants at noon weren't hanging with him. Now that he knew where she lived, he could probably take a break in surveillance and grab something at one of the cafés that lined the streets down the hill. It kind of looked like she was in for the night, and he probably wouldn't miss anything. Jesus. It was hell being a one-man team.

He thought about that last meeting with Victoria, who'd sat straight in her chair at the head of the long, carved mahogany table in the Laughlin dining room, her white hair and cobwebbed, papery skin belied by her sharp blue eyes. West had finally agreed to meet her at the Laughlin Ranch house, which he'd dubbed Laughlin Manor, which had pissed her off royally when he'd drawled the name upon entering the place. He hadn't been invited to the house since he was a child, and he couldn't help the desire to behave badly at this command performance.

Victoria had gotten right down to business. "Edmund Mikkels murdered your brother," she'd said in her incisive way. "And Teresa set him up."

"Stephen died in a hunting accident," West had reminded her, but he had straightened in his chair and paid closer attention.

"I know what it looks like. But I'm just telling you, Teresa is behind it. God knows what she's done with Stephen Tucker."

"You can't start an investigation on conjecture," he had started to say, but she'd cut him off.

"Mikkels is crumbling. With the right amount of pressure, you could get to the truth. No one else around here's interested. The sheriff's department . . ." She had flapped a hand in the air, dismissing them.

Laughlin Ranch was in the San Joaquin Valley, a little over two hours from Los Angeles. The family raised Angus cattle and sold beef across the nation. It was a huge operation and Victoria had handed over the reins first to Craig Laughlin, West's father, who'd run the ranch until his sudden unexpected death in a hit-and-run accident, and then to Stephen, whom she'd expected to be as dedicated to the operation as Craig had been. But Stephen had only been lukewarm about taking over. He lacked the fervor and true enjoyment his father and grandfather had possessed. In the few times Stephen had met West in Los Angeles before his death, he'd clearly wished for a different life.

"I'm going to join you in LA," he always promised, but it never happened, though it was Los Angeles where Stephen had met Teresa. Stephen had invited West to dinner with him and his fiancée when they were in town one evening, but West had already made other plans.

Victoria had done everything she could at that meeting, trying to get West to bring Teresa to justice and Stephen Tucker to her, but West had really only come to the ranch out of curiosity. He'd purposely slouched against the wall at the far end of the room, his jeans, boots, and two days' growth of beard making the gulf between him and his starchy grandmother appear even wider. He hadn't much cared. He owed the Laughlins nothing and vice versa.

And he'd thought her accusations were bunk.

"Mikkels was a fool," Victoria had told him. "He believed Teresa was an angel. Somehow she got to him and talked him into killing your brother."

"Why would she do that?" West had pointed out.

"I don't know. Maybe you'll learn the reason when you look for the boy."

West had known little about Stephen's wife except that she was very beautiful—and he knew that only because Stephen had sung her praises. Stephen had wanted West to come to the wedding but West had declined. Mixing with other Laughlins was something he avoided at all costs, especially since his father's death.

"I've got a picture of her," she had said. "I had many more but they're missing. She probably took them with her."

Victoria had then spread a number of photographs on the table in front of her. Reluctantly, because he'd felt her pulling him into family affairs against his will, West had walked to her end of the room. One picture was of Stephen with Teresa, the one he'd scanned, cropped, and put on his phone; the rest were of Stephen and a boy of about two.

"Where do you think she went?"

"LA," she had answered promptly. "That's where Stephen picked her up."

West had gone back to Los Angeles armed with the information that Stephen had met Teresa in Santa Monica, at a coffee shop. He'd been in no great hurry as he wasn't sure what he believed, but then he had the falling out with Roxanne and relations deteriorated with Paulsen, and suddenly he was free to look into Stephen's death.

The first thing he'd done was pay a visit to Edmund Mikkels, the neighboring rancher who was "crumbling" from guilt, according to Victoria. West didn't know the man, but when he had said who he was, Mikkels had turned white and had to sit down. "I pray every day that I wake up that it's all been a bad dream," he had told West, swiping at tears with the back of his hands. "Stephen was a good man."

West had asked him about the hunting accident, but apart from the enormity of his grief three years after the fact, there had been nothing that pointed a finger at Mikkels as being in on some wild conspiracy with Teresa to kill Stephen.

West had been pretty sure he was feeding into Victoria's own grief and paranoia and had been ready to say sayonara, when she had admitted that she had given Stephen's personal computer to a local computer expert and asked him to open some files. The guy had easily accessed the files as Stephen hadn't set up password protection on the computer itself. Stephen had kept a file that simply said "Accounts" where he'd listed the passwords for his two e-mail accounts, bank accounts, online shopping stores, you name it. Most of the passwords were in code themselves, so Victoria had skipped over those and had directed the expert to open other files. That's how she had come across the list of Laughlin heirlooms categorized with their relative worth. The date on the file suggested it was somewhere around the time Stephen had given Teresa the bracelet and Victoria was convinced Teresa had seen the list and pressured Stephen into giving it to her as a gift.

He had stopped at the ranch after meeting with Mikkels. After explaining about the computer, Victoria had said, "Teresa as good as stole the bracelet. I never said as much to your brother, but he had no right to offer up a Laughlin heirloom. Lord knows what that woman's done with it. I suppose I should consider myself lucky that the rest of the jewelry's still in the safe-deposit box. Stephen was asking about it before she killed him."

"If she wanted more heirlooms, why would she have him killed?" West had tried to reason with her, but his logic had fallen on deaf ears.

"She took the most important one with her. Stephen Tucker Laughlin. He's worth more than all of them put together."

West had been resistant to helping her, but with an insight into Teresa's grasping nature, he'd told her he would see what he could do. He took the computer to a hacker buddy who broke into Stephen's e-mail accounts and learned someone, after his death, was corresponding with someone else in Martinique.

An e-mail that originated from a Fort-de-France Internet café had started him thinking he should help find Tucker, if for no other reason than to assure himself that Stephen's son was all right. But it was Teresa's response that sent West to Martinique:

im on my way. take care of t and the b.

West had read that as "take care of Tucker and the brace-let." It boiled his blood to think Teresa was bartering it for Tucker's care. Seeing it on Callie Cantrell's arm had made him see red, and it had been all he could do to keep from shaking her senseless and demanding she turn over Tucker. But she wasn't Teresa, unless Teresa led two lives. She'd said a friend named Aimee had given it to her, but he was almost certain she was lying.

He'd left for Martinique with only half-formed plans in mind: hanging out at the Internet café in question, if it still existed; asking questions of the patrons and personnel; showing Teresa's picture around; checking with the local police. He'd called upon Pete Dorcas to help pave the way for him with the local police, but so far that plan hadn't panned out. Dorcas was only willing to stick out his neck so far for West and a call to the gendarmerie was asking too much.

But then he'd gotten lucky, catching sight of Teresa, or the woman he'd assumed was Teresa, in his binoculars on his second day. If Callie wasn't Teresa, she had to know something about where Teresa was. The bracelet, and Callie's unwillingness to tell him the truth about it, was evidence of that. No other answer made sense.

He ordered a chicken salad sandwich and a bottle of water at an outdoor café, wolfed down the sandwich, and drank half the bottle in one gulp. He finished the last swallow of water standing over a recycle bin and then tossed the plastic bottle inside.

Then he retraced his steps to Callie's apartment, checking

his phone on the way. It was eight P.M., the dusky, gold evening light a memory. It was still hot, however, and he wondered how long it would be before he got a shower.

He realized her lights were out. Was she still there? Probably. He decided to wait around a while and be certain. A light came on around ten and he saw her silhouette walk through the room, but then she doused it again, most likely returning to bed. Around midnight, West gave up and caught a cab to his hotel. If something nefarious happened in the wee hours of the morning, so be it. But he doubted there was much chance of that happening and now that he knew where she lived, he could start again tomorrow.

Chapter Seven

Andre received the call from Daniella around nine, listened for a few moments, then said, "Okay," and hung up, his gaze flicking to Teresa. "Lumpkin's headed north. Daniella will follow him until you take over. Call when he lands somewhere."

Teresa knew enough about Robert Lumpkin's habits to figure his final destination would be a bar in Venice or Santa Monica. She gathered up her purse and got to her feet. "Should I take the Xterra?" she asked, as Daniella had the Chevy.

"Yeah."

Teresa's pulse was starting to jack up. The thrill of the hunt. Andre was looking at her in that intense way he had. Once upon a time that expression had gotten her juices flowing; all she could think about was Andre and sex . . . sex and Andre. And then they would work their magic together. A long time ago . . .

Reading her mind, Andre came over to her and stood in front of her, running his hands down her arms, fitting her up against him. She had been slipping her right foot into one of her heels, but she stopped, waiting, anxious to go.

"You smell good enough to eat," he said, inhaling deeply the citrus flavor of her perfume.

She quivered when his hand slid from her arm to her hip. Behind him, she sensed Naomi and Clarice move into the room. Good God, if Andre tried to claim her before she went out on her mission she might start screaming and never stop. He'd done it before. He had amazing radar when it came to sensing what she was feeling and he was feeding off her own adrenaline rush.

But she couldn't stomach the thought of making love to him now. Her feelings for him had been eroding over time, like water eating away at rock. He'd grown obsessive and full of strange beliefs. It was just . . . over.

Biting the inside of her cheek, she kept her face expressionless, fighting her claustrophobic anxiety. It was the thought of Tucker, safe, sound, and waiting for her, that kept her from losing it.

Then Andre's cell phone rang and he made a sound of impatience, taking a step away to answer it. At his curt "Yeah?" Teresa exhaled. So did Naomi and Clarice, though they probably didn't realize it.

Teresa could hear the tinny sound of Daniella's voice but couldn't make out the words. Andre grunted an "Okay" then snapped at Teresa, "You've got a phone?"

They shared cell phones except for Andre. "Yes," she said, recognizing his growing anger. He'd wanted to screw her, claim her right then and there, but he wanted to get Robert Lumpkin more. He didn't know about the other cell phone that she had in her own name or the studio apartment she'd been renting for two months now.

"He's in Venice at a place called Ray's," Andre said.

"I know it," Teresa said. Andre's eyes narrowed at her incautious answer. He clearly wanted to ask her how. Teresa preempted him. "I met Jonathan there a time or two."

It was a lie. Jonathan Cantrell would no more have gone to

a dive like Ray's than fly to the moon. He liked the Peninsula Hotel, swank nightclubs on the Sunset Strip, expensive rooms with cabanas, pools, and girls in bikinis carrying trays of drinks, and humidors of cigars. Oh, yeah. Jonathan had liked the high life. He'd wanted to marry her and how Andre had laughed when she'd told him. "Well, he can't have you," he'd said, and Teresa, in those heady days before the handmaidens, had thrilled to his possessiveness. Jonathan had been the big mark before Stephen Laughlin, though there was something special about Stephen, from Andre's point of view, that she still didn't quite understand. She'd thought about it a time or two, but then had decided she didn't really care. Stephen had been a sweet guy, truly in love with her, or at least the Teresa he believed her to be. Whatever Andre's reasons for targeting Stephen were, they were his own.

Now she headed for the door, wondering if this was the last time she would cross this threshold. Hoping it was the last time.

She'd wanted to be that Teresa, the one that Stephen Laughlin had fallen in love with. She'd even thought she could be, for a while. That was when her love for Andre died, those few years she'd played at being Stephen's wife. Swept into the part of Teresa Laughlin, she'd repressed thoughts of her old life so deeply that she'd almost forgotten them herself. She'd even gotten pregnant, and had managed to keep it a secret from Andre. She'd lived in fear that he would drive to Bakersfield or Fresno, or somewhere in the Valley, and then decide to cruise on up to Laughlin Ranch, but he never had. But then he'd been too busy amassing the handmaidens; she just hadn't known it.

Then one day it was over. "Get the money and get back here."

She'd heard the underlying warning in his tone, knew her time was over. She'd already drained her account with Stephen and had Tucker's and her passports ready when

Edmund told her he'd set up the hunting date. She'd been teasing him in heated meetings with a lot of sexual petting, telling Edmund she couldn't truly be with him while Stephen was her husband. She'd put the idea in Edmund's head without him knowing it that if Stephen were gone, say, then they could be together. But she hadn't realized how primed he was, how ready to jump to have her. She'd been home at the ranch, actually having dinner with Victoria in the dining room, a chilly affair that nevertheless alibied her completely, when they heard the news. Stephen had given her the bracelet just two days earlier.

Victoria was beside herself, and Teresa was shattered as well. She hadn't realized until the deed was done how much she'd fallen for Tucker's father. Stephen's death appeased Andre for a while, giving her enough time to fly Tucker to Martinique, and then return to Los Angeles. Andre had been disgusted with the paltry amount she'd come away with from the Laughlin affair after such a long time—she'd purposely left the bracelet with Aimee—but he hadn't been as upset as she'd expected.

Strangely, it was more like he'd pretended to be upset, and she realized there was something else going on he wasn't copping to. Some long-range plan that she wasn't privy to, apparently. Or maybe he was tired of the Laughlin plan. Andre's interest in anything was notoriously short.

Whatever the case, Stephen was gone, and she was sorry that she'd been a part of it. She'd thought that was the worst of it, but that was before Jonathan resurfaced and followed her to their house. Teresa had been so rattled to see him loping up the stairs to the front door after her, calling her name, she'd practically slammed the door in his face. He'd yelled through the panels at her that he wasn't leaving and had made such a nuisance of himself that she'd had to step outside and confront him.

She'd tried to convince him that she didn't live at the

house, that she was just visiting a friend. He almost believed her. He wanted to punish her for leaving him, but even more than that, he wanted to pick up where they'd left off.

She couldn't do either.

After she'd finally agreed to meet with him the next day, she'd gone back inside and encountered Andre, who was cool, cagey, and surprisingly encouraging. She hadn't known then what his plans were for Jonathan Cantrell. She hadn't known then she would be the one to execute those plans. A shiver ran down her spine as she thought of the little boy who'd died because of her. Because of *Andre.*

"What's your plan?" Andre asked suddenly from behind her, yanking her from her reverie.

"I'll—show up at Ray's and see what happens."

He turned her around abruptly just as her hand was reaching for the front doorknob. His lips were pinched. "This isn't a long-term one, Teresa."

"I know what it is."

His eyes narrowed at her neutral tone, as if he were trying to fathom her thoughts. He was so good at reading her that Teresa blanked her mind to anything but the moment at hand. "Do you have the drugs?" he asked.

She nodded.

"Good. See you later tonight . . ."

"Uh-huh."

No. Not tonight. Not ever again. A few more hours, she told herself, thinking of the money in the Bank of America account. She had a debit card tucked away deep inside the seam of the stuffed bear that Stephen had won for her at a fair. She'd told Andre she'd won it herself so that he wouldn't take it from her. He hated any of them having personal possessions. Two days ago she'd swept up the bear and taken it to the apartment, pulling out the debit card and hiding it under a rock beside the garage.

As Naomi handed her the keys to the Xterra, the best car

of their small fleet, she thought of the plane ticket she'd purchased with that debit card. A ticket that was placed on the kitchen counter of her studio right next to the rolling suitcase, which was packed and ready.

If all went according to plans, she could be in Martinique tomorrow.

Her heart was thumping as she collected her debit card then drove north to Ray's, a ramshackle cabana bar near the beach. It was frequented by the college crowd and in the summer it was full of bikini tops and short shorts. If Robert Lumpkin was headed that way, it was guaranteed that he was looking for tits and ass, and the short white dress she was wearing showed lots of both.

She was going to make a statement when she walked in. People were going to remember her. Her hair was always a giveaway unless she dyed it a mousier color, which she had once or twice. Her jaw set as she thought about how many times she'd gone after a mark for Andre.

Well, this was the last. And she was going to do it her way.

She knew what Robert Lumpkin looked like per Daniella's description: late forties, balding, sporting a few extra pounds but prone to sucking in his gut as he was feasting his eyes on whatever hot young thing caught his eye. He drove a ten-year-old, green Ford Explorer, which she spotted immediately in the full lot. She had to circle around and find a space on the street, a fifteen-minute enterprise that had her champing at the bit.

The men in the young crowd looked at her with initial interest but when she didn't catch their gazes their eyes drifted back to their dates. Lumpkin was easy to find; the only man fitting his description was sitting at the bar. He picked up on her as soon as she walked in and it was simple to stop near him and feign looking toward the back of the bar as if searching for someone.

"Who you waitin' for?" he asked.

She slid him a sideways glance. "Some friends," she said in a cool tone. Didn't want to seem too eager.

"You see 'em?"

"Not yet."

He pointed to the empty bar stool next to him and said, "You can wait here. The place is gettin' pretty full."

She pretended to mull that over, then, as if considering it to be her only option, slipped onto the stool. The hem of her dress hiked all the way up her thigh and she made a half-hearted attempt to bring it down a bit. She was curious if he would offer to buy her a drink. From what Daniella had said, he was tight as a frog's ass.

The bartender cruised up and Teresa tapped her lips with one richly painted red fingernail, pretending to decide. Maybe if she gave him enough time he might say something, but Lumpkin, though maybe fighting with himself, lost the battle with near chivalry and kept his money in his wallet.

"White wine," she said.

"Chardonnay okay?" the bartender asked.

"Do you have a decent sauvignon blanc?"

"Not really," he admitted, flashing her a smile.

Teresa smiled back despite her electric nerves. "Chardonnay'll be fine."

Not to be outdone, Lumpkin said proprietarily, "The reds are pretty good here."

Teresa half-turned his way. "Not with this white dress. I'd have to be stripping it off and washing it immediately." She'd drawn out the word "stripping" and Lumpkin looked like he was going to slobber all over himself.

Her happy juice was in her purse: a sprinkle of Rohypnol in water, more commonly known as *roofies*. She thought of how many times she'd played out this scene, how many men she'd knocked out and robbed. Normally Andre would want to play the mark for all he was worth, keep him on a string until she could squeeze every last dime out of him, but this

was Robert Lumpkin and from Andre's perspective, he was
better off dead. He was basically their landlord. And after the
way Jonathan had found them out, well, Andre wasn't taking
any more chances.

Something shifted, she brooded. Ever since Stephen's
death, Andre's directives had changed. No longer was it just
about the money. Now it was all about taking the money *and*
killing the mark. There was some new kind of enjoyment on
Andre's part that hadn't been there before. His appetites
were changing as was the frequency of the headaches that
plagued him.

Something's very wrong with him, she thought, sipping
her chardonnay. It was time to leave. Of course, that didn't
mean she couldn't roll this loser first . . . and take the money
for herself. Her debit card was in her tiny black purse, along
with several twenties that Andre had given her for this job.
She'd laid her purse on the bar, and now she pulled it toward
her and pulled out the stick of red lipstick, adding another
glossy layer as Lumpkin nearly pissed himself watching her.
He probably didn't have a ton of money on him, but she'd
take what she could get.

She was getting the hell out of Dodge tonight.

"So, how is it?" Lumpkin asked, meaning her drink.

"Passable," Teresa said.

He leered at her. "You're a connoisseur, huh."

"I like the good stuff," she admitted with a smile. "But I
definitely drink too much of it."

"Yeah?"

"I get a little crazy sometimes. My ex loved it, but man,
I don't remember some really important parts, you know?"
She leaned a little closer to him, a confidante, then pulled
away again. She wasn't wearing underwear beneath the dress
and she wondered if she should thrill him with a Sharon
Stone move à la *Basic Instinct.*

Lumpkin chugged down the rest of his beer and ordered

another. Teresa figured it was just a matter of time before he had to empty his bladder and hoped he would do it before he drained the next one. No way she was going to put her happy juice into a glass he was finished with.

Sure enough, he swallowed about half of the new beer, fought back a belch with limited success, then said he'd be right back, looking back at her a couple of times as he hurried to the men's room, worried that she would leave. It was the perfect moment to Sharon Stone him and she did, turning on her bar stool just so . . . spreading her legs for a straight view to her hoohaw before she recrossed them.

He practically had a heart attack as he stopped and gaped, then stumbled over his feet as he went to relieve himself. As soon as he was out of sight she glanced around to make certain no one was looking. The bartender had his back to her as did the man seated on the other side of her, talking to his date. She surreptitiously pulled the happy juice from her purse with her left hand. The bottle was tiny enough to hide in her palm. Sliding his beer directly in front of her with her right hand, she then transferred the bottle from left to right and plucked her cell phone from her purse with her left. She set the phone on the table, then feigned texting while she un-snapped the top of the bottle with her thumb and sneaked liberal drops into Lumpkin's beer.

She'd barely gotten the beer glass placed back in front of his spot again before he was scurrying back to his bar stool. "I'm Robert," he said, practically panting as he held out his hand.

"Julia," Teresa answered, squeezing his palm warmly. She hoped to hell he'd washed, the rat bastard.

"How many of those have you had?" he asked.

"My first." She knocked back the rest of it and signaled for the bartender.

"Things are gettin' kinda crazy already, aren't they?" He

glanced down in the direction of her crotch in case she failed to remember what she'd done.

"Crazy's not a bad thing, the way I see it. My ex taught me that."

"That who you were lookin' for?"

"My ex? Oh, hell no. He can go fuck himself."

"Yeah. He can go fuck himself." Lumpkin laughed like a hyena. He was leaning toward her so much he was about to fall off his stool into her lap, and he hadn't even taken another drink of his beer. It never occurred to him to wonder what Teresa saw in him. Like so many other men, Lumpkin thought more highly of himself than he ought to.

Teresa touched her glass to his. "Cheers."

"Cheers!" He swooped up his beer and tossed it back, mimicking her. When the bartender brought her second chardonnay, she took an experimental sip, lifting an eyebrow at Lumpkin. "I'd better go slower, or the night might end too soon," she said with regret.

She set her glass down then delicately touched the corners of her mouth with her index finger, before running her tongue in a full circle around her red, red lips.

Lumpkin followed the movement, his own mouth hanging open. "Hope your date doesn't show."

"I was just meeting a girlfriend, but it looks like she's not going to show. Figures. She's flaky that way."

"Yeah?" He wasn't really listening. He was staring, glassy-eyed, taking her in.

Teresa bantered with him for about ten minutes more, then asked, "Tell me about yourself, Robert."

"Not much to tell." He shrugged. "I was in home building, but I'm an invest-chor now. Investor." He giggled at his inability to pronounce the word. "Real estate."

"Oh, yeah?"

"Own some property in . . . around here. A couple of

houses. Think-ging about buyin' inta . . . um . . . condos, er, apart-apartments."

"Sounds like you do well for yourself."

"You bet. I doan mean to brag, but I've saned a pretty penny."

"You've saved a lot."

"Hunh," he agreed, staring ahead for a moment as if in a daze.

"You wanna go somewhere?" she asked softly in his ear.

"Yeeaahh . . . but I gotta go to . . ." He slid off the chair and swayed on his feet. Teresa pulled out his wallet and put some money on the bar for both of their drinks, then tucked a hand under one of his arms and propelled him toward the door. He was still able to walk pretty well; he would be flat out soon enough.

She'd learned that no one really expected a woman to roofie a guy; it was mostly the other way around. They would remember what she looked like after the fact, but since she had no plan to actually harm Lumpkin, she would just take his cash and leave him asleep in his vehicle. When he woke up, she doubted that he would want to even tell anyone what happened. He would feel too foolish.

Andre, of course, would be out of his mind when he learned she'd merely taken Lumpkin's pocket change and left him sleeping it off. He'd believed her earlier excitement had been because she was ramping up to kill Lumpkin, which was Andre's thrill, not hers.

Whatever. Her blood was pumping. She did like the game.

They staggered together to his vehicle. She got him into the car, laying his unconscious body across the front seats. Quickly, she ripped the money from his wallet. Naturally he didn't have that much cash on him. He'd also been lying about his real estate assets, she was pretty sure. He was, after all, just waiting for his mother to bite the big one so he could have her house. Andre wanted to kill him to assure that wouldn't happen.

Teresa had a hard moment while she wondered if she should have covered her tracks more, booked a more circuitous route. She'd thought of flying to Caracas, Venezuela, since Martinique wasn't that far from South America, but the expense had been prohibitive whereas she'd gotten much less expensive flights through Miami. Still, if Andre found a way to track her he might figure out where she was going. After all, it was where they'd met.

But she was getting on that red-eye tonight. She didn't plan to stay in Martinique long anyway. All she needed was enough time to pick up Tucker and flee somewhere else. Somewhere far away where they could build some kind of life together.

And just because she wasn't working for Andre anymore didn't mean she had to give up her ways. Maybe, if she was really, really, *really* lucky, she might meet another guy like Stephen Laughlin and this time she would make it work.

Chapter Eight

Callie awoke with the sensation of a mild hangover. Grimacing, she turned her face into the pillow. Memory jolted a swift heartbeat later and she sat up fast, her eyes flying open. Tucker. The Bakoua Beach Hotel. *West Laughlin*.

She threw back the covers and, shivering a little, hurried to the loud, clinking air conditioner sticking out of her bedroom window. Switching off the machine, she almost instantly felt sticky, subtropical heat pervade the room. The bathroom was hot and Callie turned the shower to cool and washed her hair thoroughly. She had been too tired the evening before to do more than rinse the dirt off her body and apply some antibiotic ointment to the scrape on her leg.

Stepping from the shower, she wrapped the towel around her head and grabbed a second to wind around her torso. She walked back into her bedroom and looked at the clock. Six thirty A.M. Early, but still a highly likely time for Tucker to be out and about. The free rein Aimee gave the boy worried her, but apart from a comment she'd made to the woman suggesting maybe Tucker shouldn't be allowed to roam so far afield, given his age, a comment that hadn't been received well, Callie had been unable to offer any other advice.

She pulled on a blue tank top and pair of khaki capris, then brushed her hair and waited for it to dry. She kept checking the clock, anxious about Tucker, and then realized belatedly that it was Friday and Tucker, who attended pre-K three days a week, should be in school. She wondered if he'd come looking for her yesterday. Undoubtedly, unless Aimee kept him at home or he was with his friend Michel on Michel's father's fishing boat.

She drew a deep breath. Okay, so, Tucker was taken care of for today. But what about West Laughlin? He knew approximately where she lived and he wouldn't be too thrilled about the way she'd run out on him yesterday. Was he waiting outside somewhere? Or maybe he was off chasing some other lead in his search for Teresa. Anyway around it, though, he surely would come back.

And what if for some reason Tucker showed? She wouldn't put it past Aimee to keep him home from school if she so chose to. She had only met the woman once, but she had not been impressed by her parenting skills. And Callie had promised Tucker pastries. Just because she didn't have them anymore didn't mean the boy had forgotten. The thought of him suddenly appearing, and possibly leading West straight to him, made her pace the room. She would leave, go down to the open market again, wander around. If Tucker showed up when she wasn't home he would leave. Surely West wouldn't interrogate any child who happened to be in her neighborhood?

She hesitated. What should she do?

What she wanted to do was have a face-to-face with Aimee. She had a lot of questions. She'd always had a lot of questions where Tucker was concerned, but now she had even more.

What if West is out there and follows you?

Callie gritted her teeth, mad at herself for being so indecisive. Before her marriage she'd made decisions for herself
all the time, good, bad, or indifferent, and hadn't second-
guessed her every thought, even when she was still with
Bryan, and God knew he'd been no good for her. But being
with Jonathan had subverted her own personality, first because she'd tried to be a perfect girlfriend and wife, then
because of Sean. She'd kept up her fake life, buried her true
self, because she'd known that if she challenged Jonathan,
he would have used Sean as leverage against her. She'd
known it then. She knew it now.

But there was no need to be so compliant any longer. She
needed to protect Tucker. Even if he was Teresa Laughlin's
son, she wasn't ready to turn him over to West.

Tying back her hair with a rubber band, she then crushed
her ponytail into the top of a straw hat, smashing the hat onto
her head and effectively obscuring the color of her hair. If
West saw her up close he would know it was her, but from a
distance, maybe not.

She grabbed up her cell phone from the bureau drawer
and headed out. As she was locking her door behind her, she
recalled the small binoculars snapped onto West's belt. Well,
he might be able to tell who she was, even with her meager
disguise, but she would do her damnedest to take note of
anyone watching her.

She walked back down the hill, toting her plastic carryall.
In the narrow streets she saw no one who looked like West
Laughlin, but maybe he was there somewhere. At the open
market, she was glad her sunglasses were dark enough to
keep anyone from following her eye movements as she
checked her peripheral vision, searching for West or any
man with a pair of binoculars to his eyes. Nothing.

She bought the same pastries she'd purchased the day

before, tucking them into her bag. She strolled around for an hour. By the time she thought it might be all right to embark on her quest, it was after eleven and the sun was reaching its zenith, beating down on her.

She walked away. First in the complete opposite direction as Tucker's house, then through a coffee shop with a front and back door, turning around and walking to the end of the block, then zigzagging back to Tucker's neighborhood. Her steps lagged as she drew closer, her attention heightened. She thought of the African meerkats always on alert and smiled to herself. If everything turned out okay she would buy Tucker a stuffed meerkat if there was such a thing. Probably on the Internet somewhere.

As she approached the neighborhood where his apartment was, she stopped. Now she had the problem of facing Aimee. Tucker's "mother" wasn't exactly warm and fuzzy. She'd made it clear she didn't appreciate any interference by Callie, and though Tucker seemed oblivious to the tension between them the one and only time they'd met, it was there big-time.

A mangy-looking mutt gave a halfhearted wag of his tail as she passed by an open doorway and three solemn-eyed children came outside to stare. Callie smiled but they didn't respond. Feeling like the outsider she was, Callie turned the corner to Tucker's street.

A breeze swept up from the bay, soothing her perspiring forehead and dissipating some of the shimmering heat. Beside the steps to Tucker's apartment building stood a huge, gnarled, and broken jade tree. Callie could smell damp earth and an odor she realized later was coming from an overloaded garbage bin farther down the alley.

She stopped at the bottom step, clutching the sack of pastries with tight fingers. Though it wasn't that far from her apartment as the crow flies, there was a world of difference in the relative value of the properties. She'd been highly aware that there was an invisible line somewhere between them, and she'd sensed that Aimee recognized the difference and resented her for it.

Callie climbed the stairs, opened the outer door, and walked down the narrow hallway that led to the back apartments. Aged wallpaper was peeling away from the corners, and the overhead light gave off only the weakest illumination. Dirt had collected on the glass shade and Callie wondered when, if ever, the landlord had last cleaned the outer areas of the building.

She knocked on Tucker's door, wishing her heartbeat would assume a normal rate again. There was no reason to work herself into such a state. Tucker had lived without her for over five years, for Pete's sake, and soon she might be just a memory to him. It wasn't as if his whole life was at stake, or that she could do anything about it even if it were.

The door cracked an inch, a chain lock showing through the opening. Aimee Thomas peered out.

"*Allo?* Ah, Miss Cantrell," she said, recognizing Callie, making no effort to open the door farther.

"Hello, Ms. Thomas," Callie answered. "Is Tucker at school? I bought him some pastries from the bakery and I wanted to give them to him."

She tried hard not to appear as if she were trying to peek beyond the dark-haired woman barring the doorway, but she couldn't help a glance over Aimee's head. From the limited vision provided by the cracked doorway Callie could only tell there was no one in the living room.

"Yes, he is at school." Aimee was slim, attractive, and seemed *too expensive*, for lack of a better term, for her surroundings. Her hair was short and severe and her eyes were large, liquid dark pools filled with suspicion. Callie had assumed she was French, though she'd thought she'd heard some words in English from behind the front door before Aimee had answered it. As soon as Aimee saw Callie, however, she'd cut her cell phone conversation short and switched entirely to French.

"Could I leave the pastries?" Callie asked. "I told him I would bring them to him."

Reluctantly Aimee took the chain off the door and stood back, allowing Callie entrance. Callie stepped inside before she could change her mind. This grudging hospitality was more than she'd expected, after talking with West and learning of even deeper mysteries surrounding Tucker than she'd already thought. Aimee hadn't been friendly the previous time they'd met, but she'd built her up to something more in her mind since yesterday.

Pulling the white bakery sack from her plastic carryall, Callie held it out to Aimee, who was still standing by the door as if regretting allowing Callie inside.

"Tucker likes you," Aimee stated flatly.

"We're friends."

Callie and Aimee stared at each other, equally uncomfortable. Maybe Aimee's cavalier attitude to child rearing had to do with the fact that she wasn't Tucker's mother. Maybe she didn't really care about Tucker the same way a mother would.

The moment spun out and a tiny line formed between Aimee's brows. Callie's palms felt sweaty and her heart pounded as she wrestled with herself. She'd walked through the door intending to ask some questions of the woman, but she could feel herself chickening out. But that was what the old Callie would do. The one under Jonathan's thumb. She didn't want to be that Callie anymore, so she asked quickly, before she could change her mind, "Do you know someone named Teresa Laughlin?"

She had to hand it to the woman. Apart from a widening of her eyes and the faintest intake of breath, she managed to keep her composure. But Callie could tell she'd scored a direct hit.

Barely missing a beat, Aimee said, "*Non,*" suddenly very French.

"Never heard the name?"

"*Non.*"

"Huh. Maybe I made a mistake."

"I theenk you did."

"I was told I look like this Teresa Laughlin whose son's name is Tucker. It seemed kind of random, but coincidental. . . ." Her pulse was rocketing now. She'd managed the first few lines of her mental script but now her throat was tightening, her own sense of right and wrong playing havoc with her role-playing. She could feel heat climbing up her neck.

Aimee's mouth worked. She seemed to want to ask a question but couldn't find the words. Finally, she let fly a string of rapid French, finishing with, "What do you want with Tucker? You are too friendly weeth heem."

"He gave me a bracelet with lavender stones. I tried to give it back to him but he insisted I keep it."

Her head snapped around in shock. "What? That's my bracelet! He can't give it to you." Her face turned dark red. "I've been going crazy." No French accent now, Callie saw. Aimee seemed to recognize that fact because she forcefully calmed herself down. "Tucker must have taken it, but it ees mine."

"I'll make sure you get it back," Callie said, which she had no intention of doing until she knew more. West hadn't tried to wrest the bracelet away from her, but she believed it was a Laughlin heirloom and even though it had been in Aimee's possession, that didn't necessarily make it hers.

"When?" Aimee demanded.

"I'll come back later with it. After Tucker gets home?"

"He'll be back around three," she said, her expression dark. Callie sensed she was holding her anger in with difficulty and decided to beat a hasty retreat.

At the door, Aimee said in perfect English, "I don't know what you're after, but Tucker is not for sale."

"Of course not. I—"

"I will see you at three," she said in that same flat voice, closing the door behind her with a slam.

"Holy shit," Callie whispered to herself. She started to walk away, then retraced her steps and pressed her ear to the door. She heard a string of swear words in English and then footsteps pounding her way. Quickly, she racewalked to the front door of the building and let herself outside. Her heart was pounding so hard she could practically see it.

Minutes passed, but Aimee did not appear. Maybe she'd just been pacing inside the apartment. There was a back way out and Callie wondered if she'd left that way. Callie thought about retracing her steps and examining the area, then changed her mind.

One thing was clear: Aimee knew the name Teresa Laughlin. It followed that Teresa was Tucker's mother and the woman West was seeking. Aimee was likely a temporary caretaker. Maybe through some kind of foster care on the island? But Tucker hadn't come with the bracelet, so it was more likely she knew Teresa.

"Curiouser and curiouser."

Looking around herself, Callie saw no evidence of a man spying on her. No West Laughlin, as far as she could see. She headed back toward her apartment, taking a circuitous route just in case there were unseen eyes as she drew near. She slowed her steps and changed her mind before entering. There was something she wanted to do.

She was on the street in front of her apartment building and she started walking faster again. She hadn't looked at her building, so if anyone was watching, maybe they wouldn't notice that her steps had slowed. By anyone, she meant West, as she didn't think there was any other player in this drama, other than possibly Teresa, who might be a thousand miles away or more.

She waited for a cab and when one finally stopped for her, she asked if he knew where the nearest Internet café might be. He nodded and drove her down the hill and about ten blocks away from the bay.

The place didn't have a name as far as Callie could see, and it was right next to a sandwich shop, so Callie got herself an egg salad sandwich and ate half of it, tossing the rest away. Then she checked in at the desk of the Internet café and was assigned to a cubicle with a PC in the second row. Her back was to the door and windows, and she glanced furtively behind herself as she sat down.

It would be so much simpler if William called with information on the Laughlins, she thought as she brought up Google. Maybe there was nothing to find, but there generally was something if you were dealing with a family with as much money and prestige as it sounded like the Laughlins possessed.

She hit on them right away. Victoria Laughlin was the matriarch in charge of Laughlin Ranch, Inc., a renowned cattle ranch in the San Joaquin Valley of California. Nearest large city was Bakersfield, but the town of Castilla was closest to the ranch, right off I-5. Though a working ranch, it was also the site of a Western-style restaurant, Laughlin BBQ, which served up beef and lots of it. There was also a gift shop attached to Laughlin BBQ called The Bull Stops Here where one could purchase barbecue equipment, aprons and the like, and red meat enthusiasts could order T-bones, rib eyes, and roasts off the Internet or become a club member for a constant supply.

Callie's eye swept over the business information quickly. Then she clicked away from it, searching for more information about the family itself. She finally found a link to the family's history and learned the tragic story of the Laughlin men. Fifty-some years earlier, Benjamin Laughlin, Victoria's deceased husband, took the cattle ranch from its modest beginnings to the mass-producing mega-beef business it was today. Their son, Craig, took over after Benjamin died from a heart attack at sixty-four, but unfortunately Craig only lived another ten years before his own death in a single-car accident. Craig's son, Stephen, was next in line, and he, too, died unexpectedly while on a hunting trip with friends. The article didn't specify but it sounded like Stephen had been accidentally shot, and that tragedy had occurred about three years earlier.

Callie logged this information as truth, since it jibed with what West had told her. Stephen Laughlin left behind a wife, Teresa, and a son, Stephen Tucker. Victoria Laughlin was the current head of the family and CEO of the company, but she was eighty-three years old and rarely seen these days. The current face of Laughlin Ranch, Inc. was Teddy Stutz, the overseer/manager of Laughlin BBQ, The Bull Stops Here, and all Laughlin concerns.

There was a picture of a red-cheeked, middle-aged man smiling widely at the camera, wearing an apron with a comical snorting bull sliding to a stop in front of a huge sign for Laughlin Ranch.

What struck Callie was how at odds West's description of his starchy grandmother was with the whole Laughlin Ranch publicity. Ted Stutz, whom everyone just called Cal, which the article said was because the ranch was located in California—if it had been in Texas, he would have been known as Tex—seemed the epitome of the outdoorsy cowboy type.

Callie checked some more links, looking for additional information, and came upon Victoria's background. Ben Laughlin had seen her on a trip East with college friends and apparently was smitten as he wooed her to the West Coast against her family's wishes.

"She came to regret that decision," a familiar male voice said behind her head and Callie jumped.

"You scared me," she said, turning around to meet West Laughlin's eyes. He was in khakis and a navy T-shirt that showed off his tan, muscled arms.

His gaze drifted to her chin and he said softly, "That's one helluva bruise."

"Yeah?" Her throat felt tight but luckily her voice was normal. Wondering if Aimee had seen the bruise earlier, she said, "I had an encounter with a thug yesterday."

"Thug," he repeated. "Hmmm. Sorry about that."

"*Il ne pas de quois.*"

"I thought you were just going to the bathroom."

He sounded too, too casual. "I was. But I changed my mind."

"You took the ferry back." It was more a statement than a question.

"Yep. You followed me?"

"Tried to," he admitted. He was sober, not the hint of a smile, and she found herself thinking he looked danger-ous . . . and somehow more attractive.

"You found me here," she said.

"Okay, I followed you from your apartment." He lifted his hands in a "you got me" stance.

"You were at my apartment?" Her heart clutched. How had she not seen him?

Did he see me go to Tucker's this morning?

"I knocked, but you weren't there. Then I saw you coming down the street. I waited, but you cruised on by. Where were you coming from?"

Did he really not know? Or was he just toying with her?

"I should have told you I was leaving."

"That would have been helpful. But then you didn't want me to know where you lived."

"Well, I don't know you, Mr. Laughlin," she pointed out,

closing down the computer. She'd already paid for her time so she was free to leave, except he was standing in her way as she got to her feet.

"Oh, I think we got past the Mr. Laughlin phase a while ago. I coulda filled you in on that." He gestured to the now blank screen.

There was no way she could pretend she hadn't been checking up on him, and well, she didn't see any reason she should. "Did you call William Lister?"

"No."

"No? Why? Still have phone problems?"

He ignored that. "You done here?"

"Guess so." It felt too close, standing next to him, but he was blocking her way to the exit so unless she wanted to circle all the way around, she had to wait for him to move.

Seeing her discomfiture, he took a step back and swept a hand toward the door. She had to brush against him to pass by and her upper arm touched the taut muscles of his stomach. It felt electric and she realized she was too aware of him as a male by far.

The look he sent her made her also realize that he knew what she was feeling. She didn't like it one bit.

Except she did. Sort of.

Out the front door into the heat, Callie inhaled a deep breath and let it out slowly. Tucker wouldn't be at her apartment for another hour or two, if he showed at all, so she had some time to ditch West.

He followed you from your apartment. He may know exactly where Tucker lives.

"So, are we going to your place or mine?" he asked conversationally.

"I wish I could help you, I really do, but . . ." She spread her hands.

"Take me to the friend who gave you the bracelet."

"I don't think she's around."

"Why don't you find out," he suggested in a tone that suggested he was at the end of his patience.

"Y'know, I don't have to put up with you. I thought about it last night, and I don't owe you anything."

"It's not a coincidence you look like Teresa," he said. "Something's going on. You know more than you're saying. We can just keep lobbing this back and forth between us, or you can cut through the bullshit and tell me the bald truth."

"There's no bullshit."

"It's *all* bullshit," he disagreed.

"I'm a victim in this," she reminded him in a low voice. "I didn't ask for you or any of your theories. I should just call the gendarmerie."

"You want the police? Call 'em." His tone suggested *bring it on*.

Callie had really been just delaying while she came up with a game plan, but she didn't have one and she wanted to know more about him anyway. "We'll go to my place."

"Finally."

"Don't push me, Mr. Laughlin . . . West. Don't push me."

Looking as perturbed with her as she was with him, he walked out to the curb and raised an arm to hail a cab.

Chapter Nine

Plans are in motion, speeding toward a bang-up finale, my friends. Years of patience are going to pay off. It's finally my turn. There's money to be made, and wrongs to be avenged. Oh, sure, it's complicated. And dangerous. But that's what life's all about, right? Otherwise we just go through the motions, step by step, on our way to the grave-yard. Well, that's not how it's going to be for me. I'm going to grab what I need, and if that starts with Teresa-fucking-Laughlin, all the better.

Daniella's legs quivered beneath the table where she sat, hands folded tightly on the tabletop, her expression full of fear. Andre's eyes glittered with fury, disappointment, and cold excitement, a sure sign that there would be hell to pay later. She had to look away, couldn't meet his gaze. She'd never been good at hiding her emotions like Teresa, or Jer-rilyn, or Naomi, though she was a better strategist than Clarice, who didn't seem to know jack shit about anything. What the fuck was she doing, telling Andre that there was only one God? Of course there was, but saying something like that to *The Messiah* was like throwing gas on a fire. Didn't she know that?

Daniella loved being with Andre, but she didn't kid herself that he was an easy man. Some of his rules were just plain crazy, meant for his own pleasure and no one else's, but then she'd had a lot worse and at least he took care of them all.

Unfortunately, she'd really screwed the pooch this time, one of her stepmother's favorite expressions just as she was about to backhand Daniella. Last night, while she'd followed Teresa, keeping an eye on her to make sure she did what she was told, per Andre's orders, she'd let Teresa get away. She'd been parked near the bar and had settled herself behind a Dodge Hemi truck with a view to Robert Lumpkin's car. From there, she had seen Teresa weave out with the man, had watched as she'd shoved him into the front seat of a beat-up, piece of shit Ford Focus. Then Teresa had ripped some money from Lumpkin's wallet, and had walked quickly away and around the building to the opposite street where the Xterra was parked. Daniella had made the mistake of checking on Lumpkin first, wondering what Teresa's overall plan was because she was pretty sure Teresa was supposed to dispose of him somewhere else. He wasn't dead, which she knew was probably what Andre had really wanted, and she was surprised Teresa had defied him. She had heard the Xterra fire up, just as she was opening the driver's door for a peek. Lumpkin's leg had popped out and she had hurriedly shoved it back in. He had been slumped over the seat, his body awkwardly bent over the console and into the passenger bucket seat. Teresa had definitely knocked him out, but that was as far as it had gone, apparently.

It had been Daniella's bad luck that a man and his date had walked outside the bar and caught a glimpse of Lumpkin after she had gotten his leg back inside and was just shutting the door. "He okay?" the guy had asked.

Panicked inside, Daniella had said, "Yeah, I don't know. He kinda pulled the door shut and just fell over. I knocked on the window and when he didn't respond I opened the door and he kinda flapped a hand at me."

"Maybe we should call 911," the date said. She was a small woman, shivering in the brisk night air.

"Y'think?" he asked, clearly not interested in getting that involved.

Daniella meanwhile had been worried about her fingerprints. She'd yanked open the door without thinking. She didn't have a record, but she was Lumpkin's tenant of record. Shit. What had she been thinking? And where the fuck had Teresa gone?

They had all stood there a moment, and then the man said, "If he waved at you, then he must be okay."

"Maybe he's just sleeping it off," the date suggested. "At least he's not driving."

"I think he was kinda pissed I opened the door," Daniella said.

"God, it's cold. You think it was the Arctic, not LA." The date had shivered and the man put his arm over her shoulders.

"Okay, well . . . whatever," he said, then turned the woman with his arm and they had walked away, their momentary interest fading off.

Once out of view, Daniella wiped down the door handle, then immediately ran to the Chevy. She drove around the block to where the Xterra had been parked, but it was no surprise to find an empty space at the curb. Teresa had been long gone.

In a painful quandary, Daniella had nervously squeezed her hands and cracked her knuckles, then she'd put the car in gear and headed toward the airport. While Teresa had been inside Ray's with Lumpkin, Daniella had unlocked the Xterra with one of their extra keys and rifled through the bags tossed into the backseat. Andre didn't trust Teresa, who had been a real closed-off bitch since the Cantrell business, which was just weird because Teresa didn't even like Jonathan Cantrell. She never liked anybody, except maybe that Laughlin guy—she'd married him, for God's sake—but even he hadn't affected her as much as Cantrell. Well, of course, the kid had died in that accident, and that hadn't been part of the plan. Still, Teresa had never shown she cared much about anything but Teresa, so Daniella had assumed she'd get over it.

Of course, Jerrilyn had changed after being Mittenberger's mistress for so many months. She had become quieter, more watchful, and almost sort of fake-friendly. Andre had noticed it, too, though he pretended not to. Daniella just hoped Jerrilyn maybe really cared about the guy. One less handmaiden to fight off. Meanwhile, Naomi was still her bossy old self and Clarice was just a blank between the ears. If Teresa was really gone, and Jerrilyn was falling for some other guy, then definitely things would be better.

As those thoughts had filled her head, her hand had encountered a small folder in the bottom of the second bag. She'd pulled it out and recognized an airline packet just as she heard Teresa's voice. Daniella stuffed the folder at the bottom of the bag and backed out of the Xterra, banging her head on the doorway in the process. Head pounding, she'd raced away, hiding behind the huge, black truck.

When Teresa, after a few moments with Lumpkin at his car, had racewalked to her car, Daniella had been torn. She was supposed to follow her, but always before Teresa had driven the victim's car away, letting him wake up miles from the scene of the crime, if he woke up at all. Teresa would then walk to a nearby bar, call a cab, and have them drop her at the original location. She never knew she was being followed, and she always acted in the same way.

But this was new with Lumpkin, so that's why Daniella had looked.

She'd arrived at LAX forty minutes later, knowing Teresa only had about ten minutes on her, tops. It was one helluva big airport, but she'd seen Delta written on the folder and a time, just after midnight. Maybe the flight wasn't for tonight, but why else would her bags be in the SUV? She'd already broken protocol and Andre would not be forgiving.

So, she'd gone to the Delta counter and been shocked to see Teresa right there, big as life, at the ticket counter. Taking a huge risk, Daniella had circled around the other passengers waiting in line who gave her dirty looks like she was cutting, then had walked behind Teresa just as the woman handing Teresa back her ticket was saying, "Check with the gate agent when you get to Miami. It's tight, but doable, I think."

Now Daniella was faced with a glowering Andre whose left eye was ticking. A bad sign. Maybe he was having one of his headaches, or maybe he was just that enraged.

He said, "What am I going to do with you if you can't do one job?"

"She was supposed to move him to somewhere else. I don't know why she didn't."

"She was supposed to take care of the problem."

"She didn't move him."

"She was supposed to *take care of the problem,*" he stressed.

Daniella nodded. Maybe that's why Teresa had balked; she didn't want to kill him. Daniella, herself, hadn't been asked to commit this ultimate act of allegiance. She was pretty sure she wouldn't be able to, and maybe Andre had guessed that, or maybe her time just hadn't come yet. If it meant pushing herself to the front of the pack, maybe she could . . . maybe . . . God, she hoped so.

"We are all going to have to find Teresa now," Andre said, his eyes dark and flat as they gazed hard at her.

Behind her, she felt someone come into the room and glanced back to find Naomi, her eyes bright. She was almost as fervent as Andre sometimes.

"When you find her, what's—"

"*We* find her," he corrected patiently.

"Going to happen to her?"

"You know, when we do bad things, we must be punished."

"I don't do bad things," she blurted out.

"You failed The Messiah," Naomi said. Daniella's quivering turned to an out-and-out shaking. Naomi shifted behind her and said, her breath stirring the hair at Daniella's crown, "Jerrilyn is on a weekend trip with Mittenberger."

"Get her back here," Andre said. He hated being thwarted in any way.

Naomi didn't question him, just turned on her heel and went to do as she was bidden. How Jerrilyn would explain to her mark that his mistress had had a change of plans was Jerrilyn's problem. Daniella had enough of her own.

"What if I can't find where she went?" Daniella asked, cringing inside at her scared tone.

"You will find her," he said.

Daniella nodded, lowering her gaze. She could tell him right now. She should tell him right now. But she needed to at least pretend that she hadn't been lying. She would take the Chevy and drive around for a while, then she would find a way to explain how she'd learned Teresa had driven to LAX and that she was on her way to Miami and beyond.

West had accepted a glass of lemonade and they were both standing on her balcony, looking over the street below. Time was passing and she needed to get him out of her apartment soon, but he was clearly in no hurry to leave.

He would probably be happy to wait all afternoon and evening and into the next day.

"So, your grandmother married a cattle rancher and moved out west," she said, continuing the conversation that had sprung up from her search at the Internet café.

"Who's this friend, Aimee?" he asked.

Callie just shook her head. There was no way out of this. The bracelet was too big of a giveaway.

Her phone suddenly started ringing from inside her purse, which was sitting on a table inside. West's gaze slid to her purse and then back to her eyes. "No phone, huh," he said.

"Excuse me." She hurried inside and ripped her cell out of her purse. "Hello," she answered, expecting it to be William and it was.

"You want information on the Laughlins . . . ?" he asked carefully.

"Thanks, I already took care of that." She saw West casually walk back inside.

"May I ask why?"

"Don't worry about it. I really can't talk now. I'll call you back later."

"I'm assuming you mean the Laughlins of Laughlin Ranch."

"I believe so. Gotta go. Thanks."

She clicked off and turned to face him.

"So, you lied about the phone, too," he said.

"You know, I don't know what's going on here, either," she said. "I don't know how I got involved with your family problems, but I did, apparently. Now I just want it all to go away. I've only got a few more days in Martinique, and I would kind of like to spend them relaxing and preparing to go back home. No offense . . . *West* . . . but you need to leave me alone."

"Tell me about the bracelet, who gave it to you, and I don't just mean their name. I want to know who they are, and why they would give it to you. Believe me, I know it's a Laughlin heirloom, or, actually, if you want to get technical, a Brantley heirloom as Victoria was a Brantley before she married my grandfather. Call the gendarmerie if you have to, but I'm not leaving till I get those answers."

Through the door Callie heard a clatter of footsteps on the outdoor stairs. She whipped around. *Oh, God, no! It's too early!*

West's head turned, too, following her. Then there was the sound of a small fist pounding on her door.

"Calleee! Calleee!" came through in a muffled cry.

Like an automaton, Callie walked to the door, twisted open the handle. Tucker flew inside and hurled himself at her, throwing his arms around her.

West stared at the boy clamped to Callie's thigh and then lifted his eyes to meet hers. She was surprisingly calm, matching his gaze with a challenge in her own blue eyes, although there was trepidation as well.

Outrage burned through him as he set his unfinished glass of lemonade on a glass-topped side table. Damn it all. This had to be Stephen's boy.

So, maybe the woman in front of him was Teresa after all. From what he'd discerned, Teresa would easily assume someone else's identity, if it suited her purpose. The back-story about Callie Cantrell could be all true, but it didn't mean she was Callie.

The boy was looking at him, having recognized there was someone else in the room. "You must be Tucker," West said.

He looked like Stephen . . . same dark hair and blue eyes, a Laughlin brand as much as any mark seared into cattle hides.

"Tucker, this is Mr. Laughlin," she introduced.

"*Allo.*" Then Tucker screwed his neck around to look up at her. "You are *amies?*"

"We just met yesterday," she said. Her voice was wooden. West could tell she'd shut down but he sensed that she was ready to claw his eyes out if he so much as spoke to Tucker in a way she deemed incorrect.

But to hell with her. He wanted answers. "So, is she your mother?" he asked.

The boy turned to him fully and sized him up and down as Callie seemed carved in stone. "We are *amies,*" he said scornfully, as if West were really dense.

"Friends," she said.

"Friends," the boy repeated, as if memorizing the word.

"But not your mother," West reiterated.

Tucker looked confused and "Callie" said, "He lives with his mother."

Tucker shook his head emphatically. "She not *mon Maman.*"

She gave the boy a look and said, "Tucker, you've always called Aimee *Maman.*"

"*Non,*" he insisted.

"So, this woman is not your mother, and Aimee is not your mother," West clarified, holding on to his patience with an effort. He didn't much like being played for a fool.

"I'm Callie Cantrell," she insisted.

"You don't live with your mother? Teresa?" West pressed Tucker.

His tone shut the little boy up tight. He just stared at West and "Callie" snapped at him, "He lives with Aimee."

"And Jacques," Tucker said solemnly, never taking his eyes off West.

"Who's Jacques?" West asked.

"Jacques is the wharf cat who's adopted Tucker," she filled in.

Tucker asked, "*Qui?*"

"Jacques is your *chat*," she clarified.

Tucker nodded his head several times. "He eat rats."

"Can I meet Aimee?" West asked the boy.

"I'll take you there," she inserted tautly before Tucker could respond.

"Nooooo," he cried, running to the other side of the room and plopping down in one of her rattan chairs, holding on tightly to its arms. "I stay."

"What are you doing home so early?" she asked. "I thought you were at school."

"Ahh . . ." His small shoulders lifted in a very Gallic shrug. "*Maman* . . . um . . . Aimee forgot. We leave *école* soon."

"School was early out? But Aimee was there when you went home just now," she reminded. "You went there first."

"She was there," he said, but his eyes slid away.

"Tucker, was Aimee there when you got home?" she demanded.

"*Oui*. I eat what you brung me. *Merci!*" He suddenly jumped up and darted past West to the balcony.

"You're welcome," she said.

She was nervous, it was clear. Didn't want to hardly look at him. Well, fine. But the jig was up now, at least where Stephen Tucker Laughlin was concerned. He'd already been convinced she'd been connected with Teresa, and now, after seeing Tucker, nothing she could say would convince him this boy wasn't his brother's son.

As if reading his mind, she said, "I'm not Teresa."

"Yeah?"

"But I haven't been completely honest," she admitted.

No shit, sister.

He saw her hug herself and it caused her breasts to swell over the square neckline of her blue top. Dragging his gaze away, he looked instead around the room.

When he'd first followed her into the apartment, he'd looked around with a cop's eyes, sizing it up. It was clearly a rental. The flower-printed cushions were faded and slightly worn although the pillows were plumped and clean. The small table and chairs were rattan, beaten up at the legs by a vacuum cleaner, if he was reading the whitened, scarred wood correctly. The kitchenette cabinets were functional but the laminate was peeling up just a teensy bit at the corners of the doors. Still, it was comfortable. And probably a helluva lot cheaper than his room at Bakoua Beach; he'd purposely kept back the information that he was staying at the hotel, not wanting to scare her when she had inadvertently chosen his hotel as yesterday's venue. Now he was glad he hadn't been forthright. He was pissed off at her. He'd wanted to believe in her. *Had* believed in her, but she'd hornswoggled him on damn near everything and he'd believed he was beyond being hornswoggled by a good-looking woman again.

Just goes to show you, he thought darkly.

He'd gotten a call back from Dorcas, his ex-partner, who'd wanted to know what he was looking for. "The car that went over on Mulholland about a year ago," West had reminded him a bit impatiently.

"Yeah, Cantrell. Got it," Dorcas had said. "The husband and kid died. Wife survived. But what are you doing?" Then, before he could answer, "You on some kind of private case?"

"For my grandmother," he had said, seeking to squelch any further questions.

But Dorcas wasn't known for taking hints. An ex-college linebacker, Peter Dorcas kept his block of six foot three, two hundred fifty pounds in fighting shape from a five-day-a-week workout at the gym. West had also been a regular gym rat, but he was a much leaner build and not quite as tall. ce his falling out with his captain, which had included an IA review that had proven nothing other than showing Paulsen for the demigod he was, West had slacked off the workout routine, had been in search of whatever he wanted to do in this next phase of life with or without a job in law enforcement.

Dorcas had responded with, "Bullshit, pard. You're workin' on sumpin-sumpin, ain't ya?"

"Ex-pard," West had said. "Just dig into the Cantrell accident and get back to me. And send me a picture of the wife, if you can."

"Where you at?"

"Martinique."

"Where the Sam Hill is that?"

"An island in the Caribbean."

"What the fuck, man?"

"Just get me the info." He had then told Dorcas the number to call him back, adding, "And anything you can find on Mrs. Cantrell would be appreciated." Then he had clicked off as Dorcas had tried to complain about the extra work. As yet, his ex-partner hadn't phoned back, but it was a lot earlier in Los Angeles, so maybe he would check in later.

"We can walk Tucker back," she said, as if it were the last thing she wanted to do.

"Noooo!" said Tucker, who was pressed up against the wrought-iron balcony rail, looking down at the passing cars and pedestrians, vehemently shaking his head. "I not go back!" A torrent of French followed this, which West couldn't understand. Neither, apparently, could Callie because she said, "Speak American, Tucker."

That stopped the boy short. "American?"

"Mr. Laughlin and I don't know that much French. I think you were saying you're going with Michel," she encouraged.

He glanced at West and said solemnly, "Michel is *mon amie*."

"Michel's father, Jean-Paul, is a fisherman and the boys like to go fishing with him," she explained.

She wouldn't meet his gaze any longer. West said, "All right, let's go."

Over Tucker's continuing protests, they headed for the door, and finally the boy stomped his way across the room and preceded them into the outer hallway.

She could feel sweat forming down her back and between her breasts as they walked up the hot streets. She felt slightly light-headed, but maybe that was because she was anxious. Having West meet Tucker had ratcheted up the danger level.

Tucker, after getting over not wanting to leave Callie's, was in the midst of a fishing tale that was half in French, half in English. "Big fish . . . big, big *poisson*," he said, stretching his arms wide.

"That big, huh," West said. His first comment since leaving her apartment.

"Big more," he said proudly. He smiled widely, a gap showing in the line of his lower teeth where he'd already lost a tooth.

But when they got to Tucker's apartment, Aimee was not there and the door was locked. Tucker ran down the hall and knocked on another door. A fortyish woman with a round shape and a big smile came to the door and ushered Tucker inside as if it happened all the time, which it probably did. Upon seeing Callie and West, she said, "*Allo?*"

"We were looking for Aimee?" Callie gestured toward Tucker's door.

"She is out. Tucker stays with me when she is out. Ummm . . . *comprendez vous?*"

"You're his babysitter. He comes to your place when Aimee is away."

"*Oui.*"

"Come in!" Tucker called to her.

"Next time, buddy," she said. "Merci," she added to the woman, then she was alone in the hallway with West.

Callie walked out of the apartment building and once they were on the street, she opened her mouth again, but he interrupted her.

"I know. You're not Teresa."

"That's not what I was going to say," she said.

"Well, who the hell's Aimee, and did she really give you the bracelet?"

"Tucker gave me the bracelet."

"Tucker gave it to you." He was surprised.

"He just brought it to me one day."

"Oh, sure."

"I'm not lying," she flashed. "About this, anyway."

"Well, what have you lied about? Or maybe I should ask what you haven't lied about. Whatever's shorter."

"Tucker found me. He picked me out at the pier one day when he was with Jean-Paul. I thought Jean-Paul was his father, but then it became clear that his son, Michel, and Tucker are friends. Tucker acted like he . . . I don't know . . . knew me."

"Knew you." He sounded disparaging.

"Hey, I'm telling you the truth here. This is what happened. I was about a week into my vacation and I just ran into him. He came toward me, skipping, and then he saw me and just beelined . . ." Her throat closed at the memory of Tucker giving her that first, enthusiastic, big hug, as if he'd just discovered something wonderful. "I was kind of taken aback, but he was so adorable. If Teresa's his mom, maybe he saw a resemblance," she added unsteadily. "I thought

Aimee was his mother, but she is not, apparently. I found out he lived near me and we started this relationship, call it what you will. I needed him, too. I *need* him too," she corrected.

"What does Aimee think of you?"

"Of me, or of Teresa? She doesn't like me much. I don't know what she thinks of Teresa, but I asked her about it this morning."

"What do you mean?"

They'd been walking down the sidewalk but now he stopped short and Callie had to stop as well. "I went to the apartment this morning. Weren't you following me? You didn't seem surprised to find out where Tucker lived."

When she waited for him to respond, he admitted, "I saw you coming from that direction."

"I knew Tucker was at school, so I went to see her."

"What did she say about Teresa?" he demanded.

"She pretended not to know her, but she was taken aback when I said 'Teresa Laughlin.' I told her I had the bracelet and she really got upset and insisted the bracelet's hers." He was staring at her with cold blue eyes, intimidating enough for her to have to look away. "I didn't want to tell you about Tucker until I was sure everything was on the up-and-up. That's why I was at the Internet café today."

"Where is she now?"

"I don't know. I think Tucker's lying about going home first. But he said he had the pastry. . . ." She shook her head. "I was relieved to see the neighbor's a babysitter. Tucker just has so much freedom. Half the time he runs home by himself. I've tried to walk with him, but he just takes off and leaves me in the dust. He has zero supervision, as far as I can tell, which makes me crazy. I've told myself I should call Child Services, or whatever they are here, a dozen times, but I haven't yet. I don't know why. Well, yes, I do. Selfish reasons. I don't want to risk not being able to see him, but if something happened to him . . ." She couldn't finish the thought, it was too terrible.

"How long do you plan on staying on the island?"

"I told my attorney that I would leave this week," she answered, "but I might have lied to him, too."

West began walking again and Callie fell in step beside him. She couldn't discern his mood. Finally, he said, "Tucker is my brother's child. I'd bet my life savings on it."

"You believe I'm not Teresa."

"I don't know who you are. Right now, I don't really care. But I can tell you're concerned about Tucker." He paused, and then added, "Somebody should be."

Chapter Ten

Daniella was hot, thirsty, and irritable. Why was it her job to always clean up the shit? She was glad Teresa was gone. Glad! She'd hoped she'd be gone for good, but Andre had other ideas. They were all supposed to be involved.

She'd been at her "search" for two hours. She wasn't sure why she was delaying. She was going to have to tell Andre where Teresa had gone, and what did she care anyway? Let him find her. Let them all find her. This wasn't going to end well for Teresa no matter what, so why was she delaying?

She shook her head and put the Malibu in gear, heading back to their house. She didn't like sharing Andre, and she was letting Teresa's defection play out because she wanted her gone. One less handmaiden to fight with. But was that the smart way to play this? It was so hard to tell.

Daniella felt a lump in her throat. She wanted Andre to herself, but could she ever admit that? Noooooo. She was just a handmaiden, and he was The Messiah, and she was sworn to share him. That's the way things stood. If she even tried to act like she was worth more than the rest of them, a whole pile of shit would rain down on her head. She would be told she was unworthy and maybe she was, but she didn't care. She just wanted him for her. Was that so bad? He was such a beautiful man, and he did possess true spirituality.

But that's why they all wanted him. Daniella had seen the way the other handmaidens slid glances at each other when they thought no one was looking. She pretended not to notice, but jealousy and envy came off Naomi, Jerrilyn, Teresa, and even Clarice, that little snot, in waves. You could practically touch it. No matter what they said, they all wanted to be Andre's chosen one. He knew it, too, the bastard, and he reveled in it. It was enough to break Daniella's heart.

She'd thought there was a chance things were breaking open when she'd realized there was something weird going on with Teresa. She'd stopped being all sassy, smart, and in control, and had gotten all depressed, even though it made Andre mad. It was like she'd moved to some other astral plane, detached, saying less, being more secretive, sometimes barely getting out of bed. Noting the change, Daniella had been secretly happy. Maybe she'd just go the fuck away forever.

And now she had . . .

Why haven't you told Andre about Miami?

Daniella's hands clenched the steering wheel. She wanted to smoke a cigarette but didn't dare. If Andre were to catch the scent of it on her, he would lock her into that cold room in the attic. That was the punishment if they weren't pure, which was kind of a joke because they could drink and ply their marks with drugs, so who cared about cigarettes?

Andre. Smoking was not for the handmaidens. Purity. Ha. Like any of them were pure. Even Clarice, with all her talk of God, was a fake.

But they're all prettier than you.

Daniella burned inside. Maybe she *would* have that

cigarette. Maybe she'd run away like Teresa, but would Andre even come after her like he would for Teresa? Hell no. She was the little brown wren who kept the outside world from invading their nest. She knew that's why Andre had chosen her. Without her, who would keep the disbelievers safely away from them?

But then again, without Andre, who would *she* be?

The thought of never having him in her bed again made her want to weep. She loved making love with him. Loved feeling him moving inside her, their bodies one. No, she didn't like it when the other handmaidens watched. She didn't want their love on display. She wanted it to be private. Special. Just for the two of them. Jerrilyn was a born exhibitionist and thrashed, moaned, and bucked for all she was worth whenever it was her turn, but Daniella kinda thought it embarrassed Andre a little. She was chosen the least often for their circles of love, but it was torture whenever she was. Jerrilyn had a way of staring straight at Daniella with that hateful little smile that made Daniella lower her gaze in shame.

Sometimes she dreamed of killing them all.

She drove the last few miles back to the house and turned into the drive. The Malibu was the only car they allowed in the driveway, just in case the neighbors were paying attention.

Switching off the ignition, she pocketed the keys, staring up at the sun as she exited the car and headed for the front door. Andre would ask her a thousand questions about how she'd tracked Teresa, which she had no answers for, but she didn't care. She should have told him last night and didn't quite understand why she hadn't.

Entering the house, she stopped short upon seeing Andre standing in the hallway in one of their prayer robes and nothing else. The lapels were parted, showing a swatch of skin from neck to crotch, displaying his stiff, eager cock, which was standing up like a flagpole. Clarice came giggling out of his bedroom, also robed, and she fell on him, taking him into her mouth and lavishing him with her tongue.

Daniella's stomach revolted, and she could feel her cheeks burn as Andre's dark eyes regarded her calmly, a little smile playing on his face. She managed to keep from screaming at them though she wanted to fucking *kill* Clarice.

She said in a monotone, "Teresa took a flight to Miami and she's catching a connecting one to somewhere else."

"*What?* Where?" Andre pushed Clarice away from him.

Daniella felt a surge of delight and power. "I don't know." She fought the smirk that stole across her lips as she witnessed Clarice's hurt expression. But the dumb bitch just moved forward and put her mouth back on his now flaccid member, trying to revive it. *Good luck with that, whore.*

Andre was lost in thought, or maybe Clarice's attention was sending him to a rapturous place, which made Daniella clench her teeth.

"I know where she is," he said after a moment. He patted Clarice impatiently on the head until she backed away, then brushed past her as if she were a piece of furniture, which cheered Daniella no end. "We'll have to go get her."

"We?" Clarice asked, gazing up at him.

"We'll meet in the prayer room with the robes. . . ." He was walking away from them. "One hour. Then we'll see about flights."

Daniella knew now why she'd delayed telling him about Teresa. Though Andre carefully locked up their money, occasionally he would take out thick rolls of cash and they would go on some mission. There was generally a downside to these sprees, and somehow Daniella always got the short end of the stick.

The last time they'd all gone somewhere they'd ended up in Las Vegas where Andre had picked up Jerrilyn.

With a sinking heart Daniella worried Andre was looking to expand his flock. They might be getting rid of Teresa, but someone new would be coming their way. The thought of sharing him with one more woman sent a cold spike of fury into her heart. She was going to have to do something about that.

No one was going to take care of her except herself.

Maybe killing someone wouldn't be that hard. In fact it might be downright easy, if it was one of the other hand-maidens.

Callie stood in the living room, trying not to stare too hard at West, who was back on the balcony, looking over the street much as Tucker had. She didn't know what to do with him. He'd lost all trust in her. She understood why, but she didn't trust him, either. In fact, how did she know he was who he said he was? He'd asked for her ID, but she hadn't asked for his.

Do you really think he's lying to you about being West Laughlin?

No, but . . . there were a lot of unanswered questions.

"That article on the Internet didn't mention you," she said. It had been a while since they'd said anything to each other and for a moment he didn't react.

Then he half-turned.

"It mentioned your family . . . your father, brother, and grandfather, and Victoria. But there was no West Laughlin."

"I told you why."

"You're the black sheep. Right. Could I see your ID? Your passport?"

He turned around and regarded her fully, crossing his

arms over his chest and leaning indolently against the rail. "Now you want to make sure I'm who I say I am? You're a little late to the party." But he reached into his pocket and pulled out his wallet. A moment later he slipped out his California driver's license and handed it to her. As she studied it, he said, "My passport's in the safe at my hotel room. I was warned about pickpockets."

She handed his license back to him, and he lifted his brows. "It's you," she said.

"You're not going to accuse me of faking it?"

"That would be your line," she told him. "You thought Teresa was capable of that."

"That particular article only mentioned who was in direct line to inherit, not the rest of us."

"Of us?"

"My father had a brother, Jason, who was practically ex-communicated by Victoria and my grandfather. Apparently Jace was one of those guys who follows cults. I understand it's a personality type. Some people can't live without being part of a group with a leader whom they can follow. After the fallout, he left for the South Pacific and never returned. Also, Stephen's mother, Talia, wasn't mentioned. She must be still around somewhere. She was still married to my father when he died and I don't think she'd give up on the Laughlin money that easily. I've read Wikipedia and most of the other sites about the Laughlins as well," he added dryly. "Interesting you chose the one about who's in line to inherit."

"You didn't give me time to even look before you showed up. I don't give a damn about who inherits. You still think I'm Teresa," she accused.

"You're connected somehow."

"Hate to disappoint you, but we're not."

"Uh-huh."

Her temper flared at his all-knowing attitude. "I never

even heard of the Laughlins before you showed up. And for someone who acts like they don't give a damn, you're pretty quick to go to the money yourself."

That scored a direct hit. She could see him getting angry. "So, that's not the reason you're after Tucker?" he grated. "Because he's next in line?"

"I . . ." She could hardly get the words out. "That's what you think? Really? You think I would—"

"Teresa would," he cut in, before she could work herself up to full outrage.

"Tucker is a wonderful kid, despite God knows what kind of care he's gotten. Maybe Aimee's not so bad. She's done something right with him."

"Stephen Tucker Laughlin is the sole heir to the Laughlin fortune," he said.

A coldness settled into her soul. She knew firsthand about the kind of ugly infighting that went on when one member of a family inherited and the others were ignored.

"That's another reason Victoria wants Tucker. He's not only her flesh and blood, he's also next in line to take over."

"He's also five!"

"Victoria never thinks she's going to die, so she probably expects to still be around when he's old enough to take over."

"But it won't happen that way," Callie argued.

"You and I know that," he agreed.

"You can't let Tucker be caught in the middle of that."

"I'm just giving you the facts."

"You need to step in and protect him. Maybe . . . maybe the reason your grandmother picked you to find Tucker is because she really wants you to take over."

"When pigs fly." He straightened from the rail and came back into the living room. Callie took a couple of steps away from him, too aware of the space he took up. "I am not connected to Teresa," she said.

"You are. But I'll grant you that you might not know how yet. You're too good at playing this part."

"I'm not sure what that means."

"I'm good at getting to the truth. That's all I'm saying. Whatever happens happens, and whoever's standing in the way might get hurt."

"Does that include Tucker?" she challenged.

"He's the one innocent in all of this."

Callie didn't respond. The one thing she did believe was that West was on the side of the angels where his nephew was concerned. "Okay," she said, not really sure what she was agreeing to.

"If you're not Teresa, then where the hell is she?" he asked softly. "And why is this Aimee taking care of Tucker?"

Callie shook her head. Even when she'd believed Aimee was Tucker's mother, the relationship had seemed off.

"Teresa must've given the bracelet to Aimee," he said. "Maybe as payment for taking care of Tucker."

"How could she leave her son with anyone in the first place?"

"Teresa clearly doesn't have your maternal instincts," he said. "Maybe Victoria's right and something went down with Stephen. Maybe she knows something about that accident that she shouldn't, and that's why she left and couldn't take Tucker with her."

"It's still not enough," Callie said.

He exhaled. "I'm going to have to watch Aimee's apartment, hope that she comes back soon."

"Actually, I'm supposed to meet her back at her apartment at three with the bracelet."

"You're giving it back to her?" he asked.

"Well, it's not mine, and I sure as hell don't want it."

"It's not hers, either."

"So you say, and I believe you, to a point. But Tucker took

the bracelet from her and gave it to me, so that's where it came from. Maybe she owns it rightfully."

"Doubtful."

"But it's yours to take from her?"

"That's what Victoria wants. It's hers."

"But you said it's possible Stephen gave it to Teresa, and then if she gave it to Aimee . . . I mean . . . you don't have any claim."

"Let's just go back at three and see what happens."

"I think it would be better if I went alone."

"Fat chance of that," he said. "Whoever you are, Callie Cantrell or somebody else, I'm tired of either searching for you or following you around. We're going together."

Chapter Eleven

Fort-de-France. The pier. Blue-green water and the scent of the sea. Teresa breathed in deeply and closed her eyes. She was tired, rumpled, and afraid. For years she'd blindly followed Andre in whatever endeavor took his fancy, all the while thinking she was doing what she wanted. Without Andre she hadn't wanted to live.

Rubbing the back of her neck and lifting her hair off her nape, she swallowed and picked up her bag. She'd had the cab driver drop her at the pier, just in case anyone was watching her, which was absurd, really, but she still went with the subterfuge. She sat on a bench for a while, then made her way to a taxi stand, thinking about Aimee's apartment and Tucker. She hadn't made a return flight. She didn't know where she was going next.

All she knew was that she was taking Tucker with her.

Maybe I should get a room first and a cool drink.

She hated the idea of using any of her hard-earned cash. Grifting had always been an easy way to replenish diminishing funds, so she told the driver to take her to the hotel closest to the address she gave him for Tucker's apartment and drop her there. Fifteen minutes later, she was plunking down her credit card for the one-night stay, wondering how much time she had before Andre would come looking for her.

She shivered. Part of her almost wanted him to come after her. A crazy part of herself that just couldn't give him up. But no. It would be too dangerous for Tucker, who would fall into Andre's killing sights by virtue of being Stephen Laughlin's son.

That was the endgame, she figured. The Laughlins. Though Andre tried to be cagey about whatever he was really planning—calling himself The Messiah, going through all those crazy rituals—she knew him well . . . or at least the Andre he'd once been . . . and it was all about the money, really. She'd played along because she'd loved him so much.

What the fucking hell had been wrong with her for so long?

Dropping her bags inside the rose-and-cream room of the boutique hotel, she glanced at the bed longingly. A bath first, and then to climb between clean sheets where no one would wake her.

She succumbed, knowing she shouldn't, knowing she might only have a short amount of time before the hounds were chasing her. But if all went well, it would be a while till Andre figured out exactly where she'd gone. He didn't know about Tucker, so he might not think about Martinique and any connections she might have.

Turning the taps, her smile was hard as she thought back to the last time she'd been here. She'd been falling in love with Andre, playing a game of cat and mouse with him. In those days, he'd been freer, not as involved in his ultimate quest as he'd subsequently become. He'd talked about getting what was rightfully his, but there'd been lots of time and for a brief moment she'd thought he might chuck the whole plan and settle down with her on this beautiful island. She already knew then how to go after a mark and separate him from his cash. She'd actually tried her wiles on Andre and had learned that he was too savvy. He had been onto her, but instead of being angry, he had wanted to join forces with her, and it had been what she'd wanted too.

That's what had done it for her: recognizing a soul mate. She had given herself over to him heart and soul and they'd screwed like rabbits even while they were picking out her next mark, whimsically always referred to as "Mark." It had been dangerous and fun as they set up each stupid sap. Sometimes she'd acted like Andre was her boyfriend who had beaten her mercilessly in the past. Sometimes she'd played a working girl who was on the run from a terrible life of near slavery. Sometimes she had been just a lonely woman after a sad breakup. It didn't matter what story she told, she had always finished with needing money and, of course, she had wanted to leave with "Mark," her would-be savior. It was truly amazing how gullible men were.

They had worked their game long enough to start to feel the heat, and that's when Andre had suggested they move to Los Angeles. Teresa had initially been reluctant. She liked their life on Martinique, even though they'd had to lie low a few times when one of their Marks had caught on too early to the scheme and gone to the authorities.

"Just one more," she'd begged, hoping to delay leaving.

It had been a hard sell but then Andre had chosen her last Mark, pointing him out across the restaurant lounge of the Bakoua Beach Hotel. "He's been hanging at the bar, and I've been listening. Family has money," he'd whispered in her ear. "Make him fall in love with you."

She'd loitered around the hotel, watching Mark for an entire day, keeping out of sight and eavesdropping wherever she could. He wasn't much of a talker when he was sober, but once he had a few drinks, information had started spilling out. His brother and sister had been pissed off because dear old Dad had left him much of the fortune. He'd worked for the company, which was in real estate development. Everything had been going and blowing and he and Dad were putting deals together right and left and getting out at just the right time. His grasping siblings could just kiss his ass; they were getting nothing.

He'd given himself this trip to the Caribbean as a means of self-congratulation. He'd already been to Barbados, St. Croix, and St. Lucia, and now he was about as far south as he was going, though he'd thought about a stop in Venezuela. Problem was: dear old Dad wasn't doing so hot, so Mark was going to have to head back and play the part of the dutiful son.

Teresa had originally planned to step into the room in her long, backless black dress, but, sizing him up, she'd changed for a more conservative knee-length sundress the color of pink champagne. She'd walked through the bar and stood at the edge of the covered patio, looking out toward the bay, pasting a forlorn expression on her face.

Then she'd turned an about-face and walked up to the bartender, asking if he knew what time the ferry docked at the Pointe du Bout side. "Looks like I've been stood up," she had said. Mark had sat on her right, nursing his third drink that she'd seen.

"You need a ride somewhere?" he'd asked.

"Probably the airport," she'd said sadly. "This was supposed to be our engagement trip, if you can believe that. But it's hard to compete with a dead wife. I think he's changed his mind, and he's already left me."

He had looked her up and down. "Then he's an idiot."

She had smiled.

"Sit down and let me buy you a drink first. Then we'll get a cab together." He had smiled at her and she had noticed how handsome he was. "I'm Jonathan Cantrell," he had said.

"Teresa."

"Just Teresa?"

"DuPres," she had said, using her maiden name.

They hadn't gotten a cab together. They'd gone straight to his room. Since she'd been with Andre she'd managed to get her dates dead drunk and rob them before anything but a sloppy petting session ensued, but with Jonathan, she'd never had that chance. Before she knew it they had both gotten naked and she was in the middle of an energetic lovemaking session, which had only fueled the thrill of the game. Thinking of Andre finding out had sent shivers beneath her skin and intensified her orgasm. She didn't even have to fake it. She had determined she wouldn't tell Andre, then thought maybe she would. No, she couldn't . . . it was too dangerous. . . .

She had stayed with Jonathan Cantrell the whole night and into the next day. She'd tried to call Andre, but Jonathan was on her like a blanket, so instead of merely rolling him she became his island lover.

The next night Andre had shown up at the hotel lounge and she'd felt his eyes burning into her as she'd sat with Jonathan's arm draped possessively over her shoulder. She'd met his gaze and shaken her head. There was nothing she could do. When Andre left she had been scared that it was over with him. She had really loved him so much.

But then there was Jonathan, so maybe she could get over Andre?

Jonathan had taken her on an incredible shopping spree, showering her with jewelry and designer couture and treating her to sumptuous dinners in restaurants all over the city. She'd had more booty than she'd ever gotten before and she was trying to figure out how to haul it away with her and escape when Jonathan was called home: dear old Dad had died.

Jonathan had wanted her to come with him back to Los Angeles. She'd been sorely tempted, but had demurred. She had told him she really, really wanted to go but she had things to wrap up in Martinique. Yes, she was a US citizen. She had spun him a tale of being from a small Ohio town when in reality she'd been the daughter of a Gulf Coast fisherman and a beautiful, promiscuous thief and had simply rolled into the same life as her mother.

As soon as Jonathan was on a plane, she had gone back to Andre. They had a huge fight and she could still feel the way he'd wrapped his hands around her neck, squeezing and squeezing, until she'd felt real fear. But then he'd seen the swag she'd returned with and new thoughts circled his brain. Maybe a long-term mark wasn't that bad of a plan. Maybe she could hook up with Jonathan Cantrell again when they got to Los Angeles. Andre would find them a special home base, and Teresa could continue to work her magic.

She'd thought about how Andre had almost strangled her. There was a dangerous side to him that she thrilled to, but she knew he was balanced on a knife's edge and sometimes he went too far. Just thinking about it had made her want to throw him down and ride him. Adrenaline junkie. Yep, that's what she was, but she'd never considered it a bad thing.

She had sought Jonathan out in Los Angeles. It wasn't hard, as he lived large. His father's death had coincided with a dip in the real estate market and though Jonathan had pretended like it was just a blip on the investment highway, while they had continued their relationship Teresa could tell he was losing money. Some of those real estate deals that had seemed like such a great deal had gone south in a hurry.

She'd had to walk away from him. He had sensed that she was pulling back and had tried to hang on, following her and spending damn near every minute with her, also spending damn near every dime of his fortune.

It was difficult to get free but she had managed it.

She'd grown tired of Jonathan, anyway. Too needy, toward the end. She'd been glad to be back full-time with the man she loved, even if Andre had grown a little too . . . the most fitting word was: superstitious. He had rules and regulations for every behavior. Like a grown-up version of "Don't step on a crack or break your father's back." It had been noticeable enough that she'd read up on it and figured it had to be some form of obsessive/compulsive disorder.

Still . . . she had loved him. Even when he had started referring to himself as The Messiah. Whatever floats your boat, she had thought. She had a few quirks herself.

When he had commanded her to scrape up an acquaintance with Stephen Laughlin, she'd thought he wanted a repeat of the Cantrell situation and she'd gone along. But Andre had wanted to cut ties with her during the sting, and though he didn't say so, she had sensed Stephen wasn't just your average mark. Andre didn't call him Mark; he called him Stephen. Teresa had started to understand this was the endgame.

So, she'd scraped up Stephen Laughlin's acquaintance. It wasn't as easy as some. He had been that rare guy who had been interested in a long-term relationship. A quick, hot affair had held no interest for him. She'd had to play the game a while before he did more than take her on dates and actually talk to her across the table.

How was she to know that Stephen would be a good guy? One who fell for her hard but was always nice to her. And the Laughlins had *big* money. They were in the cattle business and their acres of land and beef cattle in central California supported a multimillion, probably billion-dollar business. When Stephen had asked her to marry him, Andre had been thrilled. "Jackpot," he whispered, but though Teresa had tried to keep from going that far, Andre had pushed the whole thing. There was another level here that she didn't quite understand, and she had actually started feeling kind of bad about fooling him so much. But she had stuck by her love for Andre and decided to go for it, and so she had married Stephen, becoming Teresa Laughlin.

And then she'd gotten pregnant. *That* wasn't supposed to

happen. She'd thought about an abortion but never seemed to find the energy to do it. She was living on the Laughlin ranch at the time and only talking to Andre every week or so on her cell phone. He had seemed perfectly content to let the whole thing spin out, and Teresa had found herself getting very used to playing the part of Stephen Laughlin's beautiful wife. That his grandmother, Victoria, and his mother, Talia, both pure bitches on wheels, had hated her only added to her sense of satisfaction with the whole thing. The longer she had stayed, the less she had wanted to leave.

But then Andre had dropped the bomb. "You need to kill him."

"*Kill* him?" she'd laughed, thinking he was joking. "What are you talking about?"

"If he dies, you inherit everything."

"Oh, I don't even think that's true." She'd swept a hand across her burgeoning stomach, chilled to her core. If Andre knew about the baby . . .

"It is. Don't question me. Just do it."

He'd hung up on her and she'd stood for long moments, frozen like a statue. Surely he didn't mean *kill* him, she'd told herself. That's not what they were about.

But he had meant it, and as time passed and he heard nothing from her, he started texting that he was coming to do the job himself. At eight months pregnant, she couldn't have him see her, so she had told him that she was working on the project.

"How?" he'd demanded. "Give me your plan."

"Stephen has some friends who like me a lot. One in particular, Edmund Mikkels, likes me a little too much. I think I can . . . work on him."

"Do it," Andre had said, and in the background she had thought she heard a woman's voice.

"Are you with someone?" she had asked, jealousy rising like bile in the back of her throat.

"I'm your messiah," he had said. "Don't ever forget."

She hadn't been sure what that meant, but she sure as hell didn't want some skanky whore moving in on her man, so even before she delivered Tucker, she had started working on Mikkels. With thoughts of ripping the woman's hair out by the roots, she had gone into full grifting mode: always being a little too friendly to Edmund, touching him on his arm, his back, brushing her breasts against him, finding ways to play the damsel in distress like the time she put two tires in the ditch outside his ranch/farm. The Mikkels family was deep into agriculture and Teresa had let Edmund know that she found the Laughlins' singular investment in cattle repellant.

The subtle pressure had worked. Teresa could almost pinpoint the day when Edmund's interest in her had changed from mild interest to out-and-out lust. Didn't matter that she was pregnant. He would wait, and then they would be together.

When she went into labor and gave birth to Tucker she forgot every plan. Seeing that little baby just drove them from her mind. She fervently began to wish she could just be Stephen's wife and Tucker's mother.

But Edmund Mikkels had been well and truly wound up and ready to go. If he even wondered about her new baby, he hadn't acted like it. With Andre renewing his threatening texts if she didn't get moving, she had stoked Edmund's determination by complaining that Stephen just didn't understand her, that he seemed to go out of his way to make her unhappy. Lies, all of it. But Edmund had focused on freeing her from her marriage prison with laserlike intensity. Teresa had barely had to do more than whisper a few words in his ear, he had been so amped to play the white knight . . . even if that included murdering his good friend.

She had been the one who had gotten cold feet. Stephen's death was supposed to be an automobile accident, a hit-and-run echo of what had happened to his father, but she hadn't been able to bring herself to do it. Stephen just didn't deserve it. But Andre had been growing crazily determined so when Stephen's friends invited him on a hunting trip and Edmund met her eye, she had swallowed back her own misgivings and just let it happen.

And then the hunting "accident." She'd never heard the true particulars and didn't really want to know. There had been a group of them, all experienced hunters, though Stephen had a tendency to "shoot golf," as he joked, more than actual game. After being rushed to a hospital for a bullet wound in the back that ripped through to his front chest, Stephen had slipped into a coma and died. The bullet had done too much damage. His organs had shut down. Game over.

Edmund's remorse had been so huge that everyone had believed it had been an accident. Stephen had inexplicably stepped in front of him when he'd been aiming at a deer. The man's tears had even made Teresa wonder exactly what had gone down but she hadn't been about to ask him. They'd barely had the funeral before Andre had demanded that Teresa come home. "Shouldn't I stick around for some part of the inheritance?" she had asked. Wasn't that the plan?

Andre wouldn't listen. Get back here now, he'd texted, but she'd demurred because of Tucker. She told Andre that she had to wait or she would draw too much suspicion to herself. Not that it was easy living with Victoria Laughlin, who sent her cold sideways glances, or that she enjoyed any of Talia's frequent appearances. That woman had been trouble, pure and simple. But at least Talia had left Teresa's baby alone, as she wasn't exactly the maternal type, whereas

Victoria had been proprietary of Tucker in a way that had alarmed Teresa. She'd realized she had to get Tucker away from all of them.

That's when she'd thought of Aimee, the only person she truly trusted to help with Tucker and keep her secrets. They'd met when Teresa first arrived in Martinique, and if not fast friends, they at least were like-minded, though Aimee wasn't nearly as successful at grifting as Teresa was.

When she called Aimee and told her that she needed to hide her son from the Laughlins and Andre, Aimee had balked at first, but then she'd slowly come around to agreeing to care for him, once the bracelet was offered up as collateral. Like Talia, Aimee's maternal instincts weren't exactly in the A-plus range, but money was a really good incentive.

"I will pay you back, but you can't sell the bracelet," Teresa had warned sternly. "That's a deal breaker."

Aimee had eventually acquiesced and Teresa had been relieved that things had worked out so well because there was no way she could have the bracelet in her possession when she faced Andre again. He would immediately take it from her, and she wasn't interested in giving it up.

Parting with Tucker had been wrenching. He hadn't wanted her to leave him, but she had consoled herself with the thought that she would only be back with Andre for a short time. She had told herself she would return for Tucker within the year, and they would make a life together. She hadn't been quite sure how she would convince Andre to let her go, and she had steeled herself for the confrontation to come, but she was going to make it happen.

But to her shock, when she had gotten back to Andre, he'd picked up several other women who were now living with him in the house she'd once shared with him alone. *The handmaidens*. It had been unbearable. She had been torn between jealousy and fury, and though she knew she'd made the right choice where Tucker was concerned, she had let herself fall into the drama, determined to win Andre back for herself.

What the hell had been wrong with her? Why did it take so goddamn long for her to see the truth about him?

She'd never been thrown over for another woman, and she didn't react well to the new situation; she could be honest with herself about that now. The handmaidens had really pissed her off, sucking up bunches of the money that *she* had earned for Andre and herself. She couldn't bear them, and she had complained mightily to Andre about them, but it had all fallen on deaf ears. In the end, she had resolved to make the best of it and get back to Tucker as soon as possible, but she had fallen into the new routine, playing that Andre was The Messiah, conning Marks out of cash and gifts, her mind constantly trying to find ways to oust the handmaidens and be first in Andre's favor.

And then . . . the urgency to rescue her son had disappeared. Her whole life with Stephen had faded into the background, begun to feel dreamlike and distant, like it happened to someone else. Her reality was being under Andre's watchful eye, and dealing with the handmaidens whom she had begun to hate with a passion that had been buried in a kind of numb state of repression she'd come to accept as the norm. Then the death of the Cantrell boy. At her hands. She'd woken up as if someone had slapped her. What she and Andre had once had in Martinique was long gone and the man who now owned her heart and soul wasn't the same one who'd joined in their wild adventure together once upon a time. This Andre was a taskmaster who demanded total obedience and strange rituals that she had endured, even while she had begun secretly squirreling money away, sensing some formless future where she would run away with Tucker, a loose plan that had become fully formed over the last year.

Teresa lay in the tub, her hair wound into a loose topknot,

her eyes closed, her pulse running light and fast. She didn't fool herself that she'd gotten away from Andre. Picking up Tucker was merely the first step.

But she was here. In Martinique again!

Maybe she didn't have to pick up Tucker immediately, she mused. Aimee knew she was on her way, but she hadn't been specific about when she was arriving. Maybe there was time to run one more con. She and Andre had gotten away by the skin of their teeth, but it had been years.

She smiled to herself, feeling a rush of excitement at the thought. A few hours and maybe she could pick up a new Mark.

Chapter Twelve

The walk to Tucker's apartment was only about fifteen minutes but on the way West's cell phone rang. He snatched it up and frowned at the number.

"No international service, huh?" Callie commented.

"What've you got," West answered the cell, shooting Callie a sideways look.

Yeah, you're a liar too, she thought.

The bracelet was in her carryall. She was giving it back to Aimee. Whatever the story was on how Teresa had obtained it, it wasn't her affair. She just wanted to be rid of it once and for all.

West was making monosyllabic replies, which started to piss her off. He'd actually stopped walking and Callie had slowed to a halt as well. They were now standing on the sidewalk, close to the buildings, standing back from the wheels of the parked vehicles that were humped up off the street.

After what felt like forever he finally clicked off. "A friend of mine," he said.

"Yeah?"

"I do have international calling," he admitted.

Callie shrugged.

"I didn't want to give you an out until I knew more about you. You could have had me calling anyone."

"Only my attorney. Or the Cantrells' attorney, if you really want to get down to it." Briefly she thought of Derek and Diane and their insistence that Jonathan had left more money and/or assets than what she knew of.

"Who was that?" she asked, nodding toward the cell phone he was dropping in his pocket.

"A friend at the LAPD. My old partner."

"What did you ask him to get?"

"What?"

"You answered, 'What've you got?' so . . ."

He didn't immediately answer as they started walking again. She could tell he was rolling things around, debating on how much to tell her, which only pissed her off all the more.

"I asked him to look up the Cantrells and the accident on Mulholland."

She felt something flutter inside her chest. Fear . . . grief . . . remembrance of those terrible moments. She swallowed. "Did he find anything?" she asked lightly.

"Probably nothing you didn't know. There were partial prints found on the car that hit your vehicle, on the door handle and steering wheel. There's no match in the system, so far."

"Nobody told me anything about the accident," she admitted. "I was in the hospital and by the time I got out . . ." *After a month at Del Amo . . .*

"The case is still open," he assured her. "The car that hit you was stolen and it was left at the scene. Whoever rammed into you ran and got away. Maybe they were fairly new to the criminal life, took the car for a joyride, hit you and after your car went over the edge, they just ran. Couldn't cope with what they'd done."

"That's the prevailing theory," she said. Her chest felt tight. Memory was torture.

"I asked Dorcas for a photo of Callie Cantrell. He's sending me one."

"You still don't believe I'm me?"

"I just asked for the photo."

"Keep telling yourself that," she muttered angrily. "You're still trying to tie me into all of this."

"You're here in Martinique," he pointed out. "Fort-de-France. Where Teresa sent an e-mail to a local Internet café. The one you were at this morning," he added. "You're a doppelgänger for her, and you're friends with a boy named Tucker, who, I'm pretty sure, is Stephen Tucker Laughlin. You're wearing a Laughlin heirloom." He indicated the bracelet. "You might not be Teresa, but you're something."

"I chose Martinique because it's where Jonathan and I spent our honeymoon, that's all." She was beginning to wish she'd never listened to the voice inside her head that had thought a trip to Martinique was just the ticket.

But West was on his own track. "When I figure out what the connection is, I'll let you know."

"It's a coincidence. And don't tell me there are no coincidences."

"There are no coincidences."

"What'd I just say?" she demanded and he gave a short bark of laughter, grinning like the devil.

Uh-oh, she thought, looking away. She couldn't afford to like him too much. West Laughlin was far too attractive in a way that seemed to worm itself inside her. He was so different from Jonathan, who'd been handsome and clever, but cold and calculating beneath his pretty exterior. She reminded herself that she didn't know West Laughlin well enough to make any kind of informed decision on what kind of man he was. They were stuck together for the moment, both interested in Tucker's welfare, but that was as far as it went.

They'd lapsed into silence and though Callie was starting to feel tense, West seemed as unaffected by her as she was affected by him. Great. These digging little thoughts about him had to be repressed. She had to quit noticing the strength in his hands, the hard muscles of his arms, the faint stubble on his jaw . . . *Good enough to gobble up*, one of the teachers at the elementary school where she'd worked before her marriage would say whenever she saw a particularly handsome father of one of her students. Not exactly a PC kind of remark, but then Debra hadn't been a PC kind of gal. She'd been named as one of the causes of the Peterkin divorce and had been slowly eased out of her position at the school. Didn't stop her from marrying Adam Peterkin once he was free, though they divorced a year later. Callie should have learned her lesson from Debra, but she'd gone ahead and married Jonathan anyway, expecting to live happily ever after.

She would not make the same mistake with West Laughlin. If Debra had seen him she would have wanted to start gobbling. Hopefully, she, Callie, was a heckuva lot smarter now. Not that West had shown any interest in her apart from her connection to Tucker, which was good news for the immediate future. She just didn't trust her own susceptibility.

Andre stared at Naomi impatiently, his jaw tightening by degrees, which tickled Daniella to no end. Naomi, Andre's right-hand woman, who never, never, never argued with him and always did exactly what she was told, had dared to ask why they were putting on their robes so early in the day.

"Jerrilyn won't be able to make it," Naomi had pointed out, which had only increased Andre's ire.

"Your sister, Teresa, set the timetable," he snapped. "We have flights to catch later."

Clarice breathlessly jumped in, "Maybe we should just go ahead without Jerrilyn."

Andre closed his eyes as if willing up a patience he didn't possess. He was already in his robe and his hair was pulled back at his nape with a leather thong. The ankh around his neck glittered briefly in a thin line of sunlight that sliced through the gap in the curtains. "We will wait for one hour. Get her here," he told Naomi, who immediately turned to her cell phone and placed another call as she walked out of the prayer room.

Daniella had already donned her robe, as had Clarice, but Naomi, the stupid cow, was still in her jeans and a light sweater. She, of all of them, should know better, but then maybe she'd thought she might need to go out and drag Jerrilyn back by her hair.

It would be interesting to see what happened first: Jerrilyn's return, or Andre's urgency to go after Teresa. Would he be able to go ahead without one of his precious remaining handmaidens? Daniella certainly hoped so. Without Teresa and Jerrilyn, there would just be the three of them.

"This is it," Callie said, indicating a somewhat tired-looking apartment building. West examined the stucco exterior while Callie led the way inside.

Aimee and Tucker's apartment proved to be on the ground level. West followed Callie down a hallway that currently smelled of cooked corn and burnt chicken. The carpet was worn but clean. When she got to the third door on the west side of the building, she raised her hand to knock on cream-colored panels that had begun to yellow. The place seemed cared for in the main, but it had been a while since anyone had put any real money or elbow grease into it. Callie's rental was several rungs up the ladder.

Before she could knock he heard a woman's voice raised in anger or frustration, coming from inside. Immediately he held up a hand to stop Callie, who froze in place, then leaned into the door, placing his ear against the panels.

In a mixture of French and English, a woman, most probably this Aimee, was berating someone up one side and down the other. When he heard a young boy's response he figured it was Tucker.

Furious, he took over, slamming his fist in a loud *slam, slam, slam* against the door. Immediately the woman's voice cut off. A few minutes later, footsteps crossed toward them and she called out, "Who is there?"

West looked at Callie who said, "It's Callie Cantrell. I told you I'd be back at three."

She opened the door without hesitation. "You have the bracelet?" she asked, then snapped her gaze to meet West's. Her dark hair was wet as if she'd just taken a shower and she wore a pair of gray capris and a black, sleeveless T-shirt that showed off her well-muscled biceps. She looked like a woman who took her time at the gym seriously. She was about the same height as Callie, around five foot seven, but there the resemblance ended. Aimee was dark and swarthy while Callie was fair, with blue eyes and burnished hair. And Aimee was staring at him in surprise and defiance.

Behind her, Tucker came racing up, ducking under her arm to squeeze up to Callie. "You come for me?"

"I . . ." Callie cut herself off.

"I'm West Laughlin," he said, sticking out his hand. Aimee gazed down at it and reluctantly shook with him. If she recognized the name, she was great at concealing it.

"Aimee Thomas." She snapped her hand back as quick as she could.

"I go fishing with Michel," Tucker declared, dancing into the hallway with delight.

"Tomorrow," Aimee said quickly. Then to West and Callie, "Jean-Paul takes them feeshing on his *bateau*."

He sensed Callie sending him a sideways look at Aimee's suddenly strong French accent. "You want the bracelet," he said.

She yelled at Tucker in French, then said, presumably for their benefit, "Get back here."

The boy grabbed Callie's hand and said, "Come in, come in."

She followed after him and West brought up the rear, though it was clear Aimee didn't want him to be anywhere near the forthcoming transaction.

"The bracelet belongs to my grandmother," West said as an opening salvo.

"It ees mine. A gift," she answered.

"Come see my room," Tucker declared, and Callie looked helplessly to Aimee while West said expansively, "Go ahead. Ms. Thomas and I have some things to talk about."

Aimee's dark eyes flashed at him, but she just shrugged. Playing it both sides against the middle. She didn't want Callie anywhere near Tucker's room, but she didn't want to completely piss off both Callie and West until she got her hands on the bracelet.

"I've got a few questions for you," West said, when he was alone with Aimee.

"I do not have to talk to you."

"You speak English as well as I do. Let's get past that at least. You know who I am and what I want."

"I do not," she stated tartly.

"Okay, fine. We'll play it your way. Stephen Laughlin was

my brother. He's dead now, and his widow, Teresa Laughlin, is suspected in his death. Tucker is Teresa's son, and I'm looking for Teresa."

She was staring at the floor, clearly trying to come up with something to say. "You are talking, but it makes no sense."

"Tucker isn't your son. He's Teresa's," West said again.

"*Non*. Reediculous. He is mine."

"Teresa brought you the boy and told you to take care of him. Where is she?"

"You are crazee!"

"He's a Laughlin. DNA will prove it. I don't want to fight with you, but if his mother's abandoned him, I'm going for custody."

"You are trying to steal my son!" She drew herself up in outrage.

"Where is she? How long's she been gone?" West demanded.

"Get out, and take that nosy beetch with you!"

"I've already been to the police," West lied. "They're looking into it and it's only a matter of time before they're asking the questions, not me."

Aimee appeared ready to claw his eyes out but she restrained herself. He watched her, was aware when the moment occurred that she decided to capitulate some. "She did not abandon him," she finally said.

"Where is she?" West pressed.

"The States. Somewhere." She met his gaze with hot, dark eyes. "The bracelet belongs to me."

"Teresa gave it to you. For taking care of Tucker," he said. When she didn't answer, he took that as an affirmative. "I don't believe it's a gift."

She sucked in an angry breath between her teeth. "I don't care what you believe. It's the truth."

"She's gonna want it back, so you'd better hope it's collateral for some other kind of payment."

"You have no right to question me."

At least the heavy French accent was gone. Progress, if infinitesimal. West had been through his share of interrogations and knew how much persuading went into them. The threat of the police had reached her whether she wanted to admit it or not, otherwise she'd have thrown him out by now.

"I don't really give a damn about the bracelet," he said. "You can have it, for all I care. All I want is the boy."

"He's not for sale."

"I'm not talking about *buying* him. He's a Laughlin. I'm talking about keeping your ass out of jail, Ms. Thomas, if it comes out that there's something criminal going on here."

"There is nothing criminal! She asked me to take care of him, and I have."

"And she's paying you for your services."

"Au pairs get paid for taking care of children," she snapped.

"So, you're an au pair. That's your job?"

"*Oui!*" She calmed herself down, sizing him up. "And I work at a clinic part-time for extra money to support Tucker."

"Tell me where Teresa is, and I'll give you the bracelet."

"I told you. I don't know where she is."

"I heard you. I just don't believe you. What is your deal with her? For how long?"

"I have guardianship rights."

"Yeah? I'd like to see that documentation."

He half-expected her to jump up and bring him the papers. She was so definite that she was in the right that he felt she must have something that said as much. But she didn't charge to get the proof.

"You want the authorities to come down on you?" he

asked. When she remained stubbornly silent, he asked, "How does she contact you? Still by e-mail?"

She couldn't quite hide her shock at his knowledge though she tried to pass it off as if she were just thinking things over. "We call."

"You have a cell number." Now they were getting somewhere.

"No. She calls me from different numbers. I don't call her."

"She's on the run," he said. "When was the last time you heard from her?"

She shook her head.

"I don't know everything that's going on here," West said in a softer voice. He didn't want Callie and Tucker to overhear any more than they already might have. "But that boy is a Laughlin, and Teresa's wanted back in California to explain some things about her husband's death. You know anything about that?"

She shook her head again. It was as if she'd decided it was safer not to talk at all.

"Whatever she's doing, whatever she's done, you're going to find yourself right in the center of it. I don't know what you do for a living other than take care of Tucker, but if it's anything other than on the up-and-up, it will be exposed."

Callie came out of Tucker's room at that moment with the boy racing around her to stop in front of Aimee, who was so involved in her own internal struggle that she scarcely noticed.

"I go to Michel's now?" he asked.

"Tomorrow . . . *demain*," she said distractedly.

"But we go *matin*," he cried.

"That's tomorrow," she said, then walked to the door, a plain invitation to leave. Tucker was still pleading with her as they were ushered into the hallway and missed the way she hissed under her breath, "Don't come back."

* * *

They were deep into chanting, all looking pious and worshipful, when Jerrilyn deigned to join them, much to Daniella's disappointment. She'd really believed something might change, but of course not.

Jerrilyn had walked in wearing skinny jeans and a black, stretchy Lycra tube top paired with a matching black sweater. Her breasts stood out like torpedos, more plastic than mammary gland, but the look of boredom in her eyes couldn't be disguised. Maybe there was hope yet, Daniella thought as Andre stopped chanting abruptly and they all subsided as well. Daniella pretended not to be watching so avidly, putting an expression of mild interest on her face. She hated Jerrilyn the most, she decided. She was so . . . classless.

In a voice that could cut ice, Andre ordered, "Go to your room."

Jerrilyn turned on her heel, but though it was beneath her breath, they all clearly heard, "Fuckin' A."

"Come back here!" Andre roared.

She turned around slowly, her gaze flicking in disdain toward Clarice, Naomi, and Daniella before she walked up to Andre and met his stormy eyes with clear rebellion. "What do you want, Messiah?" she asked silkily.

To Daniella's growing horror she then watched Jerrilyn do a sexy striptease, sliding out of the sweater and thrusting those abominable breasts forward, then crossing her arms over her chest and pulling the tube top from her pants, wriggling herself free so her breasts sprung out like jack-in-the-boxes.

Whatever punishment Andre had been thinking of exacting—Daniella had prayed she'd be thrown in the isolation cell until she was reduced to tears—his sexual desire ran rampant and he grabbed her and shook her even while she laughed at him. Rolling her eyes toward them as if to say, "See?" she started fake moaning as he stripped off her jeans and threw her onto the mat.

Daniella shut her eyes and closed her ears to the animal sounds issuing from their throats but her traitorous imagination saw them writhing around at her feet as Naomi and Clarice took up the chanting once more.

She rolled her fingernails into the palms of her hands and pressed as hard as she could. She was never going to have Andre to herself. He was always going to want the pretty ones. He had no control over Jerrilyn or Teresa, and they could play him sexually with no effort at all. Naomi and Clarice were both pretty too. She was the only one who wasn't. She was the workhorse. And even the times Andre made love to her, she'd always sensed he'd been somewhere else.

Naomi nudged her hard in the ribs because she wasn't chanting. Reluctantly, she joined in.

I'll tell Robert Lumpkin, she thought. *I'll tell him about Teresa and Andre and the rest of them.*

Forcing herself to open her eyes, she didn't look at the pornography in front of her. Instead, she gazed down at the little half-moons filled with blood on her palms left after her fingers unfurled.

Chapter Thirteen

West and Callie returned to her apartment, both of them lost in thought. Callie still had the bracelet and though West had thought Aimee would do about anything to get it back, she'd been more concerned with just getting them out of her home. Maybe that was because, despite what she said, she knew the bracelet really didn't belong to her.

"At least you know I'm not Teresa now," she said as they entered her apartment.

"Unless you're in cahoots with Aimee." Her head whipped around in disbelief and he chuckled. "Kidding."

She relaxed a bit. "Aimee," she said disparagingly. "You heard through the door how she was berating him because he left the preschool with the neighbor lady, Marie, who has a key to the apartment. He took the key, let himself in, and then let himself out again without locking the door."

"That's when he came to your place?"

"Apparently. Marie thought Aimee was home because Tucker brought the key back and said she was."

West's brows lifted. "So, he's a liar and a sneak," he said, half-amused. "And a thief. He took the bracelet," he reminded her when she looked about to object.

"He's just a little boy."

"Yeah, well, he's Teresa's, and he's been living with Aimee. Neither one of 'em's up for mother of the year. Don't worry," he added, seeing real concern cross her face. "We're going to get him out of there."

"How?" she asked.

"Don't know yet." For all his hard talk with Aimee, he was aware he didn't have a leg to stand on. According to Aimee, Teresa had entrusted Tucker to her care and West had no proof otherwise. His threat about bringing in the authorities was basically bullshit since Teresa was the boy's mother. The way Aimee let Tucker wander the streets might be enough to nick her on child endangerment issues, but that wouldn't necessarily guarantee putting Tucker into West's care, so he was reluctant to go that route yet.

Callie opened the doors to the balcony to get some air through the stuffy rooms and West followed her outside, aware of the way her dress flowed around her knees and tucked in at the waist as she turned her face to a capricious, little breeze that lifted the edges of her hair. Beyond, the sun was a line of gold on the western horizon.

West had taken this job because he'd been incensed at Stephen's conniving widow, at the way she'd taken Stephen and the Laughlin family. Not that he gave a damn about the Laughlins, but the injustice of it had stuck in his craw. He hadn't thought of Tucker in any real sense other than he was Stephen's son and he needed to be found, safe and sound.

Now, however, Tucker was a real person and the job had become personal. His initial sense of injustice had been replaced with determination and a feeling of urgency. He needed to do something, embark on a course of action, but without Teresa, he wasn't sure exactly what that plan should be.

He wondered if Tucker even spoke to his mother. He'd never said anything about her to Callie, as far as he knew. How old was Tucker when she'd dropped him off? Twoish, three? It had been almost three years since Stephen's death.

What was their relationship at this point? he wondered. Maybe nothing.

They'd been standing silently, side by side, for several long moments but when West turned toward Callie, she faced him.

"What if she never comes back?" she said.

His thoughts were clearly traveling along similar pathways. "Stephen met her in LA. Maybe I have to start from that end."

"And leave Tucker here?"

He heard the horror in her voice but had no answer for her. "What's her real relationship with Aimee?" he mused. "Are they friends, relatives? They're in contact, but she knows where Teresa is."

"What if, after this, she doesn't let me see Tucker anymore?"

She didn't try to hide the fear in her eyes. He had to stifle the urge to run his hand down her cheekbone and jawline, touch the pulse at her throat. Pull her into his arms and hug her tightly.

"I mean, clearly, I have no rights where he's concerned, and I don't even have a life here, really, but I can't imagine being separated from him. I'm supposed to leave and I just can't. Not now."

"How long are you planning on staying?"

"I don't know."

West heard uncertainty and a bit of anguish in her tone. He understood. This job was tugging at emotions he'd thought long buried. He didn't want to feel connected to the Laughlins, and even being with Callie made him feel raw in a way he didn't like or trust.

"Maybe Tucker'll shake loose and come see you," he said.

"What if she stops him? What if she moves now that she knows we know? What if she's talking to Teresa right now and making plans to leave?"

"I'll watch her apartment tonight. Maybe confronting her will bring things to a head."

"Tucker's supposed to go on Jean-Paul's fishing boat tomorrow. I've never actually met Michel's father, but I've seen him from afar. Didn't want to get in the way. He's a big, bearded guy. Seems good with Michel and Tucker. He must know Aimee, though."

"What's the name of his boat?"

"*Sorciere de Mer*." She suddenly shivered. "I should put the bracelet somewhere safe. Yesterday at the pier, a pick-pocket tried to take my carryall." She walked back inside to the carryall, which she'd left on a small end table, dug through it, and pulled out the bracelet, holding it out to him. "I think you should take it."

"You keep it. I don't have a place to put it."

"I don't want the responsibility."

"Put it back and I'll take it to my hotel safe later."

"How far's your hotel?" She reluctantly slipped the bracelet back into her bag.

He opened his mouth to answer, hesitated, then said, "Bakoua Beach."

Her gaze jerked to his face. "You're staying *there?*"

"Yes."

"And you couldn't tell me this yesterday?"

"I didn't trust you yesterday."

"And today?" she asked, an edge to her voice.

"Well, you're not Teresa," he said lightly, walking in from the balcony.

"There's a ringing endorsement."

He regretted the flash of betrayal he saw in her eyes, but it couldn't be helped.

"We both want what's best for Tucker. That's the bottom line."

"You sure you believe that. I could be covering up some other agenda."

"Yeah. You could be. But you care more about Tucker than anything else."

She looked away from him and he saw her lip quiver. After a moment or two, she pulled herself together and said, "Y'know, I think I need to be alone for a while, if you don't mind."

"Why?"

She slowly shook her head, her expression hard to read.

He had to resist the urge to argue with her. He didn't want to be at odds with her. He'd liked having a partner. "Look, I'm sorry I didn't tell you about the hotel."

"It doesn't matter."

"It clearly does."

"I just . . ."

"What?"

Callie made a frustrated sound that seemed to reach from her soul. "You need to take the bracelet. I don't know who it belongs to, but it's definitely not mine." She grabbed up the piece of jewelry from her purse and thrust it into his hand.

"Hey," he said, frowning.

"I don't mean to be rude, but I don't know what we're doing here. Whatever happens, I have a sense that it's not going to go well for me. You're trying to get Tucker away from Aimee and Teresa, and in the care of your grandmother. I'm trying to . . . just put my life back together."

"You want what's best for Tucker, too. We're on the same team," he said, watching her.

"I'm glad you trust me that much."

Her tone suggested she felt just the opposite. "I didn't mean to upset you," he tried one last time as she walked to the door and held it open for him. As an invitation to leave, it was pretty plain. His own steps were slower as he followed in her wake.

"Call it waking me up to reality," she said. "I don't know

what the hell I'm doing, and I'm leaving soon, and I don't want to."

"I thought you weren't on a timetable."

"I'm not . . . exactly. I want Tucker to be safe. That's all I want."

"That's what I want."

"Good."

"All right, I'll go," he said. "I'll let you know what I find out from Aimee."

She nodded. "We'll talk tomorrow. It's fine. Good-bye."

"It's not fine."

"West . . ."

Hearing his name on her tongue got to him more than he cared to admit to himself. He wanted to argue with her but it was clear she'd made up her mind. Feeling like he should stay and fight, he nevertheless stepped into the hall.

She caught herself in the act of wringing her hands and had to force herself to stop.

"I know how you feel about Tucker. I get it. He's a great kid," West said.

"A sneak and a thief?"

"Yeah, well, and a liar." He smiled and she looked away, as if she suddenly couldn't bear even interacting with him. "What is it? For God's sake, what happened?"

"Nothing. Nothing that can be helped. It's just that, I don't know how this is going to end up for Tucker, and it worries me, and I have no say in it anyway." She moved to shut the door behind him, then stopped herself and added urgently, "Do call me tomorrow. Please."

She shut the door with a distinct click.

West stood a moment, staring back at the door. Then he walked away slowly, sensing he was missing something big. He told himself to shake it off. He'd never understood Roxanne, how did he expect to understand the enigma that was Callie Cantrell, someone he'd known just over a day?

"Damn." Why did it feel much harder to leave her than his ex-girlfriend whom he'd been with for nearly two years?

As soon as West Laughlin was safely in the outer hallway, Callie locked the door behind him, then paced backward into the room, pressing her hands to her cheeks. She was overwhelmed by a familiar grip of panic, the same sensation that had haunted her days and nights after the accident, the same feeling that had been the root cause of her trip to Del Amo Hospital.

She was losing Tucker and it echoed how she'd felt after she'd lost Sean.

You can't lose Tucker. He's not yours.

She caught herself in the act of wringing her hands again and had to force herself to stop, drawing her fingers into fists and hurrying to the bathroom where she looked at herself in the mirror. Anxious blue eyes stared back at her. Her pallor was chalk white.

It had hit her like a cold slap. In the middle of the conversation with West. Here she was half-interested in the man, thinking about him romantically, when all she should be thinking about was herself . . . and getting well and staying well . . . and how she would survive after she left Tucker.

She closed her eyes. She couldn't do it. Already. She knew herself too well. In the beginning she hadn't worried about her association with him, her overriding need to mother him, because it had all been a fantasy. She'd believed Aimee was his mother and she had no right to any piece of him.

But then West Laughlin had entered her life and had made her believe she had a stake in what happened to Tucker. Unconsciously on West's part—she got that. But it didn't matter because she'd suddenly believed she had a chance in there somewhere to be something more to Tucker.

She suspected her romantic notions about West had more

to do with an inner agenda she wasn't even facing. It was one thing to throw that idea in West's face, another to realize he wasn't that far off the mark. Yes, the man was attractive, but really?

Don't you want him because he's linked to Tucker?

Of course she did.

Swearing softly at her own reflection, she shook her head. Then she headed back to the living room and her carryall, yanking out her cell phone and punching in all the numbers required to connect with William Lister's phone. It was a crying shame that he was the only person she could think of to call. The friends she'd made when she was a teacher's aide had faded away during her marriage. She'd received a couple of sympathy cards after the accident, but she'd shoved them aside, too raw, too destroyed to look outside of herself. She'd managed a call to her mother, which had been stilted and uncomfortable, a duty dispatched with relief on both sides.

Mostly she'd just slept and slept and slept at Del Amo, the private hospital that she'd checked herself into voluntarily after the psychiatrist who'd seen her when she'd woken up to learn her family was gone had suggested it. She'd been teetering on the edge of sanity after Sean's death, so lost in despair she was paralyzed.

The call went straight to voice mail. "It's Callie," she said. "Call me when you can," then clicked off.

What to do? She'd been here nearly a month and had easily passed the hours, but she felt the tick of every second.

Because she'd lost Tucker.

"I haven't lost him," she argued aloud.

Yes, you have. He's Teresa's or Aimee's or West's or Victoria's. He's a lot of people's, but he's not yours.

She sank onto the end of the bed and fought back the desire to race back to Aimee's. When Tucker had taken her into his bedroom, she'd wanted to grab him and fiercely hug him close. She had forced herself not to. Tucker wouldn't allow it anyway as, like a lot of children, any physical contact had to be on his terms. She could want to squeeze him with love, but he would squirm and twist and howl for her to let him go.

And she'd had one ear to the door anyway, listening to the rise and fall of Aimee and West's voices, eaten up with curiosity. But Tucker caught her attention. "Where is it?" he had asked.

He'd been babbling away about his room and his meager assortment of toys, when he'd suddenly stopped and looked at her. "What?" Callie had asked, dragging her attention back. He had pointed to her arm. "Oh, the bracelet? It's in my carryall."

"*Maman* want it," he had said soberly.

"Did you take it without asking?"

"It mine," he had insisted again, but he didn't sound quite as sure as he'd been before.

"Aimee said it's hers."

He had shaken his head emphatically.

"Was it your real mother's?" she had asked cautiously.

He had kept shaking his head. "It mine!!"

"Okay. Okay. Where did you get it? Aimee's room?" She'd known she was pressing him and probably shouldn't, but if he gave her any information at all . . .

"A box with the key," he had admitted, giving her a guilty look before sliding his gaze away.

"You found it in a locked box that you opened with a key?" He'd nodded once, still not looking at her.

"Was there anything else in the box?" she had asked casually.

"*Une libre avec* . . . Tucker," he had admitted. "Some . . ." He had seemed to be searching for a word, then fell on it with relief: "stuff."

A book with Tucker and some stuff?

A passport? Callie had wondered. "What stuff?"

"Moneee . . . *papier* . . ."

"Paper?" she had repeated in English. Then, "Papers?"

"Knock knock," he had suddenly said loudly.

Callie hadn't wanted to be put off track, but when she asked him about the papers again, he had said again, louder, "KNOCK KNOCK."

"Who's there?" she had asked dutifully.

"Lena."

"Lena who?"

"Lena on my shoulder."

"Who told you a knock-knock joke?" *In English, no less.* "Aimee?"

"Knock, knock."

"Tucker . . ."

"KNOCK, KNOCK."

"Who's there?"

The second time through had been exactly like the first, and Callie couldn't get any more out of Tucker. The way he had laughed at his own joke, whether he understood it or not, had made her smile and the feeling of maternal need was so strong it shook her a bit.

She had almost been glad when Tucker ran back into the other room, causing West and Aimee to back off from each other, two fighters returning to their corners.

She hadn't told West about her conversation with Tucker. She'd meant to, but then she'd been too aware of him and had become overwhelmed and now . . .

Now she was just sick with worry that it was all going to go sideways. They'd confronted Aimee and though that had seemed like a good idea, and maybe it was, it could very well mean that Callie would never be able to see Tucker again. There was no guaranteeing that West would prevail in his quest to "save" the boy. What if Teresa came and scooped him up? What if Aimee managed to sneak away with him?

What if those moments with Tucker telling a knock-knock joke were the last ones she spent with him?

"Stop it," she told herself. This kind of circular fretting was soul-destroying and only escalated her fear. In the morning West would be back after watching Aimee's apartment and maybe something would have changed for the better. If Tucker went fishing with Jean-Paul and Michel, at least things would be the same, and maybe that was okay.

The thought of waiting for answers till morning made her stomach clench.

She had a sudden memory of the last class she'd helped teach before she quit working. It was third grade, and the bell had just rung for recess. She had to stand by the door, blocking the kids' escape, until they all sat back in their seats. "You need to all wait a moment and then line up," she'd told them, knowing they would hurtle themselves in an unruly bunch through the door if she let them.

One little boy had moaned aloud, "I can't wait! I can't."

Now she knew the same feeling.

West placed the bracelet inside his hotel safe, set the pass code, and closed the door. He went down to the bar and ordered a sandwich and fries, barely tasting one bite. He didn't want to be here. He wanted to be with Callie, but she'd basically tossed him out and closed the door behind her.

He unclipped his binoculars from the waistband of his chinos, tossed them on the bed, then yanked his cell phone from his pocket. Dorcas could only help him so much, but there was someone who might get the political ball rolling, in case it came to that.

Bracing himself, he listened to the ringing of the phone, marveling how clear her voice was when she finally answered. "Hello?" Victoria greeted him suspiciously.

"It's West. I may have a line on Tucker."

"You found Teresa?" she asked eagerly.

"Not yet. But I'm pretty sure Tucker's being taken care of by one of Teresa's friends. . . ." He'd been going to say "associates" but he didn't want to send Victoria into orbit before he was able to direct her. Had to be careful with the terminology.

"Who is this friend?"

"Her name's Aimee Thomas. . . ." West went on to say that he'd met the boy and though he was a couple of years older from the picture Victoria had given him, it appeared he was Stephen's son.

"She just *left* him in Martinique with some stranger?" Victoria declared in disbelief.

"I believe Aimee may be a temporary guardian."

"Where is Teresa?"

"Still working on that."

"I want Tucker back here, safe and sound."

"That's the goal," West agreed easily. "But it may take some doing."

"She took him to a foreign country to make it hard for us to find him. I'll call Gary and we'll get something done."

"Gary is your lawyer?" West guessed.

"Yes. Gary Merritt. His firm has a local office just for the Laughlins," she offered up proudly. "You're sure this boy is Tucker? Have you talked to him?"

"I haven't asked him about his mother, if that's what you mean."

"But he's well. Being taken good care of?"

"Yes." West had to mentally cross his fingers. Tucker's freedom to do as he pleased could be dangerous to his health, but so far he looked like he was thriving. "I need to ask you a question. Stephen met Teresa in Los Angeles. Do you know where?"

Victoria sniffed. "Some nightclub."

"Do you remember the name of it?"

"Didn't you just say the boy's in Martinique?"

"But Teresa isn't," West repeated with forced patience. "I need to find her, or Tucker stays with Aimee. When I get back to LA, I want to backtrack on Teresa."

"I don't know the name," she said in disgust after a moment of thought.

"Maybe one of Stephen's friends will remember." *Edmund Mikkels,* he thought with a grimace. He needed to get to the bottom of that hunting trip, and not just for Victoria. Now he needed to know for himself, too.

"Maybe you can bargain with this woman, Aimee," Victoria suggested.

"I wouldn't count on it." His voice was dry.

"There are ways," she insisted.

"Unless there's been some kind of legal document drawn up that says otherwise, Teresa is Tucker's legal guardian, correct? That's what you said."

"Yes, of course," she snapped.

"Well, I can't just kidnap Tucker."

"He's a true Laughlin," Victoria said. "Part of our family. If Teresa's abandoned him, we have every right to make sure he's safe with us."

"I'm pretty sure you know that's not true."

"Stop telling me what you can't do, and start telling me what you can."

West had to count to three to keep his temper under control. "I can alert the authorities that I believe he's been abandoned and get that process started. It would force Aimee to prove she's legally responsible for him."

"What are you waiting for?" she demanded.

"She may have the proof," he said. "We don't know where Teresa is. We don't know what kind of deal she made with Aimee, if any." He thought about telling her about the bracelet, then immediately rejected that idea. In his mind, Victoria was on a need-to-know basis only. "If the authorities get involved, who knows what that means. He's not on U.S. soil. There could be a legal wrangle that lasts for years."

"You've given up," she accused.

"Not by a long shot. But call your lawyer. Talk to him about it. See what he says about Tucker's situation and what our options are if Teresa never shows up. I'm not giving up on my brother's son," he added firmly.

There was a long pause, and then she said stiffly, "Thank you."

It was the most real feeling he'd ever gotten from her and after he ended the call, he sat on the end of his bed and tried to remember all the reasons he didn't like his grandmother. There was a long list, but for the life of him, at this moment, he couldn't recall one.

Chapter Fourteen

Teresa sat at the bar of the Royale Caribe, conscious of the man seated with a brunette at a table just in her peripheral vision. She'd caught his eye and he'd held it for several seconds. It was just too bad that she only had this one night. A little more time, and she might be able to get something going, but time was what she didn't have.

It was midnight on a Friday night and the bar was full of late nighters still enjoying the pool and drifting in for a drink, the women in bikini tops and sarongs draped over their hips. The men were casual as well, Bermuda shorts and flip-flops or deck shoes, Tommy Bahama shirts, everybody enjoying tropical drinks, the mood festive.

Teresa wasn't in the right frame of mind. Her thoughts kept touching on Tucker, then Andre, then the ticking of the clock. She had to leave tomorrow. She'd made that clear to Aimee, who had suddenly become obstinate and damn near hostile, telling her she couldn't just take Tucker away.

Oh, couldn't she? Where the hell was this coming from? Tucker was her son and Aimee knew good and well that Teresa was on her way. She'd told her about her ticket, she'd called her from LAX and on her stopover in Miami. It wasn't her fault Aimee was so bad about picking up. She'd left messages, and she'd explained about the handmaidens and Andre's current descent into madness.

"Calls himself The Messiah," Teresa had reminded Aimee. She'd told her this before but the woman could be so damn dense sometimes. It was like she heard one word out of three.

But Aimee was focused on Tucker, not Andre. "You can't take him."

"I sure as hell can. What's your problem?" Teresa had just held herself back from screaming at her.

"There is a man here asking about Tucker."

A cold finger had traced a line down Teresa's back. "How? What do you mean?"

"He was asking about you. He wants Tucker. If you take him away, he'll find you. He says he's a Laughlin."

"Well, he can't have him!" she'd declared furiously.

"Tucker doesn't know you anymore!" Aimee had snapped back.

"I'm picking him up tonight. Get him ready."

"This man knows where I live. He'll see you."

"I don't give a flying fuck. I'll call you back." She'd hung up in a fury, but it was also mixed with fear. She'd thought she only had to worry about Andre, and though that was certainly enough, the idea of one of the Laughlins on her trail twisted her insides into a knot.

She'd taken a cab to the Royale Caribe in Pointe du Bout. She wanted to hook someone. She wanted to seduce some loser, walk away with a roll of cash, and have no one be the wiser.

For a brief moment she'd considered just grabbing Tucker and leaving, but then she'd headed to the hotel.

The guy with the brunette was getting up from the table. The girl placed a hand lightly on his arm and they headed for the elevators. The guy threw her a look that said he was sorry he wasn't available, and Teresa felt a spurt of anger.

She paid for her glass of chardonnay and left the hotel. A cab pulled up and dropped off a young man and woman, and Teresa climbed inside. She would go back to her hotel and prepare for the next day. She had a ticket for herself to Dallas through Miami, and one for Tucker as well. She'd foolishly left Tucker's passport with Aimee, afraid to keep anything with her when she went back to Andre. She hadn't expected her friend to turn on her.

As they were heading out, she realized the Bakoua Beach was ahead on their left. "Bakoua Beach," she told the driver, who looked unhappy that his fare was cut short.

She wasn't ready to call it a night yet and she'd had a lot of luck at Bakoua Beach.

At seven A.M. there was a knock on Callie's door. She knew without a doubt it was West and she'd already been through the shower and dressed. She crossed to the door hurriedly, regardless of the trepidation she felt. He wouldn't understand the conflicted feelings she was experiencing. Hell, she barely understood them. She wanted to know about Tucker, but she was worried the more entangled she became in his situation, the worse it would be for her in the end.

And then there was her attraction to West himself, which only complicated everything. Too bad he wasn't old, ugly, or as mean and harsh as she'd originally thought. As it was, he was good enough to gobble up, and if she ever let down her guard and he sensed her feelings, he would undoubtedly believe it was just more of her hidden agenda. And well . . . yes . . . she wanted to be with Tucker, so that was certainly driving her too.

He looked a little rumpled when she opened the door. A developing beard darkened his chin. "Tucker's on the boat with his friend Michel and the father, Jean-Paul."

"You saw them leave?"

"I followed them to the boat a couple hours ago."

"You watched Aimee's place all night?"

"Surveillance sucks," he said with faint humor. "But at least we know where Tucker is for the day."

She pulled the door open wider. "Come on in. I've got coffee, or we could go out for breakfast."

"Coffee'd be great," he said, walking past her and dropping onto the couch. "I'll have a cup before I head back to my hotel and catch some sleep."

"You want me to watch Aimee's, in case Teresa shows up?"

"We don't have any real intel on Teresa. She could be in Timbuktu. I need to think up a plan to find her that's more proactive than just watching Aimee's apartment. I'd like to exert some pressure on her." He yawned. "After I get some sleep."

Callie went through the process of filling the small coffeemaker that she had on her kitchenette counter. "Sorry I was so abrupt last night."

"Sorry I didn't tell you I was at the Bakoua."

"Let's start today fresh. I want to help Tucker. I just was feeling . . . raw." She glanced back at him to see his gaze was steady on her. Her heart jumped a little and she returned to her task.

"I talked to Victoria," he said.

"Oh?"

While she watched the coffee drip through the filter into the carafe, he brought her up to speed on that conversation.

"So, you're planning to go back to LA?" Callie asked when he'd finished.

"Eventually."

"I don't want to leave Tucker. Aimee could take him away." Anxiety ran along her nerves, making her voice tight even though she was trying to sound calm and reasonable.

"Victoria's working on it. I don't know how much effect her lawyer will have internationally, but maybe we can get a

DNA sample, if nothing else. Establish he's a Laughlin and go from there."

"Doesn't mean she'll stay put." She poured them each a cup of coffee. "Cream and sugar?"

"Black's fine. Thanks."

She carried his cup to him and handed it over, briefly touching his fingers as she made the transfer. She had a sharp memory of the same electric feeling she'd had with Bryan when they were young and in love/lust. She'd never had the same sensation with Jonathan but she'd assumed it was because she was older and smarter, ready for a more mature relationship. What a crock that turned out to be.

They drank their coffee in near silence. When West was finished, he put the mug down and got to his feet, stretching. "I've got some phone calls to make. I'll come back tonight and we can put our heads together and come up with some plan." It was a statement, but he was looking at her questioningly.

"Sounds good."

"What time do you think Tucker will be back?"

"I don't have any idea. I only met Aimee the one time before yesterday. I really only saw Tucker when he would show up at my place."

"Give me your number and I'll call you."

Callie met his eyes. Their lies about their phones crossed her mind and she was pretty sure he was thinking the same thing, too. She recited her number as he punched it into his phone and he gave her his as well.

"We'll talk later," he said as he left. "Maybe if we work together, we can figure out how you figure in to all this. Maybe it is coincidence," he said quickly, expecting her to argue her side again.

Perversely, when he showed a conciliatory side, she immediately went the other way. Teresa . . . Jonathan had said.

It hadn't been Marissa. Her deceased husband had known Teresa. It was time she gave him that information.

She opened her mouth to do just that, but he was already heading for the door.

Tonight, she thought, hating herself a little as her mind had already started worrying about what she was going to wear as if she were getting ready for a first date.

It was afternoon by the time Teresa rolled over in her bed, lifted the sleeping mask she'd purchased at the hotel store from her eyes, then thought grimly about what she needed to do today. She had to leave with Tucker. Had to in order to be safe. But she didn't want to. Not now, not when she was getting her mojo back without fucking Andre.

What had she seen in him for so long? What magic had she thought he possessed?

And Aimee . . . the conniving bitch had *argued* with her again about Tucker when she'd phoned her this morning!

"Answer," she'd snarled into the phone, prepared to go knock down her door if necessary, but finally Aimee had picked up her end of the line. "Well, finally," she'd said testily. "I'm here and I'm taking Tucker with me tonight. Don't even ask. It's too long to go into. Just get him ready. You've got the passport?"

"Ye . . . e . . . ss . . ."

How long has it been since I've seen my son? she'd asked herself. More months than she wanted to count. "Is there another problem? I warned you I was on the way, when I was in Miami yesterday."

"People are looking for you," Aimee reminded.

"I know. I'll deal with it. Did the man asking about me give you his name?"

"West Laughlin."

Teresa hadn't known how to react. "West Laughlin?

Stephen's . . . half brother? How could he be here? I don't even know him."

"Well, he knows you and he knows about Tucker, and he's with a woman that Tucker can't stay away from, probably because she looks like you."

"What are you talking about?"

"Tucker found this woman at the outdoor market, I believe. She resembles you. Her hair's the same and she looks a lot like you in the face, too. Tucker keeps going over to her place." In a tighter voice, she had added, "He gave her the bracelet."

"*What?*"

"He's lucky I didn't whip his hide. He stole it from me."

"He gave the bracelet to this *woman?*"

"That's what I said. She's working with Laughlin. They came together. They must have tracked you here."

"Impossible. I've only been here a day!"

"They came here and he threatened me. Said he would look into my background if I didn't tell him where you were."

"You have to get that bracelet back!"

"He wants Tucker, Teresa."

"Tucker's my son," she'd practically shouted into the phone.

"They're dangling the bracelet like bait. You want it back? Get it yourself. But you pay me what you owe me," she had added tautly, as if Teresa could forget.

"I can't believe you lost the bracelet!" she'd yelled at her. She'd counted on the money it would fetch. It was part of her plan. And the money she'd gotten off the fat man with the expensive boat last night hadn't been near what she'd hoped for.

"Tucker took it from me and gave it to them," Aimee had corrected angrily.

"What did you tell them about me?"

"Nothing. But they'll be back."

"Jesus, Aimee."

"You can't come here unless you want to face him."

She'd been incensed. If she didn't have the bracelet she didn't know what she'd do. "I can't pay you until I get the bracelet back."

"Then you won't get Tucker."

Teresa had damn near thrown her phone across the room. She'd wanted to strangle Aimee. "Well, I'm going to come get him, so you'd better get him ready."

"He's not here." And then she'd gone on to explain he was on a fishing boat with a friend of his and the friend's father. That hadn't set well with Teresa, either. She only had so much time.

"So help me, Aimee, I'm taking Tucker back to the States tonight. I've got a ticket and we're catching a flight to Miami."

"Are you taking him to Andre?"

"What are you, stupid? You know I can't do that. Andre wouldn't know what to do with a child, especially Stephen's child. I'm not going back to Andre."

"But he's the man you love." She had sounded concerned, though Teresa had known it was a fake. Aimee had always found Andre attractive, and she was probably just hoping Teresa was done with him.

"You're working off old information," Teresa had told her. "Andre's not the same man he was."

"You said he was the most beautiful man in the world."

"I said a lot of things," Teresa snapped back at her. "I was a lot younger. So were you. No, I'm taking Tucker far away from everything."

"Andre will find you," she had predicted.

"No, he won't. He'll give up on me. He's got the hand-maidens now. It's not the same."

Aimee had subsided into silence for a moment, then said, "I don't know about these handmaidens. You and Andre were a team."

"Yeah, well, that was years ago. I know you had a thing for him, but you wouldn't feel the same now," she'd added, giving Aimee a dig. Aimee hadn't been able to keep her eyes off Andre. She'd lusted for him in a way that had made Teresa laugh behind her back sometimes. It wasn't that Aimee wasn't pretty enough. It was that she was just so focused and humorless. God. Being around her had been exhausting, and she could see things hadn't changed in the intervening years.

"Tucker is on Jean-Paul's boat," Aimee had then revealed.

"What?" Teresa had been incensed. "You knew I was coming! You shouldn't have let him go."

"You told me to treat him like my own son. You told me that," Aimee flashed. "He wanted to go. What was I supposed to do?"

"Keep him close. When will he be back?" Teresa had demanded, cutting through any further explanations.

"Tonight."

"When, tonight? Give me a time."

"Whenever Jean-Paul returns," she had said in that uncaring way of hers that drove Teresa crazy.

With an effort, she'd held on to her patience and had managed to pry the name of the boat out of Aimee, who never seemed to offer up information unless she was asked directly.

"Call me when he's back," Teresa had ordered, then hung up in a fit of pique, grinding her teeth together as she recognized she would probably have to change those airline tickets. And these people who were looking for her? West Laughlin and this woman? Why were they in Martinique now? How had that happened? Were they watching Aimee's place? It was a possibility, she supposed, unless Aimee was lying to her for her own purposes.

Climbing out of bed, Teresa took a long, hot shower, fighting the weariness produced from long days and nights without the proper amount of sleep. Last night had been fun, if not as productive as she'd hoped. The big lunk had a lot of money to spread around and he was happy to do it, buying Teresa food and drink and promising all manner of things. They'd gone to his boat, which actually had a very nice queen-size bed in a room below. She'd debated on whether to drug him first and forgo the sex he was expecting, but in the end she'd gone through with it, thinking of the experience as a kind of purge against Andre. The latest Mark wasn't much of a lover and it had taken a few tries for him to even show some proper enthusiasm; his dick was a wet noodle that only halfheartedly rose to the occasion. But they'd finally managed and afterward, when he'd suggested another drink, it had been easy to lace his with the roofies she'd smuggled into her suitcase. She'd worried about that a little, but the small bottle of "shampoo" she'd taken with her sailed right through, and it worked like the proverbial charm.

With Mark out cold, she had done a quick inventory of what he had on board the boat, but apart from a well-stocked liquor supply, there had been basically nothing of any value but boat paraphernalia. It had kind of pissed her off. She'd always picked up hotel guests in the past, not boaters. Even though the boat itself had to be expensive, there had been nothing to steal. Angry, she'd emptied his pockets and netted herself about three hundred dollars. He had a bank card, but she didn't know the PIN and as soon as he woke up and realized he'd been rolled, he would cancel any one of his credit cards, though she had looked longingly at his black American Express.

Nope. They would be on her trail too fast. And she already had enough searchers to worry about.

She had to get Tucker out of here. Had to move fast. But he was on that other goddamned *boat.*

Unsettled, she packed up her belongings and checked out of her hotel, leaving her bags with the bellman. She re-booked them on the latest flight out to Miami that she could get and maybe there was still a chance they could make it.

Restless, she took a cab to the pier and sat around several different outdoor cafés, waiting. Hours passed and as they did, her nerves tightened. She had visions of Andre on his way to her. Maybe on a flight from Miami at this very minute. Or maybe he was already here, going back to their old haunts, searching the crowd for her.

Suddenly afraid, she headed into a tourist shop and purchased a scarf to wrap loosely around her head, disguising the color of her hair. It wasn't enough, but it was something.

Where the hell was that damn fishing boat? How long did it take?

Her anger at Aimee intensified as she waited. How could she let the bracelet fall into Tucker's hands? What was wrong with her? She was too lax, too trusting. Goddammit! The woman was half-French and gave new meaning to the term *laissez-faire.* She and Teresa had been friends, or maybe frenemies, back in the day, but that was long ago. Aimee had hustled a bit herself, but hadn't lived for the thrill like Teresa had. She'd lacked the imagination and the talent.

Still, she'd been there for Teresa when she'd shown up with a toddler in tow, and she'd agreed to keep the bracelet as a form of good faith. Teresa had made it very clear she always wanted the bracelet back. How could she let Tucker get his hands on it? Of course, Aimee didn't know its true value; Teresa had made sure of that. She'd had it appraised at one time, and the figure she'd been given had enough zeroes to take care of Tucker and her needs for years to come. But she

couldn't have the bracelet with her when she was with
Andre; he would have taken it from her. Even while she was
compiling her secret nest egg, the bracelet had always been
the cornerstone of her financial plan. And it was hers.
Stephen had given it to her.

God . . . damn . . . *it!*

She had to find this lookalike and get the bracelet back.
And who was this West Laughlin? They couldn't take *her*
son away. What gave them the right to even think they
could?

And fucking Aimee. Was it too much to ask for her to just
take care of her son for a little while? She acted like Teresa
should just fork over the small fortune they'd agreed upon
even when she was the one who'd screwed up with the bracelet!

Pressing her palms to her face, Teresa tried to contain her
anger and fear. Aimee was only a small part of the problem.
Andre and the handmaidens . . . they were the bigger issue.
She could feel them behind her like the hounds of hell.

Damn them all, she thought viciously, dragging her black
sweater closer to her neck to combat the kicky, little breeze
that had sprung up. She'd dressed in black slacks, blouse,
and sweater. Only her scarf was colorful, a touristy purchase
that was a map of the island in sea greens and blues.

A man on the dock was standing by a dark post, watching her. Aware that there was always an underworld in every
tourist haven around the globe, no matter how lovely the
place was, she paid for the latest cup of coffee she'd been
dawdling over and walked away. She'd been a part of that
underworld more often than not herself, and she had great
respect for it.

If only life had been easier for her, she wouldn't have to
go to these lengths.

But there's a thrill there, isn't there?

Yes . . . most of the time . . . Even last night with Mark

had sent her nerves thrumming, gotten her juices flowing. But then a dark cloud enveloped her as she thought back to the accident on Mulholland and the little boy who shouldn't have been there.

She wished this Jean-Paul and the *Sorciere de Mer* would show up. *Sea Witch,* huh? Hunching her shoulders, she kept moving forward, reminding herself to be patient. She wouldn't be able to just snatch up Tucker, if she found him, but she would at least know when he got home.

And she would get to see him again. The thought brought a hotness to her throat even as it worried her. She loved him. She truly did. He was the only thing that mattered. Except . . . how was she going to go about grifting saddled with a son?

"*Mademoiselle.*" The male voice came out of the darkness, startling her. She scurried away from it. What the hell was she doing? It felt like it had grown dark in an instant. She needed a lighted bar and a group of people, not this aloneness, yet she didn't want to get too far from the pier. Where the hell was the boat?

Hearing footsteps behind her, she picked up the pace. She could see the lighted sign and string of lights ahead. Another café, with a man plucking on a guitar. Too far from the boat dock, though.

Had Aimee lied to her?

Suddenly certain she'd been had, she pulled out her cell phone and plugged in Aimee's number. *You better damn well answer,* she thought, listening to it ring on her end. When it went to voice mail, she clicked off and dialed again, only to have the same thing happen. This time she left a message: "I don't give a damn about those people, I'm coming your way, and if—"

Abruptly she ran into a wall of flesh that had moved from the shadows.

"Whoa. *Pardon-moi.* I didn't see you." Looking up, a half-gasp formed on her lips. She stumbled backward, and in the uncertain light along the docks, gazed at the person in surprise. "What are you—"

The hit came from behind. Teresa crumpled to the ground and dimly heard rapid French shooting back and forth between two people. Vaguely, she understood they were thinking of getting rid of her. *No!* She tried to struggle, but apart from a moan, she couldn't move.

And then she was helped to her feet and half-carried away. A rag of some kind was placed over her mouth and nose, and there was a terrible, chemical smell, and then nothingness.

Chapter Fifteen

Daniella stood in the empty prayer room and felt humiliation and building rage. She was alone. Left behind once again. Given all sorts of platitudes while the birds with the beautiful plumage flew away and the wren stayed behind.

It had been over a day since Jerrilyn had finally wound down and stopped screeching like a cat in heat while she and Andre had sex in front of them, all the while looking at the rest of the handmaidens through slitted eyes, a smile curving her lips in satisfaction. Daniella had forced herself not to react, and when the torture was finally over, all the handmaidens had headed to their rooms to get ready for their next great adventure. Daniella had yanked her robe from over her head and quickly hung it in her closet. Then she'd thrown on a pair of jeans, a short-sleeved T-shirt, and a zip-up cardigan that she could take off for airport security. Dressed, she'd quickly and efficiently finished packing a medium-size suitcase. She'd tossed in shorts, capris, T-shirts, several sundresses, underclothes, a pair of sneakers, her sandals, and the black flats she could team with anything. Her makeup bag had gone in next along with other toiletries, a brush, and a comb.

The first one ready, she had sat down at the table and

waited impatiently. The rest of them had trickled out, though Jerrilyn had taken a leisurely shower and yawned, dressed in her own satin, blue robe.

"You'd better hurry," Daniella had told her, and she'd rolled her eyes and sauntered back to her room.

Andre had come out, looking incredibly handsome in a loose white cotton shirt, chinos, and deck shoes, his hair still wet from his own shower and pulled back into its habitual leather thong. He had a three-days' growth of beard that made him look rakish and Daniella had felt something inside her turn to liquid.

He's the prize you're fighting for, she had reminded herself. *You can't do anything to hurt him.*

He had smiled at her and sat down next to her, which had set her heart aflutter. His ankh lay on top of his shirt, and he'd picked up the cross and tucked it inside his collar. She had been able to see a vee of dark skin and she'd leaned forward without thinking and kissed his warm flesh.

And then he had said with regret, "I'm going to need someone to stay behind and watch over things."

"Not me," Daniella had blurted.

"I think so." He had taken both her hands in his. It was so rare to have his undivided attention, to have him be so nice to her, that she had been disarmed in spite of herself. "We'll take care of the defector in our midst. Maybe you can think of a way to rid us of Robert Lumpkin."

"Teresa was supposed to do it," she moaned, searching for some kind of rebuttal.

"Yes, she was. And we all know how that turned out. I'm counting on you, Daniella."

Now, she wished she'd fought harder to be part of the posse leaving for Miami. It was so unfair! But Andre had asked her directly and what could she do?

She would have liked to be there when Teresa got her comeuppance. She suspected Teresa might have to die. What other punishment would fit her crime? Surely, they wouldn't bring her *back?*

No. Teresa was done for. Had to be.

And here she was, twiddling her thumbs and waiting. Recalling her earlier plan to tell on them all to Robert Lumpkin, she shook her head. She could do that in a heartbeat to the other handmaidens, but she couldn't risk losing Andre.

Maybe you can think of a way to rid us of Robert Lumpkin. . . .

Well, she didn't possess the same arsenal as Teresa had in looks and sexual allure, but she had a brain and a wild imagination.

Smiling coldly to herself, she went back into her bedroom to get ready. She knew Lumpkin's cell number, and he knew hers as well, but if she called him from a pay phone and played a game of hide-and-seek, it might work.

Halfway across the bay to Pointe du Bout and West's hotel, Callie began to feel she should have rethought going out with him tonight. West was too damned good-looking by half, and his undeniable attraction coupled with the heat and exotic beauty of Martinique had awakened the adventurous part of herself, that same part that had been sure marriage to Jonathan would be a good idea. If she knew what was good for her, she'd keep that part far away from West Laughlin. Since he'd burst into her life the day before and they'd embarked on this uneasy partnership, he'd circled her thoughts in ways unhealthy to her well-being. Their relationship needed to begin and end with Tucker.

She glanced over at him. He'd taken a taxi to her place and when she'd protested that she could have met him at the Bakoua, he'd said he was in the neighborhood anyway. He was in tan pants and a dark blue shirt that she'd noticed made his eyes even bluer, and she'd made a point of not looking at him directly as they decided to catch the ferry rather than take a taxi. Now he was standing beside her at the ferry's rail, lost in his own thoughts, the wind tossing his hair. The heavy hum from the ferry's engines and the loud and constant splashes of water as they cleaved their way forward made Callie raise her voice to be heard.

"What were you doing 'in the neighborhood'?" she asked.

"I get better phone reception in Fort-de-France, for some reason. I was talking to my ex-partner."

"About what's going on here?" She spread her palms to include the area at large.

"About Teresa. She met my brother in Los Angeles, so I asked him to find out where she was living before she was married. Her maiden name's DuPres."

"What happens if you find her?" she asked.

Strands of hair whipped in front of her face and she tried to brush them aside. She froze when West reached forward with one finger and slid soft filaments away from her lips. "I want to look her in the eye and ask her about Tucker, and Stephen, and Edmund Mikkels."

"Mikkels is the man who accidentally shot your brother."

"Victoria would tell you it wasn't an accident, but that's probably a fantasy on her part. She thinks Teresa and Edmund were involved, and that might be closer to the truth."

"It's pretty hardcore to set up your husband's murder."

"Teresa may have just left with Tucker to get her life together. On the other hand, she could be purposely keeping him away from the Laughlins. I just want to know."

"She is his mother, for better or worse," Callie pointed out. "If I thought someone was trying to take Sean from me, I'd commit murder before I let it happen."

"If I pushed Aimee harder . . . put the bracelet in her hand, say, told her she could keep it if she gave Teresa up . . . maybe then she'd tell us."

Callie's gaze was trained on the waters of the bay and the horizon. "I didn't get the impression it's up to you to decide what happens to the bracelet."

"You got that right. Victoria would have a cow if she thought I was giving it up."

"But you'd do it anyway."

"Sure. Whatever it takes. I'm only helping Victoria because we have the same basic goals: to find Teresa and make certain Tucker's safe. I'm out of her plans to win custody."

"She's his great-grandmother and wants custody?"

"He's a Laughlin."

"But how does that work, I mean, if she succeeds? Tucker's an energetic boy and she's how old?"

"Eighty-three."

"And there's no one in between who might be . . . more suited?"

"There's Talia, Stephen's mother."

He said it so carefully, she sensed he was trying hard not to give his feelings away, yet his very effort was more telling than words. "You don't like her."

"I don't know her. I don't know any of them, and that's just the way I like it."

"You like being the black sheep."

"Maybe a little," he said after a moment.

"Tell me more about your family history," she said. "Who are the Laughlins and all that."

"Didn't find enough on the Internet?" he asked, a small smile teasing his lips.

"You were the one who pointed out the site I was on wasn't giving me the whole story."

He nodded. "My grandfather started Laughlin Ranch. Bought up the land in the thirties from farmers who were defaulting on their loans during the Depression. He was ruthless and smart. A real pain in the ass."

"That a trait that runs in the family?"

A quick smile. "I'd have to say yes. Laughlin Ranch is a cattle ranch, one of the biggest in California, right there in size and proximity to the Harris Ranch. You know that one?"

The Harris Ranch in the San Joaquin Valley between Los Angeles and San Francisco was one of the largest in the nation. They shipped beef all over the world. If the Laughlins' was even half the size of the Harris Ranch, it would be enormous.

"I know it," she said. How could she not? Drive that stretch of I-5 and the section with the cow manure stench went on for miles. You couldn't have a hundred thousand head of cattle without it.

"My grandfather expanded and competed with Harris Ranch, even to the point of building an inn with a restaurant and gift shop, just like them. The main Laughlin house is a two-story ranch. Big, with miles of fences. I spent some time there as a kid. My father would take me upon occasion, and Stephen and I would run all over the place. My grandparents didn't like it, but they just stayed out of the way whenever I was there. I didn't catch on to this for years, but by the time I figured it out, I wasn't going there anymore anyway. My mother put her foot down. I think she got over Craig, my father, pretty damn quick when he bent to my grandparents' wishes. Saw him for what he was instead of what she wanted him to be. She only allowed him to take me to the ranch, mainly because she's always liked horses and wanted me to have that experience."

"But you got the Laughlin name."

"Some kind of bargain that my father insisted upon, apparently. But Mom didn't like them much. Any of them. After she was let go, she was hired by a veterinary clinic, working with large animals, and she married one of the vets and changed her name, so we never had the same one anyway."

"Does your grandmother run the ranch now?"

"In essence, though not on a day-to-day basis. She wanted

Stephen to run it, but he wasn't in love with the idea. He was more interested in investments and numbers, that kind of thing. He saw the ranch's value, of course, but he was never hands-on like my grandfather and father. He came to me a couple of years ago and asked if I'd be interested in taking over."

"Really? That was for him to say?"

"Hell, no, but he thought he could convince Victoria. I told him he was crazy and I didn't have any interest anyway."

"Who runs it on a day-to-day basis?"

"Main foreman's name is Stutz. He's been around for years."

Callie nodded. She'd seen the name on the website. Even though West was repeating some of what she'd just learned about his family, it was interesting to hear his take on it. "Your father died in a car accident?"

"Yeah. He and Stephen's mother, Talia, were driving home from dinner after drinking too much. They were in a fight, apparently, that started at the restaurant. He was weaving and eventually drove off the road. She survived. He didn't."

"Oh." Callie thought back to her own accident once again, feeling sweat collect along her spine and her hands go cold. With an effort she pushed the memory aside, compartmentalizing it, storing it under lock and key on a shelf in her mind.

"My father shouldn't have been behind the wheel. It was totally his fault. I went to the memorial service, but it was clear I wasn't wanted. My mother warned me, but I went anyway. After that I learned my lesson and stayed away from Stephen and his family."

"So, when Victoria called you about Teresa . . . ?"

"It was the first time I'd heard from her since Stephen's death. Actually, pretty much the first time she'd called me directly. I was surprised, to say the least, when she identified herself. I went to see her just for the kick of it, in the beginning. What the hell, I figured. She's a stone-cold bitch, but it was so out of character I was interested."

The memory made his mouth twitch with repressed humor. "I'll introduce you to Victoria. She lives on the ranch, but she's no rancher. She's more like her name: rigid, uptight, Victorian."

"When would this mythical introduction take place?"

His gaze slid over her face. "If I can find Teresa and work a deal with her, that's probably where Tucker will end up. I figured you'd want to keep in touch."

"Of course. It's a lot of ifs, though."

"One way or another, we're going to make sure Tucker's safe."

Callie tried to imagine how she would fit into Tucker's life but couldn't. "Why are you the black sheep?" she asked. "I mean why, specifically?"

"I think I just explained it."

"So, it's just because your mother wasn't married to your father? It wasn't anything you did."

"You're trying to make a distinction between a bastard and a black sheep. The Laughlins consider it one and the same. Craig had to make a choice, and he chose his wife and Stephen."

"He could have still kept you as part of the family," Callie said.

"Not if he wanted to share in everything Laughlin, which he did. He wasn't about to let his brother, Benjamin Jr., inherit everything. According to my mother, there was always fierce competition between them."

"So, your father ignored both you and your mother, then spent a lot of his time fighting with his brother over money?"

He shrugged. "Craig and Ben Jr. were antagonists, near as I can tell."

"But you and your half brother were close?"

"Stephen and I were friends," West allowed. "Not really close, but we kept in contact. It wasn't brother against brother, like Craig and Ben Jr."

"What happened to Ben Jr., is he still around?"

"Nope. He had a falling out with the family—I don't know exactly what happened—but he was practically ex-communicated by my grandparents. Made my father happy, though. Craig got what he wanted all along: to be the only Laughlin heir. After my grandfather died and it was just Victoria in charge, Craig was worried that there would be some forgiveness handed out. He made another halfhearted attempt to contact me. Said he wanted me to be a part of the ranch with Stephen. I was working my way up to detective at the LAPD and told him to go screw himself. Again, Victoria would have never allowed it anyway."

"So, when your father died, Stephen was the only heir."

"There was some provision in the will for me, but I refused it. Now, I guess it will all go to Tucker once my grandmother dies."

"Does Teresa know that? She must."

"It wasn't any kind of secret. Maybe that's why she's stashed Tucker with Aimee, waiting for him to grow up a little. As the Mama Bear, she would be in a good position to run things eventually, so maybe she's just biding her time until Victoria dies."

"It doesn't sound like you really believe that," Callie ventured.

"I think it's a little too long term for Teresa to plot. After Stephen's death, I think she just ran."

Callie thought of William Lister and Derek and Diane. All she'd heard about for the last year was Jonathan's will and how they felt things were unfair. "What if your grandmother changed her will?"

"What? To cut out her great-grandson? No way. Victoria wants to leave everything to him."

"But if Teresa were plotting to get her hands on some of the Laughlin estate after Victoria dies, then she would need to make certain Tucker was safe," Callie said.

He nodded.

"Well, he's not safe with Aimee. Not completely."

"Maybe Teresa doesn't know that. Like I said, if she's planning that far ahead, I'd be surprised."

"But your grandmother's health is good," Callie said.

"Far as I know. She's certainly still as imperative as ever."

The ferry's engines turned to a low whine as it slowed and aimed for the dock. Small, round lightbulbs were strung in loops from pole to pole, throwing illumination on the people lined up to catch the ferry back. It was after eight o'clock and Callie suddenly felt famished.

They caught a cab for the short ride to the hotel. There was a steel drum band on a dais at one end of the outdoor patio and an older couple was swaying in each other's arms, though there wasn't really a dance floor. Tables were lit by candles and the dark water of the bay shimmered beneath the outdoor lights. Callie and West were seated close to the water and she could hear the lapping waves and smell the dank, briny scent. She'd worn a tan, sleeveless dress and flat sandals, but looking around at some of the other women she felt a little underdressed.

"I think I'll find the ladies' room before we order," she said.

"What would you like to drink?"

"White wine."

"You're not going to leave, are you?"

She gave him a look and saw the flash of white of his smile. "No."

"Because I'm buying."

"I'll be back. I promise."

She walked inside, thinking about yesterday's escape to the ferry and Tucker. It hadn't been that many hours ago, but now she trusted West Laughlin, at least in regard to Tucker. It was herself she couldn't trust now, her dangerous attraction to the man.

Her phone rang inside her carryall. William. Finally. She slowed her steps and answered, moving toward a corner of the bar that was unoccupied as the man and woman who'd been seated at the nearest corner table were just leaving.

"There you are," she said into the receiver.

"I haven't got anything further on the Laughlins, if that's why you're calling."

"In part. I just . . ." Now that she didn't feel quite so out of control about Tucker and West Laughlin, she didn't really have anything to say.

"Have you decided when you're coming back?" he asked, filling in the gap. "I can set up a meeting with Derek and Diane for next week."

"I'm still not sure about my travel plans, so don't do it yet."

"So, this is still about your interest in the Laughlins." He sounded wary.

"In a way."

"Callie, I should inform you that I can't be your lawyer and also be Derek and Diane's, at least in this instance where you're fighting each other."

"Oh, you're choosing them," she said in surprise. She should have expected as much, but it got to her.

"They feel there's been a misappropriation of funds. Not by you, per se. By Jonathan. I told them I would represent them in the matter."

He didn't sound happy about it, but that hardly helped Callie. "Duly noted," she said dryly.

"You should check with your accountant, when you get back."

"Jonathan's accountant," Callie corrected, thinking of the man she'd only met once.

"Find out about Jonathan's financial dealings. It would be to your benefit to come back soon and get this resolved," he said.

"Thanks for the advice."

She hung up just as she felt someone come up close behind her. She edged away, feeling hurt and angry. William Lister, though not exactly a friend, was someone she'd felt she could count on. He'd been the Cantrell family attorney and that apparently did not extend to her, now that Jonathan was gone. He'd defected to Derek and Diane, the only true Cantrells left.

She started to turn around when a male voice with an American accent whispered harshly in her ear, "There you are. Don't move, or I'll bring the police down on you, you thieving whore."

"What?" She automatically tried to step forward but the corner table was in her way. To her alarm, his hand gripped her hip, holding her in place.

"No, don't turn around. Just ease yourself to the side and walk out through the front doors. I'm right behind you."

"There's—this is a mistake."

"I saw you with tonight's date. I have a gun. Don't make me use it."

A *gun?* He put slight pressure on her hip to turn her toward the front of the hotel. She didn't fight it. Her gaze ran wildly over the other customers around the bar, hoping one of them would notice something was amiss. What if she just screamed? *Never get in a car with a kidnapper. Don't let them take you. You have a much better chance staying alive.*

"I don't know you," she said, her voice shaky.

"Stop it. You're making me angry. You don't want to make me angry."

His voice was cold and hard. Her brain had practically shut down, but she got that he thought she was someone else. *Teresa.*

"My name's Callie Cantrell." She tried to turn to look at him but he was a brick wall of anger.

"I don't give a damn what you call yourself today. I want my money back, and I want you in a cell. What the fuck did you give me?"

She shook her head, afraid to argue with him, her brain racing.

"Come on. We're going to the boat. . . ." She felt something hard in the small of her back and she took a step forward.

Chapter Sixteen

Callie's heart raced as she moved forward. This couldn't be happening. They were right in the hotel lobby. It would be laughable if it wasn't so frightening. Was he thinking of taking her hostage? Where was his car? Her heart was galloping in her chest. "You've made a mistake," she said again.

"No."

"I'm not Teresa, if that's who you think I am."

He whipped her around and glared into her eyes. He was tall and had a close-cropped salt-and-pepper beard surrounding a florid face. His clothes were casual but expensive. His anger was palpable, but she'd never seen him before in her life.

And he got a jolt looking her square in the face, too. She saw it in the widening of his eyes. "What are you up to?" he demanded.

"I told you. I'm . . . Callie Cantrell."

"Shut the fuck up. This is some trick!"

"No . . . no trick."

"Who are you?" he demanded. "Where's Tara?"

Tara was close to Teresa. Callie's mind jumped from thought to thought. "I don't know. I don't know."

They were deep into a tense conversation. To the outside world it might appear as a lovers' quarrel. "You know where she is. This is some game."

Callie just stared at him mutely. She didn't have any argument that seemed to wash. But since it was the second time in two days that she'd been mistaken for another woman, she suspected there was some connection between Tara and Teresa. "When did you see Tara?" she asked.

"Last night." He glared at her, unwilling to admit his mistake just yet.

"You were with her last night?" Callie repeated, her pulse leaping.

"Ah, you know her!" He jumped on that.

"No, I'm looking for someone who looks like me as well. Her name's Teresa."

"Old Sal said you were hustling here before, about six years ago. He recognized you, too."

"But it wasn't me," she reminded him, and he stared into her face in consternation.

She realized the hard object pressed against her spine was not a gun but the end of a table knife, which he now held loosely in his hand.

"What's going on here?" West's voice rang out behind him. The guy whipped around, sizing West up.

"It's all right," Callie said quickly, before the situation could get further out of hand. "He thinks I'm someone named Tara."

"Yeah?" West assessed the man coldly. She realized he was poised on the balls of his feet. He looked dangerous and determined, and she was glad to see him.

"You part of this con?" the man asked West.

"No con." West carefully gestured toward Callie, not

making any sudden moves. "Her name's Callie Cantrell. I'm sure she told you that." He flicked a look to her over the man's shoulder and she nodded vigorously.

The man slowly started to relax his belligerent stance. "Egan Rivers isn't a man to toy with," he said.

West said, "You've just made a mistake."

"If I have, I apologize. Remains to be seen." He kept his gaze on West several moments longer, then shook his head and stalked back inside, toward the far end of the bar.

"You okay?" West clipped out, his eyes following Rivers.

"He was with someone named Tara last night who looks like me."

He gave her a quick look. "You think Teresa's here?"

"Maybe. What do you think?"

"I need to talk to him."

"I want to go with you."

"You're white as a ghost," he said, already in motion.

"I'm fine," she answered stubbornly, following after him as he swept through the bar fast, his strides eating up the distance. She had to pick up the pace to catch up with him. Rivers was already out of sight, having charged through the bar and out the side door that led to a series of stairs down to the private docks behind the hotel that were shared by the Bakoua Beach and several other hotels that ringed the bay. West burst through the door, but Rivers was moving fast down the steps as Callie slammed through after them.

He thought I was Teresa. Teresa must have used the name Tara and had taken him in some way.

Egan Rivers moved quickly for a big man. West raced down the steps two at a time. "Hey!" he called.

Rivers threw him a dark glare over his shoulder and kept moving.

"Hey, slow down," West called. "I've got some questions for you."

His answer was to double his speed.

Behind West, Callie said, sounding out of breath, "Teresa must be in Martinique!"

"Damn it." West didn't really want to tackle the man, but he sure as hell wasn't going to let him get away. The boats were lined up with narrow wooden docks running off the main access. Rivers turned onto one, took two steps, then seemed to think better about revealing his destination because he stopped short and turned, his arms up, his fists clenched at his sides, his face full of belligerence.

West slowed immediately. He was sure the man didn't have a gun, but there was no reason to test that theory if he didn't have to. He eased to a stop and lifted his hands. "Hey, look, I don't want to fight. Just want to ask a question or two." He heard Callie coming up behind him, her sandals slapping the boards, her breath coming fast. He wished she'd gone to the table instead of chasing after them, but there hadn't been time to negotiate the point. "We're looking for someone named Teresa who resembles Callie and has a connection to Martinique. You thought she was someone named Tara, which sounds a lot like Teresa. Maybe they're one and the same."

"You're both in it with her," he said, glaring at West, then Callie, who had moved to just behind West's right shoulder. Rivers slowly dropped his hands, but his stance was still confrontational.

"Not sure what you mean," West said.

"The scam, man." He pointed a finger at them. "I'm calling the police."

"We're not involved in any scam. I thought Callie was

Teresa at first, too, but she's not. The hair's the same . . . body build. But you know she's not the woman you're looking for."

Egan Rivers had been breathing hard, too, and now he inhaled a long deep breath. "I don't really give a shit what your deal is."

Callie said, "You can maybe help us find her. That's all we want."

"You met Tara last night?" West asked.

His face turned a brick red in remembrance. "Picked her up at the hotel bar." He gestured to the Bakoua Beach. "I spend a lot of time around here, Pointe du Bout, Trois-Îlets," he said, referring to the entire area on this side of the bay. "Had an Internet sales business that I sold. I bought that boat." He inclined his head toward a vessel with a shiny, navy-blue hull toward the end of the dock. "She came on to me last night. We had some serious fun but she slipped me something. I was out cold. Got up this morning and all my cash was gone."

"Who's Old Sal?" Callie asked.

West looked at her, but Rivers answered readily enough. "Man, he's been around Trois-Îlets for years. Maintains the docks, does some work around the hotel grounds. Everybody knows him. He asked me this morning about Tara. When I told him about her, he said she used to work this area, five, six years ago."

"Work this area? That's what you meant about a con?" West asked.

"Yep. Went after guys with money. Sal said she'd been gone a while, but he recognized her right off." He was staring at Callie now, examining her closely. "What happened to your jaw?"

West's gut twisted with remorse as Callie said, "And here

I thought I'd managed to cover it up with the miracle of modern makeup."

Rivers actually smiled and the rest of his aggression melted away. "Guess you're not with her."

"We're not," West said.

"Wanna come to *Castaway* for a drink? That's what I'm gonna do." With that he turned and headed for the boat, the stern of which was backed to the dock. West looked at Callie who nodded. He took her hand and they moved forward together.

Rivers led the way onto the boat, then gallantly offered a hand, helping Callie aboard, as West brought up the rear. It was about forty-some feet and had a back salon with a built-in banquette with red cushions and a bar surrounding a tidy galley. There was something stripped down and masculine about it, function over form, that spoke of Egan Rivers's apparent bachelorhood.

"What'll you have?" he asked Callie as he slipped behind the bar.

She glanced at West, then said, "White wine?"

Rivers declared sourly, "I think that bitch drank all the chardonnay. No wait. There's one more bottle." He pulled out a bottle from the refrigerator, uncorked it, then brought up three plastic glasses from a lower cupboard and filled one for Callie. "I'm having Maker's Mark," he said to West. "That work for you?"

"Sure." As Rivers set up their two glasses, West asked, "Old Sal told you that Tara used to work these hotels?"

"Yep."

"Where can I find him?" West asked.

"Oh, he's around. Mostly during the day."

"What else did he tell you?"

Rivers slid a glass to West, picked up his own, took a deep swallow. "Look, I'm sorry I threatened you," he apologized to Callie. "I don't like being taken, y'know? She stole from me. Didn't get a lot, but I think she drugged me. But we had some fun, first, so maybe I shouldn't care."

"What kind of fun?" West asked.

Rivers gave him a knowing look. "The best kind."

West had an instant mental image, but it was of Callie and himself. "Old Sal say anything else?" he asked, dragging his thoughts back.

"She and her partner left when things started to get hot. They just disappeared one day."

"Partner?" West asked.

Rivers rubbed his beard and grimaced. "Sal caught him on a boat once, watching Tara and some other guy getting it on. Mostly she picked up guys and went to a hotel room, but this time was on a boat. The partner was spying on 'em, but Old Sal caught him at it and called him out. Peeping Tom just sauntered off, like no big deal. The guy who owned the boat heard their voices but was kinda busy. When he surfaced and found Old Sal, he was outraged, but he was into Tara, or whatever her name is, and let it go. Wasn't gonna give her up. Later, he told Sal he was pretty sure she knew the guy was watching them and played into it. Made me worry about last night a little, but hell, Tara was doing things to me at the time that I wouldn't've wanted to give up, either, even if I'd known." He lifted a hand to Callie, a silent apology. "Sorry about scaring you. I wanted to kill her after talking to Old Sal."

West reached for his cell phone and the big man turned back to him. "What're you doing?" Rivers asked suspiciously.

"I want to show you a picture, that's all." West clicked on the phone and scrolled through his photos until he found the one with Teresa in it. Cautiously, Rivers moved close enough to get a good look at it.

"Looks just like her, but then so does your girl."

"That's Tara?"

"That's what I said. Who's the guy?"

"My half brother. Stephen Laughlin. The woman in the picture's name is Teresa Laughlin."

"She his wife?" he asked.

"She was. Before his death."

"Oh hell, man. What happened?"

"That's what we're trying to find out," West said grimly.

Callie's heart stuttered as she sipped at her glass of wine and listened to Rivers's tale unfold. Thoughts danced in the back of her mind.

Teresa picked up men at bars in Martinique . . . Teresa . . . Martinique . . . Jonathan . . .

She suddenly remembered seeing some papers Jonathan had left on his desk. A quick view before he came back into his office, swept them up and yelled at her for being a sneak. She'd tried to defend her innocence, but he'd been coldly furious and she'd left the room, injured. She'd forgotten that fact. It happened right before the accident. Had it been something about the money Jonathan had spent from the mortgage? No, it was . . . an address?

An address for Teresa DuPres.

Oh, God. Her head hurt. This was one of the missing pieces she'd tried so hard to remember after the accident. Jonathan knew Teresa. She could still practically hear Jonathan calling out to her at the coffee shop that day, "*Teresa!*"

It had never been Marissa. It had been Teresa. Teresa DuPres Laughlin.

Rivers was leaning against the galley cabinets and now he focused on Callie. "Where do you fit in to all this?"

Callie felt like she was in another world. "I—don't. Not really. I just got mistaken for Teresa. . . ." Even to her own ears, her voice sounded strained. She could feel West's attention sharpen on her.

Jonathan knew Teresa. West's Teresa! It wasn't just a vague thought in her head. He'd had her name and an address written down. He must've met her in Martinique, maybe fell for her. She recalled how shocked he'd seemed when he'd called out to her that day and then realized he'd made a mistake. But he'd pursued her anyway, hoping for sexy, dangerous, morally ambiguous Teresa, a woman who fit into Jonathan's adrenaline-charged world of wealth, sex, and fantasy far better than Callie ever could. He'd tried to re-create her with Callie, but it hadn't worked. She'd been a poor substitute, a pale copy of the real thing.

"You okay?" West asked.

It seemed so obvious all of a sudden. Her marriage to Jonathan failed in large part because Callie couldn't measure up. Not that she was blameless. She'd wanted a fantasy too: Jonathan Cantrell, handsome, sophisticated, worldly. "I'm fine," she said tautly.

"If she's working these parts again, you'll find her," Rivers predicted.

"Old Sal mention what this partner looked like?" West asked.

"You'll have to ask him yourself."

"I'll do that."

Callie could feel a buzzing in her ears. She'd barely touched her drink, but she felt half drunk. Could she remember that address? Could she, if she tried really hard? It had been in California . . . Venice, maybe? Not Los Angeles, but a nearby suburb?

"Your brother meet her here?" Rivers was asking West.

"At a Los Angeles bar," he answered.

"Ahh, so, that's where she went," the bigger man said. "But now she's back."

"Do you mind if I walk outside to the prow?" Callie asked. "Just want to look at the bay."

"Have at it," Rivers said.

West looked like he wanted to follow her, but she headed him off with, "I'll be right back."

She tried not to hurry, but she needed some time to herself to think. West had maintained all along that there was a connection between her and Teresa and now she knew what it was. There was a chance she could possibly be making more of this than there was, but she didn't believe it. Right down to her heels she knew Jonathan had wanted her to be Teresa.

He booked their honeymoon in Martinique because that's where he'd met Teresa. And Callie had thought it was so romantic, had even come back here because it was when she'd been so happy! She'd wanted to reconnect with those feelings and it had all been a lie!

You came because of Sean . . . not because of Jonathan, she reminded herself.

She shook her head, unwilling to even cut herself that break. She'd been such a blind fool. It was embarrassing.

She had to move carefully over the narrow walkway along the side of the boat. Her face felt hot, emotion firing her blood. She turned her face to the breeze, seeking relief, but her thoughts churned forward relentlessly. On the one hand she wanted to sit down and collapse, give herself time to process all her feelings. On the other hand she wanted to jump up and down, scream, tear at her hair, and have an out-and-out fit at her own susceptibility.

She needed to tell West what she'd figured out. Needed him to know about the connection between Teresa and Jonathan. They had to have known each other before she was married to Stephen. They met in Martinique, she was certain, but had their affair ended here? Or had it spilled over to Los Angeles? They were both in the same city for a time. Had they reconnected? Maybe even *after* he was married? After *she* was married? With an uncomfortable lurch of her stomach, Callie recalled how Jonathan had always been on the phone, making "secret" calls that he never explained. She'd tried to ask him about them a time or two, but he'd always brushed her off.

Oh, God. There was more to her connection to Teresa than she'd ever dreamed.

She stood on the prow, looking across the water, feeling slightly sick. To her right, a man and woman were standing in the rear of the boat next to her. The cabin lights illuminated the bay so that the water glowed light green. His arm was slung over her shoulders companionably as they both sipped wine from fluted glasses. They glanced over at Callie and she nodded to them though she barely saw them. Her vision was turned inward.

She needed to ask West when Stephen met Teresa.

What about Tucker? Has she come back for him? What if she takes him away?

What if she's trying to do that right now?

Vaguely, she realized something had been bumping against the boat. She started to turn back, fired by the certainty that Teresa was taking Tucker away, when the woman in the boat next to her let out a scream that sounded like a siren. A chill ran up Callie's back. She shot a glance at the woman and saw her stumble back from the edge of the boat, her hands clasped to her chest while the man tried to steady her. Her gaze was fixated on the water.

A body floated into the light. Not a swimmer. Someone wrapped in a black dress and sweater. As Callie watched, the face turned slowly upward, mouth open, dark reddish-blond tresses sliding across the slackened flesh of a familiar face.

"Holy Mother of God," Callie whispered as the woman's

Chapter Seventeen

The fog that enveloped Callie was a familiar one. It had crept in slowly after she'd woken in the hospital after Sean's death, hampering her recovery, causing all the doctors and nurses to cast her worried looks. It had been the main reason Dr. Rasmussen, the psychiatrist assigned to her case when her recovery veered into depression, had suggested a stay at Del Amo Hospital. Callie had checked herself in willingly enough, if you could count the fact that she remembered next to nothing in those weeks following the accident.

Now it was trying to come back, oozing toward her, numbing her brain and blanking out the vision of the face she'd seen in the water. Not her face, but enough like it to give her a sense of being outside her own body. But she knew the fog wasn't a friend and she wasn't planning to let it take her over again. She fought it back with cold, hard logic, tamping down her own emotions, and she was better at it this time.

Three hours after the body was discovered and identified by Egan Rivers as his mysterious Tara, the gendarmerie finished their initial investigation. A young man in a uniform with a respectable command of English had questioned Callie who'd managed to say that she'd only seen the body floating in the water after the woman on the adjoining boat had started screaming. If he noticed her resemblance to the corpse, he didn't mention it. Maybe it wasn't as startling as Callie felt it was. Maybe it was her own association with Teresa that made everything feel so personal and chilling.

She was a little hazy on the sequence of events since the body floated up. Another gift of the fog. She knew that West had been locked in conversation with the authorities as had Egan Rivers. She wasn't certain exactly how much West had revealed about his own quest to find Teresa, but she thought she'd heard him mention he was a policeman recently with the LAPD.

The body was pulled from the water and carried to a waiting ambulance, which raced away from the premises heading toward the morgue. West had tossed a jacket over Callie's shoulders as she'd been plagued by shivers that wouldn't quit. He'd left her for a few moments to pick up the jacket from his hotel room and bring it to Rivers's boat, which was where the initial interviewing had taken place. After West had helped her return from the boat's prow, she'd practically fallen into a chair in the salon and she'd been there ever since. It was kind of a surprise when, as the questions slowed down, someone mentioned the time and she realized how many hours had passed. The fog took away the dimension of time as well.

Now, West's face floated into her view as he bent down to look into her eyes. "Ready to go?" he asked her.

"Are we allowed to?" Her voice was steady and careful. She sounded more in control than she felt.

"They're finished for tonight. I told them I'd go down to the station tomorrow. They'll do an autopsy and run DNA, just to be sure, but it's Teresa."

"Did you tell them about Aimee?" she asked, as he helped her to her feet.

"I said she was taking care of the victim's son."

"What'll happen to Tucker?" she asked, her heart clutching.

"If Victoria gets her way, he'll be on the next airplane to Los Angeles."

Callie absorbed that with mixed feelings. Yes, she wanted Tucker to be safe, but it meant a complete upheaval from everything the boy knew. And she wasn't sure where she fit into that picture, if at all, which wasn't maybe the most pressing issue, but it sure as hell mattered to her.

They said good-bye to Rivers, who had poured himself another stiff drink and was drinking it down as if he were on a mission. He nodded curtly in response.

"The police are treating it like an accident for the moment," West said as they walked back up the steps to the hotel. "No one's actually said 'homicide,' but the thought's there."

"What do you think?"

"Don't know yet. But I need to get you to stop shaking. Come to my room. Take a shower."

I should go home, she thought as they walked through the hotel bar, but she let him guide her into the elevator and up to the third floor. She obediently followed him inside and went straight to the bathroom, stripping off her clothes and stepping into a shower that was just shy of uncomfortably hot.

For reasons she couldn't quite grasp, her thoughts turned to her first love, Bryan Tapper. How she'd followed him to Los Angeles and supported him while he auditioned for roles and music gigs, how he'd become seduced by the fast-paced lifestyle, living it up with sex, drugs, and rock and roll, and how Callie had been forced to give him up to his new woman to save herself. Her thoughts then turned to Jonathan, and she was almost embarrassed at how easily she'd been seduced by him, a man who, as she now believed, had never really wanted her.

And lastly she thought about Teresa DuPres Laughlin, who'd apparently seduced and conned men right and left for

her own pleasure and personal gain but had ended up floating lifeless in Fort-de-France Bay.

When she came out of the shower she tugged down one
of the Bakoua Beach bathrobes from its peg on the back of
the bathroom door and tied it around herself. Then she
stepped into the main room to find West standing on the balcony, talking on his cell phone. His room overlooked the
bay where dots of lights from the myriad anchored boats
gave the inky water the look of a starry sky.

Seeing her, he cut the call short and walked back inside,
closing the sliding door behind him. "Victoria's calling her
lawyer to get the paperwork started to become Tucker's
guardian. She doesn't want to hear that Aimee may have
rights bestowed on her by Teresa."

Callie didn't immediately respond. She was too discombobulated to make plans and strategize. She felt slightly
untethered, and it reminded her uncomfortably of how she'd
reacted after Sean's death.

"You look like you could use a drink," West said. "I don't
have any wine, but I've got Jack Daniel's."

"No, thanks."

"You sure? I'm having one." He pulled out a glass and
poured two fingers into it. Then he gazed at her again, brows
raised.

The fog was threatening to overtake her and she wanted
to be overtaken, but it wouldn't be a good thing right now.
Maybe a stiff drink was what she needed, so she nodded and
West poured her one. She sat down on the end of the bed and
he brought the glass to her, pressing it into her hands and
then seating himself next to her. He smelled slightly briny,
from all the time on the boat, and she inhaled deeply, wanting to clear her head. Taking a large swallow of the liquor,
she let it burn down her throat. The shudder that ran through
her caused her to clamp her elbows in tight, which made the
robe gap at her neckline, revealing the tops of her breasts.

West couldn't stop himself from glancing at the deep vee of skin. When he dragged his gaze upward, Callie met his eyes. They stared at each other.

"You've still got the bruise on your chin," he said.

She touched a hand to her jawline, then finished the rest of her drink and leaned back on one elbow to set the empty glass down on an end table. When she looked back she saw West had finished his drink and was slowly passing the glass back and forth between his two hands.

"I'm sorry," he said, not looking at her.

"For?"

"Scaring you. Attacking you."

"I remember you kissing me."

West inhaled slowly, then set the glass down on the floor at his feet. He turned slightly to look at her. She was lying back on both elbows.

In her mind's eye she could already see them rolling around on this king-size bed, his hard contours pressed against her softer ones. Was that what she wanted? Yes. Definitely. But was it what he wanted?

"You think 'Tara' was with other men besides Egan Rivers?" she asked, more to keep herself distracted from her own thoughts than because she wanted to talk about Teresa anymore.

"I think it's Teresa's m.o. Depends on how long she was here. Aimee acted like she hadn't seen her in quite a while, but then, I don't think she and the truth are great friends."

She opened her mouth to tell him that he'd been right in thinking there was a connection between herself and Teresa; it just wasn't the way he'd thought it was. But her attention was focused on his face, the blue of his eyes, the beard that was darkening his chin.

"You can't look at me that way," he told her.

She almost asked, "What way?" but she already knew what he was seeing. *I want to gobble him up,* she thought, sensing a lifting in the fog. Her gaze shifted to his lips and he leaned down until his face was mere inches from hers.

She reached forward and ran her index finger over his lower lip.

"Oh, man . . ." he said.

"I want to feel . . . something," she whispered.

He leaned in and kissed her hard, though she sensed that he was holding himself back. But she wasn't interested in waiting. Right now, she just wanted to *feel*. Running a hand around his neck, she drew him forward. His tongue touched her lips and she opened them and gave entry, falling onto her back at the same time, forcing him to lean over her.

"Is this . . . ?" He didn't finish the sentence.

"What?"

"What you want?"

For an answer she brought his mouth to hers again, and then he was atop her and pulling the tie of her robe free. A moment later he was drawing a line of warm kisses down her throat and between her breasts.

She squeezed her eyes closed, willing her brain to stop, reveling in the moment. She was sick of being sad, broken, and lost, and she was glad she'd found him, and Tucker, and a reason to start again. She wanted West to make love to her. Right now. And for it to go on and on forever!

She felt the scratch of his beard tickle and tease her neck. She inhaled deeply from the top of his head as she threaded her fingers into his thick hair. Letting out a groan, he slowly levered himself up to take in her naked body lying atop the white, open robe.

Quietly she moved forward, reached for the bottom of his shirt. She yanked it free and helped pull it over West's head. Hard, tan muscles that slid beneath his skin begged to be touched. Running her hand slowly from his chest down to his flat abs, she paused at his belt buckle, her eyes sliding up to meet his. He was tense, holding back, letting her set the pace. It gave her a power she hadn't expected, a thrill Jonathan had never let her experience. Pulling his belt buckle free, she smashed her lips to his and they both fell back onto the bed. His urgent kisses left a trail of fire down her neck and chest, and she squirmed beneath him as he sucked one taut nipple into his mouth.

"Please . . ." she moaned.

She heard the tearing of foil and wanted to almost laugh at the craziness that had engulfed her. Protection was the furthest thing from her mind. Then she felt his weight shift back toward her. A warm, liquid sensation began to fill her as he gently eased himself inside. She ran her inner thighs up the side of his hips and wrapped her legs around him as she began to slowly match his rhythmic thrusts. Her hands gripped his taut back, pulling him nearer, needing his closeness. Faster and faster. Her body shivered and suddenly she was there, sensation exploding in her core, shooting through her. She heard him groan and then shudder within her, collapsing against her, their twin heartbeats galloping madly.

"My God," he expelled.

"Exactly my thoughts," she said, and they both felt each other's silent laughter.

Daniella drove the Xterra out of the LAX parking lot, griping a bit under her breath at the amount she had to pay to the bored woman at the booth, and also about the damn pain in the butt it had been to find the vehicle. She'd had to keep pressing the panic button on the remote. She could hear it, but it wasn't close enough to see at first, and she suffered the annoyed stares of other people in the lot. Well, screw them. She'd been pissed off about being left out of the trip to Miami and then, on top of it, to have to locate the SUV that Teresa had just abandoned . . . well, it just wasn't fair.

It was after ten before she got back to the house, and then she walked around for a few minutes, frustrated, anxious, and annoyed. Always, she was the one left behind to mop up. Always.

She wanted to get laid. That's what she wanted. And if it wasn't going to be Andre, maybe some nameless guy at a bar. She didn't have a mark like the rest of them. Oh, no. That wasn't her job. So, she didn't have a regular sex life. In fact, she damn near didn't have any sex life at all.

Her thoughts about finishing the job Teresa had started with Robert Lumpkin faded away. She was tired of doing things for other people. She needed something for herself.

Snatching up the keys to the Xterra, she headed toward the strip of bars along the beach in Venice where she'd first met Andre.

An hour after making love, Callie still lay cradled against West. He was lying on his back and her arm was thrown around him, her cheek pressed against the skin of his chest, softly prickled by the whorls of hair she couldn't see in the darkness. She never wanted the moment to end. Stretching languidly, she tried to remember the last time she'd felt so relaxed and couldn't. The fog had lifted, but she sensed it hovering just outside. When she thought about Teresa's body, it grew closer, but being here with West kept it away.

She needed to tell West what she'd remembered about Jonathan, but she almost didn't want to. She didn't want to alter anything between them. Making love hadn't been anything she'd planned on, especially not to a man she'd only known a few days, but now she didn't want anything to destroy this new and fragile joy.

But nothing good would come from putting off the inevitable either.

"West," she said.

His hand lifted to smooth her crown. "Mmm-hmm."

"There's something I need to tell you."

"Okay."

"When I first met Jonathan, he called out to me like he knew me. He called me a name, and I wasn't sure what it was until today. It was . . . Teresa."

She felt him tense. "What do you mean?"

"I think he knew Teresa. When he called out to me, I wasn't sure whether he said 'Teresa' or 'Marissa,' or something else, because he moved right on when he realized he'd made a mistake. He never explained, and I never thought too much about it. Then you called me Teresa, and I don't know, it kick-started my memory."

"You think your husband knew Teresa," he repeated.

"Jonathan chose Martinique as our honeymoon spot because he'd been there before. He told me it was one of the best places on earth. I thought so too. Sean was conceived here. It's a beautiful place.

"But tonight, after Rivers was talking about this Old Sal and how he thought Tara, or Teresa, had been here before . . . it made me think that Jonathan met Teresa here and how you've been saying all along that there's a connection. I didn't see how, but then on Rivers's boat I thought maybe I did after all. Maybe Jonathan picked Martinique for our honeymoon because he was trying to relive the relationship, or maybe he hoped she'd show up, or something. Right before the accident, I saw some papers on Jonathan's desk. I didn't mean to look at them, they were just there, but he caught me at it, and he was really upset. I think it was something about Martinique and Teresa. I'm pretty sure. An address, maybe? I don't know. But then the accident happened and I forgot everything that occurred right before the crash. It took me a year of recovery to plan this trip to Martinique."

She could tell he was listening hard. "You think he was conned by her?"

"I think he never got over her, whatever their relationship was. And I think something in those papers got into my head. I caught a memory of it again last night. It has to do with Teresa and Jonathan. Maybe they reconnected?"

"In LA?"

"He spent money he didn't have on something," she said, reminded of what William had told her. "Maybe it was on her, or at least the search for her. But then he died in the crash."

West considered for a long time, then said, "Teresa met Stephen in LA, but they moved to the ranch."

"Maybe Jonathan was looking for her, and for a lot of that time she was married to Stephen."

"And then he found her?" West questioned. "After Stephen was gone?"

"Maybe after she left Tucker in Martinique," Callie posed. "William asked me to dig through all of Jonathan's papers and find out anything I can about where some missing money might be. As soon as I go back, I'm going to do that, and see if I can find out anything else, too."

"When are you planning to go back?" he asked.

"Well, I don't know. I didn't intend for things to happen . . . as they have."

His grip around her tightened briefly and then relaxed. "Me, neither. But I'm glad they did."

"Me, too," she admitted, unable to stop the smile that reached her lips. He wasn't saying it, but she sensed he wanted what had started tonight to continue as much as she did. She was a part of this, a part of Tucker's life.

"The police are talking to Aimee tonight," he said. "I wanted to be with them, but I don't have any authority and anyway you looked . . ."

"What?"

"Undone. I couldn't leave you." He kissed her shoulder and she quivered, nestling closer to his warmth.

"What's going to happen next?" Callie asked.

For an answer, he pulled her atop him and let her hair fall all around his face as his lips met hers. One hand skimmed down the curve of her back. She felt herself heat up from the inside out.

"I mean, what's going to happen to Tucker, and you, and me . . ."

Brushing her hair away from her face, he said, "As soon as I can, I'm going to take Tucker and head back to the States."

"And . . . *moi?*" she asked lightly.

"It looks like Teresa, with or without her partner, moved her hunting grounds to Los Angeles after she left Martinique. Maybe your husband caught up with her and wanted to start up again."

He spoke diffidently, but Callie said, "Don't worry about my feelings where Jonathan is concerned. We were long over before the accident. Sean was the only reason we stayed together. When I go back, you want me to see if my memory's correct, and there's something there about Teresa?"

"If Rivers is right, Teresa was good at conning people. She got my brother to marry her. If your husband maybe found her again, after being conned himself, he might have felt more like Rivers does, like he was taken."

"I don't think it was like that. As I said, he wanted her back. That's why he married me. He was trying to re-create something that never really existed. If I could just remember everything it would help, but it's just out of reach."

"Maybe when you go back."

"What are you going to do?"

"I'm going to get Tucker to the ranch, make sure he's okay, then check with Edmund Mikkels again. I want to know what Teresa was doing all the while she was on the ranch. Was she any part of Stephen's death? Who did she hang out with there? Somebody must know something."

"What if there's a snag about taking Tucker from Aimee? What if she fights for custody?" Callie worried.

"She'll lose. Victoria is a formidable opponent. Once Tucker's DNA comes back, and it's clear he's a Laughlin, Aimee won't have a chance. And if she kicks up a fuss, I'll offer her cold, hard cash to go away, if I have to."

"When do you think I should fly to LA?" she asked, hoping against hope he would say it was best if she stayed, knowing it wasn't true as she would only undoubtedly complicate things with Aimee.

His hand cupped her buttocks and slid down her thigh. She could feel that he was hard and ready to go again and it sent a thrill through her.

"Not today," he said, his hips moving seductively, and with a soft sigh Callie slid her hands down to hold him hot against her.

PART II

Chapter Eighteen

Sorry, Teresa, but you had to go. You were long past your pull date. And based on the amount of bad stuff you did, it's amazing somebody didn't beat me to the punch long ago.

But you left a bit of a problem behind, didn't you? That boy of yours. You sure as hell were begging for his life at the end, but unfortunately, I don't think I'll be able to help you out there. He's an obstacle, and you know better than most what to do with obstacles, don't you? You gotta remove them.

Callie sat in the chair across from Dr. Rasmussen, intent upon keeping herself from wringing her hands, cracking her knuckles, or playing with her fingernails, all the little signs of anxiety that had plagued her before. It wasn't that she was afraid to meet with her psychiatrist. Actually, she welcomed it. Dr. Rasmussen had been nothing but supportive after the accident and had been instrumental in putting the pieces of her back together. But if Callie were going to be an integral part of Tucker's life she needed to convince everyone, especially Victoria Laughlin, that she was the right, the most perfect, person for the job of his teacher/nanny, and Dr. Rasmussen's approval was key to meeting that goal.

"Tell me more about Tucker," the doctor encouraged Callie. The psychiatrist, wearing a cream-colored blouse teamed with a gray jacket and a matching gray pencil skirt, sat with her legs crossed in the chair facing Callie. Her eyes were benign over a pair of half-moon glasses, and her steel-gray hair was cut short and feathered around her face, which was remarkably unlined.

Callie hoped she looked as at ease and natural as Dr. Rasmussen did, though every nerve was strung tight. She hadn't met Victoria yet, hadn't met any of the Laughlins, as West was still in Martinique, finalizing Tucker's move to California. She needed her first impression to be a good one.

"There isn't much more to tell," she said. "When we became friends I didn't realize he was being taken care of by someone other than his mother."

"And now, after his mother's death, Tucker will be living with his uncle and grandmother."

"His grandmother and great-grandmother. I'm not sure about his uncle. West Laughlin lives in LA and Laughlin Ranch is outside of Castilla. That's where I'll be going."

"They're home-schooling and you're the teacher."

Callie wanted to lick her dry lips but refrained. "Tucker will be matriculating into first grade, but he needs to catch up a little first."

The doctor shifted position, uncrossing her legs. She looked at the file she held in her hands. "I haven't seen you in a while."

"I was away for over a month, and I just got back a little over a week ago. I went away to gain some perspective. Like I said earlier, I chose Martinique because it's where Jonathan and I honeymooned."

"When you were at Del Amo, you blamed Jonathan for

the loss of your son. You said he deliberately drove too fast when you asked him to slow down."

"He's not the reason I chose Martinique," she answered. "But, yeah, Jonathan always drove too fast."

"You said that if Jonathan had been driving slower, Sean would have survived," the doctor reminded.

"Well . . . yes. I said a lot of things."

"Do you still blame him for your son's death?"

"I know we were run off the road, but yes . . . partially. I'm not going to lie about it."

She regarded Callie over the tops of her glasses. "How are you feeling now?"

"Good. Much better. Almost as good as new."

Did she sound too eager? She cut herself off before she could start babbling and really blow her chances.

"Callie, I sense you're here because you want me to give you a good recommendation. Something you can take to the Laughlin family to prove you're fit to be Tucker's teacher."

"Your word would definitely make a difference," she said diffidently.

"I believe you would be a good teacher. I'm just not sure about your emotional connection to the boy."

Callie had known it would come down to this and she'd practiced her response. "I understand. It's tricky. But meeting Tucker helped me get back to where I am now. I was broken; I totally own that. And I know Tucker's not mine. I just don't want to lose contact with him. And from the Laughlins' point of view, they need someone during this transitional time and Tucker already knows me."

Her words started rushing toward the end and she had to take a careful breath when she was finished. She knew, as well as Dr. Rasmussen, that she wanted something more out of her relationship with Tucker, but was that so wrong? She loved Tucker. Was he a replacement for Sean?

Maybe . . . at some level. Probably. But she just didn't care. She wanted to be with him.

"The Laughlin family knows about Sean and the accident?"

"West Laughlin does. I don't know if he's told his grandmother yet."

"Tell me about Mr. Laughlin."

Callie had brushed over her association with West on purpose, aware that her feelings for him could be used against her in her quest to be with Tucker. Knowing she was retreading some of their earlier conversation, she said, "He thought I was Tucker's mother because of my appearance, and because I was Tucker's friend. When he and I realized we were both looking out for Tucker's best interests, we began working together."

"But what about him as a man? I don't have a sense of what you feel about him and his relationship with Tucker."

"West's good with him. He's a good man."

Dr. Rasmussen left that for a moment and said instead, "He's leaving Tucker in his grandmother's care and you plan to move into the Laughlin home in Castilla with the family."

"It's a big house. I'll have my own room."

"Mr. Laughlin works here, but will make the trip back and forth as he plans to be a part of Tucker's life too?"

"Yes."

This was the arrangement she and West had worked out before she'd caught the plane home. She'd thought—hoped—West would be right behind her with Tucker, but there had been legal hang-ups. He'd told her that Aimee had fought tooth and nail to keep Tucker with her. She hadn't even believed Teresa was dead and had demanded to see the body. Even then, shocked as she was at the sight of her deceased friend, she'd claimed Tucker was her responsibility. The wrangle was still continuing but the last Callie had heard Victoria's legal team had prevailed, and Aimee had reluctantly already relinquished Tucker's passport, which had been in her possession as Callie had suspected.

"Aimee kept saying over and over again, 'But she owes me money. She owes me money,'" West had told Callie just yesterday. "That's why she's hanging on to Tucker. She wants payment."

"The bracelet?" Callie had asked.

"Oh, I think she'd prefer a cash payment for its value," he'd answered dryly.

"What about Teresa? Do the police know anything more?"

"They found her belongings. She'd left them with the bellman at her hotel. She bought two tickets to Miami, one for herself, one for a Stephen Laughlin, leaving that night. She had to have contacted Aimee if she was taking Tucker, but Aimee won't say anything. I think she's afraid it'll look bad. I'm going to try to persuade her to see things my way."

It had been over a week and there was still no clear evidence whether Teresa's death was an accident or something else. There was a contusion to her head, which could have happened aboard a boat, and there was a chain mark around her neck, as if from a necklace, but there was no chain. From what West had gleaned, the chain mark wasn't considered significant in her death. More likely she'd slipped, hit her head, and fallen into the water. Or it was possible someone had purposely hit her over the head and tossed her overboard. The theory was she'd been on a boat, but that vessel had yet to be found. Jean-Paul's boat had been thoroughly examined, but there'd been no sign Teresa had ever been aboard it.

"Victoria's elated that Tucker will probably end up in her and Talia's care," West had said as their conversation wound down. "She brought up Tucker's schooling and I told her about you. Victoria will vet you, so get ready for the hard questions. That's just how she is."

And that's when Callie had realized she needed to make an appointment to see Dr. Rasmussen who'd managed to fit her in this morning. If West's grandmother got hold of the fact that she'd spent a month in a mental hospital, she could see how dim her chances might become. Of course, West didn't know about that, either.

She answered several more of Dr. Rasmussen's questions with responses that appeared to be unsatisfactory to the psychiatrist, but eventually their session wound down, though the doctor pressed upon her the need to return. Callie agreed to make another appointment, though in truth she never wanted to be on the couch again. Yes, she'd needed help after Sean's death, but that didn't mean she felt comfortable talking about her feelings. Upon occasion, she'd felt some of the mental health professionals had twisted her words, looking for meaning where there wasn't any, expecting some terrible truth she refused to give them.

Was she paranoid? Maybe a little, but she wasn't interested in blindly following anyone in her life ever again. She'd done that with Jonathan, and before him, Bryan. If nothing else, those relationships had taught her to be cautious and careful about what she revealed.

You let West in pretty quickly, though, didn't you? Don't congratulate yourself too much, just yet.

She drove back to the Mulholland house and went into Jonathan's den, seating herself at the massive antique desk that he'd said was a gift from his father. Inside one of the file drawers were the bank statements from all of his accounts, as far as she knew. She'd gone through them several times, but nothing had jumped out at her. Maybe he had another account somewhere else but it had never surfaced. This one, held jointly in their names, still had a substantial balance that was slowly being depleted. Callie had always kept a separate checking account and had mostly relied on it since Jonathan's death, but her funds weren't going to last forever. With her name on the joint account, the money was hers, though she suspected Derek and Diane would argue that fact. They seemed to believe all things Cantrell now belonged to them and Callie should just get the hell out.

Glancing at the clock, she saw that she had a couple of hours until her next appointment at William Lister's office. She'd finally called him the night before to let him know she'd returned. He'd immediately wanted to set up a meeting with Derek and Diane, and she'd had to talk fast to get him to put off seeing them until the following week. The last thing she wanted to do was talk to either Cantrell sibling, especially since she'd dug through all of Jonathan's papers and found no trace of where he'd spent the money, nor had she discovered anything about Teresa and Jonathan. It was discouraging, really. She'd been so sure there was a Jonathan-Teresa connection. Maybe she just hadn't found it yet, but whatever the case, she didn't want to deal with either of the Cantrells just yet . . . or really ever.

But with West's admonition of Victoria's vetting still ringing in her ears, she knew she needed to meet with William and convince him that she was mentally strong and ready to move forward. Next week she could face the Cantrell lions, but not today.

And next week West might be back with Tucker, she thought as she headed into the kitchen to find something for lunch. Then she could leave this house and all the Cantrells behind forever.

"Can I get you anything before we land?"

Andre momentarily lifted his head to make eye contact

with the pretty flight attendant with the big blue eyes. He tried to smile at her, pull out the old charm, but the synapses between his brain and mouth seemed to have frozen. "No," was all he said, and she moved away to check on another passenger.

He closed his eyes and bent down over his clasped hands, deep in prayer to his gods. Even with his eyes shut, he could see there were flaky edges on the periphery of his vision, a crumbling that had begun bothering him some time back but that he'd dismissed.

Now, he dismissed it again, lost in a weaving world with colors so bright he had to open his eyes to get some relief from their blasting power. His gods were sending The Messiah messages.

The flight was circling LAX. The day was gray, clouds mixed with smog. He contrasted it to the lovely, tropical morning he'd left in Martinique, but memories of the unsatisfactory trip were dark and painful and he pushed them aside. Things hadn't gone as planned and it was the handmaidens' fault.

Reaching inside his shirt, he crushed the ankh against the flesh of his palm. Teresa was dead. He thought he should feel more satisfaction at her death, but in truth he already missed her. Yes, she'd tricked him and run away and death was the price. But once upon a time they'd been partners. She'd done so many things right. Without her, there would have been no other handmaidens. She'd shown him how good it was to sit back and let her do the work, and when she'd been gone so long, so very long, embedding herself into the Laughlin world, he'd been forced to find new "Teresas," although none of them were anything close to her.

Now, who would carry that torch? His mind skipped over the women who had pledged their souls to him and he felt faint despair. Naomi, Clarice, Daniella, and Jerrilyn . . . none of them could be counted on. The ultimate goal was about to be realized and only Teresa would truly have understood. To the rest, it was just another con.

His mind suddenly swept away from the topic, as if overrun by floodwaters. He'd had this sensation before, of being washed away from this reality to another one. When his inner vision finally cleared he saw he was standing in a roomful of skulls. They stared at him and spoke to him without chattering their teeth.

You're too late, they said. *Too late.*

"No!"

His vision cleared and he realized he'd lost time. He wasn't on the plane anymore, he was in baggage claim. What had felt like an instant must have been thirty minutes or more.

Looking down, he saw that he'd already collected his bag. Turning, he strode outside into a warm LA afternoon. He and the handmaidens had taken different flights and he didn't know who was back and who wasn't. Now he punched in Naomi's number, then Daniella's, and when they both went to voice mail, he turned in disgust to the taxi stand.

They were useless to him any longer. He was moving to a new phase and they were baggage. Dangerous baggage.

But it wasn't too late, no matter what the skulls warned.

He needed to close down things in Los Angeles and move on.

The cab dropped him at the house and he strode up to the front door. He was leaving them, but still they needed to remember that he was The Messiah. He looked forward to a prayer meeting with anticipation.

Pulling out his key, he unlocked the door and then stopped short at the sight of the dumpy-looking man standing inside. The man turned and stared at him as well, his gaze dropping to the bag Andre held in his hand. "Who are you?" the man demanded.

Andre had never actually met Robert Lumpkin, but he knew without asking that this man thought he was their landlord even though Lumpkin's mother, Irene, was the actual owner of the house. Beyond him, Daniella stared, wide-eyed, shaking her head as if to say it was no fault of hers the man had shown up.

"Just how many people are living here?" Lumpkin demanded, turning back to Daniella.

"Just me . . ." she quavered.

She was such a whiny rat. She would buckle under the slightest pressure.

"Daniella's my fiancée," Andre said smoothly, striding toward her. He didn't know where the rest of the handmaidens were, but he hoped to hell they weren't about to show up now. Sliding an arm around Daniella's narrow shoulders, he added, "I have my own place. I just got back from a trip and couldn't wait to see her."

"The rent on this place is too low. Do you know how much this house is worth? How much you'd pay if I fixed it up a little, like the others around here?" Lumpkin asked, hooking a thumb in the direction of the neighbors to the west. "Twice as much, that's what."

"You're Daniella's landlord?" Andre asked.

"You got that right."

Daniella managed to squeak out, "His mother is."

Lumpkin scowled at her fiercely and said, "I run things for my mother."

"Well, I assume you signed a lease," Andre said to Daniella.

"Yes . . . yes . . . it's . . . I'll go get it."

She slipped from under Andre's arm as Lumpkin, his

bluff called, declared, "No need. I have a copy. But it clearly states that I need to be informed of the names of all tenants."

"You mean your mother needs to be informed," Andre pointed out as Daniella scurried away.

Lumpkin looked ready to burst a blood vessel, but didn't take it any further. Instead he headed for the door. "The lease is up in January," he snapped, a final volley meant for Daniella as he headed through the door.

Immediately Andre went in search of her and found Daniella cowering in her room. "I didn't do anything," she said, trembling. "He just stopped by. I couldn't keep him out. I didn't know what to do."

"I phoned you from the airport," he said. "I had to take a cab."

"I—I didn't get the call. I don't know where my cell phone is."

Andre closed his eyes and pinched the bridge of his nose. He needed to find patience . . . serenity. "What have you been doing since we've been gone?"

"I picked up the Xterra, like you wanted. I've just been around here."

"What made Lumpkin stop by? And don't say it was just random chance. He's never done that before."

"Maybe . . . maybe Teresa led him here? She wasn't doing what you wanted, you know. Maybe she set him on us . . . as a last mean thing."

"A kind of 'fuck you' on the way out?"

Daniella bobbed her head eagerly.

"It's so easy to blame the dead, isn't it?" Andre asked silkily.

"Teresa's . . . dead?" she warbled.

"Yes, darling. Don't act like you didn't know what the plan was."

"I just didn't know for sure, that's all."

Andre wanted to smack her lying face into the wall. Instead he stalked down the hall to the prayer room.

"Who did it?" Daniella's question floated after him. He could tell she was slowly following after him.

Andre thought of the handmaidens who'd gone with him, Clarice and Naomi. Jerrilyn hadn't made the flight but had said she would catch up to them, something she hadn't managed to, as far as he knew. And Clarice and Naomi had proven worse than useless. "That's something you don't need to know," he told her brusquely.

"Do you know?" she queried, which sent Andre's blood pressure into the stratosphere. He was glad to be done with her, glad to be done with all of them.

"Where is everyone?" Daniella asked. He'd stopped and she was right behind him.

"Doing what I asked of them," he said, though in truth, he didn't know where they were right now. They'd taken separate flights over and back on his orders, but it had left them a lot of leeway. Maybe too much . . .

He turned around to face her. On one side was the prayer room, on his other, the door to the attic. Daniella was looking hopefully at the prayer room, but her expression dimmed as Andre unlocked the attic door.

"Go on up," he ordered her. "I'm tired, and I need to think."

"Oh, Andre, please . . ." she murmured, looking at the steep stairs with despair.

"Who am I?" he demanded, grabbing her arm and shaking it hard. "*Who am I?*"

"The Messiah," she whispered briefly, bowing her head and turning obediently toward the door. He released her and as she reached the stairway, he slammed the door and locked it again. Briefly he wished he'd taken her to the prayer room first, but that thought flickered away. He really didn't want Daniella. She was too ordinary. Jerrilyn, now, she had that hot, sinuous body and kick-ass attitude, and Clarice, apart from all her "only one true God" bullshit, was a wide-eyed, sexy innocent. And then there was haughty, beautiful Naomi, who was tall and statuesque, but for some reason Andre generally felt his dick wilt around her. She was too mothering. Always worried about how he was feeling.

It was Teresa who'd done it for him all the time, he thought with regret. Teresa who'd craved the adrenaline charge as much as he did. Teresa who'd been the only woman he'd truly loved.

Only now she was gone for good.

Daniella had asked which of the handmaidens had killed her. He didn't know, and he didn't care. He was just sorry she was the one who was gone.

Chapter Nineteen

William's receptionist ushered her toward the conference room, which surprised Callie until she realized, looking through the glass, double doors that Angie pushed open, that she'd been ambushed. Seated across from each other at the polished, rectangular, mahogany table were Derek and Diane Cantrell. William sat at the head and he half-rose as Callie stopped short just inside the room. Angie tiptoed back out, softly closing the doors behind her.

Feeling the heat rise in her face, Callie gave William a hard glare.

He looked pained, but Derek was the one who spoke up first. "Oh, don't blame him. Diane and I descended upon him once we learned you were having this meeting."

You shouldn't have told them, Callie thought, keeping her gaze on William, who urged her to take a seat as she came around the table.

"I'll be right back," William said, suddenly breaking for the doors as if the hounds of hell were at his heels.

Bastard.

But then he warned you that he couldn't be your lawyer, too, she admonished herself. *You should have listened.*

Derek Cantrell looked a lot like Jonathan, lean and

sandy-haired with hazel eyes and a slow smile that could turn supercilious at a moment's notice, a trait Callie hadn't seen in her husband until it was too late. Diane had darker hair and eyes and a darker personality as well. She possessed none of her brothers' veneers of charm. She was tough, prickly, and determined in a way that had always made Callie somewhat nervous. Surprisingly now, as she did an internal check of her emotions, Callie realized she didn't really give a damn anymore what Diane thought.

"William says you've packed up," Diane started in. "Did you pack up my brother's things too?"

"C'mon, Diane. Dial it back a bit," Derek said in that lazy way that was meant to put Callie at ease. Good cop, bad cop. Derek played it to the hilt though Callie wasn't sure Diane even recognized the game. She, herself, wasn't buying any of it.

"I've packed up my own clothes and some personal belongings," Callie answered. "Everything's still in the house, the furniture, household items . . . it's all there."

"I don't give a damn about your decorating tastes. What about his personal things?" Diane demanded.

"They're still where he left them, untouched."

Her eyebrows lifted at Callie's taut tone. Callie could read her mind: *What happened to the mouse Jonathan married?*

"Girls, girls, no need to fight." Derek glanced over his shoulder through the glass doors that led from the conference room to the rotunda outside where William was talking to Angie. His back was to them. He clearly didn't want to be any part of their powwow. She couldn't really blame him for that. She didn't want to be, either.

"What do you want?" Callie demanded, looking at Derek.

"Um . . ." he said, at a loss. He'd probably expected Diane to bully her way into getting what she wanted and for Callie to cede it over with both hands.

"We want to know what happened to the money," Diane said, in a voice that made it clear she thought Callie was deliberately being dense. "You've put us off long enough."

"I've told you. Outside of the joint account I had with Jonathan, there is no—"

"You're lying," Diane cut in harshly. "Don't think you're just going to waltz away with our money."

Anger feathered along Callie's nerves. "You've had accountants on this since Jonathan's death. You probably did even before that."

"I did," Diane admitted. "We did," she added, nodding toward her brother. "I know Jonathan made some bad investments. I know he burned through a hell of a lot of the assets, and they weren't his to burn. I don't give a shit that Father left everything to him," she snapped out as she saw Derek open his mouth to argue. "It wasn't right and it wasn't fair and if you think we're going to just walk away and let you take our money, our *inheritance,* you'd better check yourself back into that mental hospital again because you're fucking nuts."

"Jesus, Diane," Derek said uncomfortably.

"Stop acting like such a hero. You're in this with me." Diane glared at him.

"Apart from Jonathan's and my joint checking account, there is no money," Callie reiterated. "You think William hasn't kept me informed of what you want? If there was any money, believe me, I'd hand it over to you."

"You're not even a good liar," Diane declared.

"Since I'm telling the truth, something I understand you may not recognize, I don't think you're the best judge."

"Well, ouch," she said, lifting a brow, then reminded, "You haven't signed the final papers yet."

"I will soon, and the house will be yours."

"Why don't you sign them right now?" Diane suggested.

Callie threw a glance toward the outer office again.

William had moved away from the receptionist, but, as if he felt her gaze, darted a look at her before turning away. "I'll look them over once William gives them to me. I'm not doing it today."

"You're stalling," Diane said.

"Call it anything you want."

"Okay, how much is in that joint account?" Diane demanded.

"Diane, give us a break," Derek murmured.

"Not as much as you're apparently looking for," Callie answered her.

She pressed, "Was there an account for Sean? Where's that money?"

"Jonathan didn't look that far ahead," Callie said coldly. "You know all of this already."

"I know what you'd have us believe while you've been out 'finding yourself' on that tropical island."

Callie fought her rising temper. She'd told herself not to let the Cantrells get to her. She was almost done with them. They had no hold on her. But Diane was really a piece of work. "I'll be out soon, and you can go through Jonathan's things then."

"What kind of guarantee do I have that you won't strip the place before you go?" she asked.

"Diane!" Derek barked.

She lifted a palm. "She's not signing the papers. I don't believe she ever intends to."

Callie got to her feet at this last challenge. The way things were going, she was beginning to feel Diane was right: maybe she wouldn't sign the papers. She didn't care about the house, but she was really getting irked at being treated like a gold digger.

"Where are you moving?" Derek asked.

"Ask William. I'll leave my address with him."

"This have to do with the Laughlins?" Diane asked.

Callie couldn't help jerking in surprise. *William*, she realized. *He told them I asked about the Laughlin family.* She momentarily wondered if that was ethical, then decided it didn't matter one way or the other. "My plans aren't set yet," was all she said as she slid her chair under the table and walked to the glass doors.

"We're not done here," Diane warned.

Callie didn't bother to answer. She flicked a look at Derek, who wouldn't meet her eyes. She was almost more disgusted with him than Diane because of the way he hid behind his sister's skirts, always pretending to be the good guy. "It's almost too bad there isn't any money," she said as she pushed through the doors. "I'm starting to wish I could fight you for it, because God knows Jonathan never wanted either of you to have any of it."

Callie's righteous indignation followed her back to the house, but slowly dissipated as she wandered into Jonathan's den and reseated herself at his desk, staring out the floor-to-ceiling windows to the expanse of sky beyond. The room faced out over the cliff to the sky and down to the snaking freeway far below. Today that sky was dusty gray, which fit her mood. For all her words about fighting Jonathan's siblings, she really just wanted them out of her life. She wanted to move on.

She hoped to high heaven that Victoria would deem her fit to be Tucker's nanny/teacher, and she could move to Castilla and the Laughlin ranch, at least for a while. If it didn't happen, Callie wasn't sure what she would do. She really didn't have a plan B. Hopefully, West would have some influence over his grandmother, but given his relationship with her, it was hard to know which way Victoria would jump.

Either way, she couldn't really make plans until he returned to Los Angeles.

* * *

West prowled the pier, letting his gaze slide over the white spires of sailboat masts, thinking of Egan Rivers's and Jean-Paul's power boats, the *Castaway* and the *Sorciere de Mer.* Could Teresa have been a guest on either one of them? The gendarmerie had looked closely at Rivers and Jean-Paul and had ruled them out. From what West had gleaned from them, Teresa's body hadn't been in the water that long.

So, no . . . she'd been on some other boat.

The body was definitely Teresa's, however. The hospital where Teresa had given birth had sent her records, and Tucker had been given a DNA test. Victoria's people had worked their magic and the results had come back with the match in less than a week, record time, especially given the delay of international political rules and regulations. The body pulled from the bay was Tucker's mother, and Tucker was also related to West, who'd insisted on giving a DNA sample himself.

Aimee had been a problem even after she'd viewed Teresa's body herself. She'd insisted that she had guardianship of Tucker, which had created its own whirl of demands and accusations, and she might have won that battle except that West's DNA was a hereditary match . . . and he also offered her a cash settlement if she signed off.

Aimee had seen the writing on the wall and had reluctantly taken the money and handed over Tucker's passport. West had been in constant contact with Callie, who wanted to come back and be with Tucker. West had been about to tell her to purchase the airline ticket when he'd gotten an unwelcome surprise: Talia Laughlin, Stephen's mother, had called him on his cell phone—she'd gotten the number from Victoria—and announced she was already at the Fort-de-France airport. As Tucker's grandmother, she'd been sanctioned by Victoria to come and escort the boy home, which pissed West off, no end. He would have liked a little heads-up.

Callie would have been the better choice. Tucker knew

her and cared about her and vice versa. But Victoria was already making political moves behind the scenes. He could practically read his grandmother's mind: she wanted Tucker under her control, not West's and Callie's, and any roadblock to her plan would be viewed as a breach of familial duty and trust. If West wanted Callie to be chosen as the boy's nanny, he would have to go along with her plans.

Victoria hadn't changed all that much from when he was a boy.

Unfortunately, the police investigation into how Teresa had fallen into the bay wasn't moving at the pace West wanted. The pressure from Victoria's people only concerned what happened to Tucker; they had little interest in how or why Teresa had died. And since Teresa's death wasn't a clear homicide, though West had been assured the gendarmerie were looking into it, the investigation was at a standstill.

So, while West waited for the legal okay to take Tucker back to the States with him, he was doing his own search into what had happened to Teresa. She'd been planning to leave the night she died, but what had she been doing beforehand? Aimee insisted she hadn't met with Teresa, but West sensed they'd at least spoken to each other. He suspected Aimee had been more forthcoming with the authorities, otherwise they would be grilling her more diligently, but she'd been pointedly disinterested in giving West any information.

Which also pissed him off.

Shortly after Callie had flown home, Dorcas had sent West the asked-for picture of her. Too little, too late, but West had studied Callie's photograph for reasons that were far more personal. She'd gotten under his skin in a way that both elated and worried him.

Dorcas had also had some other surprising news. "Paulsen's in deep shit with Gundy."

"How?" West had asked. Lieutenant Randall Gundy was

Paulsen's immediate superior and generally a pretty hands-off kind of guy.

"You know what a prick Paulsen is. Well, you're not the only one who's gotten on his bad side, and he's been playing kinda fast and loose with his own rules and regs. Has his favorite detectives, as you know, of which you and I aren't among. Really torked Gundy and now Paulsen's under the microscope. I'm thinking you're getting your old job back."

West had hardly known how to take that. He'd been so burned by Roxanne's father he'd walked away with no regrets. Still, his "job" for Victoria was coming to a close and he was going to be looking for another. Vaguely, in the back of his mind, he had both Callie and Tucker as part of his future, but he hadn't known in what capacity. Victoria would fight tooth and nail if he should make any move to adopt Tucker or become his legal guardian, which was an idea definitely swirling through his thoughts. Not that he knew the first thing about being a parent, but Callie did, and she was always part of his nebulous plan as well.

"Glad to hear it," he'd told Dorcas, even while those thoughts coalesced. "Maybe you can get me some more information, now that I'm almost legitimized." And he'd gone on to give him a brief recap about his search for Tucker, the discovery of his sister-in-law's body, and the questions surrounding his brother's death as well.

Dorcas had whistled. "Jesus, man. Wasn't this supposed to be a kind of forced holiday?"

West had ignored that. "It looks like Teresa was a con artist of some kind. Working alone, or with someone. She moved from Martinique to LA, and she lived at the ranch in Castilla with my brother for a couple of years. She met Stephen at an LA club. When I get back, I'm gonna try to follow her trail, see what she did."

"You think she's a homicide?"

"It feels like it to me," he had admitted. "But maybe she

fell off the boat by accident. The gendarmerie aren't saying what they think. It's just a little convenient that she's suddenly dead when I start looking for her."

"Well, okay, man," Dorcas had said dubiously. "If Gundy asks about you, I'll tell him you'll see him as soon as you're back."

"Thanks."

It was after his conversation with Dorcas that West had decided to use his free time to launch his own investigation. The only picture he had of Teresa was the one he'd shown Callie. But he now had a good photo of Callie and they looked enough alike that he'd decided to use it to canvass the pier as well, see if anyone remembered seeing Teresa on the pier the day she died. He hadn't had it in his possession when he'd interviewed Sal DeGregorio—Old Sal, as everyone called him, who'd emigrated from the States years earlier—and asked him about Teresa, but it hadn't mattered. Sal had recognized Teresa from the picture of her with Stephen.

"Ahhh . . . yeah. . . ." he had said, nodding. "That's her, all right. Who's the poor fool with her?"

"Her husband," West had responded. "My brother."

"Sorry, man."

"It's all right. What can you tell me about her?"

It turned out Sal had a lot of stories about Teresa. "Had a whole bunch of different names," he'd reminisced. "I tried to tell people to steer clear, but sometimes a man just wants what he wants and he don't wanna listen to Old Sal."

"She picked up men and used them."

"That's about the size of it, though some of 'em came back for more."

"I heard you thought she had a partner."

"Oh, yeah. One of those guys with laser eyes. He was a watcher who liked what he was seeing. She knew it, too. Part of the fun, I'd say. But I didn't see him this last time."

West had quizzed Old Sal further, but that was about the extent of what he knew. When West had asked if he remembered any of the targeted men's names, Old Sal dolefully shook his head. "They didn't want to tell me. Didn't want me spoiling their affairs, I guess."

Now West looked around, trying to put himself in Teresa's shoes. Why had she come to the pier? As a tourist? Or maybe to pick up a new target? Could she have known that Tucker was on the *Sorciere de Mer?*

"If she talked to Aimee," West said aloud. It was frustrating to have his hands tied by the twin facts that he was a foreigner and he no longer possessed his LAPD identification, although the idea that he might get it back was taking hold.

It was hot. Late afternoon. He ran his fingers through his hair, pulling it away from his face. The gesture made him think of Teresa and Callie's fiery blond hair. So noticeable. It was what had drawn him to Callie in the first place.

Taking out the photo, he canvassed more tourist shops and cafés along the pier.

He was about to give up, when one of the vendors suddenly pointed to the picture and said, "*Oui.* I sell her a *foulard. Pour* the hair, *non?*" He gestured to his own head, miming wrapping it with something.

"She covered her hair with a scarf?" West asked, excited by the acknowledgment that she'd been on the pier.

"*Oui.* Yes. A scarf. Theese one." He pulled a brightly covered fabric rectangle from a rack of many. The design was a map of the island in blues and greens.

West thought about it hard. It was a disguise. She hadn't wanted to be seen. *By whom?* he wondered. *Egan Rivers? Her friend, Aimee? Someone else . . . ?*

"Did you see her with anyone?"

"Mmmm . . . a man, maybe? No, a *femme . . . ?*" He gave West a Gallic shrug and held out his hands.

"Thanks a lot," West said, realizing he'd tapped the man out.

She'd been on the pier and her actions solidified his theory that her death wasn't an accident. Once Tucker was safely in his custody, he was going after Aimee again with some more questions. He'd teased her with the promise of some good old American dollars for Tucker, and he was about to up the ante.

Chapter Twenty

Naomi, Clarice, and even Jerrilyn were already robed and in the prayer room when Daniella was released. She'd had to use the large bowl purposely left in the attic as a chamber pot. She could feel the back of her neck heat when she brought the bowl down and emptied it with all of them watching her as she passed by on her way to the bathroom. Pulling her robe over her head, she seethed with resentment that burned through her veins like lava.

She met the others and they all stood in their places waiting for Andre, though Clarice had moved into Teresa's old spot.

"What did you do to get sent to the attic?" Naomi asked her, but Daniella didn't answer.

"She brought Robert Lumpkin here," Clarice said, shrugging apologetically to Daniella.

Jerrilyn gave Daniella a scathing look. "Jesus Christ, don't tell me you did that on purpose."

"I didn't," Daniella said, but the sound of her voice wasn't convincing.

"You know what this is? It's bullshit," Jerrilyn declared. She ripped off the robe and stood naked in front of them. In a stage whisper, she said, "You know he's fuckin' crazy, don't you? Seriously mad. I don't mind playing the game, but you gotta know when it's over."

Naomi looked affronted. "Shut the hell up." To Daniella and Clarice she snapped, "Jerrilyn's just pissed because Mittenberger got sick of her. Took his toys and went back to his wife."

"Not true. You're such a fucking bitch." Jerrilyn got in Naomi's face and they glared daggers at each other.

"Don't be mad," Clarice said in a little girl's voice but her gaze traveled between them avidly.

Naomi snarled, "We all know you've been playacting the whole time."

"Like you haven't been? All of you . . ." Jerrilyn swept a look to Clarice and then to Daniella.

"I love Andre!" Clarice vowed hotly.

"You can't even call him *the Messiah* 'cause you know he's not," Jerrilyn pointed out. "How long's that going to last before he decides you're a liability, like Teresa?"

"Teresa did bad things," Clarice said, her voice shaking with anger or maybe fear.

"Yeah, like the rest of us deserve halos. You're the worst, Clarice," she sneered, "because you actually think you're something special. Go home to Mama."

Clarice's mouth opened and closed like a fish. "You're terrible!" she cried.

"I'm a realist," Jerrilyn declared loftily, stalking away to her room. "You're the stupid little whore."

"Jerrilyn!" Naomi was stiff with outrage.

"Yeah, yeah . . ." Jerrilyn waved at them airily, not bothering to turn around as she stepped into her room and slammed the door.

Daniella was transfixed. Jerrilyn was leaving?

Clarice was blinking back tears. "Where's she going? I hate her!"

"Where's Andre?" Daniella asked.

"He's late," Naomi said distractedly. "I'll be back." She hurried after Jerrilyn, knocking lightly on her door. Whether Jerrilyn let her in or she just bullied her way, Daniella couldn't tell. But that left her with only Clarice whom she really decided she didn't like. But she couldn't afford to make an enemy of her, especially now, when she'd really screwed the pooch again because Lumpkin had stopped by.

It just wasn't her fault that he'd seen Andre, but no one cared.

Maybe it was *your fault*, the devil on her shoulder pointed out gleefully.

She inwardly sighed. She'd just been so mad that they'd all left her behind that she'd gone out looking for someone to show her a good time. But after a few missed opportunities where no guys seemed interested in her, she'd gone back to Ray's and, lo and behold, there was Lumpkin, hanging out at the bar, talking to the bartenders with one eye on the door. Had he really thought his dream girl in the red dress would come back? Probably. Stupid ass.

But seeing him had made her reverse her decision about him once again. After all, he was *right there*. Maybe she could finish the job Teresa had begun. She didn't have a plan in place, but she could improvise, couldn't she? But just as that thought had crossed her mind, Lumpkin had spied her standing there and she couldn't miss the disappointment and annoyance in his expression when he realized it was Daniella. Oh, yeah. He wanted Teresa. Of course he did.

"What are you doing here?" he had asked her as she walked into the bar, trying to put some enthusiasm in the question. He couldn't quite manage it.

"Looking for you," she answered, stuffing her resentment down. "Or looking for someone," she had amended, smiling. She'd really tried with her appearance that night. Her figure was good. She had nice legs and her breasts weren't bad, and though she hadn't gone home to change, she was wearing a

pair of black slacks and a low-cut pink sweater that did her
proud. Lumpkin's eyes had lingered at her chest and the
fuzzy material. If he hadn't been such a toad, she might have
put one of his hands on one of her breasts just to see the look
on his face.

"What are *you* doing here?" she had asked him a bit flir-
tatiously.

His gaze had sharpened on her, as if noticing her for the
first time. "Just winding down after a hard day."

"What made it so hard?" she had asked, stressing the last
word just a teensy little bit.

"Tenants . . . like you."

"You have other properties?" She'd almost said, *Your
mom have other properties?* but had caught herself at the
last moment.

"Oh, sure. Lots of 'em."

She had been pretty damn sure he was lying, but he was
warming up to her. Over the course of the next hour, she had
watched him knock a few strong ones back while she'd
sipped a glass of chardonnay. She'd wondered if she could
make him her mark. She never really got the adventures that
Teresa and Jerrilyn and sometimes Naomi embarked on.
Andre wanted her to stay out of trouble. Even Clarice got
guys who went gaga over her innocent thing, but she pretty
much always bungled those jobs, never seeing the real
dough Andre was looking for. In truth, Clarice didn't know
how to do much of anything but give Andre the occasional
blow job and cry and the like.

She was an annoying piece of shit.

"I don't make a practice of hanging out with my tenants,"
Lumpkin said.

"I don't hang out with my landlord," she retorted. She
had taken out a tube of lipstick from her purse damn near
the exact shade as her sweater. His eyes had avidly watched
her as she ran it around her lips. She had snapped the cap

back on and smacked her lips. "Maybe we should . . . think about changing that rule?"

"Well, I know where you live." He had given her a predatory smile. "We could go there."

Daniella had felt a thrill of anticipation. Not sexual. Good God, she hadn't wanted this ugly bug anywhere near her. The anticipation had been that she might find a way to end his life and make Andre proud of her. "Let's go to your place. I don't know where you live, and maybe it's time I found out."

He had rolled that over for a moment and then shrugged his agreement.

They had walked outside together and he tried to play grab-ass with her, which really cooled her off. "You okay to drive?" she had asked him dubiously.

"What? You think I'm drunk?"

No shit, Sherlock, she'd thought. He was so unattractive, she was already starting to rethink her plan. She'd just been so angry about everything, and there was Lumpkin. She had known Andre wanted him out of their lives permanently and she'd thought she could do it. *But could I? Really?* An icicle thrill had shot through her at the thought. *Could I? Maybe?* Andre would praise her and make love to her and tell her how valuable she was. *But could I?*

"I just think it's better if I follow you," she'd told him, her teeth chattering with sudden fear at the thoughts swirling inside her head.

He'd snorted in agreement, then asked in surprise, "That yours?" when she turned toward the Xterra.

The hairs on Daniella's arms had shot up, electrified. Did he remember Teresa driving it? "A friend's."

"Who is he?"

"Who says it's a guy?"

He had waved at her, gotten in his vehicle, and then led her back toward his mother's house. She had been creeped out thinking he was planning a "date" with her with Irene in the house, too, but he had driven several blocks past and into an apartment complex that needed a serious paint job. In the light of one lamppost at the edge of the parking lot, she had been able to see the corners of the building were splintered, raw wood graying from the elements.

She'd realized immediately she shouldn't have come. She didn't want to be alone with Lumpkin anywhere and certainly not at some rundown apartment.

She had driven right on past the apartment building and back to their house. She'd half-expected him to follow her home that night, but he hadn't. Not then, anyway. He'd waited until today, right when Andre got back, and that hadn't gone over well.

Now she asked the same question she had earlier, "Where's Andre?" as Clarice stomped out of the prayer room and plopped down in a chair at the dining table.

"I don't know," she declared petulantly. "He was here and told me and Naomi that you were in the attic. I thought he was going to get Jerrilyn, but she's here."

"Is what Naomi said about Mittenberger true?"

"I sure hope so. I hope she disappears in a puff of smoke! She doesn't belong with us."

"Neither did Teresa, anymore," Daniella reminded.

Clarice darted Daniella a look. "I didn't do it, if that's what you're thinking. I didn't like her, but it wasn't me."

"You got to go to Miami at least."

"We went farther than that. We went to Martinique." She was triumphant.

"Huh . . . where's that?" Daniella had to ask but she felt herself burn anew with indignation and fury.

"An island in the Caribbean." She looked around as if expecting someone to be listening. "We all met there, but Andre wasn't around. Naomi seemed to know what she was doing and just took off. I never saw Jerrilyn."

"What did you do?"

"Me? Nothing. I hardly left the airport. I thought we were . . . I don't know, I thought it was a game. I mean, I know it was a game. We weren't really going to do something criminal!" She laughed shortly.

"But Teresa's dead, right? That's what Andre said."

"I don't know. Yeah . . . yeah, I guess she is. I heard someone talking about the woman's body in the bay, so it was Teresa, right? I went right out and caught a flight home as soon as I heard."

"But didn't you just get back?" Daniella blurted out. "You haven't been here."

"I—I went home for a little while." She glanced away and Daniella could tell she was hiding something. "What were you doing with Lumpkin?"

"Hey, it's not my fault he came here," Daniella said, the lie tasting bitter in her mouth. "You think Naomi or Jerrilyn killed Teresa?"

"I don't know. Maybe she just *died*." She clapped her hands over her ears.

"Y'all went there to kill her. One of you did it," Daniella pointed out.

"I would never *kill* someone." Clarice looked shocked at the idea.

"Come on, Clarice. You didn't all take a trip just to play games," Daniella argued. "If you don't want to tell me, fine. But don't act like I don't know what I'm talking about."

Clarice glared at her, but Daniella glared right back. Finally, Clarice said, "Teresa was evil. It's good she's gone."

"Andre liked her best."

Abruptly she got up from the table and stalked off. "If you just want to be hurtful, I'm leaving!"

Daniella watched her leave with mixed feelings. They always got the plum jobs, while she got the shit ones. Even Clarice. And it was just because she wasn't as pretty. Maybe not as seasoned as the rest of them, minus Clarice, who was a naive train wreck waiting to happen, but all of them were out-and-out whores, no matter what story they told themselves. If Andre said go have sex with whomever, they just went off and did it, and even if Clarice tried to act like her shit didn't stink, if he ordered her to kill someone, Daniella bet she'd at least try to please him. Naomi would definitely do it, and Jerrilyn, that mean sex addict, she'd go right ahead and pretend it was her idea.

And Teresa had already killed. First the guy she'd married. Then the one who'd tracked her down and found her at their house. Andre had made her kill him, but Daniella kind of thought that had been the beginning of the end for Teresa . . . and maybe for all of them.

Jerrilyn's raised voice, followed by Naomi's, sounded from Jerrilyn's bedroom. They were quarreling, and Daniella tiptoed forward to listen in. Before she heard more than the fact that Naomi was ripping on Jerrilyn about running out, with an underlying threat/reminder of what had happened to Teresa, which Jerrilyn just laughed at, Andre suddenly came through the front door. He was walking with purpose down the hall and nearly ran over Daniella before turning toward his own bedroom, not even stopping to acknowledge her or the argument he had to have overheard. He didn't say one word to her, which deflated Daniella, although she felt better when he also ignored Clarice's cheery "Oh, there you are!"

The door to his room slammed shut.

This was not usual Andre behavior. Though usually if he was going to close himself in his room he took one of them with him.

Snubbed, Clarice tried to pretend it didn't matter though she practically racewalked to the sanctuary of her own room. *Ha!* Daniella thought, cheered immensely that she was so crushed.

Clarice probably did kill Teresa, Daniella thought uncharitably. It would be just like her to act like it was all so terrible, that she was so pure and innocent, when all the time she was the one who'd drugged Teresa's drink, then threw her over the edge of a boat, if that's what even happened, since no one was really filling her in.

A few minutes later Jerrilyn appeared in black slacks, white blouse, and a black cardigan sweater, a small suitcase in hand. "You're really leaving?" Daniella asked her.

"Happy, are we?" she asked. "He's all yours, honey . . . oh, and Naomi's and Clarice's and whoever he picks up next."

Irked, Daniella shot back, "You just can't face him because Mittenberger cut you off and all that time's been wasted for nothing."

Jerrilyn raked her with a cold glare. "You're all deluded. This is nothing but a joke."

She slammed out of the house. Daniella ran forward to peer through the front windows, half-expecting Jerrilyn to steal one of their cars, but she stopped at the edge of the street and whipped out a cell phone, not one of the ones Andre had gotten for them. One of her own.

She's been planning this, Daniella realized with a start. On the heels of that, she felt jubilant. "Good riddance," she muttered.

She turned to see Naomi standing in the doorway to Jerrilyn's room, still in her prayer robe. Daniella could tell she was furious, though she didn't say anything as she strode in the direction of the prayer room. Daniella followed after her, curious, her gaze lingering momentarily on Andre's closed door. What were they supposed to do now?

Clarice reappeared a few moments later, but she stayed far away from Daniella, as if afraid she would probe with more questions. Well, she would, if she thought Clarice might actually tell her something.

And then Andre came out of his bedroom, but not in his

robe. He was wearing a pair of slacks, a loose white shirt, and suede boots. "It's time," he said, looking faintly regretful as he noticed them all standing in the prayer room.

"You're going out?" Daniella asked, disappointed.

He gave her that *look,* the one he bestowed on them whenever they questioned him. "There's work to be done."

"Jerrilyn just left," Naomi said in a voice that could have cut ice. "She's not coming back."

"She never fit in," Andre said.

His casual dismissal caused Daniella to look from Naomi to Clarice and back again. They all were confused.

"You don't want to . . . go after her?" Clarice asked.

"I have to be somewhere tonight. In the meantime, just stay here and wait for me to call."

"What about our jobs?" Naomi asked. "I thought I was going to Laguna Beach to pick up where Teresa left off."

Andre nodded. "Yes, yes, of course," he said, as if he'd totally forgotten the directive.

"And I'm supposed to have lunch with Todd Bridgewater tomorrow," Clarice said reluctantly. *Staying true to form,* Daniella thought with disgust. All Clarice wanted was Andre.

Kind of like you? her inner bitch pointed out.

"When will you be back?" Naomi asked.

Another no-no, and one Naomi never did. Daniella held her breath, waiting, hoping Andre would chastise her. Maybe shake her like a rag doll until her stupid head snapped and rolled around on her neck.

But he just headed for the door, saying, "I'm taking the Xterra. You've got the Malibu and the Civic."

"How long will you be gone? What about money?" Daniella blurted out, unable to stop herself though she might earn another trip to the attic. But there were still bills to pay and they had to eat.

"I left the safe open," he said. "Don't worry. I'll take care of you."

The safe was *open?*

"What if Lumpkin comes back?" Daniella asked.

Andre hesitated, turning back to them. She watched as he looked from Clarice, to Naomi, to Daniella, a small smile playing on his lips. "Well, I'll be gone now, won't I? If he sees Clarice or Naomi, just tell him they're your friends and they don't live here. Just keep on doing what you're supposed to," he added. "Everything's come down to this and we're all going to be fine."

The door slammed behind him and Daniella suppressed a full-body shiver. Immediately she ran to his room and checked the safe. Inside she saw about three hundred dollars. She pulled out the money, worried at the small sum that wouldn't last long. As she turned away, she caught the dull, golden glow of one of the ankhs, lying on the floor. He'd been in such a rush he hadn't noticed it had dropped to the ground. *Was it Teresa's?* she wondered. He'd never given one to anyone else that she knew of. Before the others could find it, she slipped it over her head and under her robe, warmed by its coldness against her skin.

She had a feeling Andre wasn't coming back.

Gary Merritt, Victoria's lawyer, was the one who finally called West to tell him everything was set for him to bring Tucker back to the States. It was six P.M. and he was seated at the hotel bar, just finishing the Bakoua's take on a chicken salad sandwich served with mango, pineapple, and papaya when he got the call. Merritt assured him that Aimee had already been told and that he and Tucker were booked on the last flight out, the same one Teresa had planned to take.

He signed the meal to his room and was just leaving when he saw Talia Laughlin crossing toward him. He stopped short. Their relationship, such as it was, had always been an uneasy one; she didn't really want to deal with her husband's bastard son.

"There you are," she said.

He held up his phone. "I just got a call from Gary Merritt, Victoria's lawyer."

"I just spoke to him too. Looks like everything's set, but I just got here. Let's go tomorrow."

West looked at the slim, raven-haired woman with the sharp features. He remembered Talia from when he was a kid and invited to the ranch by his father. He'd been aware then that she was watching him like a hawk, though he hadn't understood all the ins and outs of what had transpired. To her credit, she'd never been outwardly awful to him, though he was pretty sure she and his mother had had words.

On his first trip to meet with Victoria to discuss finding Teresa, he'd been reintroduced to her. She'd been civil enough and had professed to being as interested in having Tucker back as Victoria was, though he'd since come to realize maybe she wasn't quite as eager as she'd have him believe.

West wasn't exactly sure how Tucker's guardianship was all going to play out, but he was determined to have Callie be at the ranch. Tucker needed someone completely on his side.

"It's best to get Tucker away from Aimee as fast as possible," West told Talia now.

"What's her stake in all this?"

"Money."

"Well, of course." Her lips tightened, then she shook her head. "Well, fine. I haven't even really unpacked, so I'll be ready. When are you planning to pick Tucker up?"

"Now."

"Oh, dear. I hope you know I'm going with you, but I really need to get something to eat first," she said.

"You can order at the bar," he said.

"Oh, can I?" She lifted her brows at his proprietary manner.

"Or you can go somewhere else and Tucker and I will meet you at the airport."

"You're just a joy to get along with, aren't you?"

West shrugged, and she said, "Fine," sat down at the bar, and ordered the exact same sandwich West had just finished.

An hour later they were on their way. The taxi driver double-parked outside the apartment building but assured them he would find a spot and stay for as long as they needed. He and West exchanged numbers, then West led Talia into the dark hallway outside Aimee's apartment. Before he even had a chance to knock, Aimee swept open the door and stared at him coldly. "I know," she bit out, stepping back to allow them entry. She and Talia, both slim and dark, looked each other up and down warily.

"Talia, this is Aimee Thomas," West introduced. "Aimee . . . Talia Laughlin. And here's Tucker," he added when the boy charged into the room, but came to a skidding stop near Aimee.

"Where is Callee?" he asked West.

"She's back home in Los Angeles. That's where we're going." He pointed to himself and then Tucker.

"I want Callee," he whispered, looking down at the floor.

Talia stepped forward and said, "You're going to go to a ranch with cattle and horses and cowboys."

Aimee's face was a thundercloud. She tried to put an arm around Tucker but he slid sideways, out of her reach. Warily, he came closer to West. "Michel go too?" he asked.

"No, Michel's not going!" Aimee snapped. She stalked across the room and swept up a small suitcase that looked as if it had been purchased new. Then she grabbed an envelope from a side table and held it up. "His passport. Still good."

She moved forward and slapped it into West's palm, then stood back and crossed her arms.

"You've been evasive about Teresa. You had to have talked to her during her last trip here," West said.

"You want answers, talk to the gendarmerie."

"I want answers," he agreed.

"Not my problem," she said coolly.

West would have liked to interrogate her some more, but this clearly wasn't the time and the place, and it was more important to tiptoe away with Tucker than antagonize her. He pulled a thick envelope from inside his coat pocket and exchanged it for the one she held out to him. She took the money without saying anything. It was a generous amount, but if it was enough to keep her from trying to gum up the works, that was fine with both him and Victoria.

"I'm sure you've taken good care of him," Talia put in a bit desperately. West could tell she was worried he was going to somehow screw things up.

"How are you related?" Aimee demanded of her.

"I'm Tucker's grandmother," she said. "He's my son's son."

Hearing that, Tucker pressed himself into West's leg, as Aimee silently assessed Talia. "I stay with you and Callee?" Tucker whispered to West.

"Yes, but first we've got to fly on an airplane to where she is," West said firmly when Talia opened her mouth to apparently argue the point. He grabbed up Tucker's suitcase and asked, "This all?" Aimee nodded curtly, and then he herded both Tucker and Talia out the door ahead of him.

Andre drove carefully, aware that something wasn't quite right inside his head. If he thought about it, it worried him a little, but most of the time he ignored it. Naomi was always jabbering about a doctor she knew whom she wanted him to see, but he wouldn't trust any one of the handmaidens to choose anything for him.

He'd had an epiphany, of sorts, about Teresa. He was pretty sure which one of the women had killed her, though he wasn't certain it was a true memory or something his brain had manufactured. The way the handmaidens had all acted on the trip, as if it were some vacation that he was just paying for, had really sent him into a dark funk.

But now, as he drove to Laughlin Ranch, his ranch, he had a glimmering of what had happened.

His cell phone rang and he stared at the screen. His mouth curved into a feral smile, and he answered, "Miss me already?"

"It's laughable, the way everyone thinks I'm someone else. I should get an Academy Award," the caller said.

"Teresa was good at that too," he reminded her, knowing he was purposely goading her.

"She certainly thought so," was her cool response.

"I have to go. I don't want to be pulled over because I'm talking to you on a cell phone."

"Have you got everything ready for me? Everything I need?" she asked.

He thought briefly of the prayer room, the robes, rites, and sex, and had a moment of melancholy, realizing he wouldn't be able to pick among the handmaidens any longer. But were they really worth it, anyway? There was so much bickering, backstabbing, and disruption, and his head couldn't handle the noise of it all. Besides, he was moving into a new phase, the place he'd been driving toward for most of his life. He was almost there.

"The rest of them will have to be gotten rid of," she reminded him. "Isn't that what you said?"

He grunted his agreement, though her high-handed manner annoyed him. She should know better than to test him. "Whose boat did you use to take Teresa out?" he asked.

A hesitation. "You really want to know all the details?"

So, it was her. He'd thought so. "No."

"It'll be just you and me, right?" she questioned.

No . . . it could never be just one woman. Maybe he could have been faithful to Teresa, but not to anyone else. But she didn't have to know that. "Just you and me," he told her.

"I'm thinking about what I want you to do to me," she said suggestively. "Where I want it . . . *how* I want it. You get me?"

That woke up his slumbering dick. "I get you."

She trilled with laughter. "Just as long as you're okay," she said as she hung up.

The reminder of his health sent his cock into a quick downswing. Damn her. Damn them all.

It was definitely time to move on.

Callie awoke in the middle of the night, trying to capture the stray thought that had been circling around her fragmented dreams. She reached for her cell phone, the smartphone she'd left in LA when she'd taken off for Martinique, and reread West's last text, which had come in around ten P.M., her time. He was spending the night in Miami with Tucker. They'd missed a connecting red-eye flight to Los Angeles, and were staying at an airport hotel. Tucker had been asleep on his feet and West was getting him settled. They were scheduled to leave the next morning and would arrive on the West Coast around noon. Reading between the lines, Callie thought Tucker had to be discombobulated over leaving everything he'd ever known. She wanted to call West, but figured it was best to let him call her.

Climbing out of bed, she walked into the kitchen, flipping on the under-cabinet lights. A Keurig machine sat on the counter, something Jonathan had purchased and she'd thought she'd never use. Now she pulled down a mug from the cupboard and set it under the machine's spigot. She selected a tiny bucket of decaf coffee, dropped it into its cylindrical, fitted slot, shut the top, and pressed the button for the size of cup she wanted. Immediately, a stream of hot coffee began pouring into her mug.

Jonathan . . . she thought. That's what she'd been thinking about.

As soon as the brown liquid slowed to a stop, she picked up the mug and carried it with her into the den, switching on the desk lamp, which offered a circle of soft light on the mahogany desktop.

Instead of seating herself in his chair again, she walked over to the credenza and slid back one of the doors. Inside was a small box that held Jonathan's keys, his wallet, the Mercedes's registration, their proof of automobile insurance, a number of pens, change, and other small items: the personal detritus left from the accident that she'd collected and never put back in its proper spots. Callie had paid no attention to any of it, but now she picked up the ring of Jonathan's keys, wondering what they all went to. That's what she'd been thinking about. Secret places where he could hide money, or papers, or who knew what. Derek and Diane were sure there was a cache of something somewhere.

She took the keys to the desk, examining them under the light. There was a house key and the one for the Mercedes, and a defunct one for the safe-deposit box that had been drilled after his death and revealed a copy of the legal papers that left the house to the Cantrells. There were two other keys as well. One was to his father's office, which Jonathan had retained after his death and which Callie had paid for until the lease's end, about two months before she'd left for Martinique. The last key was a mystery. She'd thought it might be to the private bathroom within that office, but she'd never checked it.

Setting the keys down, she returned to the credenza,

pulling out the box itself. A stack of envelopes fell out and slid onto the carpet. Bank statements from this last year that she'd glanced through and then shoved haphazardly back into the credenza.

She hadn't really examined them closely since she'd been home. In fact the latest month was still unopened. Jonathan had been gone over a year, and the joint account was solely hers now. There wasn't any other bank account that she knew of.

Picking up the stack, she brought it and the box to the desktop too. Pushing the box aside, she grabbed the un-opened envelope of the bank statement, ripped off a corner, then slid her finger inside and tore it jaggedly open. Unfold-ing the document, she glanced over the charges, most of them from her time on Martinique. It made her heart beat fast to think about Tucker and West arriving soon. Her rea-sons for going to Martinique had all been about her past, but she'd found a future there, instead.

She smiled as she recognized the line of purchases, fol-lowing her own progress via her debit card. Two-thirds of the way down she noticed a charge that wasn't hers and imme-diately zeroed in on it. "Security One annual fee."

"Well, that's wrong," she said aloud. She'd cancelled the house alarm system. It wasn't with Security One and they'd changed to wireless. And in any event, there hadn't been an annual fee. They'd paid by the month.

Fine. She'd call them in the morning and get them to re-verse the charge. Stacking the envelopes, she set them aside, then picked up the ring of keys again and looked at the mys-tery one. She supposed she could give it to Derek and Diane, let them try to figure out where it went.

"No." Dropping the keys back in the box, she then gath-ered up the bank statements and shoved them back in the credenza. She was a little sorry she'd told Derek and Diane

the house would soon be theirs. Though it didn't feel like
home to her any longer, as time went on, she was getting less
and less interested in leaving it. She just didn't feel like
being that helpful, and the way she saw it, there was no set
time she had to vacate. If they wanted to push her out and
take possession, they could just go ahead and start legal pro-
ceedings.

Maybe she'd just let them do that.

Chapter Twenty-One

Callie waited outside the TSA checkpoint, wringing her hands. Realizing what she was doing, she released her grip and shook her wrists. Geez, Louise. She had to relax.

Ten minutes later she caught her first glimpse of Tucker walking beside West. His head was down and he was taking giant, swinging steps. She could tell he was tired.

"Tucker," she called, though her eyes strayed to West, who saw her and started to smile.

That smile was devastating and she literally felt herself go weak at the knees. *Oh, my God,* she thought, her own smile spreading across her face.

"Calleeeeee!" Tucker called, immediately running toward her.

She swept him up. "I'm so glad to see you!"

"*Moi, aussi.* When do we see horse?" he asked.

"Ummm. Soon . . . ?" She looked to West for support and noticed the middle-age woman with the fixed smile who was walking behind West but staring at Callie.

As if realizing Callie was looking at her, she stepped around West who'd stopped when Tucker had jumped into Callie's arms. "I'm Talia. Laughlin," she added, reaching out a hand. "Tucker's grandmother."

"Oh, well, hello," Callie said, shaking her hand. What did this mean?

"Victoria sent Talia to escort us both," West explained neutrally. Callie couldn't get a bead on his feelings, but she thought he wasn't all that thrilled with the arrangement.

"Are we . . . all going to the ranch?" Callie asked.

"I'll have to join you there later," Talia said. "I want to go home first, but I also want to make sure this little man gets acclimated." She smiled widely at Tucker, who turned away from her, burying his face into Callie's shoulder.

A flash of annoyance crossed Talia's face, but then she was all graciousness again. West's hand brushed purposely, she saw, against Callie's as they headed toward baggage claim, and her skin felt electrified. They waited at the carousel and when Tucker pointed out his suitcase, Callie grabbed it at the same moment West collected his bag. Then she dutifully helped Talia as her monstrosity of a bag lumbered toward them. Talia pulled out her handle and wheeled her bag away, giving them a wave as she headed out to the taxi stand.

"My car's in the lot," Callie said. "And I brought a booster seat for Tucker."

"Booster seat?" Tucker screwed up his face in a question.

"Nothing you've had to date," Callie said, to which West snorted his agreement. "It's the law here," she added in case Tucker took objection to the idea. "A cool, special seat."

"Cool, special seat." Tucker held up his hand to high-five her.

Callie threw West a smile, realizing this had to be his work. He acknowledged that with a return smile. She found herself holding his gaze, felt her blood heat a little, and wrenched her eyes away first.

They'd already worked it out that she was going to drive to West's apartment where he planned to pick up his vehicle as well, and then she would follow him the two and a half hours it would take to reach Laughlin Ranch outside the city of Castilla.

"You'll have to give me directions, too, in case I lose you," she reminded.

"Sure. But you won't lose me."

Hoping there was a double entendre in his response, Callie led the way through cool October sunshine toward her Lexus with Tucker traipsing along beside her, regaling her with his impressions from their trip—the airplane was loud, the flight attendants gave him snacks, the people in front got mad when he kicked their seat, a baby cried and it hurt his ears—his hand in hers, his arms swinging. Even while she was attentive to him she was supremely conscious of West: his beard-darkened chin, the curve of his lips, the breadth of his shoulders. It had been less than two weeks since she'd seen both of them, but it was long enough to make their time in Martinique seem slightly surreal.

"Seeing you's been good for him," West said, glancing at Tucker meaningfully.

Only for him? As soon as she thought the words she wanted to kick herself. There would be time to sort out their relationship later. Right now Tucker was the main concern.

West directed her to his apartment, which was just outside of Santa Monica on Wilshire Boulevard and inside the Los Angeles city limits. It was a complex of about forty units and West's was a second-floor corner unit. As soon as they stepped inside he dropped his bag and she got a look around the cream-colored walls and brown carpeting, noticing the absence of furniture apart from a massive television set and leather couch.

"I've been stuck in early post-college American," he admitted.

"You need a healthy stretch of HGTV."

He glanced at the television. "You'd think I'd have time to watch it, but it doesn't happen."

"Big TV," Tucker said, impressed. "We stay here?" He was already snatching up the remote.

"Just long enough for me to change," West said, picking up his bag and heading toward the bedroom.

Callie eased the remote from Tucker's fingers and switched through the channels until she found Nick Jr.

"There'll be a TV at the ranch, too," she assured him. From down the short hall she heard the rush of the shower and had a mental vision of West's naked body under the spray.

"I want to see horses," Tucker reminded Callie.

"Me, too."

Callie had already stowed a small bag in the Lexus. She didn't know exactly what to expect from this first meeting with Victoria, but she'd packed for an overnight just in case. She knew Tucker would not want her to leave, and though she would like to stay with him as well, the decision wasn't up to her. The fact that West was taking his own car suggested he didn't trust they would be on the same schedule, either.

A few minutes later the shower shut off, and ten minutes after that West came out wearing jeans, cowboy boots, and a cream-colored suede shirt. He looked so different that she couldn't take her eyes off him. "I didn't pack my ranch gear," she said. "Wait. I forgot. I don't own any."

He gave her his slow smile and she wanted to throw herself into his arms and kiss him madly. Spreading his hands, he said, "This is me."

"I like it," she said, and there was a whole wealth of meaning packed into her words that she hadn't meant to convey.

"You ready?" he asked.

"Where's your bag?" she questioned.

"I've got to come back tonight. Looks like I'm going back to my old job. Meeting with my lieutenant tomorrow."

He threw a look toward Tucker, who was engrossed in *Yo Gabba Gabba*.

"Oh. I put an overnight bag in my car, just in case," she admitted.

"Good. I wanted you to." He hooked a thumb toward Tucker, and said softly, "It was kind of hard on the plane. He doesn't really know about Teresa, but he senses something's up."

Callie nodded, staring at the back of Tucker's head, wanting to drag him close to her.

It took a little bit of convincing to disengage Tucker from the television and herd him back to Callie's car. Leaning in the window, West gave her quick directions to the ranch, which mostly consisted of which exit to take off I-5. "All you really have to do is follow the signs," he said, then he headed to a black Explorer, backing it out of a numbered parking spot that was lined up beside others in a carport that stretched the length of the building. He aimed the Explorer toward I-5 and Callie followed behind him as they began the trip north to Laughlin Ranch.

Andre stood inside the floor-to-ceiling windows of the rambling two-story house with its rustic, wood interior and looked out onto the main acres of the ranch. Miles of fencing and a scattering of barns and outbuildings were visible as far as the eye could see. He could almost taste the wealth and had to hide how much he coveted all of it. By rights, it should be his and he intended to have it.

The old woman in the crisp white blouse, tan slacks, and sensible brown shoes with her frost-white hair and imperious manner regarded him like an insect on a pin. She was standing in the archway of the dining room, one gnarled hand clasped hard around the handle of her cane. One tiny push and she would fall over and clatter to the floor.

He couldn't stop laughing inside at the image.

"Mr. Stutz is on his way," she said for about the third time, as if that would scare him. "He's the man in charge of Laughlin Ranch."

"Since my cousin's death," Andre said.

"Since my grandson's death," Victoria corrected. "Whether he was your cousin or not is still in question."

"Take your DNA samples, check my identification, look at me. All I heard all my life was that I looked just like my father."

Andre met her gaze squarely. On the one hand, he felt like he should be nice to her. She was his grandmother, too, after all, and just because she and her husband had kicked his father out of the family didn't mean she would disown him. Now that he was back, he couldn't see why she wouldn't put him in Stephen's place. His father was her first born, Benjamin Jr., and it stood to reason that Andre would be next in line to inherit. Whatever bad blood had transpired among Victoria, Benjamin Sr., and his father shouldn't affect Andre's relationship with his grandmother now.

On the other hand, he hated her with an intensity he couldn't deny. His father, crazy bastard that he'd been, had chosen his Tahitian wife and a life as an ex-pat, and therefore been rejected by Benjamin Sr., Victoria, and Laughlin Ranch, Inc. It was no way to treat family. His father had always acted like he'd made the choice and would do it again, but on the two occasions he'd actually flown back with Andre in tow, Andre had overheard him fighting with Ben Sr. who'd been adamant that Ben Jr. was disinherited forever.

"You do bear a resemblance," she allowed, and he thought it about killed her to admit as much. She moved into the dining room but he stayed where he was, looking out at the expanse of prime real estate that would be his, by hook or by crook.

When Andre's father had said he didn't care that he'd been disowned, Andre had believed him, too young to understand the pain beneath his father's cavalier attitude. But Ben Jr. had cared, and even the worshipful flock that Ben Laughlin Jr. brought together on the Tahitian island of Moorea, the group of women who attended his needs and loved their priest with all their hearts, hadn't completely fulfilled him. He was their Messiah, and after his death, they looked to sixteen-year-old Andre to take his place. Andre had happily stepped into his father's shoes, but he hadn't been interested in a life of near poverty, so in the end he'd taken off, leaving his mother and the other heartbroken women of his tribe to mourn Ben Jr.'s death from cancer.

He'd planned to sneak away but his mother caught him before he could make his escape. He'd expected her to rail at him for running out, but all she said was, "You have a mission to fulfill. To take your rightful place. Go back . . . and make those people pay."

He'd promised her he would, though he'd taken a circuitous route before he found his way home. Too bad his mother had also died before seeing her son on his rightful throne; he'd gotten news of her death last year from one of his father's disciples when he'd placed his annual call to her on her birthday. That had made him want to take over the ranch immediately, but he'd had to wait. But now he was here and he wasn't leaving. Sure, Victoria had refused to let him in last night when he'd shown up on her doorstep, even after he'd explained who he was, but she'd allowed him to come back this morning. *Allowed* him . . . Things were going to change very soon.

He finally turned away from the window and walked into the dining room where she sat regally at the head of the table. "I don't know what you think is going to happen," she said in that crisp way he was coming to loathe. "Even if you are who you say you are, this is not your home. Your father—"

"My father made an error of judgment by leaving. On his deathbed he asked for you. He knew his father was gone, but that you were still here. He wanted to come back to you."

"I doubt that's true." She was firm.

"He came back twice, with me. I remember being here."

"Your name was Andrew, not Andre," Victoria said coolly.

"Andrew is the name on my birth certificate, in honor of my great-grandfather, but my mother always called me Andre."

"Your mother," she said, and something implied in her tone crystallized the hate inside him he needed to keep under control.

"Yes."

There was a rap on the back door and both he and Victoria turned their heads toward the kitchen, which was through a butler's pantry from the dining room. Andre heard the cook-*cum*-housekeeper-*cum*-all around assistant to Victoria open it, and a male voice call out, "Victoria? You there!"

"That's Cal now. Mr. Stutz," Victoria said, rising from her chair and thumping her way toward the kitchen. "I'm here," she sang out in a warm voice that implied she was close to the ranch manager. Another thing that would need to change.

Andre didn't follow her. Instead he moved from the dining room back to the great room with its soaring rafters, antlered chandeliers, and stretches of windows that framed the rolling grassland. He knew the cattle were kept far away from the house and that the ranch hands drove pickups to the barns and outbuildings. There was a picturesque barn on a slight ridge where horses had been kept when he was younger. He remembered riding them with Stephen once. He wasn't sure if there were still some there.

Hearing approaching voices, he turned to see a tall,

middle-age man with sun-weathered skin in jeans, boots, and holding a Stetson walk into the great room with a familiarity that put Andre's teeth on edge. "Hello, there," he said, in a friendly manner, holding out a hand and moving toward him. "I'm Cal Stutz. I understand you say you're Ben Jr.'s boy?"

"That's right. Andre Laughlin," he said, shaking the man's calloused palm.

"Andre," Cal repeated, turning to Victoria, who'd followed after him, and raising a brow. "Well, I guess I don't go by my given name, either. Some people call me Ted, but I prefer Cal, for California. I've been ranching here all my life. My son's Teddy."

Andre fought down his immediate dislike of the man and managed a tight smile, but Cal had already turned his attention to Victoria, again.

"Teddy's here," he told her.

"In town, or at the ranch?" she asked, sounding surprised.

"Here at the ranch. Got him working for me, for a while. We'll see how long that lasts." He switched back to Andre. "So, how long are you staying?"

The presumption that he would be leaving outraged Andre. "I plan to make Castilla my home. It's where I'm from."

"Uh-huh." He just managed to keep from exchanging another glance with Victoria. "Well, looks like it's old home week for a lot of people. You'll get to meet your cousin and your . . . I don't rightly know. Is Tucker a second cousin, or a first once removed? Dang, but that one's always been a poser."

"If you are Andrew Laughlin, then Tucker is your first cousin, once removed," Victoria said with certainty.

Andre knew about the boy, and he didn't like the warm tone to Victoria's voice when she talked about him.

"That sounds fairly distant," he said, fighting back the urge to remind her yet again that he *was* Andrew Laughlin.

"He's my great-grandson," Victoria defended.

Andre had pretty much dismissed the boy as a threat to his inheritance. Sure, the kid was Craig's grandson, but by all the laws of inheritance that should matter, Andre was the one in direct succession, not Stephen, nor Craig's bastard son, West, nor the issue of either of them. But Victoria wasn't greeting Andre with open arms the way she should whereas she seemed to be anticipating this child's arrival. Cold snakes of fear wriggled through him at the thought that he might have already been usurped and that set off splitting pain inside his head. He had to turn back to the vista of land to hide his expression.

"When are they showing up?" Cal was asking.

"Later today. Maya's got Tucker's room ready, and also the nanny's, who'll be arriving with him, I'm told."

"Something wrong with the nanny?" Cal asked, hearing the disapproval Victoria didn't try to hide.

"I'm just not certain she's the right choice. We'll see." Clearly she didn't want to talk further in front of Andre. In a louder voice, she said primly, "Mr. Laughlin, I need to be sure you are who you claim to be—"

"Your grandson," he said tightly, fighting through the pain.

"And that will take some time. I have your number and my lawyer will call you once the verisimilitude of your claim is established."

Cal said, "Ma'am, I sure love it when you use big words."

Victoria actually laughed and Andre ground his teeth together. Luckily, the first wave of the attack was subsiding and he was feeling better.

"When Teddy gets here, let me know," Victoria said.

"He hasn't changed any," Cal admitted a bit dolefully. "Still walking that line between what you should do and you shouldn't."

"Hmmm . . ." Victoria didn't seem to know what to say to that.

Andre turned back around, wondering what that was all about, but of course they didn't tell him. And then to add insult to injury, Cal said to him, "Come along, son. I'll walk you to the door. And you get off your feet, now," he told Victoria.

"Don't nag me," she said, but a smile threatened her stern lips.

Andre had no choice but to follow Cal Stutz to the door, and he hated every second of it. By the time the door was closed firmly behind him, his blood was boiling. Victoria—*his own grandmother*—was way too friendly with the help. This wasn't right. It needed to be stopped. He was going to stop it. And they needed to learn that he was The Messiah, and he was going to have his rightful place at the head of this family, even if he had to kill for it.

West was about a half hour from the I-5 turnoff when his cell rang, and he answered through the Bluetooth receptor at his ear. "Laughlin," he said, reading the number and seeing it was Pete Dorcas.

"Where you at, man? Thought you were coming in," his old partner said.

"Tomorrow. I got stuff to do today."

"Yeah? Well, stuff's happenin' here. Your French friends are callin'. You know, the ones you told to call you here? Even though *you're* not officially here and so they call me? They say they're lookin' at a homicide."

"They're certain?" West asked, ignoring the jab. He'd pressed the gendarmerie as much as he could and given them Dorcas's number. He had purposely been vague about his liaison with the LAPD, letting Dorcas field the calls and be the go-between. For that price, he had to put up with some shit from his partner.

"Head injury killed her, but someone had choked her

with some kind of chain. Maybe didn't kill her, but it wasn't friendly, either."

West nodded. "There were marks on her neck, but I didn't get a good look." He'd practically been shoved aside by the French authorities. "Why'd they take so long to get back to me," he grumbled.

"'Cause maybe they knew you were fudgin' some about your job?"

"Did they send a copy of the autopsy report?"

"Not yet."

Before he'd left Fort-de-France, West had notified the police that Teresa had been seen on the pier, and they'd thanked him for the information and said they were looking for the boat she'd been on. "Did they say anything else?"

"Nope. You can call 'em tomorrow. Now, you also asked me about the Cantrells."

West's interest sharpened. "That's right. You find something interesting?"

"Here's what I know: There's a brother and sister left. Their father's the one made the money. Older brother got it all, until the accident that killed him. Now, it's split between the deceased older brother's wife and his younger brother and sister. House is with the wife, but it's supposed to go back to the family, according to Diane Cantrell, who showed up at the station in person and made it pretty clear she doesn't much like the wife, Kelly . . . no, Callie, and this Callie is still living at the house and Diane is working to legally evict her. I talked to the family attorney first, a William Lister who apparently told this Diane that we were on the case, so Diane shows up at the station and just goes off. I listened to her as long as I could stand, then gave her your name. Told her that *you'd* call her."

"Thanks," West said dryly.

"Like I said, man. This is your baby."

West glanced in his rearview mirror to Callie's silver

Lexus, which was following at a safe distance behind him. He felt kinda sleazy, checking up on her now, and he sure as hell didn't want to hear anything bad at this point. He wanted Callie. Had from the moment he'd first seen her and thought she was Teresa, which was probably the kind of thing that should send him to a therapist's couch. And he knew, deep in his gut, that he'd never felt this way about Roxanne . . . had never felt this way about any other woman.

"And he wasn't happy with the wife, either, according to the sister," Dorcas was saying, and West snapped back, realizing he'd maybe missed something important.

"Who?"

"The younger brother. Derek Cantrell. Ain't you listenin'? According to Diane, Derek wants Ms. Callie out too. The house is worth a few mil but Ms. Callie's not budgin'."

"But the house is hers."

"Not supposed to be. I'm just sayin' what they said. Diane thinks Ms. Callie has always been after the family money, and now she's got the upper hand."

West thought about what Callie had said about her husband, Jonathan, knowing Teresa. It had been constantly in the back of his mind ever since she'd mentioned it. He just needed some time to be able to follow up, and to date, time was the commodity he hadn't possessed. He wanted to know more about Jonathan Cantrell, for sure, but first things first.

"I'll call Diane back," West said, not sure when that would be exactly.

"That woman's a piece of work, for sure. Kinda hot in that bitchy thrown-you-down-on-the-ground-and-stomp-on-you-before-screwing-your-brains-out way. Maybe too scary to act on, though. Y'know?"

"But you think she's telling the truth?" West asked, trying to keep the thread of the conversation on track. Dorcas had a tendency to categorize women by how they'd be in the sack, which was sometimes colorful, and always beside the point.

"She believes what she's sayin'. Don't necessarily make it true."

West let the matter of Diane Cantrell lie for a moment. "Teresa Laughlin was living in Los Angeles when she met my brother. She met him at a bar. I don't know which one yet, but I'm going to find out. This was about six years ago. I think she might've come back to LA after his death. She probably had a California driver's license. See what you can find on her. I want to know where she lived, what she did." *And if she continued her relationship with Jonathan Cantrell in there somewhere.*

"It's not like I'm sittin' on my hands here," he protested.

"I'll be at work tomorrow, and if I'm reinstated, I'll get on it myself. But anything you could find out would help."

"Yeah, yeah." A pause. "Gonna be good to have you back."

"Gonna be good to be back."

He clicked off the Bluetooth, glanced back again to Callie's car. Five minutes later he saw the exit for Castilla, put on his blinker, and took the off ramp.

Callie inhaled a deep breath as she followed West's Explorer off the freeway and toward the town of Castilla. She'd seen the sign on the freeway extolling Laughlin Ranch beef and the Laughlin BBQ restaurant. Now, she saw more signs for the barbecue and one for the gift shop, The Bull Stops Here, but they bypassed the main section of the town and turned onto a road that ran dead east, which presumably led to the ranch itself.

What a complete change for Tucker. She slid a look to her rearview mirror and saw his head was bent forward. He'd conked out almost immediately once they'd hit the freeway. Too much excitement, too much worry about what was in store for him. Callie wished she could protect him and decided if there was any way possible, she would spend the night at the ranch tonight. She was basically his only stability in a strange new world.

Her gaze next touched on her shoulder bag, which was sitting in the passenger seat. Besides her clothes and toiletries, she'd stuffed the bank statement with the automatic charge from Security One inside as well. She'd called Security One before she left the house, but they hadn't picked up and she hadn't bothered to leave a message. It would be one more nagging annoyance she'd need to deal with when she finally decided to cut ties with the Cantrells once and for all, but it could wait. Everything could wait until she was certain Tucker was settled.

Of its own accord, her mind went back to that last meeting with Derek and Diane, which made her grimace with distaste. Luckily, her attention was jerked back to the present when she saw West's Explorer crest a small hill and disappear. Half a minute later, she followed after him and then before her was a thick grove of California black oaks that spread for a number of acres, only petering out when it reached a series of rolling hills that seemed huddled against today's gray skies. Up to this point, the landscape had been virtually flat grassland, but here was an oasis of green that she suspected had been purposely planted. West's Explorer turned north into a long lane bordered by the oaks. Callie followed and a wide canopy of branches reached overhead as they drove along the extensive drive, which suddenly opened to the Laughlin ranch house sitting like a queen on a throne at the end of a long carpet. The two-story structure had two wings, which pushed backward from the drive.

There were several trucks parked to the east side and West pulled up next to one.

Exhaling, Callie slowed to a stop beside his car and switched off the ignition. West was already out of the Explorer and now he came to her window, throwing a glance back toward Tucker whose eyes were trying to open as Callie slid the window down.

"Home, sweet home," West said dryly, and pulled open her door.

Chapter Twenty-Two

From his vantage point at the top of one of the hills about a quarter mile away, Andre trained his binoculars on the ranch house. Because of all the damn trees he had limited vision to the front of the house; he could see for miles out the back with the paddocks, fencing, and in the distance the small, hazy shapes of cattle. The sky was overcast and the temperature was cooling off, the weather system more like that of January than October.

He watched a dark-haired man get out of the car. His cousin, West Laughlin, Victoria had said, though he wasn't really a Laughlin and therefore didn't count. From everything Andre had been told Benjamin Sr. and Victoria were too uptight, repressed, and infused with a different century's morals to consider as a rightful heir any child from Craig's dalliance with one of their employees.

He might have to take care of him, but he wasn't really the problem. The boy, though . . . the way Victoria obviously felt about him . . . he was going to have to be dealt with.

He watched West open the door to the silver Lexus that had followed his Explorer to the front of the house. A woman stepped out, her red-gold hair shining in the late afternoon sun.

A jolt ran through him and he gasped, "Teresa!" before he realized this had to be the nanny.

Teresa is dead. She's dead. Never to return.

But for a moment, watching the woman, he wasn't entirely sure.

The front door was opened by a tall, rangy man with salt-and-pepper hair and a weathered face. Callie inadvertently squeezed Tucker's hand a little tighter as the man stepped back and said, "Well, come on in." Even though he oozed bonhomie she hadn't felt this nervous since she'd first met Jonathan's sister and brother, and that hadn't gone well.

"I'm Cal," he said, sticking out a hand. "You must be the nanny."

Callie reluctantly released Tucker's hand to shake Cal's. "Callie Cantrell."

"Cal and Callie," he responded with a grin. "That's gonna make things hard around here."

"I hope not," Callie said lightly.

"And you must be the little man Victoria's been expecting," Cal said, bending down to Tucker's level.

Tucker gazed at him solemnly and stayed silent.

West brought up the rear and Cal stood up and thrust out his hand again. "Good to see you again, son," he said. "Your grandmother's in the dining room."

"Thanks," West answered.

Cal glanced down again at Tucker, who had reclasped Callie's hand. He chuckled. "Cat got your tongue, huh?"

"No." Tucker frowned at him, then looked up at Callie.

"It's an expression," she told him. "A funny way of saying that you're being kind of quiet. Tucker's first language is French," she added for Cal's benefit.

"Well, *parlez-vous français!*" Cal declared, amused.

"Cal is the Laughlin Ranch manager," West said as they moved through the foyer and into the house.

Callie caught a glimpse of the great room with its curved beams, river rock fireplace, hanging lights made from deer antlers, and an expanse of oak flooring that was artfully arranged with groupings of couches and chairs before she was ushered into the dining room with its cathedral ceiling and massive plank table of black walnut.

At the end of the table sat a woman with silvery-white hair swept up and clipped at the back of her head. Her strong face was webbed with tiny lines, but her blue eyes were sharp and intense. "I prefer a straight-backed chair," she said. "You must be Mrs. Cantrell."

"Please call me Callie," she answered.

She would have walked toward her and offered to shake her hand, but Victoria pointed to a chair and said, "Have a seat," then turned her attention to Tucker, who was clamped onto Callie's hand like a vise. As soon as Callie started to sit, he grabbed the next chair, but Victoria said, "No, come here, Tucker. Let me get a look at you."

"Try not to scare him," West suggested with a faint smile.

"I'm not going to scare him," she snapped back.

"You already are. Give him a chance." West looked toward Cal, who was standing at the door that obviously led to the kitchen. "He's been wanting to see the horses since we got here."

"Horses," Tucker repeated, perking up. He looked from West to Cal.

"Well, c'mon then, boy," Cal said, strolling into the next room. "I was just about to head outside."

Tucker slid from his seat but wouldn't leave Callie. "You come too."

"Would it be okay if I stayed here?" Callie asked him.

"No. Come!"

"I'll be right here when you come back. I promise," she said. "I just want to talk to West and your great-grandmother."

Tucker's eyes slid carefully in Victoria's direction.

"Why, I think I see a palomino stallion out there," Cal called from across the kitchen. "I'm headin' out the door now. Better hurry!"

"You stay," Tucker warned Callie, edging away.

"I'll stay," Callie assured him, and then he ran after Cal as if shot from a cannon.

"Cal's kind of like Jean-Paul to Tucker," West observed, watching them leave.

Victoria frowned. "Who?"

"Someone Tucker knew on Martinique," West said. "I brought you a present," he told her. "It's in the glove box. I'll go get it and bring in Callie and Tucker's bags."

He left before she could answer, but she didn't seem to want to anyway. If she objected to hearing Callie had brought her own bag, she didn't say so. Her gaze was centered on Callie. "I don't see any reason to waste a lot of time," she said crisply. "I can see that Tucker's fond of you, and that having you around is necessary, at least for now, but I think it would be better for all of us if you planned on this being a very temporary position."

Even though it's what she'd half-expected to hear, it was a blow. "I just want what's best for Tucker."

"I've looked into your background. You were an elementary school teacher's aide before your marriage. You lost your husband and son in a terrible car accident last year, and you spent some time in a mental hospital, recovering."

"I spent nearly a month," Callie responded. "I checked myself in voluntarily."

Victoria eyed her thoughtfully. "Do you really think you're ready for the challenges of teaching Tucker and taking care of him?"

"Yes. If you're asking if I'm mentally well enough, yes."

"I sent Talia down to that island to help bring Tucker home because I'm not as mobile as I used to be. She's here some of the time, but she has a condominium in Santa Monica. If I entrusted you with Tucker's care, you would be doing most of the work by yourself."

"I understand."

"You look a lot like his mother," she said.

"I think that's what drew him to me, in the beginning. My hair."

Callie heard West reenter through the front door and drop the bags on the wood floor. A moment later he appeared in the dining room aperture, holding the bracelet.

"Ah," Victoria said as West laid it on the table in front of her.

"So, what have you been talking about?" he asked, looking from Victoria to Callie.

"Mrs. Cantrell's employment," Victoria said. She hesitated for a moment and Callie held her breath, preparing for the worst, but all she said was, "We've worked out a trial arrangement." To Callie, she added, "You're welcome to stay at the ranch. It will probably be best for Tucker."

Half an hour later, West pulled Callie into the great room as Victoria said she was going to get ready for a meeting later with Gary Merritt at his satellite law office in Castilla. The lawyer also had an LA hub, but since Victoria was one of his major clients, he made certain he was available in Castilla when she wanted to meet with him. Maya, who served as Victoria's companion as well as a cook and housekeeper, went to help her.

A few minutes later, Maya returned and said, "A lot of excitement," folding her hands under her ample breasts as she gazed at West and Callie a bit suspiciously. She was round where Victoria was gaunt, and she was a good thirty years younger than the older woman.

West observed, "It's not my place to say anything, but you might need some extra help around here, now that it's not just Victoria."

Maya said, "My daughter lives in Castilla. If I need someone, she'll come right out. Now, would the boy like something to eat when Cal brings him back?"

"Peanut butter and jelly?" Callie suggested.

West informed her, "He's been living on it for days, but it never seems to get old."

Maya said, "We have beef here. Does he like hamburgers?"

"I really don't know," Callie admitted.

"I'll start with peanut butter and jelly," Maya conceded, then headed into the kitchen. It was the first time Callie and West had been alone since Martinique, and West pulled her into his arms.

"What if your grandmother catches us?" she teased.

"You think she doesn't suspect?"

"It's more like I don't want to put it in her face unless she's ready."

"You want me to let you go?"

"No," she admitted, holding on to him tightly. But when he kissed her lightly on the mouth, just enough to remind her how good it had been, she eased out of his embrace before things could heat up. "You didn't bring your bag in," she observed.

"I thought I might stay tonight, but some things have come up with my job. I don't want to leave you and Tucker here alone, but . . ." In lieu of continuing he reached for her again and his hand swept up into her hair. She tilted her chin up, and this time the kiss was warm and more insistent.

"Okay," she said a bit breathlessly when he reluctantly released her. "Just hurry back."

He nodded. "There are a lot of loose ends that need to

be tied up around here. I really want to talk to Edmund Mikkels, but there's not time today. Last time I saw him, he wouldn't say anything, but he wasn't a happy man. Victoria said he was crumbling. Maybe he's ready to talk about Teresa. But I have more things to check at work, too. You good to stay here?"

"I'm packed for a night or two," she said. "But there are things I need to take care of in Los Angeles as well. I'll see how it goes, but I may have to go back for a day or two and then return."

"We'll figure it out."

He leaned in and kissed her a third time, this one quick and hard, then let her go, closing the door behind him as he left.

Callie picked up her bag and headed upstairs, finding the room that was laid out for Tucker with a number of age-appropriate toys lined on the shelves and a dark brown comforter on the bed designed with running horses. She continued on and saw the door was open to the very next room. When she stepped inside she found the decor to be more nondescript: a queen bed with a cream-colored quilt and an antique, oak dresser with a matching oval mirror above it. There was an en-suite bathroom with a shower, vanity, and toilet room done in cream and light green.

Hearing voices downstairs, she realized Victoria and Maya were heading out the door together and she figured Maya was also Victoria's driver.

Callie went back downstairs, grabbed Tucker's suitcase, and took it to his room. By its size, she figured they were going to have to get him some more clothes and soon, and by the look of the weather, he was also going to need something warmer than the shorts and T-shirts he'd worn in Martinique.

She had returned downstairs to the great room when she heard the back door slam open and the familiar pound of running feet. Tucker never went anywhere unless it was at full tilt.

"Calleee! Horses and *le chats!*" He ran toward her and they met in the dining room.

"They have cats?" she asked.

"Furrall cats," he said. "In the barn. They catch the mouses."

"Feral cats," Callie said.

"Uh-huh." He then did a U-turn back toward the kitchen and the back door.

Before he could go through it, the door opened again and a man in jeans, boots, and a denim work shirt stepped in. "Hello," he said in surprise, seeing Callie standing in the doorway between the kitchen and butler's pantry.

Tucker whooped upon seeing him and said, "Knock, knock!"

"Hey . . ." he said, seeming even more startled to see the boy. To Callie, he said, "My dad said Victoria's grandson was showing up. I guess this is him."

"Knock, *knock!*" Tucker demanded.

"Tucker, just a minute," Callie warned.

"I'm Teddy Stutz. Cal's son." His hand shot out and clasped hers. In the next breath, he asked Tucker, "Who's there?"

"Lena," Tucker said promptly.

"Lena, who?" Teddy asked.

"Lena . . . um . . . you say," he declared, pointing at Teddy.

"Lena on my shoulder, I'm tired?" Teddy guessed.

"*Oui, oui.* Yes!" To Callie's surprise, Tucker ran to Teddy Stutz and gave him a big hug before trying to squeeze past him and head out the back door again.

"Where are you going?" Callie called as she followed him through the kitchen.

He stopped short and turned to look at her, his gaze spying the peanut butter sandwich Maya had left on a plate beneath plastic wrap. "*Pour moi?*" At Callie's nod, he yanked off the wrap, grabbed half the sandwich, then thrust himself through the outside door, yelling, "Cal! Cal!" as the door shut behind him.

"Whew," Teddy said.

"So, you've met Tucker already," Callie said with a smile.

"Just now? Oh. Yes. Looks like he's acclimating pretty well. I'm not around here all that much, but I remember him as a baby. First time I've seen him in years. He's grown up a lot."

Teddy Stutz was sandy-haired and lean with eyes a cool blue shade and a set of dimples that she could already tell he knew how to use. Or maybe she'd just grown too cynical about men.

"You look just like her, by the way, which I'm sure you've heard already."

Callie didn't have to ask whom he meant. "A few times. You knew Teresa?"

"We all knew her."

"That doesn't sound . . . good."

"She didn't really fit in very well around here, but everybody knew her. The married guys' wives hated her. The single guys were all in lust with her."

"Are you counting yourself? And which one are you, married or single?"

"I was probably the only single guy who didn't care about her. It takes one to know one, y'know?"

"In what way?"

He gave her a sideways look, seemed to think something over, then shrugged. "Well, hell, you're bound to hear anyway. I'm the big disappointment to my father. Had a little trouble when I was younger. Wild-ass kid stuff. Owed some money to some people who didn't like to be kept waiting. But that was years ago."

Sounded like he was a gambler, and she could believe

that about him in the few minutes she'd known him. "What do you do now?"

"Just now I'm working at the ranch." He shrugged. "So, what's your deal? How'd you get to be a part of this?" He circled a finger to include the whole Laughlin Ranch.

Callie told him about meeting both Tucker and West in Martinique, how West had mistaken her for Teresa initially, and how after Teresa's body was discovered, Victoria had doubled her already intense efforts to gain custody of Tucker and bring him back to the ranch. Smiling faintly, she finished with, "I didn't want to leave Tucker so I came along. Victoria seems to be a woman who gets what she wants."

"Well, she apparently wants a great-grandson. Who's the supposed guardian here? Victoria?"

"I think that's her plan," Callie admitted carefully. "I really don't know."

"What about Talia? She's a generation younger."

Callie shrugged.

"She's jonesin' for my dad, you know," Teddy confided.

"Talia?"

"Yep, he's the only reason she really ever comes back here. She and Victoria . . ." He drew an imaginary line across his neck, as if slicing off his own head. "They don't get along."

"Victoria sent Talia to Martinique to help West bring back Tucker," Callie pointed out.

He barked out a laugh. "Well, if she sent Talia, she must not trust West at all. I've never met him. What's he like?"

"She trusted him enough to start the investigation," Callie said loyally.

"Take it from someone who knows: Victoria's not going to allow some non-pedigree into the Laughlin trust, so if that's what you're thinking, you better let that go right now. Talia isn't her favorite person, but she comes from San

Francisco and her family has some deep pockets. Craig
scored when he married her, in Victoria's opinion. I don't
know that the old man felt the same way, but he's gone and
Victoria remains, so it's her rules and only her rules."

Callie didn't know how to respond so she remained silent.
She tried to get a bead on his feelings, but Teddy Stutz just
kept a secret smile on his lips, as if he knew something she
didn't, and she suspected maybe he did.

He leaned in. "I'm just sayin', there's no way to work
your way in here with Victoria running things. Once she's
gone, you might have a shot."

Callie stared at him. "You seriously think that's why I'm
here?"

"No, of course not." He winked at her as they heard the
sound of Tucker's running feet just before he burst through
the back door again.

The pain in his head was like a hammer pounding in a
stake. Andre squinted his eyes as he followed the old
woman's Cadillac to downtown Castilla, which was a hodge-
podge of buildings off I-5 with one main street. Victoria's
maid was at the wheel. At least she wasn't spending all his
money on extra employees, though he wouldn't be the same
way once he had control. He would take the handmaidens to
Tahiti, he thought suddenly. He could be a king and they
would be his queens. No squatty refugee camp like his
father's ratty kingdom had been because *they'd* cut him off.

The pleasant vision faded almost as soon as it had materialized, shattered by the continued pain inside his skull and
the remembrance that the handmaidens weren't anything
he wanted them to be.

His cell phone rang and he glanced down at it, recognizing the number as one of the handmaidens'. But which one?

He knew this. He knew it a second ago but now it escaped him. He didn't have Bluetooth on but he answered anyway. "Yes."

"I just saw you drive by," Naomi said.

Ah, yes. Naomi. He almost asked her what she was talking about before he remembered he'd told her that he was going to Castilla. Had he told the rest of them . . . no . . . He couldn't now recall why he'd told her. Wasn't she supposed to be on a job somewhere . . . Laguna . . . ? "Where are you?"

"By the hardware store."

He'd seen it on his right as he drove by, he realized vaguely. Glancing in his rearview mirror, he saw the brown Chevy parked at the curb.

"Did you see the Cadillac in front of me?" he asked.

"The white one? Yeah. Is it hers?"

Suddenly the floodgates of memory opened and he recalled spilling his plan to Naomi. Only Naomi. It was like being really drunk sometimes, or on drugs, this passage of time and loss of recall. He'd confided in Naomi that Victoria was the only person between him and his inheritance, which wasn't exactly true now that he knew about the boy.

"It's hers," he confirmed. "Follow her. I don't know where she's going, but she's plotting against me."

"Are you sure?" Doubt had crept into her voice.

"Yes," he said, instantly furious.

"It's just that your memory . . . we've talked about this . . ."

"Stop being a fucking nurse and get to the job! What happened with Laguna?"

"You said this was a priority."

He hated hearing his words coming out of her mouth, but yes, he recalled bits of that conversation now, too. "Tell me where she goes. I want to know what she's up to."

"Where will you be?"

"At the ranch." The pain was a screech inside his head. "Get rid of her."

"You mean . . . ?"

"Yes! Kill the withered, old bitch!"

He hung up, so angry he could scarcely think. He saw the Cadillac turn into the parking lot next to a brick building and noticed the discreet sign for Merritt Law, her law firm, headquartered in Beverly Hills. Of course they had an office in Castilla. That just showed how much money she had at her control, that her lawyer specifically kept a nearby office just for her.

Hate burned through him. He hoped Naomi would be as good as her word. He needed one of them, just one, to finally do something right for him!

As the businesses along the main street began petering out he made a U-turn to get back to the freeway entrance. He witnessed Naomi's Chevy turn into the lot after the Cadillac as he drove by, glad to keep the Xterra away from the scene, just in case someone had told Victoria what he drove.

Two hours later, his phone awoke him from a trancelike state where the skulls had again chattered at him without moving their mouths. He remembered he didn't want Victoria dead until he'd won her over. The timing was all wrong, he recalled, staring through the windshield in his same place on the ridge above Laughlin Ranch.

"Yes?" he asked.

"It's done," Naomi said breathlessly, and she hung up and was gone.

It was after four by the time West entered the station and his energy was flagging. The day had started early in Miami and he'd been traveling by plane or car through most of it.

He'd damn near gone straight back to his apartment when he reached the Los Angeles city limits, needing a brief nap, but instead he'd picked up a sandwich and black coffee from a Starbucks and gone in search of Dorcas and Lieutenant Gundy, both of whom were out when he came in.

"Damn," he muttered, calling Dorcas on his cell. His partner answered that he was at a nearby coffee shop, a cop favorite, with Gundy at that very moment. It was within walking distance so West left the Explorer where it was parked and hoofed over to Donny O's.

Pete Dorcas was still built like a Mack truck. Big arms, thick neck, wide chest, buzzed blond hair, and a Clint Eastwood squint that was the result of vanity, as he really needed to wear glasses for a mild vision correction but wouldn't. He intimidated practically anyone who didn't know him, which had worked well for West on more than one occasion when they'd taken down a suspect together. Now, Pete grinned upon seeing West and motioned for him to join them at their corner table. "Siddown. How's the globe-trottin' goin'? The lieutenant and I were just talkin' 'bout cha."

As West took a seat, he looked at Gundy who'd climbed from patrolman through the ranks to his current position. A tall, lean man with perfect silver hair, an expensive dark blue suit, and a knotted, yellow tie at his throat, the lieutenant gazed back at West and didn't waste any time before saying, "Captain Paulsen is being relocated and we want you to take your old position back."

West almost said, "His crimes catch up to him?" but knew that wouldn't be political. He was lucky Gundy had taken an interest in having him back. "Look forward to it," he responded instead.

Almost immediately, Gundy, who'd been sitting with a half-empty cup of coffee while Dorcas was working on a piece of peach pie, got up, shook West's hand, and said, "Get the paperwork done. Good to have you back," and was gone.

"Since when do you fraternize with the bosses? And what happened to Paulsen?" West asked.

"Since everybody wants to cover their ass. Nobody's sayin' it, but Paulsen fucked up with you. He got all personal about his daughter and took it out on you. He's also got his own boys, y'know."

West nodded. "I know."

"Too many favors being passed out. The kinda shit that happens all the time, but it finally got in Gundy's way. Today, I just ran into him here and we'd just nodded at each other when you called, so he invited me to sit down. I think he wanted to see which way the wind was blowin' with you." He snorted out a laugh. "You look like hell, by the way."

"All that globe-trotting. Anything more from Martinique?"

Dorcas scooped up the last bite of pie and said around it, "No autopsy report yet, but I did find a California license for Teresa Laughlin. Picture looks like your sister-in-law, so I'm pretty sure it's her. Recently changed her address to a studio apartment on Barrington."

"I know Barrington. Have you been there?"

"You're kiddin', right? Hell, no. I got me some pie to eat."

West smiled. "All right. Give me the address."

"It's at my desk." The waitress had already left the slip, so Dorcas checked the price, muttered about Gundy leaving him to pay for his coffee, then threw some dollars down and walked back to the station with West. He'd jotted the particulars down in a notebook and he ripped off the page and held it out.

West took it and asked, "Who's working the Cantrell vehicular homicide?"

"Osbirg and Bibbs were on it. It stalled out. Osbirg's out, by the way."

Harold Osbirg and Jay Bibbs were partners who had worked out of their department and had been favorites of Captain Paulsen. Dorcas didn't have to tell West that Osbirg had been removed because of cronyism with Paulsen. Thinking of that, West wondered what had happened to the woman who'd been teamed with Dorcas while West was on leave. "Where'd Jiminez end up?"

"She was bumped from Robbery, so that's where she went back to. She was too good-lookin' to be my partner anyway."

West yawned, thinking of Jade Jiminez. She was an attractive Hispanic woman with a humorless husband who worked for the LA transit system and thought his wife should be promoted faster than her years and ability would prove. "She is too good-lookin' to be your partner," he agreed, then headed out, wishing the paperwork was already processed so he could just get to work.

Back in the Explorer, his thoughts turned to Callie, as they did every time he was alone. He couldn't leave her with Victoria indefinitely. He knew how irascible the old woman was, and he didn't want Callie that far away from him anyway. Maybe after a while, Tucker would settle in and she could come back to LA.

Except that she loves him and he loves her, too, and they shouldn't be apart.

How the hell was this going to work? He had a vision of himself burning up the freeway between LA and Castilla every time he got a day off, and that just made him feel more tired.

He picked up another coffee and found enough energy to check out Teresa's apartment. See if there was an on-site manager who might let him inside, although without his identification he thought it highly unlikely.

He caught a second wind about the time he showed up at the apartment complex. There was no one at the manager's office, so he walked down the east side of the building to an inner corner unit, which, according to the address, was Teresa's studio. He cupped his hands to the front window and attempted to peer through a tiny crack in the drapes. He couldn't see much of anything, although he thought the room might be bare. On a lark, he twisted the doorknob and about fell over when it opened beneath his hand. Aware he was on shaky legal ground, he glanced around to see if anyone was looking, then pushed open the door.

The place was empty and the laminate floor was dusty. There were footsteps in the dust and a line where something had been dragged—bags maybe?—to the door.

He stood outside looking in for several moments, then slowly reclosed the door. If Teresa had been there, she hadn't in a while. Was it a fake address? Dorcas had said she'd recently changed it.

Shooting another look around the premises to see if anyone had noticed him, he headed back to the Explorer. Inside, he placed another call to Dorcas, but only got his partner's voice mail.

"Pete, you said Teresa Laughlin recently changed her address. Can you get me her old one? The studio doesn't look lived in."

He'd just turned the ignition when his phone rang back. Thinking it was Dorcas, he was pleased to see it was Callie's number on the screen. "Just thinking about you," he answered lightly.

"West, your grandmother was just taken to a hospital, I think in Coalinga?" she said in a strained voice. "She was run down in the parking lot of her lawyer's office. Cal is on his way there."

Shocked, West asked, "Run down?"

"Maya was hit too," Callie said soberly. "They're both in the hospital."

He was already putting the SUV in gear. "I'm on my way," he said grimly.

Chapter Twenty-Three

Well, well, well. The old bitch might actually die. That'll sure throw a wrench into Andre's plans, not to mention what it'll do to the Laughlins. Ha! Andre doesn't know that I'm following his every move. The man's nuttier than a PayDay bar but thinks he's in total control. Just you wait, Messiah . . . when you've outlived your relevance, your name'll be on the list too.

But for now, just keep doing what you're doing. Besides, there are others that need to be removed too. Luckily, Teresa's already gone, and Victoria could check out at any moment. Once she's dead, everything'll change. Sure, there are a few more heirs to knock out of the way, but I'm counting on you to help me out. Just don't have an aneurysm or something before you get the job done. I don't want to have to do it all myself.

Her mind on Victoria and Maya and West, too, Callie finished preparing the green salad that Maya had begun to make before she drove Victoria to her lawyer's just as the oven timer announced the beef roast was done. Tucker was watching television in the small den off the great room. She pulled out the roast and while it rested, she called to Tucker. She wasn't about to serve him up until she knew what he liked to eat beyond peanut butter sandwiches and pastries. When he didn't respond, she went in search of him. "Tucker, I've got roast beef and a salad ready."

He shook his head. "*Non . . .*"

"Another peanut butter sandwich?" she asked. Today wasn't the day to get him to change his ways.

"Not hungry."

"Okay." She left him and returned to the kitchen, pouring herself a glass of ice water. A knock on the back door made her nearly jump from her skin. "Who is it?" she asked, aware her heart was racing. She'd only been at the house a few hours and suddenly she was temporarily in charge.

"It's Teddy," he called from the other side of the door. He rattled the knob. "You locked it."

She turned the lock and opened the door. "Is it usually left unlocked?"

"Well, yeah." He exhaled as he entered, dropping down at the kitchen table across from where Callie had set a place for herself. "I just talked to my dad. Guess Maya has a broken leg and arm, and God knows what else. Victoria's unconscious. Pretty beaten up, sounds like."

Callie felt ill inside. "That's terrible."

"Yeah, bummer, huh." He shook his head.

"Would you like something to eat?" she asked when he eyed the roast.

"Sure. Looks good."

"Maya made everything. I just finished putting it to-gether." She went to the cupboard to pull down a plate and then sliced into the roast, putting a healthy slab on Teddy's plate and adding a portion of the dressed salad.

Teddy tucked in like he was starved. "Good stuff," he said.

Callie's cell phone rang and she leapt up to snatch it off the counter. Seeing it was West, she said, "Excuse me," then headed through the butler's pantry and dining room to the great room.

"Hey, no problem," he called after her.

"Hello," she answered her cell.

"How are you doing?" West asked, and the sound of his voice made her feel weak.

She sat down heavily in one of the leather chairs. "Don't worry about me. Where are you? Are you at the hospital yet?"

"Just got here. Had enough caffeine to keep me going. Haven't seen Victoria yet. They operated to stop a brain bleed and she's not in a room yet."

"Oh, no."

"Talia got here ahead of me, but now she's on her way to you. I'm gonna hang around a while and see if I can talk to a doctor. Maya's being released. Her daughter's here."

"Good."

Callie heard an engine approaching and glanced toward the front window. An SUV had just broken free of the oak-shaded drive and was pulling to a stop beside her car.

"I think I see the doc now. I'll call you as soon as I know something," West said hurriedly. "Bye."

"Bye," she responded, dragging her gaze from the window.

A few seconds later the front bell rang and Callie walked to the door, expecting Talia. Teddy Stutz must've already been on his feet because he was suddenly beside her as she reached for the door handle. "I don't know who it is," she said.

"Here." He moved in front of her and threw open the door. Callie had been cautious about answering. She'd wanted to make sure it was Talia first but Teddy clearly had no such compunction.

A man stood on the other side. He was handsome with a strong jaw and dark hair pulled back to a ponytail at his nape, held by a thong of leather. His body was lean and in the porch light she thought his eyes were blue. He wore a loose white shirt and tan slacks, and she realized distantly that he looked something like West.

His gaze moved instantly past Teddy to land on her. "Who are you?" he asked.

"Hey, pal, I think that's what we should be asking," Teddy said, then gave him a hard look. "I know who you are. You're Andrew, right?"

His gaze swung back to Teddy. "Andre," he stated coldly.

Teddy said in an aside to Callie, "My dad told me he came by earlier. Says he's Victoria's grandson."

Callie absorbed that. Since Stephen's death, she'd thought West was Victoria's only grandson.

Reading her like a book, Teddy explained, "He claims to be Benjamin Jr.'s son."

"I am Benjamin's son," Andre said. "I came to speak to Victoria," he added, clearly annoyed at Teddy's breezy manner.

Teddy said, "Well, sorry. She's in the hospital. You'll have to wait."

"Hospital?" He turned to Callie again. "What happened? Is she all right?"

"We're waiting to hear," she said.

"Well, I guess you should come on in," Teddy said grudgingly, waving Andre across the threshold. "We're just finishing dinner."

"Um . . ." Callie said, unsure. She kinda thought Teddy was overstepping his bounds, though she didn't see how she could stop him.

Andre strode past her and looked around, his eyes assessing everything in a way that made Callie uncomfortable. "Don't look so worried," he told her coolly. "I'm not going to steal anything. I'll just wait in here." He gestured to the great room.

Teddy said, "Victoria's not gonna be back tonight. What is it you want to talk to her about?"

"I just want to get reacquainted with my family." He flicked a look to Callie. "You're the nanny?"

"Yes. I'm Callie Cantrell. Can I get you anything? A glass of water?" There was something about his face that was pinched, as if he were in pain.

"No, thanks."

Teddy made a motion for them to return to the kitchen, though Callie was reluctant to leave Andre alone. Nevertheless, she followed Teddy back and once they were in the kitchen, she demanded, "Why did you let him in?"

"'Cause Dad said he looked enough like a Laughlin to be believable, and since Victoria's not here . . ." He shrugged. "We should be having a drink. Bet there's some bourbon somewhere."

"Let's just finish this." She sliced off a thin piece of roast beef, added salad to her plate, then sat down at the kitchen table across from Teddy. She ate a few bites of salad, but in the end was unable to face the slightly bloody slice of meat. Teddy was eating with relish, but Callie had had enough of his company. She also didn't like Tucker being in the den with Andre waiting nearby.

Sweeping up her plate, she left it by the sink, then headed back toward the great room.

"Hey," Teddy protested, but Callie ignored him.

Andre was nowhere in sight and with her heart clutching, she practically ran for the den.

As soon as she entered she saw Andre standing to one side of Tucker, just watching the boy, who was deep into some afternoon kids' program she didn't recognize.

A shiver slipped down her spine at the intent look in his eyes. She had no idea what he was thinking, but every maternal instinct she possessed went into overdrive. Andre moved his gaze from Tucker to Callie. She felt his eyes following her as she took a seat on the den couch next to Tucker and placed a protective arm around him.

Talia Laughlin breezed in with a loud sigh and dropped her bag with a clunk on the floor. She shook off her coat—the October day had grown gloomy and colder as it progressed—and said, "God, I could use a drink. Has Victoria got anything? Probably not. She's a teetotaler from way back."

Callie had answered the door, glad that Teddy had apparently left the way he'd come. Andre had eventually wandered back to the great room, so when the doorbell rang, Callie felt comfortable leaving Tucker for a few minutes to answer it.

"How's Victoria?" Callie asked, conscious of Andre somewhere behind her left shoulder.

"I've got a bottle of wine in my car," Talia said. "Let me go get it and we can sit down and talk." She glanced past Callie to Andre. "Oh, God, you must be Andrew. I'm Talia, Stephen's mother." She moved past Callie and held out her hand.

"It's Andre," he told her.

"Oh, sure. I heard that, too. Andrew, Andre . . ." She shrugged. "Whenever Ben's name came up, which wasn't often, believe me, and his son was mentioned, the name was Andrew. I'll try to remember, but don't hold me to it. I'll be right back." She let herself out and Callie stayed by the open door. When she returned she was carrying two bottles of cabernet.

"Whew," she said, carrying the bottles into the kitchen and placing them on the counter. Callie followed after her and searched through three drawers before she found a corkscrew. Talia fell on the bottle and twisted out the cork like an expert. "Come on in here, Andre," she called.

Callie had been just about to go make sure he was still in the great room when he appeared in the dining room doorway. By that time Talia had found the wineglasses and had poured one for herself and one for Callie.

"No, thank you," Andre said when she waved the bottle at him.

"Okay," she said in a voice that suggested he was making a big mistake. "So, Victoria . . . it's not looking good. Maya's a wreck. Blames herself, but it sounds like a car just blasted through the back parking lot and clipped them as they were walking toward the door. Maya was actually hit harder by the car, but Victoria's head smacked into the pavement."

"Do they know what kind of car it was?" Andre asked.

"A brown sedan. Maya didn't notice whether it was foreign or domestic. God, this wine is good. Are you going to even try it?"

She was looking at Callie, who dutifully brought her glass to her lips. She wished she could talk to West. She wanted to ask him about his cousin Andrew/Andre.

Talia went on, "It's kind of a wait-and-see game now. I hope she makes it. How ironic that she was at her lawyer's. I thought she got that new will taken care of. I don't know."

"New will?" Andre asked carefully.

Callie slid him a look. His eyes were practically boring through the back of Talia's skull as she tipped back her glass while she walked toward the bottle for a refill.

"Oh, I got it," she said suddenly, holding the bottle up but not pouring yet. To Andre she said, "It wasn't about the will. She went to see him because of you! She needs to vet you. Doesn't believe you're who you say you are, but you look just like Ben before he took off to find his bliss in the South Pacific, so I figure it's true. Were you there the whole time? We got the message that he died, but no one ever knew what happened to you or your mom."

Andre wasn't enjoying Talia's casual twenty questions. "My mother's gone too."

"Oh. Sorry." She said the words but Callie saw they were nothing more than a polite, expected response.

"My father was disinherited," Andre said.

"He sure was. By his father. Ben Sr. Victoria might've loosened up but once Ben Sr. was deceased, I don't know. Let's all hope she survives or we're at the mercy of her last choices, right? I thought she was going to give most of the ranch to Cal, but now my grandson's back." She lifted her shoulders and smiled, a silent "what're you gonna do?"

"Cal . . ." Andre repeated scornfully, as if he couldn't hold himself back. He was so transparent it was painful.

"Ted Stutz, the ranch manager," Talia said. "Everybody calls him Cal. He's a great guy and my mother-in-law loves him to pieces."

Callie thought of Teddy's comments about Talia "jonesin'" for Cal. Were they in some kind of relationship? And was that why she seemed to feel so powerful about her place in the Laughlin hierarchy?

"She wouldn't leave everything to someone outside the family," Andre said, biting off each word.

"And you know her so well," Talia said, her eyes sparkling. "But you're probably right. The bulk of the estate will be Tucker's. God, how ghoulish we sound. Talking about money when she may not live through the night." She yawned and heaved a sigh. "Okay, I'm going to take this glass with me. Third bedroom, right?" she asked Callie. "Tucker's in the first and you're in the second."

Callie nodded.

"I'll turn on the alarm after *Andre* leaves," Talia said, stressing his name with a faint smile. "Cal said Victoria's taken to locking the back door, too. About time. This place was like a robber's dream."

Callie took another sip of wine, specifically to hide anything that might show on her face after witnessing the growing rigidity of Andre's jaw. Talia seemed to be specifically goading him, which, in Callie's opinion, was pretty much like poking a snake.

West showed up close to eleven o'clock. Callie had managed to get Tucker into bed, though the strangeness of his surroundings finally penetrated and he clung to her and cried out when she tried to leave. She rocked him and whispered gently to him, going over the highlights of the day so he would remember the good things and get himself to sleep.

"Furrall cats bite," he said sleepily as he finally wound down.

"That's right, and scratch. You have to be careful."

"Careful," he mumbled.

He slipped into slumber a few minutes later and Callie eased herself out of the bed and back downstairs. Andre had taken Talia's broad hint to leave with ill grace, but had reluctantly headed back outside. As soon as he was gone, Talia checked all the doors and set the alarm. "The code's 'bullbbq,'" she'd said as she headed up to her room. "You should take Tucker to Laughlin BBQ tomorrow. Hell, maybe I'll still be here and we'll all go."

Soon after she was gone Callie saw the splash of West's headlights across the front of the house and she punched in the code to release the alarm, opened the back door, and stepped into a cool, starless evening. West shut his driver's door, spied Callie, and strode her way quickly.

Before she could say anything, he pulled her close and

kissed her. Then he buried his face in her hair and said, "God, I've missed you."

"Back at cha," she said lightly, inhaling his male scent, which she was beginning to crave like a drug. "How's Victoria?"

"Hanging in there . . . just. I talked to her doctor and he didn't want to say too much. Her lawyer showed up too. He was in shock and felt responsible since it happened at his offices. He gave me his card."

"You think she's going to be okay?"

"God, I hope so." He half-laughed. "Didn't know I cared so much about her until this happened."

He ran his lips over her face and to her mouth again, and she kissed him desperately. They were like teenagers in their secret, all-consuming need to touch, caress, and rediscover each other. She was pressed hard against the side of the building and his body lay urgently against hers but it wasn't enough. Realizing how much she wanted him felt so absurd that she started soundlessly laughing.

"What?" he asked, his mouth against the skin of her neck.

"I almost want to make love to you out here."

"I'm game."

"But what if someone comes back, like Cal, or Teddy, or even your cousin?"

She hadn't meant to curl her lip on "your cousin," but she did and West reluctantly pulled himself back from her, peering at her through the darkness. "What cousin?"

"A guy who claims to be Andre Laughlin came by today. Teddy said his dad told him that he met with Victoria earlier, then he came back again when Teddy and I were having dinner. It was Talia who actually got him to leave."

"There is no Andre Laughlin," West said.

"Sorry. He goes by Andre now, but his real name is Andrew. He says he's Ben Jr.'s son."

"Bullshit."

"Maybe not. Talia said he looked just like his father. I don't know."

"And who the hell's Teddy?" West demanded. "Not Cal's son, Ted."

"Yeah, Teddy Stutz. You haven't met him?"

"No. What was he doing here? Victoria said Cal and Ted were on the outs because Ted gambles money away as fast as he makes it."

"Huh. Well, he's here now."

He shook his head, kissed her once more, then reluctantly pulled away from her. "Okay, we'll go in."

"Maybe we can be together upstairs?" she suggested.

"No maybe about it," he responded as they headed back inside. As Callie reset the alarm, he asked, "What about this Andre?"

"I don't really know. He's . . . well, you'll probably meet him. Talia was talking to him about the Laughlin inheritance and when he heard her intimate that Tucker, as Victoria's great-grandson, would probably inherit, he stared at her in a way that gave me the willies."

"You think he wants a piece of the inheritance."

"That's what it looked like to me, and believe me, I know about people who think they deserve something they think you're keeping them from."

West didn't really want to talk any longer. He was tired and he just wanted to hold Callie, make love to her, and let it all go for a while. But this Andre sounded like a scammer. "Seems coincidental that he showed up today and then someone runs Victoria down."

"You think there's a connection?"

"What time was he here?"

"He showed up about an hour after Victoria left. He was here a while, but maybe he could have made it back to

Castilla before she was out of that meeting. Depends on how long it ran."

"You really think he did this?" West asked soberly.

Callie hesitated. "I didn't like him. I don't know. Somebody ran her down."

"Did you see what kind of car he drove?"

"I got a glimpse when Teddy let him in, but I wasn't really looking. A black SUV of some kind, maybe?"

"That's not the vehicle that ran into Maya and Victoria. Maya said it was a brown sedan."

"Maya said?"

"I talked to her before her daughter picked her up."

"Oh," Callie said, derailed a little.

West stretched and ran his hands through his hair, stifling a yawn. "What about this Teddy? Why'd he show Andre in?"

"He seemed very familiar with things around here," Callie admitted. "And I didn't know how to stop him."

He half-smiled and gathered her close again. "This has all been pretty weird for you. For all of us, but especially you." He inhaled the soft spring scent of her hair and added, "Teddy was one of the guys on the hunting trip when Mikkels accidentally killed Stephen."

"Huh. He doesn't seem the type that would go hunting."

"Yeah?"

"He's just kind of loose and breezy. Like a salesman, maybe. Trying to charm people. Talking a little too much."

"And Andre? What's he like?"

"Intense . . . can't see the humor in stuff . . . prickly. He's definitely got a hidden agenda, and I'm betting it's your family's money."

He released her to meet her eyes. "You got quite a bit for only one meeting."

She nodded several times. "I fell for my husband because

I didn't trust my first impression, even though I knew he wasn't really the way he came off. He was like Teddy, hard to pin down to the truth. If I sound like a shrink, it's because I've been on the other side of that."

"Yeah?"

"You might as well know, I was a basket case after Sean's death. Couldn't remember anything, couldn't do anything, so at one point I checked myself into a mental facility and I stayed for . . . thirty days."

He felt her brace herself for his response and understood how sensitive she felt about it. All he asked was, "Did it help?"

"Saved my life," she said promptly.

"Then it was worth it."

"Thank you." Her voice was small.

Hooking his arm through hers, he led them both through the house to the stairway that led upstairs to the west wing that held the bedrooms.

"Sometimes I still get the creeping fog when things are really bad," Callie admitted, "but less and less."

"Creeping fog?"

"I'll tell you about it sometime." They'd stopped at the base of the stairs, and she said, "Tucker's room's up to the right. I'm on the left, and then Talia's in the next room. . . ."

"There are more bedrooms though, right?"

"One more. Just past Talia's."

"Think I could talk you into joining me for a while?"

"You couldn't talk me out of it."

"Good."

They reached the top of the stairs and headed down the hall toward the room on the end. "I got stuff in the Explorer but I'm gonna get it tomorrow," West said. "Never thought I'd be spending a night in this house." She felt him slide a hand around her waist, beneath the hem of her shirt, caressing her skin. "I warn you. I'm going to pass out like the dead."

"Maybe I should let you sleep, then . . . ?"

"Like hell," he muttered, kissing her hard as they moved into his bedroom together.

Jerrilyn Stiles cooed in Aaron Mittenberger's ear as he struggled to climax beneath her. She was straddling him, but she was going to have to work on him some more, which made her want to sigh. Though she was good at getting the job done, sometimes sex was just one big bore. Not when people were watching . . . there was nothing more satisfying than seeing those stupid cows, the handmaidens, try to hide their horror when Andre decided to take her in front of them. Yep, that was fun. Got her juices flowing. Especially when that prig Clarice and angry-girl Daniella were forced to watch. Jerrilyn had really whooped it up a time or two when they were her audience. Ha! She'd even made stone-faced Naomi uncomfortable a time or two, she could tell.

But Andre himself . . . holy God, what a crazy man. Not a bad lover, all things considered. He could certainly perform when his blood was high. If she thought he was really in control of himself, she might have stuck around, but the truth was the guy was sick. Like brain-sick. Something truly off there, and she'd heard Naomi on the telephone to a doctor or nurse, or somebody who knew something about health, and there was talk of a tumor. Naomi hadn't apparently broken the news to Andre 'cause he seemed to think he was fine.

Anyway, it was time for her to leave. She'd picked Andre up in Vegas with the original thought of hanging with him a while and seeing what came out of it. The handmaidens had been a surprise, but Jerrilyn had seen she could be the queen bee of those drones with no effort whatsoever. But, like all good things, it had to come to an end. Andre was worsening with the whole "Messiah" gig, which was really old, and let's face it, he just wasn't right.

"C'mon, baby," she whispered, licking the side of Mittenberger's face. He wasn't bad-looking for a guy in his fifties, and he was wealthy as sin. No, he wasn't going to leave his wife, but then they hardly ever did, did they? And honestly, what was she going to do with him anyway? Marry the douche bag? C'mon.

Naomi had told Andre that it was over between Jerrilyn and Mittenberger, just like Jerrilyn had planned. Jerrilyn had purposely given this bit of news to Naomi with a shrug and a sigh, like it was sad, but, oh well. Naomi, of course, had hoped Andre would come down on her hard. Jerrilyn had kinda hoped for it herself. Maybe he'd want a little rough sex in front of their shocked faces, but no, he already had his plans in motion, whatever the hell they were. Jerrilyn didn't give a damn. She was done. Outta there. Ready for the next adventure.

It took ten minutes more of coaxing and cooing and rubbing and damn near making her want to scream before he managed to hold an erection long enough to climax.

"Oh, baby," he exhaled, flopping on his back as she slipped away into the bathroom where she'd left her clothes when she'd donned the hotel bathrobe. Now, she freshened up and shimmied back into her short black dress. Her Christian Louboutins were neatly placed by the tub, their red soles gleaming. Man, she loved those shoes. Expensive, but worth it. She'd seen Clarice eyeing them with envy and had thought the little whore might actually steal them, but Jerrilyn had made sure she couldn't by locking them inside a small suitcase when she wasn't wearing them.

Slipping into the heels, she examined her reflection in the

mirror. Her shoulder-length hair was dark brown, glossy, and somewhat wild now after her calisthenics in the sack. Her lipstick was scarlet and wet-looking. Beautiful. If she had a complaint about her appearance it was her eyes. A little on the small side. A little calculating, she'd been told more than once, but whatcha gonna do. The right makeup made them pop and sparkle a violent green color, and right now they were popping, all right.

Stepping out of the bathroom, she damn near ran smack into the slab of hairy flesh that was Mittenberger's chest. "What are you doing?" she demanded.

"What are you doing?" he asked back at her. "Leaving?"

"Lover, you told me you had to go home. I got places to be too."

His mouth turned down. He absolutely hated to be reminded that he had no real hold on her. "I told her I had a dinner meeting that would last late."

"It is late," Jerrilyn pointed out.

"What about this weekend?"

"That's still on. Don't worry." She air-kissed him on the cheek. Didn't want to mess up the lipstick. "I'll call you."

"Where are you going?"

This was the question he always asked. Normally, she sidestepped it. Didn't want to give away the nest she shared with Andre and the handmaidens. But now, since she had no intention of going back, she said, "I've got a new place in Venice."

"Where?"

She wagged her finger at him, then blew him a last kiss and stepped out into the hallway. She took the elevator to the lobby. The Peninsula Hotel was expensive and a haven for Hollywood stars. Sometimes, when she crossed the lobby, she got a double take, people wondering if she was "somebody." She had that look about her, she knew.

Tonight she cruised out the door and under the portico. She shivered a little as she asked the bellman for a taxi. Cold in LA tonight. She wished she had a fur. Wouldn't that be something. Draped over her shoulder.

Someone bumped into her from behind and she felt a sharp prick. "Hey." She turned around, but there was no one there. A blond woman was hurrying away from the hotel, but she had lifted her arm as if hailing someone or something. Wait a minute. She was hailing *her* cab, damn it. "Hey!" she called.

The blonde looked over. Must be a wig, she thought, thinking the blond bob looked kind of fake. She took two steps toward the woman and felt light-headed. Holy shit, what was wrong?

The blonde hurried back to her. "You okay? Sorry, I didn't realize that was your cab. . . ."

Jerrilyn thought, *Wait a minute. I know you. This is a setup.* She tried to say, "What the hell?" but couldn't get her thick tongue to utter the words.

The blonde was wiry tough and hustled Jerrilyn to the cab. She climbed in with her and said, "Too goddamned much to drink," to the driver in a mock angry voice.

"Where to?" he asked.

"My car's just a couple blocks," she said in a voice that now sounded to Jerrilyn as if it were coming through water.

The cabbie dropped them off and the blonde stuck Jerrilyn's arm over her shoulder, half-dragging her to the compact. Jerrilyn was tossed in the backseat like a rag doll.

She was unable to talk and may have actually passed out for a bit. Then she awakened and tried to talk, but she couldn't form words.

When the car finally turned into a drive, she knew where she was. Andre's house . . . she was back at Andre's house!

So, this was Andre's idea. He wasn't going to let her

go. Just like Teresa, he'd sent the handmaidens to do his bidding . . . and he meant to kill her!

She struggled to rise but was unable. The blonde opened the back door and hauled her out. Jerrilyn's head hit the concrete drive with a crack and she saw stars.

As she was dragged inside, she prayed one of the neighbors would notice, but the street was completely dark and quiet, as ever. A bomb could go off and the neighbors would just quiver behind their walls.

Where was Daniella? She was supposed to be here. Could the blonde be her with a wig? Jerrilyn couldn't even remember her abductor's face now. Where was Clarice? Naomi? Please let them come home from their jobs . . . *please!*

She was dragged down the hall and into the prayer room and laid beside another body. To her shock, she could clearly see it was Clarice, but her eyes were open and staring, her tongue lolling out. There was something smudgy on Clarice's face, and an ugly chain mark circled her neck, breaking through the skin.

Through whirling vision, she saw a gold ankh swinging in front of her eyes.

Words burbled around her . . . nearly indistinct . . . the blonde was talking.

"Teresa . . . to get away . . . smacked her head against . . . killed her. But she wore . . . ankh . . . one Andre gave her . . . gave me . . . idea . . ."

She felt the ankh pulled over her head and draped around her own neck. Then the pressure of the chain against her flesh, tightening . . . *tightening!* The blonde was twisting and twisting. Choking her. Jerrilyn tried to reach up with her hands but couldn't. She wanted to scream, but only gurgled in her throat.

No air . . . *no air!*

Through a shimmer of fading vision, she realized there was no escape and she would die. The final image imprinted on her retinae was Clarice's bulging eyes and long, limp tongue, and her last regretful thought was, *That's what I'll look like, too.*

Chapter Twenty-Four

Daniella sat outside Ray's, her thoughts dark. Lumpkin was here. Again. Just sitting around waiting for his hottie to return. And Andre was gone. She knew it in the deep, black depths of her core. They all thought she was plain and uninteresting, and maybe she was, on the outside. Inside she pulsed with heat, gleamed with brilliant light, and she could do anything.

She got out of the car and walked into the bar. She'd always been glad Andre had found her, lifted her up, kept her from wallowing in the wasted life that she'd once lived with her boyfriend, Ty. Well, "boyfriend" was a euphemism because he was a lying, cheating, fucking weasel, but then weren't they all?

Andre had shown her a life within the bosom of his family, such as it was: she'd initially thought she could live with the other handmaidens, had embraced communal living in the beginning. Why not? It was better than being treated like a stick of furniture.

But was it? She'd really just traded one kind of life for another and now with Andre gone, what did she have?

Lumpkin was seated on his same stool at the bar. For a moment she almost turned on her heel and walked out. Why should she do as Andre had bidden, when it just didn't feel like it was going to matter? Why should she care?

Because she desperately wanted to be the one he turned to in the end, and completing a big task like this one would go a long way toward getting her there.

At that precise moment Lumpkin looked over and saw her. The faint disgust on his face led her to decide once and for all. Fuck him and the other handmaidens. She was going to get rid of him for her own sake, and the world as a whole. He deserved to die. She sashayed up to him, throwing her hips in an exaggerated walk. "Wanna come home with me?"

Lumpkin's eyes narrowed. "Like the way you played me last time?"

"I couldn't go to that apartment. You were right. We should have gone to my place."

"What about your *fiancé?*"

"You think he's faithful to me?" she asked, her voice catching a little of its own accord. It really did hurt that Andre cared so little about her.

Lumpkin thought it over a moment, then said harshly, "No."

She really didn't like the man. *Really* didn't like him. "Meet me at the house. You know the way," she said, turning around and sashaying back, making sure he got a perfect view of her swinging ass, the one he thought he was going to be able to grab and squeeze. Stupid, little cockroach.

Callie re-dressed in the dark and tiptoed out of West's room, glancing back at him as she softly closed his door behind her. She walked quickly past Talia's room. She really didn't want to have to explain what she was doing up in the middle of the night. Thinking she would check in on Tucker, she moved past hers and gently opened the door to his. His room was nearest to the stairway that opened above the entire great room. After peeking in on him and assuring herself that he was asleep, she turned back. Glancing to the floor below, she had a view across the entire great room and through the massive windows that looked onto the backyard and rolling fields beyond.

The moon came out from behind a cloud at that moment and sent a strip of white light onto the yard, silhouetting a man's figure, pressed against the back window.

The scream that rose in Callie's throat nearly choked her as she held it in, hands over her mouth as she stumbled backward, away from the rail, heart jumping madly in her chest.

It took a minute before she dared to look again, cautiously easing forward to the edge of the rail. The clouds had obscured the moon again, but she was pretty sure there was no figure there.

She thought about waking up West, or Talia, but hesitated. Maybe it just was someone checking on the house, like Cal. Making certain everything was secure with Victoria at the hospital.

No. She didn't believe that for a moment.

Andre . . .

Something about his shape and the way he seemed to hunger to be inside convinced her it was the man claiming to be West's cousin. And it made sense that he was the one outside looking in. The question was: Should she do something about it? The house was locked. Andre had been gone when Talia told her the code. And what would he be doing anyway?

She hurried back down the hall to West's room, eased open the door. He was sound asleep and she hated to wake him. But should she? Was Andre a threat tonight? A threat to *Tucker?*

She hurried on her tiptoes back to Tucker's room. She needed to get him away from Laughlin Ranch. It wasn't safe. She felt it in her bones, and though she knew she would

sound a little crazy when she told West and Talia what she
believed, she didn't care.

And as for tonight . . . In her clothes, she climbed into
bed with Tucker. She knew she wasn't going to sleep
anyway, so she wanted to be right next to him if anything
should happen.

The house was completely dark when Daniella pulled
into the drive. *Didn't I leave a light on in the prayer room?*
she thought, yanking on the emergency brake. Couldn't have
the damn Malibu sliding down the drive to the street and
then rolling down the hill. She needed to think of everything
if she was really going through with this.

But the house . . . shouldn't she see some illumination fil-
tering out? Unless Naomi or Clarice had switched off everything . . . ?

Lumpkin pulled up to the curb in front of the house and
turned off the ignition. Daniella looked over at him and
thought what a toad he was. She wasn't quite sure how she
was going to kill him yet, but she was damn well going to do
it. There were knives in the kitchen. Better yet, maybe she
could knock him out and suffocate him. The thought of
being close to him, having him touch her suddenly, sent the
heebie-jeebies running through her. It was a sad, sad truth
that she still just wanted Andre.

Ah, well . . .

She positioned herself against her car, leaning on her
elbows and pushing her breasts forward, watching him ap-
proach. "I don't really want you to come in," she said.

He stopped short and inhaled a sharp breath. "That's not
what you said at Ray's."

"I said you could come home with me. We can do it in
the car."

"Hell, no. I'm coming in," he said furiously. "It's *my* house."

"Well . . . not technically," she reminded, deliberately provoking him. She knew she shouldn't really, not if she was going to get him to do what she wanted, but it just felt so good she couldn't stop herself.

"Listen, bitch. I don't know what you think you're doing, but you got no game, girl. You don't deserve to live here, and when the lease is up, you're on your ass."

"The ass you can't take your eyes off."

He actually grabbed her by her hair, but then released her immediately. "Oho, I know what you're doing. You're trying to set me up for a lawsuit. Well, it ain't gonna work." He stepped back from her as if she smelled bad.

"You want to come in the house? Fine. Come on in." She walked up the steps to the front door and inserted her key. She was infuriated with the bastard, but even as she was pushing inside and fumbling for the light switch, she realized there was no way she could actually kill him here. Not when it was *her name* on the lease. *Her name* on every car registration. *Her name* on the utility bills. No, it would have to be somewhere else, but what could she use to—

Her hand encountered a wall of human flesh and she shrieked in surprise. Whoever grabbed her arm yanked her inside, pushing her to the floor, smacking her head on the floor. She flailed and tried to get up, but the prick of a needle sent cold shivers rushing through her. "What—what?" she gasped.

Distantly, she heard Lumpkin say cautiously from outside, "Daniella?"

Fighting back a swirling dizziness, she saw him stick his head inside the door, his body outlined by the lighter outdoors. Her attacker was on him in an instant, putting something around his neck that made him choke, stagger, and gasp. In the near blackness Daniella could only make out images: his fingers clawing at his neck, his feet stamping and shifting, the hood covering his attacker's face, the smell of urine as Lumpkin's bladder gave up the ghost and emptied onto the floor.

Time passed. She must have blacked out because she awakened to find herself dressed in her prayer robe, naked underneath. She felt foggy and strange, and the woman standing over her could have been a mirage. It was a woman, wasn't it? She was in one of their hooded prayer robes, too, but her face was obscured.

The woman was dangling the chain of one of their ankhs in one hand and there were bits of flesh attached to it.

Lumpkin. Oh, God. She'd killed him with the ankh! *Is it mine?*

She sensed she wasn't alone and turned her head as much as she could muster to see two other robed figures on the floor, glassy eyes staring, mouths open and tongues flopping. *Clarice and Jerrilyn.* And Lumpkin . . . on the far side, his eyes bulging out of his head in a death mask of horror.

She shivered, glanced back at the woman. "Naomi?" she tried to squeak out.

The robed woman flung the cross aside and suddenly jumped on her, reaching inside Daniella's robe to grasp the ankh that was still around her neck. And then she started twisting and twisting. Daniella managed to fling one hand up and claw at her, but her hand was weak and only hit the woman's robe.

"You call yourself the handmaidens," the woman said calmly as Daniella felt her throat squeeze shut, her lungs scream for air. "You're a harem of whores."

And the world went black.

West awoke, blinked a couple of times, realized where he was and that Callie wasn't next to him, and threw back the covers. It was early, the gray light of morning barely creeping in. Quickly he got up and took a shower in the en-suite bathroom. Then he shaved and ran a comb through his wet hair. He had to re-dress in yesterday's clothes as he'd left his bag in the car. Then he headed downstairs and walked to the back door, disarming the alarm as he emerged into a cool morning that smelled fresh with no hint of the manure scent that sometimes blew in from the northeast, where the bulk of the massive herd and barns were located.

He grabbed his bag from the Explorer then retraced his steps. When he entered the house he was surprised to see Callie, fully dressed. "Good morning," he said.

"You got your bag," she observed.

"Yeah, I figured I'd better get ready for the day."

"Did you see anyone out there?"

"No. Why?"

"You're going to think I'm nuts, but I saw a man standing outside the great room windows last night, the back side of the house. It was around midnight, or maybe one? It worried me so I spent the rest of the night in Tucker's room."

He frowned. "Why didn't you wake me?"

"I don't know." She shook her head.

"Okay, I'll check for footprints," he told her.

"Good . . . but when you come back, I want to talk to you about Andre."

West let that sink in a moment. "You think it was him?"

"I do."

"Okay. I'll be right back," he assured her.

"I'm going to take a shower and change, and I'll meet you back here in the kitchen. I . . . West, I don't want to stay here. Without Victoria, I want to leave with Tucker and go back to LA. Call it paranoia if you want, but I don't think it's safe here."

He nodded slowly, thinking. He didn't want her here, either, and with Victoria in the hospital there was no one likely to stop him from taking Tucker away, at least temporarily. "We need to tell Talia."

He saw her relax with relief. "Thank you."

She hurried for the stairs, and West walked back outside, looking around himself carefully. He circled around the back of the house and examined the area in front of the windows, which was hard soil surrounded by grass in need of mowing. There were footprints in the grass, nothing noticeable in the soil. It did appear that someone had been walking around the house.

Back inside, he reset the alarm then waited for Callie. Forty-five minutes later he heard Tucker's high-pitched voice babbling in French and then his clambering footsteps down the stairs. He zipped into the kitchen and stopped short upon seeing him. "*Déjeuner!*" he declared.

Callie showed up right behind him, showered, and changed. "Breakfast," she translated, but he knew the word.

"How about I take you both to Laughlin BBQ? They have great breakfasts," West said.

"They do?" Callie asked, then immediately said, "Sounds like a plan. Talia told me to go there, too, but I was thinking dinner." She turned to Tucker. "What do you like to eat in the morning?"

"Croissants!" Tucker declared.

"I should have known." She smiled.

"Think it'll be more like flapjacks," West pointed out.

"Flapjacks?" Tucker perked up at a new word.

"Pancakes . . . like crepes, sort of," Callie explained.

"I know pancakes," Tucker told her haughtily. "Flapjacks," he told West as if ordering from a waiter.

"All right, pardner. Flapjacks it is." West resisted the urge to ruffle the boy's hair, knowing Tucker wouldn't appreciate it. Right now the boy wanted Callie and nobody else, but given enough time, they might become a kind of family.

The three of them walked out to his Explorer together, Tucker skipping ahead and scaring several rabbits that were munching on the front lawn.

The killer flexed her gloved hands as she looked at the four bodies lying on the prayer room floor and felt a certain amount of satisfaction. This *array* . . . was a long time coming. She hadn't anticipated the guy. He was nothing more than collateral damage, but she'd seen how he'd acted on the driveway and he was a complete asshole.

She'd put him in Andre's robe. He hadn't taken it with him and why would he? Sick man that he was, he didn't know up from sideways anymore. He was focused on killing the boy, but that wasn't going to do him any good. She knew how families like the Laughlins worked. They would close ranks and keep him on the outside. He couldn't see that, of course, because he'd never been psychologically astute and now, with whatever was happening to him—brain tumor, maybe?—tearing him apart, making him believe in his own delusions, and megalomania, well . . . he wasn't the man he used to be. She was afraid something had popped inside his head, making him believe all the shit he spewed.

He'd been so sexy and compelling once. She ached for the old Andre, and she wanted him back!

Carefully, she retrieved the ankh from Daniella's neck, then gathered up the one she'd used on Lumpkin and tossed aside for effect, the one that had once been Teresa's. The ankhs were valuable and she didn't want to leave unnecessary evidence . . . she just wanted to be able to show Andre what she'd done. Let him know how good she was at this kind of thing, how much better than the other handmaidens. With that in mind, she snatched up the small black leather bag she'd brought with her and carefully removed a box of cigarette ash.

She looked down at all their distorted faces and smiled. She'd already spread some ash over Clarice and now she did the same to Jerrilyn, Lumpkin, and Daniella.

Then she walked quickly toward the front door, gently tossing Teresa's ankh into a corner as if it had mistakenly fallen there. If things didn't go the way she hoped, she was going to have to implicate Andre in their deaths. He would know she'd done the deeds, if he could hold the thought, but he wouldn't be able to drag her down with him, as long as she was careful.

But she didn't want things to go that way. She still wanted Andre. A part of her always would.

The cigarette ash was a brilliant addition, the perfect motif for her tableau. Andre would enjoy that she'd made them sacrifices to him and, if the authorities needed to be brought in, they might believe Andre's scrambled brains had come up with the idea. He wore an ankh around his neck, and the presence of another one, the one used in the murders, would certainly put him under suspicion, but again, this plan was merely a last resort.

Before she left, she went back to the prayer room for a last look over her handiwork. The robed bodies were lining up and she was going to have to get Andre here soon or the smell of rot would be noticed.

Satisfied, she grabbed up Lumpkin's pants and searched through them for his keys. She'd left her own vehicle down the street and figured it would be fine sitting there for a while. She had a couple more targets in mind, though she wasn't exactly sure which she would do next, which would present itself first.

She locked up the house, got in Lumpkin's vehicle, turned the ignition. She drove for about five miles before pulling off on a Venice side street and slipping out her cell phone. "Hey, lover," she said when Andre answered. "You don't have to worry about Clarice or Jerrilyn or Daniella anymore. . . . Thanks for telling me all about them. They were easy to fool, just like you said. So predictable. And as a special bonus, your landlord. Time for you to come on home."

What? What was she saying? "I'm not going anywhere," Andre snarled. No one told The Messiah what to do.

"You need to come back," she said in a singsong voice.

Andre looked around the dismal room he'd booked at the Travelin' Inn in Castilla, a motor lodge with a lumpy bed on which he hadn't slept a wink all night. He'd taken a drive back toward the ranch and had seen his cousin arrive. West Laughlin. Craig's bastard who shouldn't even be around, and yet there he was, with the nanny who looked so much like Teresa it made his groin hurt. Callie *Cantrell.* What were they doing? What was their plan? He'd dismissed West as unimportant but watching him put the nanny up against a wall and kiss her and press up against her while her hands clutched at him in delirious desperation had made him burn with lust and indignation. It was *his* house! Not some out-of-wedlock cur's like West Laughlin. After they'd gone inside the house he'd tried to scrub the memory from his brain but his own imagination—visualizing them thrashing around in ecstasy with him inside her and her legs clamped around his back, both of them moaning and crying out— was infinitely worse! He'd gone back later to stare through the window, the urge to smash his way inside nearly over-whelming.

". . . know you want Victoria to die, but it's time to come back," she was saying and he realized he'd missed what had come before.

"I don't want her to die yet," he hissed. "If she goes now, the boy could get everything . . . or maybe she'll leave it all to Cal Stutz." He could hear the despair in his voice and he pulled himself together. He didn't remember confiding in her about the Laughlins, but he must have.

"Victoria won't leave the ranch to the help," she assured him.

He so wanted to believe her, but his fear was too great. "You don't know Victoria. She'll do whatever she wants, even though it's not as it should be." He glanced through a crack in his curtained window and the sudden light blasted his eyes. Quickly he dropped the curtain back and turned away.

"Where's the boy now? At the house?"

"There's a woman in charge of him." He deliberately left Callie Cantrell's name out of it. He needed to think about what to do next, and he didn't want her spoiling his plans. Was she even telling him the truth about Clarice, Daniella, and Jerrilyn? And Lumpkin? It was so hard to tell sometimes. "She's staying at the house with the boy."

"If Victoria dies, is this woman in charge of the kid?"

"Possibly."

"Make nice with her," she ordered. "You know how to better than anyone."

Andre couldn't speak he was so infuriated at the suggestion. *He* was the one who made the decisions, no one else!

"I'll call you," he struggled to get out. His head was really pounding. The wild colors showed across everything.

"Come home," she said and he resented her for that, too.

He was going to have to do something about her. Anarchy, that's what it was. He thought about the Glock he'd taken from his safe, tucked at the bottom of his bag. Bullets were inelegant but all they required was a touch of the trigger, and the Glock could fire eighteen rounds without reloading.

"How are you feeling? The headaches and blank spots still there?"

"Shut the fuck up," he ground out, clicking off the cell phone and throwing it across the room. It slammed against the wall and fell to the floor. He pressed his palms to his temples and screamed.

Chapter Twenty-Five

Callie's cell phone rang as she was following West's Explorer to Laughlin BBQ. Glancing at the screen she recognized Diane Cantrell's number and thought, *Nope*. She wasn't going to be harangued again. Not if she could help it.

West looked over at her Lexus as he pulled into the restaurant parking lot and she rolled into the spot next to him. Both Laughlin BBQ and The Bull Stops Here gift store were closer to the Laughlin Ranch house than Castilla's downtown and it had only taken fifteen minutes to get to them. Callie got out and then helped Tucker to the gravel parking lot. As soon as he touched ground, he ran toward the rustic building with its board and bat siding stained red, and a weathervane slowly twisting atop the barn-shaped building. Two branding irons were crossed above the sliding wooden door that was the entrance, and which looked heavy enough to rupture a muscle. Tucker tugged on it to no avail, but when West clasped the handle and gave it a hard yank, it slid back on well-oiled tracks.

Tucker loved everything. Talking rapidly in his own mixture of French and English, he let them know he wanted a Cattleman's Plate, which was steak and eggs and lots of it, but Callie thought he was more enamored of the name than of what he would be eating. She managed to talk him into a child's stack of flapjacks, orange slice, and a glass of unfiltered apple juice, he-man style. She had no appetite whatsoever, but forced herself to eat part of a skillet of scrambled eggs, hash browns, and sauteed vegetables labeled FOR TENDERFOOTS ONLY.

West chose bacon and eggs, and coffee that was served in a pot large enough to fill both of their cups several times over. As soon as their order was placed, West pulled out his phone and sent a text. "For Talia," he explained. "You can head back to LA after breakfast. I'll stop by the hospital and then be right behind you. I'm back at work today."

"Where we go to?" Tucker asked.

"Great-Grandma isn't well, so you and I are heading to my house until she feels better," Callie said.

"You got horses?"

"No."

"Cats?" he asked hopefully.

"We'll come up with something."

Their food arrived and while they ate, West said, "I'd like to ask this Andre a few questions, but if he's still around, it's going to have to wait. Luckily, Talia can handle things. Not that I want anything to do with the ranch," he added quickly. "But without Victoria . . ." He shrugged.

Tucker lifted his shoulders, mimicking West and grinning as he tried to cut his flapjacks and mangled them miserably. Callie helped him and soon he'd worked his way halfway through the stack.

Just as they were finishing up, the front door opened and a tall man with a shock of nearly white hair, wearing jeans, boots, and a green flannel shirt, came through. He noticed Callie immediately and stopped dead, looking like he'd seen a ghost. West glanced over at him and said, half-apologetically, "You're going to probably get that a lot."

"Who is that man?" she asked.

"Edmund Mikkels." West lifted a hand to him in greeting, adding in an aside to Callie, "Victoria said he was crumbling. I just saw him a month ago and don't remember his hair being that white."

Mikkels had to be told twice to follow the hostess to a table two over from theirs. He couldn't seem to rip his eyes from Callie. She murmured, "It's pretty clear I remind him of Teresa."

"Teresa is mine *maman*," Tucker stated positively, which brought both West and Callie's attention back to him with a bang.

"You overheard us talking?" Callie asked.

He nodded. "She dieded, but Aimee is not mine *maman*." He slid Callie a sideways glance. "You is."

Callie felt her throat tighten. "Thank you, Tucker, but you know that's not true."

He lifted his shoulders again, shrugging off her denial as if it were expected but not believed.

West said, "I want to say a few words to Mikkels before we leave." He got out of his seat and headed toward Mikkels's table just as Teddy Stutz entered the restaurant. Spying him, Tucker clambered out of his seat to chase after West.

"Tucker!" Callie half-stood, whispering harshly. The little boy ignored her, but Teddy Stutz strolled her way.

"Took the little man out for breakfast, huh. How's Victoria?"

"I thought you might know better than I, from your father."

"Cal doesn't talk to me about things that matter," he said with a short laugh. "So, that's West Laughlin talking to Mikkels, huh? Wonder why Victoria called on him. He's more persona non grata than I am."

"Excuse me." Callie hurried after Tucker, touching his

shoulder to get his attention as he was staring unabashedly at Edmund Mikkels.

"Your hair is *tres blanc,*" he said.

Mikkels, who'd been asking West about Victoria, first turned to Tucker, then Callie. His eyes were red-rimmed, but she didn't think he'd been crying. He just didn't look well all over.

"I'm sure you've heard it before, but you look just like Teresa," Mikkels said. His voice was scarcely louder than a whisper.

"Doesn't she?" Teddy Stutz said, coming up to them.

Tucker said loudly, "Knock, knock!"

"No, Tucker. Not again," Callie said, trying to pull him away.

"Knock, knock!"

Callie managed to wrangle him away from the table, but Tucker resisted, trying to escape her grasp by twisting his body. "Tucker, we need to let them talk," she said urgently.

"*Pourquoi?* I want to be there!"

She grabbed his hand and practically had to drag him outside. He was pouting a few minutes later when West joined them after settling the bill. His expression was intense and she could tell he was bothered about something.

"What is it?" she asked as she buckled a recalcitrant Tucker into his booster seat. His arms were crossed over his chest and he looked straight ahead in protest.

"Mikkels started to shake. Seeing you must've hit some chord. He wanted to apologize. Said he didn't mean for it to happen. If Teddy Stutz hadn't jumped in and changed the subject, he might've broken down completely and told me exactly what happened the day Stephen died."

"It was a bullet from his gun that killed Stephen, right? That would make anyone feel guilty."

"That, and for getting involved with Teresa in the first place. I don't know at what level, but the guy's eaten up with guilt. When I talked to him before he was morose and drinking a lot, but when he saw you . . ."

His cell phone rang and he pulled it from his pocket. "Talia," he said aloud, answering the call.

Callie could tell Talia wasn't happy about them leaving, but West fended her off by changing the subject. "We ran into Edmund Mikkels at the BBQ. He looks like hell."

Her response was so loud that West pulled the phone away from his ear and Callie could hear every word.

Talia was saying, ". . . feels damn guilty for killing his friend, and who can blame him? Probably wishes he'd never introduced him to Teresa in the first place. We all wish that, don't we? Except for Tucker, of course."

"Stephen met Teresa in a bar in Los Angeles," West corrected her.

"Who told you that?" Talia asked. "It was Edmund who introduced them because Teresa was hanging around the BBQ. He thought she was into him, but it was Stephen, and we all know why that is . . . the *mon-eeee* . . ."

"Teresa was living in LA before she married Stephen," West said, clearly processing unexpected information.

"So? Yeah? I'm telling you, she met him here."

West shook his head and said, "Investigating Teresa's death is one more reason I've got to leave."

"Fine." Talia snorted. "At least Cal's here, although he's got the whole damn company to run. I'll stick around as long as I can, but don't forget I have a life, too."

The hospital in Coalinga was a few miles south of Laughlin Ranch and West was in and out of it in less than an hour. The doctor said there was no change in Victoria's condition and there wasn't much for West to do other than ask the staff to keep him in the loop. On the drive to LA he called Victoria's lawyer, telling a still-rattled Gary Merritt about his plans to take Tucker to Los Angeles and keep him in his and Callie Cantrell's care in the interim. Merritt said he would talk to Talia, as the child's grandmother, and make sure that worked with her, but if she agreed that everything was co-pacetic, then that was legally fine. Again, West requested to be kept in the loop and Merritt assured him he would.

The last call he made was to the San Joaquin sheriff's department, asking if they knew any more about the brown sedan that had run Maya and Victoria down. "What about people in the building?" West asked, knowing he was over-stepping his bounds a little. In his experience, police officers of any kind didn't like being pressed by outsiders, even sometimes other officers. But the deputy he spoke to simply said there was nothing new so far. Once more, West asked the man to make sure he was kept informed.

He was inside the Los Angeles city limits when Dorcas called and told him a homicide suspect had been brought in that he wanted West to sweat.

"I haven't even gotten my badge back," West protested.

"It's a woman," Dorcas told him. "Shot her boyfriend in the back and now's claiming self-defense."

"Doesn't sound even close to credible," West said, know-ing Dorcas wanted him to do the interview because Dorcas was big and intimidating and West, though over six feet him-self, had a leaner build and a face that seemed to appeal to the ladies.

"Said he drugged her and held her down, and she was kind of woozy when she was brought in. Supposedly picked up his gun and thought he was comin' at her."

"I'll be there in thirty," West said. He really wanted to spend his time concentrating on Teresa, but she wasn't even truly his case, and now that he was going to be back on

the force, he would need to work on whatever cases were
assigned to him.

Andre had watched the two-car brigade leave the ranch.
He'd swallowed enough Advil and aspirin to knock out a
horse, and had brought the pain in his head under control.
This all started with Teresa, he decided. *The headaches are
her fault. They've been a bitch since that last trip to Martinique.*

A stray thought struck him.

*Maybe this was manufactured. Maybe one of the hand-
maidens did this to me. The one who killed Teresa!*

He hadn't wanted to know which one had done it. Had
told himself he didn't care, but now . . .

It was all a plot. A plot to get rid of him.

Through the binoculars he saw the Explorer and the
Lexus turn down the oak-lined drive. He got in the Xterra
and took after them, keeping a fair distance behind. Laughlin was in the black SUV and Callie and the boy were in the
Lexus.

Maybe *she* poisoned him, he thought. She was there on
the island at the time. She'd sought out Tucker, made herself
look like Teresa, plotted with *West Laughlin* . . .

A jab of pain in his head. He nearly swerved onto the
shoulder.

"Careful," he told himself, keeping the Lexus just in view.
As ever, there was a ton of traffic barreling toward the City
of Angels. The thought made him smile. Angels were looking out for him. "I am The Messiah," he whispered.

His cell rang, sitting on the console, and he glanced over
at it angrily. Naomi. Shit. He couldn't talk now. Didn't have
fucking Bluetooth and couldn't risk being pulled over. He let
it go to voice mail, knowing she wouldn't leave a message.

A few minutes later he was proved right when he heard the buzzing ringtone that said he'd gotten a text.

Cautiously, he touched the screen and read her missive:

ditched the car

He grunted. At least that was good news. He didn't trust her as far as he could throw her but she was definitely the most reliable one.

In an act of pure kindness, he decided he would wait till the end to kill her . . . after the Cantrell woman and the boy and that fucking, big-mouthed bitch, Talia Laughlin.

West signed paperwork that took him off administrative leave and put him back on the force. He was issued his badge and gun, a Glock, and practically before he entered the squad room Dorcas was on him. "She's in number three," he said, meaning the third interview room down the hall.

"You gotta be kidding. I need some time. I'm not up on this case," West said.

Dorcas slapped a thin file in his hands. "There ain't enough there to care. Read it and talk to her. You're good with the women."

"Then I need something from you," West said. "Everything you've already got on Teresa Laughlin and everything you can find. I mean everything. I want a complete murder book. The autopsy report. Fingerprints. DNA. *Everything*. I want to know what brand of toothpaste she used, you got that?"

Dorcas grinned and slapped West on the back. "Good to have you back, man."

"Whatever," West muttered, but he smiled at his partner. It was good to be back.

* * *

The minute Callie entered the house she decided she never wanted to come back here again. There were only bad and sad memories associated with it. She'd hung on because of Sean. Because this was where she'd lived when he was born. Because this was the only home he'd ever known.

But Sean was gone and her memories of him were inside her heart. There was nothing about the house that meant anything to her any longer, and apart from the satisfaction she felt in thwarting the Cantrells, there was very little reason to hang on to it.

Tucker ran past Callie and tore through the rooms much as he had at Laughlin Ranch. "We staying here?" he asked.

"For the time being," Callie said distractedly.

"I like this place," he yelled. "It loud!"

Callie half-smiled. Jonathan had always complained about Sean's lack of volume control. He had one setting: high.

For a moment she got that same niggling sensation of a memory just outside her reach. Did it have to do with Sean? Jonathan? It tantalized her and she struggled to grasp it, but it was gone too quickly.

Idly, she picked up her cell phone and examined it for new calls or texts, hoping to have missed a message from West. Diane Cantrell's number popped up again, but she ignored it. There was no voice mail or other attempt at communication, so she assumed it was just another attempt by Diane to harass her.

Thinking of Diane, the Cantrells, and the house reminded her of the charge from Security One. Pulling the statement from the bottom of her shoulder bag, she called the number again, not expecting to be put through, so she was pleasantly surprised when a woman with a tired voice picked up. When Callie explained about the charge, the woman said it was company policy to bill accounts by automatic payment and that whoever had set up the account had asked to be billed annually.

"My husband set this up," Callie told her, "but we don't use you for our alarm system."

"We're not that kind of company. We rent out security boxes, kind of like safety-deposit boxes at a bank, but we're a private company and you have twenty-four-hour access. Just sign in and use your key."

The keys. Callie was standing in the kitchen, but she automatically looked toward the den where she'd left Jonathan's keys in the box on his desk. The mystery key might very well open the security box. She almost told the woman that her husband was deceased but thought better of it at the last moment. Clearly she wasn't a signer for access to the box account, which led her to believe that Jonathan had kept it secret from her on purpose. It didn't take a huge leap of imagination to believe that, if there truly was money left over from the mortgage Jonathan had taken out, this was where he'd stashed it.

She asked the woman for the company's address and found it was in Santa Monica, a block off Lincoln. As soon as she was off the phone she texted West, asking him to call her. She knew he was at work and preferred not to phone him, but she hoped he would get right back to her. When he didn't she figured he was buried with work on his first day back. Frustrated, she glanced at the clock. One P.M. It might be hours before she heard from him.

Since there was nothing in the house to make for lunch, and she had time to kill, she rounded up Tucker and headed out to a sandwich shop she knew of that made sandwiches with croissants.

Whether it was because he was impatient and disinterested, or because he was fed up with the kind of woman whose every sentence is a lie, West didn't respond well to Bonnie Burnham's tears, wails, and clinging need. He didn't play her friend. He didn't invite confidences. He just laid out the fact that she wasn't going to leave that room until she told enough of the truth to match the crime scene evidence already collected. Although it was counterintuitive, West's distance worked like the proverbial charm and she broke in about an hour and a half, admitting that she basically shot her boyfriend in the back when he was walking away from their fight.

"He was leaving me for that fucking bitch!" she screamed as a defense.

West dropped her from his thoughts as soon as he left the room though she was still screaming. It was always about sex or money, he told himself again, his thoughts turning toward Teresa.

Dorcas swung away from his desk and computer as soon as West entered the room. "Good goin' with Burnham," he said admiringly. "New Laughlin record." Then, "Diane Cantrell is on line two for you."

"Don't have time." He sat down in his own chair and moved up to his computer screen. "You put together what I asked for?"

"She keeps callin', and I'm done talkin' to her," he said. "I'm serious here. Pick up the goddamn phone. And I sent you the file. Hard copy's on your desk."

West had already spied the murder book and now he slid it his way. "Thanks," he said. And then to show his gratitude, he made a big show of punching the button for line two. Dorcas said, "Good luck," then turned away as West answered, "Detective Laughlin," fleetingly enjoying the sound of that again before Diane Cantrell's strident voice jumped into his ear.

"Thanks for taking my call," she said sarcastically. "You're the one who ordered information on Callie Shipley. I'm just trying to give it to you."

"I was looking for information about the accident that

killed your brother and nephew and injured Mrs. Cantrell," he corrected, sensing she'd used Callie's maiden name purposely.

"She married my brother for money," Diane snapped back, ignoring him. "And she's still hiding funds that aren't hers and living in the house my brother meant to leave our family. She's no better than a thief. Jonathan was taken in by her. He collected conniving women like flannel collects lint. If I told you . . ."

West tuned out. He didn't care why Callie had married Jonathan Cantrell. He knew she'd wanted a family and was still, and would always be to some degree, devastated over her son's death.

His mind wandered back to Teresa as his eye traveled over the documents in the murder book. Where had she been between the time she and a partner had worked their con in Martinique? What had she been doing before she met Stephen at Laughlin BBQ? He'd assumed she'd been in Los Angeles because that's what Stephen had told him. So, how come she'd been hanging around Castilla? It seemed an odd place to have her hunting grounds unless she'd specifically targeted the Laughlin family. . . .

That made the most sense, the more he thought about it. Somehow she'd targeted Stephen after she'd returned to Los Angeles? She'd been living in LA before that last trip to Martinique as evidenced by her studio apartment she'd rented, so it seemed reasonable to assume LA was her home base. Was her male partner in Los Angeles, too? Maybe still here?

". . . and you can't tell me he didn't pick up Callie because she was a replica of that other gold digger. Lucky for Ms. Shipley that he was interested in a 'look' rather than any substance or character. Once upon a time I was relieved that he'd chosen Callie to marry, but—"

"You know the woman who looked like Callie?" West interrupted, his attention snapping back.

"*Know* her? No. I couldn't say that. She was slippery. Always unavailable for the family to meet. Callie Shipley, now . . . she made a point of meeting us. Her agenda was to become beloved by the family. It wasn't—"

"Ms. Cantrell, what do you think happened in the accident that killed your brother?"

His direct question derailed her diatribe for a moment, but not for long. "Well, come on, Detective. Isn't that your job? It's still an unsolved crime."

"I just wanted your take on it."

"I have no *take* on it," she said tightly. "There was a suggestion that they were racing, but Jonathan had his son in the car. He liked fast speed, sure, but come on. He wasn't completely negligent."

"All right. Thank you," West said. "I'll let you know when I have any further information about the accident."

"You called me, Detective," she reminded. "Or your partner did. I thought *you* knew something."

"I'm just getting up to speed."

Though she tried to hang on the phone, he managed to end the call a few moments later. He finished looking through the murder book, then went to the computer file and added a few notes of his own. He also listed a few questions:

Who was Teresa's partner?

How did she learn about the Laughlin family, specifically Stephen Laughlin?

Did Jonathan Cantrell reconnect with her in LA?

Whom did she meet in Martinique on her last trip and why was she killed?

What is Aimee Thomas not saying?

He circled this last question. He'd never believed in Aimee's protestations of innocence, but she had taken care of Tucker for three years or more. The Fort-de-France police had interviewed her thoroughly and though she'd been unwilling to give up Tucker, she'd been forced to in the end as she'd little legal choice but to let him go.

West had no jurisdiction over Teresa's murder, but he had the link to Jonathan Cantrell and Cantrell's death, and possible homicide, was definitely in his bailiwick.

He reread the report from the gendarmerie. He'd already noted that they'd found the boat on which Teresa had died, a rental, but the man who'd rented it had used identification in the name of John Bonner with a fake Pennsylvania address. The description of the man was vague: medium height, light brown hair, tan pants, and a light shirt. But at least he knew they were searching for a man, one who knew enough about boats to take one into the bay and maybe out to sea.

He examined the autopsy report again. It was confirmed that Teresa had died of a head injury, and that the marks around her neck from an apparent chain, maybe a piece of jewelry, had come after her death. Someone had wrapped the chain around her neck and tightened it. In a fit of fury? Because she was wearing a necklace and whoever killed her tightened it before slipping it off her head? Because it was valuable? The killer had left no fingerprints or any other identifying crime scene data. He was currently a ghost.

Teresa's DNA had been sent to the crime lab and her fingerprints had been entered into the AFIS database. West wasn't expecting much beyond a DNA confirmation since he already knew the body was Teresa's and that Teresa was Tucker's mother. He didn't think Teresa had ever been arrested, but maybe there had been some cause to fingerprint her once upon a time. In any case, this was the waiting game he was playing. The DNA would take a few weeks at the earliest; the fingerprints should be back quicker, especially if there was a match.

Noticing that Callie had left him a text, asking him to call, West checked his recent phone calls and clicked on

Chapter Twenty-Six

"*What?*" West jumped up to look at Dorcas's computer screen.

"At some point, she was inside the car that ran them off the road. Probably driving. And they didn't find anyone else's prints, so . . ."

"She did it," West said.

"Not for sure."

"She did it," he said again, with certainty. "Maybe I can't prove it yet, but I know it."

Dorcas grinned. "This is the kind of thing that pissed off the captain."

"Paulsen was pissed off because I broke up with his daughter."

"Yes and no. See, I'm glad you're back, because I've been meanin' to point some things out. You jump to conclusions, and what really chapped Paulsen's hide was that you were always right."

"Not always." West's head was buzzing with the news about Teresa.

"Always," Dorcas argued. "When you'd get that blood-hound look like you've got now. He wanted you to be wrong, but you never were."

"You're giving me way too much credit."

"Just tellin' it like it is."

"Teresa knew Jonathan Cantrell. If she ran him off the road, she did it on purpose."

"Where you goin'?" Dorcas asked as West swung away from his desk and toward the door.

"The stolen vehicle that slammed into the Cantrell Mercedes was impounded, but eventually it was returned to its owner. I'm going to check with him."

"You got that from my notes on the Cantrells?" Dorcas asked.

"You do good work, Pete. Don't let anyone tell you differently."

"And here I thought I was just a pretty face."

The doorbell rang, scattering Callie's disjointed thoughts. She'd broken down earlier and called Diane back, getting her voice mail, which was a boon. She really hadn't wanted to talk to her, but knew she needed to head her off at the pass or risk a series of ever more angry phone calls. "I'm back in LA," she'd told Diane's voice mail, not without some misgivings, but she was ready to sever connections with the Cantrells once and for all.

Hurrying to answer the door, she looked through the peephole and spied Derek Cantrell standing on the front porch. "Damn," she muttered, pulling back, wondering if it was too late to pretend she wasn't home. Damn, damn, damn. Phoning Diane back hadn't been such a hot idea, apparently, as it had sent her brother right to Callie's door.

Cautiously opening the door, she said to Jonathan's brother, "My message for Diane was just to let her know I was back. I wasn't expecting a house call."

"I won't stay long," Derek said to her, stepping across the threshold quickly as if afraid she might shut the door on him.

"What can I do for you, Derek?"

They were standing in the foyer and when Callie showed no signs of inviting him in, Derek asked uncomfortably, "Can we sit down for a few minutes?"

"We've said everything there is to say. I'm here temporarily. I told you that. I'm moving out very soon. I just need a little time. Don't push me or I could change my mind and fight you for every Cantrell dime."

"It isn't just about money. This house has been in the family for years."

"It's totally about money," she disagreed.

"Callie, don't be this way."

"This way," she repeated. "You mean, honest?"

"You don't even like this house, do you?"

She didn't immediately answer, trying to read his expression. He seemed sincere but Derek, like his brother, was a chameleon. She never really knew what was beneath their changing skins. The Security One box Jonathan had rented popped into her head and she considered telling Derek about it. She couldn't access it anyway, and really didn't want the legal wrangle. If they worked together, though, they might find a way to open the box. Whatever was inside was probably Cantrell property and there was nothing she wanted from them anyway.

As if reading her mind, he asked, "You haven't found any trace of the mortgage money?"

"Not so far."

Without being asked, Derek walked past her, but instead of going into the living room, he headed for the den. Irked, Callie followed him, standing in the doorway, her arms folded across her chest as Derek looked over the expanse of the walnut that was the desktop and the box with the ring of keys.

Tucker swooped in at that moment, skidding to a stop in

the doorway beside Callie. He looked Derek over from head to toe. "Who is him?" he asked.

"Tucker Laughlin, meet Derek Cantrell."

"Laughlin," Derek repeated, examining Tucker as thoroughly as he was being checked out.

Something about the angle of his jaw jolted a memory of Jonathan. She could suddenly practically see her husband the way he'd looked that last evening. He'd been furious because they'd learned their sitter had come down with the flu and they were stuck taking Sean with them to the soiree put on by moneyed friends of the family. Callie had said she would be happy to stay home, but Jonathan wouldn't hear of it. His face had turned brick red with annoyance and he'd sported a scowl well into the evening. Callie had spent most of her time that night trying to play cheerleader to Jonathan, hoping to keep his temper from exploding and taking out his fury on Sean.

And then the ride home. Suddenly that ethereal memory she'd been reaching for came close enough to grab. Jonathan driving fast. Looking in the rearview. The dark SUV on their tail. He'd been excited and Callie had sensed something else was going on. She'd screamed at him to slow down. She'd demanded to know who was in the other car. She'd shrieked that *their son* was in the backseat.

He'd ignored her and they'd hurtled forward to the wide curve about a half mile from their house. . . .

"Callie? You okay?" Derek was suddenly right in front of her, his hands on her shoulders.

She drew back sharply. "Fine."

Tucker's hand had stolen into hers and he was pressed against her leg, alternately gazing up at her and then at Derek with suspicion and worry.

"You looked like you were going to faint," Derek said. "What happened? What's wrong?"

"Nothing." Callie walked on unsteady legs to the desk

chair and sank into it. The keys were directly in her line of vision.

It had been a woman driving intently behind them. Callie had seen the outline of her shoulder-length hair, the tightness of her knuckles on the steering wheel.

She meant to kill us. . . .

"Calleee," Tucker said on a faint whimper.

Immediately, she reached out to him and he climbed onto her lap, his spindly legs draping over hers. "I'm okay. I just felt kind of dizzy for a moment."

"You go away," Tucker said determinedly to Derek.

"No, it's okay," Callie intervened. "Really. It's not about Derek."

"You really do look like hell," Derek said.

That made her utter a short bark of laughter. "Thanks."

"What happened?"

"I saw a vision of the past," she said, holding on to Tucker a little too tightly. He started to squirm in her embrace and she let him go.

He jumped down and looked at her. "It okay?" he asked.

"Yes, yes . . . I hear the TV on in the family room . . . the room by the kitchen," she added at the line drawn between his eyes. "Go see what's on while I finish talking to Derek."

"I stay with you."

"Well, you can, but I'm all right. I think you might be missing something on TV."

He frowned at her for another couple of moments before he moved toward the door, keeping himself facing both of them as he backed out.

"At this rate, I'll turn him into a TV addict," she said ruefully.

"What's the deal with you and the Laughlin kid?" Derek asked.

She was immediately sorry she'd said anything. "Was

there something else? I really think I should be talking to you through a lawyer."

He looked around the room as if cataloging everything in Jonathan's den. "I guess not," he said reluctantly as his gaze drifted over the box of keys. "What are all these keys to?"

"Jonathan's car . . . the house . . ."

It was then that Callie made a final decision about her life. She couldn't move on completely until she'd dealt with the consequences of her husband and son's deaths, and now was as good a time as any. "I'm pretty sure one of them is to a box at Security One." She then told him about the charge on her bill and her suspicion that maybe the box was where Jonathan had stashed the remaining mortgage money.

Derek looked excited. "You haven't looked yet?"

"I just found out and I'm not a signer."

"Well, we've got the death certificate," he said eagerly "You're his widow. They have to let you in."

"Maybe, but it's bound to be a legal hiccup."

"I could go as Jonathan," he said as if the idea had just popped into his head. "People got us confused all the time, and I can copy his signature."

"Can you?" Callie said quietly.

"Sure. I'm good at it. I mean . . . I haven't done it in years, but I'm pretty sure I haven't forgotten," he added hastily.

"I don't even have the death certificate."

"Oh, I do. You were a mess . . . but we got all that stuff done. I'm calling Diane." He immediately snatched his phone from his pocket and hit a saved number.

"I don't want to do this, Derek."

"No, no. This is good." He cut off his call before it went through. "Tell you what. I'll head out and pick up a copy of the death certificate, and I'll talk to Diane then. But I still think it would be easier just to act like I'm Jonathan. Try it first and see what happens. They obviously don't know he's dead, so . . ."

"No, thanks."

"Fine. I'll get the death certificate and we'll do it that way. Don't worry. I'll be back soon."

He was out the door before she could protest further.

West put in several calls about the stolen vehicle that had been involved in the Cantrell accident before he finally connected with Bob Vincent, the rightful owner of the Acura MDX.

"Took forever to get reimbursed from the insurance company," Vincent told him in a voice filled with gravel. "Damn bandits. The damage wasn't that bad, but since it was used at a crime scene they ran me around and around. Talk, talk, talk. Blah-bidy, blah-bidy, blah-bidy. Good luck trying to get them to stop explaining over and over again why I couldn't get my car back. Nobody would listen to me. Nobody cared that the car had been stolen, but I was out the money. And don't get me started on my insurance company. My *previous* insurance company. Bastards were just looking for a reason not to replace it."

"When was the vehicle stolen?" West asked.

"A couple of nights before the accident. I left it outside that construction job I had in Santa Clarita and when I came back it was just gone."

"What construction job?"

"Theron Construction. We were putting up mini-storage, y'know? Tilt-up concrete. Check with Michael Theron. He's the one hired the riffraff and kooks that took my car."

West questioned, "You think one of the men on the job took your car?"

"You bet that's what I think. That's what I told you people, but nobody would listen. Those guys were always looking at my car. I knew what they were thinking. It was a damn fine vehicle. But you guys . . ." he muttered. "Told me that because it was taken after hours, it was probably some random theft, but I know one of them came back for it."

West remembered Osbirg and Bibbs had been on the case. "You're saying the police didn't investigate thoroughly enough."

"I left it there because I was being a safe driver. Y'all kept acting like me having a few beers with some friends was a crime or something. I don't drive drunk, Detective. That's something Bob Vincent doesn't do."

West had clashed with Osbirg on more than one occasion and currently, with Paulsen in the doghouse with Lieutenant Gundy, Osbirg wasn't around. Bibbs had been moved to another station, but neither of them was known for being a top-grade investigator. "Can you give me names of the men you worked with?"

"Sure. Bubba, Dipshit, and Preacher." He chuckled low in his throat. "That's what I called 'em, anyway."

"Got anything more concrete?"

"Nah . . . you'd better check with Mike." Vincent then gave West the number for Mike Theron and as soon as West was off his call, he placed another one to the man who owned the construction company. That call went straight to voice mail, so he left a message, then tried Callie again.

This time she answered right away. "Hi," she said warmly.

He felt himself heat from the inside out and thought, *Boy, you've got it bad.* "Hey, how's it going? How's Tucker getting along?" he asked.

"He keeps hoping we have furrall cats, but he's doing okay. Have you heard anything on Victoria?"

"They're 'cautiously optimistic,'" he said, then explained that Talia had called earlier. "She seems to have calmed down a bit, but then she's been spending time with Cal who's divided his workload with Teddy until Victoria gets back on her feet. If she gets back on her feet . . ."

"So, it's basically good news," she said.

"Barring any unforeseen setback, looks like Victoria might be okay."

"I hope so," she said, sounding relieved. "What about Andre? Have they seen him around?"

"Talia didn't say, and she would've, if he'd been there. Maybe he left. Figured it wasn't the time to work his way back into the family with Victoria down."

"No," she said positively. "You didn't meet him. He's not going to give up."

He really wished he'd met up with Andre, the way Callie had an aversion to him. They talked about Tucker for a few minutes, and he debated on telling her what he suspected about Teresa, that she'd been driving the car that rammed her husband's Mercedes. Before he could decide, she knocked the thought right out of his head with news of her own.

"I may have found Jonathan's secret hiding place. Maybe where he kept the money the Cantrells are so sure he had." She told him about Security One, then really took him aback when she added, "I told Derek about it, and now he wants to try to get into the box by pretending he's Jonathan."

"You're kidding."

"I told him it wouldn't work, that he should just go through legal channels, but he left before I could put the total kibosh on that. He said he's coming back later with the death certificate, but I don't know. He likes shortcuts . . . just like Jonathan."

"Why did you tell him about the box?" West asked.

"Because I don't care what's in it. I just want to tie up all the loose ends to my old life."

He nodded, even though she couldn't see him, then checked the wall clock. Four P.M. "I might be off earlier than I'd planned. Just waiting on a few calls."

"That would be great," she said with feeling.

He liked the way she said that, and for some strange reason a sudden memory of Roxanne complaining that he never told her he loved her popped into his head. Put on the spot like that, he'd never been able to say it to her, and truthfully, he just didn't feel that way about her. Now, Callie, even given the short time they'd known each other, he easily could see himself saying those three words.

"I'll get there as soon as I can," he told her.

As he hung up, he heard smooching noises and looked up to see Dorcas standing behind him with an open bag of Cheetos and a Coke. "Who's the lucky lady?" he asked, grinning like an idiot, his teeth orange.

"Callie Cantrell."

Dorcas started choking on his snack and West snatched the bag out of his hands. "Give me those," he said.

"Cantrell? Man, you like to live dangerously," he said when he finally got himself under control.

West grabbed a few Cheetos and shoved the bag back into his friend's hands. He really wanted to just settle down with Callie and Tucker and keep the danger to a minimum.

South Central. Not the safest place to be in Los Angeles, but perfect for what Naomi needed: a place to leave the car. She'd driven the Chevy back to the city and stayed at a Comfort Inn in Burbank, walking to a nearby 7-Eleven to pick up baby wipes, her method of choice to wipe down the vehicle of all prints. The dent from the old lady and her companion wasn't all that significant. She'd barely brushed them and they'd toppled over. Still, she didn't want the slightest chance of being caught, so she stayed the night and most of the day in Burbank and then drove on to South Central, wearing plastic gloves. She emptied the glove box, took out the registration, then made sure all the side pockets and the area beneath the seats were clean. She'd already checked the trunk during her wipe down, and finally she simply walked away from the car, leaving the keys in the ignition. Sure, the license plates and VIN number would trace the car back to Daniella, but by that time Naomi would be long gone.

At the nearest bus stop, she chose the next one that stopped, not caring where it took her. Turned out, she ended up heading south. She managed to work her way to Marina del Rey, where she stopped at a café overlooking the ocean and bought herself some outstanding fish tacos and a glass of white wine. As she ate, she stared across the Pacific. It pissed her off that Teresa had had an exit plan. Maybe all of them did, except her. Loyal till the end . . . they could inscribe that on her tombstone after she was dead.

But she didn't plan on dying today.

It was after five by the time she got to the front porch of the house she'd shared with Andre and the handmaidens. Slipping her cell phone from her purse, she started to call Andre, then hesitated before putting the call through. If she were smart, she'd just gather her things and get the hell out. Shit was going to rain down in torrents soon, and Andre was a fucking head case. How many times had she told him to go the doctor? Fifty? A hundred? A thousand? Something was deep-down wrong in that screwed brain of his, and though she loved him in a way she'd never loved anything before, and never expected to again, he was bad news for her. If she stayed with him, she would be arrested or killed. She hadn't been the one who'd murdered Teresa, but she'd been there, and she sure as hell had wanted Teresa dead, but then, hadn't they all?

And there was no getting around the hit-and-run she'd done for Andre.

Nope. It was time to move on.

Still . . . Her thumb hovered over the send button. Just before she pressed it, she thought she heard something inside the house. Frowning, she put the phone away and pulled out her key, inserting it into the lock.

As she pushed open the door, she heard murmuring. A woman's voice. A chill slid down her spine and she hesitated just inside the threshold. It didn't sound like Daniella or Clarice . . . Was someone on a cell phone?

"Hey—" she started to say, just as the hall closet door flew open and a body launched itself at her. "What? Wha—?" Her words were choked off as a dark bag was thrown over her head. She immediately struggled but felt the prick of a needle in her arm, which sent her heart into overdrive as fear kicked in.

Struggling with all her might, she heard the clatter of the hypodermic needle against the floor as she managed to throw her attacker off her. She ripped the bag from her head, but the woman—she could feel the shape of her body more than see her in the dark—was back on her in an instant, ripping at her hair, scraping her face with her nails. They rolled on the floor and Naomi grabbed her attacker's hair and tried to slam her head against the hardwood entry hall. No such luck. The woman pulled away and cuffed Naomi with a wicked right cross.

She saw stars. And then felt lethargy enter her muscles. The prick of the needle. What had the bitch given her? Oh, God . . . *This is it.*

When she slowed down the fight, the woman released her and staggered to her own feet. Naomi stared up at her. "Who are you?" she mumbled.

For an answer the woman grabbed her by her jacket collar and dragged her down the hall to the prayer room, surprisingly strong for her wiry frame. As she neared it, Naomi smelled a faint odor of must and decay. *What?*

And then she saw the bodies. Daniella . . . Clarice . . . oh, God, *Jerrilyn!*

The cold feel of the necklace penetrated her swimming senses, then the tightening of the chain around her neck.

"For Andre," the woman said in a breathy growl.

No, Naomi thought. *Not for Andre! No! He's not The Messiah. He's nothing but a screwed piece of garbage! No . . . no . . . no . . . o . . . o . . . o . . . !*

The singing of his cell awoke Andre from the daymare he'd fallen into where Teresa's beautiful face turned into one of the chattering skulls. When he came to he was in a full sweat, seated in the Xterra outside the Cantrell house. He'd actually driven around the curve where Teresa had pushed Jonathan Cantrell's car off the road and a strange thrill had slid into his core, landing in his groin. Dimly he realized it was the first time in days that he'd felt even the most minor sexual tickle. Something wrong there. The one thing he'd always counted on was his masculine essence. It worked for him with the draw of an aphrodisiac and yet ever since Teresa's death, it had diminished, almost as if it were dying with her. And his cock was like a lazy dead worm.

Disturbed, his voice was curt. "Yeah," he answered.

"Where are you?" she asked.

He closed his eyes, willing his dick to come to life at the sound of her voice. He tried to conjure up an image of Teresa. Not the ugly skull he'd seen, but the way she'd been . . . all lithe limbs, red lips, and molten heat. Nothing. "I'm in LA."

"Good," she said. "You're getting closer. Come on home."

"I'll be there soon." He cut her off abruptly, clicking off. His head was dully pounding, a usual state these days. And no sex drive. Maybe Naomi was right. He needed to see a doctor.

He trained his gaze on the Cantrell front door. He'd followed

Teresa from the ranch. No . . . not Teresa . . . Callie. Had to keep reminding himself. He'd followed *Callie* to the Cantrell house and then he'd left for a while, needing to plan. He'd driven to a coffee shop at a mall but hadn't gotten out. The Cantrell house loomed in his thoughts, reminding him of smooth and wealthy Jonathan Cantrell who'd thought his shit didn't stink. Cantrell hadn't known he was just the latest Mark when Teresa had connected with him in Martinique. He'd thought their *love* would conquer anything. Ha. Teresa had wanted to hang on to him longer than she should, but in the end she'd left him cold, as it should be. They'd laughed about Cantrell's starstruck love for her all the way back to LA. He'd been like a dog with his tongue dragging on the ground. All he wanted was Teresa under him, in his bed. Andre had let it go as long as he could stand it. But Teresa was his, no one else's, and Andre made that clear to her when they were back together in Los Angeles. She'd eventually come to heel, but Cantrell was wilier than Andre had suspected. For once Andre had underestimated the man, who never stopped searching for the love of his life. And then years later, he actually found her again. He showed up on their doorstep and spoke to Daniella who lied that she was the only one residing there. But Cantrell wouldn't take no for an answer. Then Teresa came back from taking care of Stephen, and he was waiting for her.

As soon as Jonathan knew where they lived, he'd been marked for death, but he let Teresa lead him on a bit. She was quarrelsome anyway, unhappy with the handmaidens, and so she'd jumped at the chance to be with Cantrell. That's when he knew she had to be the one to kill him. And he made it clear that the task he set for her wasn't optional. She did it too. Ran that fucker off the road. Andre had really thought that things would get back on course after that, but instead her scheming and planning had apparently intensified. She thought he didn't know about the boy, but he did.

He just hadn't acted on the information like he should have. Like he planned to now.

A sleek, black BMW pulled into the Cantrell driveway and a man stepped out. Andre gazed at him through slitted eyes, willing the headache to dial back a bit so he could appraise who this might be.

And then the man turned and looked right at him and Andre's heart stalled for a beat. *Jonathan?* No! Yes, his mind screamed, and he realized right then and there that Teresa had lied to him. She hadn't killed him. She'd let him live so she could be with him!

But there were newspaper accounts of his death. Think . . .

Lies, Andre realized now. He was so incensed he could scarcely see. Rage blinded him.

And then she came out to greet him and Andre realized he'd been duped. She might not be Teresa exactly, but she was a close enough clone and she and Jonathan Cantrell were plotting together. Plotting against him. Plotting for themselves.

They had the boy and thought they had a straight line to *his* money!

"You can't try to get into the box," Callie told Derek firmly. She'd come outside as soon as she'd spied his car pull into the drive. The sky was overcast and it was already dark. There was a definite unseasonable chill in the air, enough that she pulled her sweater close and held it tight. "I don't care whether you have the death certificate or not. And I'm definitely not going along with any plan to have you pretend you're Jonathan."

"Diane's sure that's where the money is," Derek said. "We could at least try."

"Nope."

"Just give me the key, then," he said with extreme patience, holding out his hand.

She set her jaw. She was standing less than two feet away from him and could read the implacable look on his face, but she could be just as implacable. "Did you talk to William about this?"

"Lister doesn't need to know."

"Of course he does! Derek, for God's sake, we need to follow the legal rules here."

"Lister would just try to stop me, and I'm going to find out what's in that box," he said stubbornly.

"Derek," she said, exasperated. "I'm not going to let you do this!" Out of the corner of her eye she noticed movement approaching from across the street. Someone was coming their way, but she didn't want to be distracted. She needed Derek to listen to her. "Did you even bring the death certificate?"

Derek started to shake his head, then flicked a glance at the newcomer and he froze in shock. "Hey, hey!" he said, his mouth turning to an *O* of surprise.

Callie turned and saw Andre. And a gun. Raised. Her own mouth dropped open in shock as her brain tried to process what she was seeing. "Wha—"

Bang! Bang-bang!

Andre pulled off three shots in quick succession and Derek stumbled backward, red blood spots blooming on his shirt, his hands clawing at his chest, his face full of stunned disbelief.

Callie emitted a bleat of shock as Derek fell in a heap. She turned wide eyes on Andre as he lifted the gun again and leveled it at her face.

Tucker, she thought. *Oh, God.*

"Callee?" As if he'd read her thoughts, Tucker called to her at that moment from inside the open front door.

The gun slowly lowered and Andre shifted his gaze from

Callie to beyond her and Tucker. She seized the moment to twist around and run back to Tucker, half-expecting to be shot in the back. "Stay inside!" she yelled at Tucker, shocking him with her harsh tone.

He was standing in the foyer. His gaze moved past her. "What that sound?" he asked.

"Teresa?" Andre queried shakily from behind Callie.

She blocked Tucker's view of him, standing in the aperture in front of him. She grabbed Tucker by the shoulders and tried to turn him around, but he resisted. Callie was moving by rote. Her mind's eye was still filled with the sight of the gun barrel. And the snapshot image of confusion that had rippled across Andre's face as he'd looked her up and down.

"Where is she?" Andre's voice sounded far away.

He meant Teresa. He'd thought she was Teresa for a moment? "I don't know," she threw over her shoulder. If she could slam the door. Keep Tucker safe. Keep herself from fainting or screaming or God knew what.

On the ground outside behind her Derek was making moaning sounds.

"What that?" Tucker demanded, trying to look beneath Callie's right arm.

"Nothing!" she snapped.

"Turn around, or I'll shoot him," Andre ground out.

Callie wasn't sure if he meant Derek or Tucker, but she definitely believed he meant what he said so she slowly revolved until she was facing him again, her hands behind her, trying to hold Tucker back.

Derek had stopped moving, his eyes fixed now across the road on some faraway distance.

He's gone, she thought surreally.

Andre looked like a wild man. His eyes didn't seem to be tracking together. "Get in the car." He waggled the gun at her. "You and the boy. You drive."

"I need my purse . . . my keys . . ."

"No. My car." He inclined his head and she saw the Xterra he'd driven to the ranch a half a block down the street.

"I—I need a car seat. I don't have ID."

"Get in the fucking car!"

Tucker had stopped trying to get past her. He clung to her back, now made aware of the danger.

"He needs a car seat," she repeated. Sean had died because Jonathan had let him unbuckle himself and lie down on the seat. She'd demanded that they stop until he was rebuckled, but Jonathan said they were almost home. She'd yelled at him but all he'd done was race with the woman behind them . . . Teresa, she realized now. "Leave him here. I'll go with you."

"Nooo," Tucker whispered behind her.

"Can't do that." Andre slowly shook his head, a spasm crossing his face. "Get him in the car."

"I'll get the car seat."

"I will shoot you and then him, if you don't get in the car right now."

Tears filled Callie's eyes. "Okay . . . okay . . ." She half-turned. "Tucker, can you grab my hand?"

He gazed up at her with huge blue eyes, slipping his small hand within hers.

They walked across the street with Andre following them. At the Xterra, she saw the keys were still in the ignition. If she could get in and drive away before he rounded the car . . .

But the gun was now aimed at Tucker, so she was helpless to do anything but get Tucker buckled into the backseat. He looked so small and scared. She felt completely responsible for this, for taking him away from Martinique and the life he'd known.

She slid into the driver's seat and buckled up as Andre got in the passenger side, the gun now unerringly on her. Callie started the ignition. Her cell phone was in her purse, which was still sitting on the dining table, but Andre's was lying on the console. If she could just reach West. Find a way to call him. Andre looked like he was damn near close to collapse and if she could just get an open line . . .

"Turn around," Andre said to her.

"What?"

"Turn the car around."

She edged the SUV forward and pulled into the neighbors' drive, hoping they would come outside and see, but they were never home. As she reversed back onto the road, she ventured to ask, "Where are we going?"

"I'm taking you both home," he said.

Chapter Twenty-Seven

It's showtime, folks. All the work's been done and now I get to reap the benefits. And I'm just an innocent bystander. No one knows about me, and that's the way I want to keep it. Of course, I do have a partner in crime, but hey, if they all want to blame someone they should look at Andre and Teresa. They're the ones who put the whole plan in motion. It's endgame time now, and all I've done is pick up the ball and run with it. Now it's time to clean up the remaining mess. Can't wait to see the looks on their faces as they realize they're all doomed.

West drove north on the 101, fighting rush-hour traffic. Half an hour earlier he'd said, "I'm out of here," to Dorcas as he got up from his desk and stretched his back. It was going on six o'clock and it was looking like Mike Theron wasn't going to call him back today. He'd put a call in to Bibbs, too, but had learned the detective was on vacation. Since Osbirg was no longer on active duty with the LAPD, he was stuck with the case notes on the Cantrell homicide and they weren't all that enlightening. But if Theron didn't return his call, he might have to chase down one or the other of the two detectives who'd handled the case.

Through Bluetooth, he punched in Callie's cell number, but was sent straight to voice mail. He wanted to text her, but that would necessitate pulling over and he didn't feel like wasting a minute. He would be at her place soon enough if traffic didn't get any worse.

With time on his hands, he next phoned the Coalinga hospital, hoping to talk to Victoria's doctor directly. After being directed and redirected a couple of times, he finally connected with the man who told him Victoria had woken up briefly and seemed to know who she was and where she was. Encouraged, West thanked him, aware how relieved he was that Victoria would live. It was something of a revelation that he felt so protective of her when all she'd ever done was try to deny his existence—that is, until she'd needed him.

Freeway traffic was moving steadily, if at a snail's pace. He had to contain his impatience and was doing a piss-poor job of it when his default ringtone trilled. Snatching up the phone, he didn't recognize the number. He almost didn't answer, but finally clicked on and said, "Detective Laughlin."

"I believe we were cut off earlier. This is Diane Cantrell," she said snappishly.

Dorcas had given out his cell number to her, he realized. His partner wanted nothing to do with the Cantrell case, especially since he'd learned West was involved with Callie. Though Dorcas had been amused at that, he'd also warned West to watch himself. Getting involved with anyone connected to a case was asking for the kind of trouble West didn't need.

"Was there something else?" West asked her.

"I'm trying to help you, Detective," she said, exasperated. "Callie has now *suddenly* found a key to a security box of some kind and she lured my brother to her house but she won't let him see what's inside. She's playing some kind of game, and she's unstable. Did you know she spent over a month in a mental hospital? I know you're trying to find out what happened to Jonathan and Sean, but you're looking far afield when she's right there!"

"Are you suggesting Ms. Cantrell had something to do with the accident?" West asked in a dangerous voice.

"Oh, for heaven's sake, no." Diane backed off immediately. "But she's hiding money, and I would hope the LAPD would consider that a crime."

"What you've described sounds more like a legal issue. You might want to consult a lawyer."

"We already have," she said, ruffled. "But you need to investigate Callie. There's a pattern here, that you people seem to be missing. That's all I'm saying."

West heard a beep in his ear, signaling another call. He just managed to stop himself from saying, "*We people* will look into it," instead, ending their conversation by politely assuring her he had noted her concerns before clicking off from her and on to the next call. "Detective Laughlin," he answered.

"This is Michael Theron. You called me earlier?"

"I sure did," West said. Quickly, he explained what Bob Vincent had told him about feeling one of Theron's other employees had stolen his car, which had then been used in a homicide a little over a year earlier.

"I thought that was ruled an accident," Theron said.

That was Osbirg's fault, West thought, annoyed. The detective had assumed it was a random theft and had let the case languish because he thought digging further was a waste of time. "It's an open investigation. Mr. Vincent said he didn't know the employees' real names."

"Look, I hire men on the spot when construction is going

and blowing. Sometimes they have ID, sometimes . . . well, I just need bodies, y'know?"

West understood that he was saying he hired illegal aliens among others. "Do you remember any of the names? He called three of them by nicknames it sounded like he'd given them himself."

"I know who he meant." Theron snorted. "Bob drinks too much, but he's a good worker. I'd still hire him. You can tell him that, but he might not believe you. He got all wrapped up in the insurance problems and tried to sue them and me, and I was pretty pissed for a while. Those three, though. They didn't really want to work. Especially the one who thought he was God's messenger, or some such thing."

"Preacher?" West put in.

"Yessirree, that's what Bob called him. The guy spent way too much time on his cell. He never had wheels of his own. Got dropped off by a couple different women. Mostly pretty good-lookin'. He could draw 'em in like a magnet. Actually, now that you reminded me, I think I did see him lookin' at Bob's car once while he was on the phone. Thought he was gonna offer to buy it."

"What's Preacher's real name?" West asked, wondering if there might be something to Bob Vincent's accusations after all.

"Mmmm . . . Andrew Something. Can't remember." He hesitated a moment, then said, "Oh, yeah. That's right. Wanted us to call him Andre."

West jerked. "Andrew Laughlin?" he asked sharply.

"Mighta been," Theron allowed, rolling that over. "I think you might be right. He didn't work for me long, and he didn't work much when he was there. He was the first one to leave of those three. Huh. Like your name."

West's mind was reeling. Had to be Andre, from his description. Andre . . . the stolen vehicle . . . Teresa's finger-prints . . . the Cantrells . . . "You have an address for him?"

West asked without much hope. Transient workers didn't often give out accurate information, and he'd already heard how strange and secretive Andre was. Callie sure hadn't liked him. . . .

He had a moment of cold fear, a premonition of sorts that made him itch to call Callie again.

"Actually, I do, sort of," Theron said thoughtfully. "I heard him on the phone once, complaining about the neighbors and he mentioned the address. Carmella Lane, Laurel Canyon somewhere. I remember 'cause it's my aunt's name."

"Thanks," West said hurriedly. He hung up and immediately called Callie. Once again he went straight to voice mail.

Where was she?

He next put a call in to Dorcas. When his partner answered, he asked, "You still at work?"

"Just leaving, pal. Don't ask me to do anything."

"Can you look up Carmella Lane? Laurel Canyon somewhere. Just give me a general idea. I don't want to stop and look for it."

"This the Cantrell homicide?"

"Can you just do it?" West shot back.

Muttering beneath his breath, Dorcas went silent for a few minutes, then gave West the location, which West pinpointed in his mind. "It's a small, dead-end street," Dorcas said. "What's there?"

"I'm following a lead on the stolen car that pushed the Cantrell Mercedes over the cliff."

"You got something?" He was interested.

"I'll let you know soon. I'm going there now."

"Thought you were going home."

"Have to check on this first."

He hung up, attempted to reach Callie one more time, then tried to tamp down a bad feeling that persisted. He should have listened more closely to her complaints about his dark-horse cousin.

The house Andre guided Callie toward was a dark brown bungalow with a steep driveway that rose from the sloped street below. The place looked like it could use a coat of paint or two and one eave dipped down toward the hedge that ran along the north side.

"Turn around, then stop on the street," Andre said. The first words he'd uttered in several miles.

Callie had to jockey the Xterra to get it facing down the street toward the exit. Then she pulled over to the curb and squeezed into a parking spot. She set the parking brake automatically, aware that her hands were shaking on the steering wheel.

"Get out and get the boy," Andre ordered.

He waited until she'd climbed out and opened the back door, then levered himself from the vehicle and came around to her side, all the while pointing the gun at her head. Full night had fallen while they'd been driving.

Callie clasped Tucker's hand and they walked across the road together. Tucker was shivering. She wondered if it was because he was in a short-sleeved shirt or if it was from fear. Probably both. She was shivering too.

There were houses crouched on both sides of the street. She hoped someone would look out and see that Andre had a gun. He wasn't really trying to conceal the weapon. He was too concerned that she should understand the threat . . . and she did.

He'd taken the keys from her and now he put them back in her hand and showed her which was the one to the house. She unlocked the front door, her mind spinning. He was sick. There was no doubt about that. If she could use that to her advantage, maybe she could somehow get his phone and contact West. Andre had picked up his cell from the console and tucked it in his pocket, but she could see the end of it, as if it hadn't been pushed down far enough and could fall out.

But most important was to keep Tucker safe. Find a way to get him free.

A faint putrid scent reached her nose as she stepped inside and into a darkened hallway. Tucker squeezed her hand even tighter.

"What is that?" Andre asked, sounding like the smell was a surprise to him, too.

She'd stopped short but he prodded her in the small of her back with the gun.

She stepped forward reluctantly, almost dragging Tucker as he didn't want to move. She didn't either. Something was dead here.

She moved slowly down the hall. Doors were closed on either side and it was cool inside, almost cold. There was no heat. The smell grew stronger and Callie stopped short at a room near the end of the hall. Faint light showed from beneath its closed door.

Andre hesitated, then said loudly, "I am The Messiah!"

He moved past Callie and threw open the door. Callie got a glimpse of a large room with robed bodies lying on the floor. Staring eyes. Bruised throats. Pools of blood. Ashes poured over them. And the smell!

She made a retching sound, grabbed Tucker, and turned around, pushing him ahead of her. She didn't even have to yell for him to run. He tore for the front door, racing back down the dark hallway and directly into the woman who had suddenly thrown open one of the bedroom doors and jumped in front of him.

Tucker staggered backward and said in a scared, confused voice, "Aimee?"

Callie was almost upon them and Andre was breathing down her neck. She parroted Tucker blankly, "Aimee?"

In perfect English Aimee answered, "You're going to both have to turn around. Tucker, go in there." She pushed open a door to one of the bedrooms.

"No . . . *Callee* . . ."

"Get in there," she ordered tautly. She held something in her hand. Callie realized in shock that it was a hypodermic needle.

"Yes, go," Callie said faintly, and Tucker reluctantly moved into the room. As soon as he was inside, Aimee locked the door from the outside. The knob had been turned around to make the room a prison.

"What have you done?" Andre rasped, before Callie could even form a question.

"They're a sacrifice for you, *Messiah.*"

Callie's heart was pounding so hard it deafened her. Was that sarcasm in her voice? Why was Aimee here? Had she killed those women and that man?

"What the fuck, Aimee," Andre muttered.

"I told you to come home, but you shouldn't have brought them here," Aimee retorted. "The boy. This woman? You shouldn't have done that."

"Don't tell me what to do!" he roared.

"I love you!" Aimee shrieked back at him. "I told you when you came to Martinique that I would handle things."

Callie was between them. She felt faint . . . ill . . . could sense the fog trying to creep in. No. She had to save Tucker. . . .

"But it was always Teresa," Aimee continued her rant. "Is that why she's here?" She hooked a thumb toward Callie. "Because she looks like her?"

Callie took a slow step to the side, so that she could get out of harm's way. They glared at each other. Andre's gun hand was slack, she saw, and his free hand was pushing hard against his temple. "You killed them . . . and Lumpkin . . . Jerrilyn . . ." he muttered.

"And Teresa," she said coldly. "Your handmaidens . . . You really thought they were capable of killing for you?"

"Naomi ran down the old lady," Andre growled.

"No . . ." Callie murmured, horrified.

"Is she dead?" Aimee asked with an edge.

"She will be," Andre assured her, seeming to get some of his strength back. "Teresa killed for me."

"Always Teresa," she said in disgust. "She was supposed to kill Stephen Laughlin, but she got someone else to do that one. Couldn't quite dirty her hands. She'd had the man's child and had feelings for him."

"She killed him under my orders," Andre snarled. He looked ready to throttle Aimee who seemed not to care about the danger.

"She did murder Jonathan Cantrell, though," Aimee conceded. "But only because he found your camp here," she sneered, throwing out a hand to encompass the house. "Stupid ass wouldn't stop looking for his lovely, lovely Teresa. It's like a fairy tale, isn't it? His quest for her. He even married her *lookalike*. She didn't love you, Andre. She *never* loved you." Her mouth worked as if she were about to cry. She fought back her emotion and dragged her gaze back to Callie. "They didn't give a damn about killing your kid. Set it up from the start. A test for Teresa."

There was a beat inside Callie's head. An angry pounding. She was being goaded but the way Aimee talked about Sean's death sent blood running hot through her veins.

"He told me about it," Aimee went on, correctly interpreting the storm gathering in Callie's eyes. "When he came to Martinique. Gloated about it."

"You lie!" Andre roared.

"I'm the one who loved you," she spat at him through her teeth. "But you never even saw me. *They* were leaving you!" She flung her arm in the direction of the bodies. "But I waited for you. All that time. *All that time.* Waited while you and Teresa played your games. Conned your marks. When Teresa brought me the boy, I thought, now he'll see. Now he'll know what a cheating bitch she is. But she never told you about *him*." She gestured to Tucker's room. "Never told you she'd had Stephen *Laughlin's* son!"

"I found out," Andre shot back. "I knew!"

"Only when I told you," she reminded. "I kept him for Teresa. Planned to contact you when the time was right and turn him over. But you had those fucking handmaidens! Called yourself Messiah!"

Callie slid another step away from them until her back was against the hallway wall.

"Teresa told me she was leaving you," Aimee railed on. "Said you weren't well. And then I saw for myself." She lifted the hypodermic. "And you still didn't even notice me. You were on a mission to find Teresa and you couldn't see what was standing right in front of you. All those wasted years . . . I had to turn to others, Andre. Find someone I could count on. Because it wasn't ever going to be you and those fucking whores, was it? Even after you told me how to find them, who they saw, what they did. You said you wanted me to kill them! You don't get to be sorry now!"

Andre was pushing, pushing, pushing at his temple.

"I told you to come home," Aimee said tautly, "and look what you brought . . . *her.*" She flung a disparaging look Callie's way.

Quick as a snake, Andre reached forward and slapped Aimee. Hard. Callie was running for the back of the house before the decision even reached her brain. She had to get free! Save Tucker! Get away from them!

Aimee staggered from the blow but got a hand out, grabbing Callie's leg, tripping her. Callie went down hard, her cheek slamming into the hardwood floor. The hypodermic flew over her head and into darkness beyond. Andre slammed himself down on her. Callie witnessed his cell phone clatter to the floor and skim across the hardwood before Andre grabbed her by the hair and dragged her forward. Her hands scrabbled for the cell, caught it just as Aimee reeled toward the end of the hall, blindly searching for the hypodermic. Andre smacked Callie's head against the wood and she momentarily saw stars and went limp. It was easy to play dead. The cell phone was beneath her.

Andre was breathing hard near her ear. Then he backed off and snapped, "What's in that? You gonna roofie her?"

Callie's heart sank. Aimee had found the hypodermic.

I work at a clinic . . . Callie dimly recalled Aimee's answer to West's question about employment.

"It's something else," Aimee told Andre sullenly.

"You brought it from Martinique?" he asked.

"You think I'd risk Customs finding it? You know I barely was ahead of the gendarmerie."

"I can smell them," he said, switching subjects. "You overdosed them and now they're rotting."

Callie could feel herself quivering. Her hand cradled the phone. She ran her finger lightly over its face. She'd memorized West's number. She could call him. But she had to be careful. If she messed up digits she wouldn't get a second chance.

"I immobilized them," Aimee corrected. "Didn't you see the ankhs?"

"The ankhs?"

Callie had a brief flash of memory. A chain around the nearest body's neck. A cross at the end. She'd strangled them.

"Like the one you're wearing." Aimee's voice had changed from angry to softly persuasive as she moved closer to him. "Like the one you used to control Teresa when you were having sex."

Andre made a sound that could have meant anything.

"Yes, she told me," Aimee went on, "but I still wanted you. Kept telling myself it was just a matter of time until you realized I was the right partner. Knew the handmaidens were just a distraction . . ."

A heavy moment passed. Callie hesitated, ready to push the first button, afraid it might make a small sound in the sudden silence.

"But I was wrong," Aimee admitted. "So, I did what you couldn't, or wouldn't, and I got rid of them. And Lumpkin."

Callie pressed the first number. No sound. She pressed the second, and third. . . .

"I didn't mean for you to kill them," Andre said.

Callie pushed the fourth and fifth. . . .

"Yes, you did. Of course you did."

"No," he denied.

"Y'know, I knew you were going to say that. I knew you'd back down. That's why I had to use the ankhs. They're your ankhs," she reminded, sounding regretful. "For your whole Messiah thing. When the police get here, the evidence will look like you set them up as sacrifices. Strangled them with your own crosses . . . robed them and covered them with ashes."

"What?" Andre inhaled a sharp breath.

"You shouldn't have brought the boy here," she said. "Now, they both have to die too."

"You set me up?"

"I *loved* you. More than anyone else ever would—"

Callie quickly pushed the sixth and seventh.

"But you weren't worthy and now you're *sick!*"

Quickly she depressed the eighth, ninth, and searched for the tenth number.

BANG!

The gun exploded and Aimee shrieked. She jabbed at Andre with the hypodermic.

BANG! BANG!

Callie lost her hold on the cell and it slipped away from her. She almost cried out with fear. She saw its lit-up face inches away and reached for it. Andre was swearing viciously. He yanked out the needle from his thigh. Aimee took three steps and toppled over. Callie grabbed the phone and pressed the tenth number, praying it would go through.

Seconds later she heard the front door open at the same time West's cell phone started ringing. She'd reached him and he was already *here!*

"*Look out!*" she screamed, struggling to get her feet under her. "He's got a gun! West! He's got a GUN!"

Chapter Twenty-Eight

Carmella Lane was a short street that teed into a dead end with no streetlights other than the one near its entrance. West had found it easily enough, and had driven its length, getting a cold feeling when he spotted a black Xterra parked facing the exit at the curb. It was probably Andre's SUV. He'd looked over the other homes along the street, mostly all remodeled, pre-World War II bungalows, when his cell phone had rung. He'd snatched it up, praying it was Callie, and had been disappointed to see it was Dorcas.

"Yeah," he'd answered, his gaze still roaming from house to house.

"Man, you gotta get to the Cantrell house. Neighbor called. There's a guy dead on the driveway."

"*What?* What guy? Anyone else there?" he'd demanded, his heart clutching.

"Just the dead guy. Neighbor thought it was Jonathan Cantrell, for a moment. Spooked him. Door was wide open."

"Maybe Derek Cantrell," West had answered, thinking of what Diane had said about her brother going to see Callie. He'd climbed from his car in a sudden panic. "I'll call you back. I'm at Carmella." He'd hung up before Dorcas could say anything else.

BANG! Then, *BANG! BANG!*

Gunshots.

Coming from the brown bungalow with the steep drive and the Civic in the driveway.

West had immediately grabbed his Glock from beneath the front seat and climbed from the car in sudden panic. He'd wanted to race to the Cantrell house, but the gunfire took precedence. Where were Callie and Tucker? Who'd killed Derek Cantrell? He hoped Andre wasn't somehow involved.

He ran lightly uphill to the bungalow through a chill October wind. Just as he reached the door, he saw movement near the hedge that ran around the house. Lifting the Glock, he'd held it in front of him with two hands and was about to identify himself as a police officer when he'd seen the small form shoot out from the greenery.

"Tucker?" he'd called softly, his heart seizing with fear.

With a hiccup of fear, the boy had skidded to a stop, then had veered his course toward West. "Calleeee . . ." he'd whispered tearfully, pointing to the house.

That had been all West needed. He'd twisted the handle, readying to break down the door, if necessary, when to his surprise the knob turned in his hand. He'd opened the door when his cell phone suddenly rang and Callie's cry burst out: "*Look out!* He's got a gun, West. He's got a GUN!"

Blast!

The wood paneling near West's head exploded and he dived for the floor. "Stay down!" he screamed to Callie, shifting wildly away, anticipating another shot.

From farther down the hall he heard footsteps running away. Immediately he rolled to his feet and gave chase, stepping over a woman's body, pausing briefly at Callie who was struggling to her feet. "You all right?" he asked, trying to hide the fear in his voice.

"I'm fine . . . fine . . . Tucker's in the room . . ."

"He's outside. In the front."

"Oh, oh . . ." She heaved herself toward the front door. "I'll go . . ."

"Keep him safe. I'll be right there. Who'm I chasing? Andre?" West demanded, already turning to the back of the house.

"Yes."

"That smell . . ."

"Dead bodies," her voice trailed after him, as he burst through the half-opened door into the backyard.

West was here. He'd found her. Callie reached the front door, feeling a surge of hope and adrenaline. Tucker was outside. Safe. At the front of the house. She had to get to him before Andre found a way around.

She ran outside and felt the wind grab at her hair. "Tucker?" she called. "Tucker!"

"*Ici! Ici!* Calleee . . ." He darted from the shadows and into her arms. She hugged him close and wanted to cry with relief.

"How'd you get out?"

"The window. I climb up on bed and out. Michel show me."

"Good old Michel," she whispered. "Come on." She grabbed his hand and pulled him down the steep slope to the street. She was worried sick about West, afraid to hear more gunshots. What if Andre killed him?

No. She couldn't think that way. She wouldn't. She had to get Tucker safe.

"We've got to go down the hill. Find some help." Regretfully, she realized Andre's cell phone was still on the floor where she'd dropped it. "Maybe knock on some doors."

Tucker ran toward the nearest neighbor's door.

* * *

West led with his Glock through the open back door. It was dark in the small, hedge-enclosed yard. Was there a gate to the front of the house? Could he get away?

Mindful of the fact that he had a weapon, West edged into the yard, hugging the house wall. He felt exposed and open, but he saw nothing to hide behind.

At the back of the yard something moved. Immediately West crouched down, the figure in his sights. He stepped sideways, farther away from the door, half-expecting a hail of gunfire.

A groan met his ears as his eyes zeroed in on the prone figure lying up against the hedge. Knowing it could be a trap, he moved carefully forward.

"Help me," the pain-filled voice called weakly.

"Andre?" West responded, once again sidling quickly away after he spoke, in case the sound of his voice could pinpoint his position if Andre had laid a trap.

"She stabbed me . . . drugged me . . . I got it out . . . I got it out . . ."

As West drew nearer he made out the gun on the ground, just outside the reach of Andre's right hand. Andre was lying on his back, his arms outstretched, staring up at the sky.

West moved in quickly and kicked the gun farther out of reach. Then he bent down to him. "She stabbed you?"

"Aimee . . . hypo . . . dermic . . ."

"Aimee Thomas?" he asked incredulously. *That* was the woman Andre had apparently shot?

Andre seemed to focus on him. "West?" he asked.

"We need to get you to a hospital."

"I am The Messiah . . ."

* * *

Before Tucker could get to the house on the adjoining property the door of a dark SUV, also aimed down the hill, swung open. The interior light didn't come on, and Callie skidded to a halt, alert to danger. What was this?

But Tucker, whose young eyes seemed to see through the darkness with ease, stopped short, then ran directly toward the man stepping out of the driver's side. "Knock, knock!" he yelled, and threw himself into the man's arms.

"Teddy?" Callie asked, hearing her voice crack with relief. "God, is it really you? What are you doing here?"

"I heard there was some action going on here," he said lightly, hanging on to Tucker. "Need some help?"

"He is a bad. And Aimee is bad!" Tucker declared, pointing toward the house.

"Yeah?" Teddy Stutz asked, a hint of amusement in his voice. "Better get in the car, then, and be safe," he said, opening the back door.

"Wait," Callie said, alarm sizzling down her nerves. "Who gave you this address?"

"Oh, I think you know," he said as Tucker jumped inside.

"What do you mean?" Callie blinked in the darkness. Was that a gun held loosely in his hand?

Yes, it was a gun. Because now he waved it at her. "Get in the car, Callie."

"No."

"You want to save your little friend here, don't you?"

"You wouldn't hurt him," she said, her mouth dry.

"You don't know what I'd do. Get in, before I stop asking nicely."

West would be here. If she stalled, West would be here. "You're a part of this?" she asked in disbelief.

"I told you I knew Teresa," he said. "I knew what she was going to do long before she went through with it. The way she flirted with Edmund Mikkels . . . He was no match for her. I had to work pretty hard to make him pull that trigger, though. But Stephen had to die, otherwise he'd inherit everything."

His tone was conversational, but he'd stepped forward while he was talking. Callie jerked backward, but he pressed the gun straight into the hollow at her throat. "Get in the car," he said in a pleasant tone that made her muscles quiver with fear.

This time she did as she was told, climbing into the passenger seat. *West, where are you?* She prayed to God he was okay. But she couldn't count on him to save them. There wasn't enough time.

Maybe she could stop Teddy. Get the gun away. "Don't try anything," he warned her, correctly interpreting her hesitation. "You don't want me to wreck the car with the kid in the back, like your husband did."

She buckled herself into the passenger seat, sending a smile back to Tucker that she hoped wasn't as tremulous as it felt.

Gotta keep him talking . . .

"Why would it matter to you if Stephen had inherited?" she managed to get out.

"Have you been asleep all this time? Victoria loves my father. And she should, because he's a good guy. Me, on the other hand. The proverbial bad seed. Gambling . . . shirking work . . . stealing . . . Oh, yeah. I've earned all the labels." He grinned as he turned the ignition. Callie hoped West would hear it. Would somehow sense she and Tucker were in trouble.

"Good old Cal's never given up on his only son, though," he went on, "so, I'm next in line, as long as the dominoes all fall in place."

"Like getting rid of Stephen," she accused.

"You just don't know how hard I had to work to orchestrate that, and then Teresa gets all conflicted. Can't trust a woman," he said. "Actually, you can't trust anyone but yourself. . . ."

He pulled out and started to drive down the hill. Callie was beside herself. How was she going to save them?

"Stephen never did the job around the ranch that my dad did," Teddy said. "When I knew Teresa wanted Stephen out of the picture, I saw the opportunity. And then I knew when she was going to Martinique. I hacked her e-mail account. Who do you think told Victoria to get the computer expert? *Moi*," he said on a short laugh. "So, I went to Martinique myself and met the love-sick and thoroughly misguided Aimee Thomas." He glanced in the rearview. "And saw Tucker again. Didn't know he'd recognize me and the knock-knock joke I told. That shook me up a little."

"You were in Martinique?" Callie asked, stealing a glance in the side mirror. No sign of West and they were approaching the main highway.

"I tried to tell Aimee that Andre was a no-go, but she had to see for herself and even when the whack-job showed up two weeks ago and she got to see his full-on crazy for herself, she wouldn't quite let go."

"You're the one who got Teresa on the boat," Callie realized.

"With Aimee's help," he said with false humility. "She can be surprisingly imaginative when she has to be, but I couldn't count on her with Andre. One moment she loves him, the next she hates him. Totally dysfunctional." He smiled, then asked, "Who shot who, back there?"

Soon they would be in a busier area. Could she hit him at a stoplight? Have time to get out of the car and save Tucker? "Andre shot Aimee."

"What about Aimee's hypodermic?" When Callie didn't

respond, he said, "Oh, she tried and failed." He snorted in disgust. "You know what she uses? A little gift from me. A tranquilizer used to subdue cattle on the ranch. I just helped myself to some. It's been a boon having to 'help out' Cal during this trying time while Victoria decides whether she's going to live or die."

"You tell me jokes," Tucker accused from the backseat.

"Well, one joke," Teddy confided to Callie, as if Tucker wasn't all that bright. "The wharf rat was only there the one time when I met with Aimee."

"You're the real black sheep," Callie said coldly.

He laughed. "You just figured that out? Oh, I get it. West isn't the black sheep. He couldn't be, could he? He's the white hat in this fiction you've created."

"You're taking us to the ranch," she guessed.

"Now, why would I do that? I wasn't really counting on having to deal with the boy so soon, but Andre pushed up the timetable by bringing you both to the house. Guess it's karma, how these things work out." His smile chilled Callie to the soles of her feet. She and Tucker were doomed to die unless she came up with a plan.

Keep him talking. You need more time.

"West will find us," she predicted with more confidence than she felt.

"After he gets done chasing Andre? Sure. He'll find you. Just don't know . . . when."

She understood that he believed West would find them after they were dead.

"Then, he'll have to be dealt with, too, apparently," he added. "Victoria always acted like he didn't even exist, but that all changed when she hired him."

"How did Teresa meet Stephen?" she asked, desperate for anything to say. They were driving with traffic but they'd entered a main surface street.

"I'd seen Teresa around LA. Even in this town, she was hard to miss when she was trolling for a guy with money. I wanted to test the waters and so I told her I was part of the Laughlin family who owned Laughlin Ranch. She must've gone straight back to Andre with that information because she suddenly wanted to get real friendly—until Andre figured out I wasn't Stephen. Then they went right by me and she started hanging out at the BBQ until the real Stephen Laughlin walked in. Edmund had been dogging after her for a while and he introduced them. Something he was sorry about later."

They were behind about three cars in the outside lane, slowing for a stoplight. The curb and sidewalk were to her right. Could she do it? Leap out and round the car to get to Tucker in time? Could she yell at him to jump out? Did she dare? Traffic was stopped. But could she save him from Teddy?

She tensed, her hand stealing toward the door handle. Tucker suddenly leapt out of his seat and jumped forward, grabbing Teddy's head and clamping his teeth on his right ear. Teddy let out a howl and lifted the gun still in his right hand. Callie slammed her hand down on his forearm and the Glock discharged. A bullet *zinged* into the roof of the vehicle.

"Get out of the car!" Callie screamed at Tucker but he was way ahead of her. He threw open his door while she yanked back on the handle of hers. "Tucker, look out!" she yelled, her heart seizing as he stepped into still-stalled traffic.

"Hands up!" a familiar voice ground out. West suddenly appeared at Teddy's driver's window.

Teddy's answer was to slam his foot on the gas and ram the car in front of them. West jumped back, but then stepped forward again, his gun leveled at Teddy's head through the window. "So help me God, Stutz. Get out or I'll shoot," he snapped.

Teddy slowly dropped his gun and lifted his hands, and Callie heard still distant but approaching sirens. West had called in the cavalry.

West yanked open the door and hauled Teddy out as Tucker ran around the back of the vehicle and into Callie's arms. She could feel Tucker's small body shaking and held him close. On the sidewalk, she burbled, "How did you do that? How did you know to do that?"

His face had been buried in her neck, but now he pulled back enough to say, "Furrall cats bite. And I does, too."

Four hours later they were released from the police station and allowed to return home. West drove them in his Explorer and Tucker was nodding off in a car seat borrowed from one of the administrative assistants who'd overheard Callie worrying about the issue and had offered hers up.

"I heard the car start," West had told her earlier. "Andre was unconscious by then and I'd called for help, and that's when I heard the car. Coulda been the neighbors, but I knew it wasn't. I ran out the way Tucker did and saw you and Tucker's heads in the Trailblazer. Didn't know whose it was, but I just followed and called in the plates. Ted Stutz. Figured it wasn't Cal."

West had gone on to say that Andre was at Cedars-Sinai Hospital. He was going to survive, but he was scheduled for neurological tests. "Fast-growing tumor, squeezing his nerves," was the educated guess at this point. He'd probably been suffering hallucinations and an extraordinary amount of pain. Whether he was really Andrew Laughlin was yet to be determined, but both West and Callie were fairly certain it was true.

Aimee did not survive the gunshot wounds. Nor did

Derek, but then Callie had known he was dead before Andre had ever taken them away.

West, at Callie's request, had taken Tucker and her to his apartment. Derek's body was picked up by the coroner's van, and other officers had collected Callie's purse and phone and locked the door to her house. Diane Cantrell had been asked to identify the body and had screamed at the ME and his staff all the while she was there. She'd been given a sedative and officers had driven her home.

As they pulled into West's parking spot, Callie lifted her head from the seat rest and asked, "Are we home?"

"Yeah," West said, leaning over to kiss her lightly on the lips. "We are."

Together they gathered Tucker from the backseat and carried him upstairs to West's couch. He lay on his side, the sweep of his lashes resting on his cheeks, his chest rising and falling evenly.

"Think he'll be okay after all this?" she asked.

"He's tough," West said.

"Teddy called him a wharf rat. Made me angry, but I don't know . . . it's almost a badge of honor."

"It is," West agreed, putting his arms around her. "Teddy's going to jail for a long, long time. Did I tell you that Victoria woke up and recognized who she was and where she was?"

"That's good news."

"Mmm-hmmm." He guided her down the hall to his bedroom. "We just have to convince her that Tucker would be better off living with us."

"Are we planning to live together?" Callie asked, pulling him down on the bed beside her.

"Well, I need someone to help me with home decor."

She laughed silently, holding him close, relieved and happy to be safe in his arms. "Yes, you do."

Epilogue

Callie slid the gray, metal box from the slot and took it inside a special room within Security One. Opening the lid, she found stacks of hundred-dollar bills. Without counting, she did a quick estimate and decided a good deal of the money from the mortgage was still there. There were also two passports. She opened the first and saw her deceased husband's smiling face. The second was her own. Her name. Her state of residence. Her birth date. But it was Teresa's picture smiling up at her.

She didn't know how he'd done it, but Jonathan had managed to have a fake passport made. Had Teresa even known about it? She somehow doubted it. Whereas Jonathan had been obsessed with her and planned for them to run away together, Teresa had been just as obsessed with Andre, at least at that time.

There were snapshots as well. Digital pictures printed on photo paper, probably from the jump drive labeled MARTINIQUE, if she were to guess. They were candid shots of Jonathan and Teresa, most likely from their earlier time together. Behind them was a panorama of sky, sand, and beach. Both of them looked tan and beautiful. Not a care in the world. Nothing like the Jonathan she'd come to know who'd become surly, tense, and dissatisfied.

She wondered who'd taken the photos . . . Andre, perhaps?

She emptied the contents of the box into the duffel bag she'd brought with her. Diane could have the money. It was hers, along with the house, though she'd lost her fire over the last few weeks. It had been extinguished when she'd lost Derek.

Callie slid the empty box back into its slot, then went to the outer room to meet Victoria's lawyer, Gary Merritt, who'd greased the legal wheels to gain her access to the box. Victoria was out of the hospital, wan, but as sharp and in control as ever. She'd insisted on Callie using Gary, and Callie had been grateful for the help.

William Lister was waiting with Gary. Callie kept the pictures, jump drive, and passports, then handed over the bag of money. "You're sure?" William asked. He was looking worse for wear himself.

"I'm sure. I think Jonathan spent some of it looking for Teresa, but most of it is there."

Gary Merritt cleared his throat and reminded her again, "As his wife, it's rightfully yours."

She shook her head and headed outside into bright LA sunshine. A lot of people had thought somebody else's money was rightfully theirs, whether it was or not, and all it had gotten them was misery and death.

West was leaning against his Explorer, which was parked at the curb. The back door was open and she could see Tucker inside, his skinny legs swinging to the sound of something he was listening to inside a pair of headphones.

"You good?" West said.

"I'm excellent."

"I'd have to agree."

They'd moved into his apartment together and were looking for a new place as a family of three. Victoria hadn't liked having Tucker outside of her control but had let it happen.

"Andre's tests came back. No surprise that it's a tumor. He doesn't have long to live," West said.

Callie shivered and let herself be folded into his embrace.

Gary Merritt came out of the Security One offices and walked over to them. Callie was faintly embarrassed to be caught in a PDA, but didn't really care. She was too happy with West and Tucker.

"I just spoke with Victoria," he said.

"She said she wouldn't stand in the way of Tucker's adoption," West warned.

"She isn't. She just asked me to tell you that she recently rewrote her will."

"And named Tucker her heir, which damn near got him killed," West guessed.

"Actually, she's leaving everything to you, Mr. Laughlin."

West froze. "She wouldn't dare," he said grimly.

The lawyer smiled slightly. "She'd already signed the papers at my office. That's what she was doing there. And now that you and Ms. Cantrell will be Tucker's legal guardians, she wants everything in place. She's requesting that both of you meet with me sometime in the near future in order to go over particulars. Good afternoon." He nodded and walked away.

The look of horror on West's face as he turned to Callie made her cover her mouth to keep from laughing. "Guess you really are a Laughlin," she said.

"I'm not moving to the ranch, if that's what she thinks this is all about."

Callie's eyes danced. "I think your black sheep days are over."

"Don't bet on it," West warned.

"You just hate the idea that she might actually like you,"

Callie said with a grin, to which West grumbled under his breath.

From inside the car, Tucker yelled, "Knock, knock!"

"Oh, here we go," Callie said. "Who's there?" she called back.

"Cows go," Tucker declared.

Callie bent down and peered into the car where Tucker had ripped off his headphones and was holding tight to the stuffed meerkat she'd found on the Internet. "What happened to Lena?"

"I might've told him a new one," West admitted behind her shoulder. "With a Laughlin spin."

"COWS GO!" Tucker repeated.

"Okay, okay," Callie said. "Cows go who?"

"No! Cows go MOO!" Tucker started laughing at his own joke and Callie and West joined in.

Books by Bestselling Author
Fern Michaels

___The Jury	0-8217-7878-1	$6.99US/$9.99CAN
___Sweet Revenge	0-8217-7879-X	$6.99US/$9.99CAN
___Lethal Justice	0-8217-7880-3	$6.99US/$9.99CAN
___Free Fall	0-8217-7881-1	$6.99US/$9.99CAN
___Fool Me Once	0-8217-8071-9	$7.99US/$10.99CAN
___Vegas Rich	0-8217-8112-X	$7.99US/$10.99CAN
___Hide and Seek	1-4201-0184-6	$6.99US/$9.99CAN
___Hokus Pokus	1-4201-0185-4	$6.99US/$9.99CAN
___Fast Track	1-4201-0186-2	$6.99US/$9.99CAN
___Collateral Damage	1-4201-0187-0	$6.99US/$9.99CAN
___Final Justice	1-4201-0188-9	$6.99US/$9.99CAN
___Up Close and Personal	0-8217-7956-7	$7.99US/$9.99CAN
___Under the Radar	1-4201-0683-X	$6.99US/$9.99CAN
___Razor Sharp	1-4201-0684-8	$7.99US/$10.99CAN
___Yesterday	1-4201-1494-8	$5.99US/$6.99CAN
___Vanishing Act	1-4201-0685-6	$7.99US/$10.99CAN
___Sara's Song	1-4201-1493-X	$5.99US/$6.99CAN
___Deadly Deals	1-4201-0686-4	$7.99US/$10.99CAN
___Game Over	1-4201-0687-2	$7.99US/$10.99CAN
___Sins of Omission	1-4201-1153-1	$7.99US/$10.99CAN
___Sins of the Flesh	1-4201-1154-X	$7.99US/$10.99CAN
___Cross Roads	1-4201-1192-2	$7.99US/$10.99CAN

Available Wherever Books Are Sold!
Check out our website at **www.kensingtonbooks.com**